…r Post

BY MIKE RESNICK

MIKE RESNICK

KIRINYAGA

A FABLE OF UTOPIA

THE BALLANTINE PUBLISHING GROUP

NEW YORK

A Del Rey® Book
Published by The Ballantine Publishing Group

Copyright © 1998 by Mike Resnick

All rights reserved under International and Pan-American Copyright Conventions. Published in the United States by The Ballantine Publishing Group, a division of Random House, Inc., New York, and simultaneously in Canada by Random House of Canada Limited, Toronto.

The stories in this work were originally published in somewhat different form in *Asimov's Science Fiction Magazine, Magazine of Fantasy & Science Fiction,* and *Stalking the Wild Resnick.*

Del Rey is a registered trademark and the Del Rey colophon is a trademark of Random House, Inc.

www.randomhouse.com/delrey/

Library of Congress Catalogue Card Number: 99-90319

ISBN 978-0-345-41702-2

Cover design by David Stevenson
Cover illustration by John Harris

Manufactured in the United States of America

This, my finest work, is dedicated to
Carol, my finest friend

Contents

Prologue

ONE PERFECT MORNING, WITH JACKALS

{APRIL 19, 2123}

Ngai is the creator of all things. He made the lion and the elephant, the vast savannah and the towering mountains, the Kikuyu and the Maasai and the Wakamba.

Thus, it was only reasonable for my father's father and *his* father's father to believe that Ngai was all-powerful. Then the Europeans came, and they killed all the animals, and they covered the savannahs with their factories and the mountains with their cities, and they assimilated the Maasai and the Wakamba, and one day all that was left of what Ngai had created was the Kikuyu.

And it was among the Kikuyu that Ngai waged His final battle against the god of the Europeans.

* * *

My former son lowered his head as he stepped into my hut.

"*Jambo*, my father," he said, looking somewhat uncomfortable, as usual, in the close confines of the rounded walls.

"*Jambo*, Edward," I replied.

He stood before me, not quite knowing what to do with his hands. Finally he placed them in the pockets of his elegantly tailored silk suit.

"I have come to drive you to the spaceport," he said at last.

I nodded, and slowly got to my feet. "It is time."

"Where is your luggage?" he asked.

"I am wearing it," I said, indicating my dull red *kikoi*.

"You're not taking anything else?" he said, surprised.

"There is nothing else I care to take," I replied.

He paused and shifted his weight uncomfortably, as he always seemed to do in my presence. "Shall we go outside?" he suggested at last, walking to the door of my hut. "It's very hot in here, and the flies are murderous."

"You must learn to ignore them."

"I do not *have* to ignore them," he replied, almost defensively. "There are no flies where I live."

"I know. They have all been killed."

"You say that as if it were a sin rather than a blessing."

I shrugged and followed him outside, where two of my chickens were pecking diligently at the dry red earth.

"It's a beautiful morning, is it not?" he said. "I was afraid it might be as warm as yesterday."

I looked out across the vast savannah, which had been turned into farmland. Wheat and corn seemed to sparkle in the morning sun.

"A perfect morning," I agreed. Then I turned and saw a splendid vehicle parked about thirty yards away, white and sleek and shining with chrome.

"Is it new?" I asked, indicating the car.

He nodded proudly. "I bought it last week."

"German?"

"British."

"Of course," I said.

The glow of pride vanished, and he shifted his weight again. "Are you ready?"

"I have been ready for a long time," I answered, opening the door and easing myself into the passenger's seat.

"I never saw you do that before," he remarked, entering the car and starting the ignition.

"Do what?"

"Use your safety harness."

"I have never had so many reasons not to die in a car crash," I replied.

He forced a smile to his lips and began again. "I have a surprise for you," he said as the car pulled away and I looked back at my *boma* for the very last time.

"Oh?"

He nodded. "We will see it on the way to the spaceport."

"What is it?" I asked.

"If I told you, it wouldn't be a surprise."

I shrugged and remained silent.

"We'll have to take some of the back roads to reach what I want to show you," he continued. "You'll be able to take a last look at your country along the way."

"This is not my country."

"You're not going to start *that* again, are you?"

"*My* country teems with life," I said adamantly. "*This* country has been smothered by concrete and steel, or covered by row upon row of European crops."

"My father," he said wearily as we sped past a huge wheat field, "the last elephant and lion were killed before you were born. You have *never* seen Kenya teeming with wildlife."

"Yes I have," I answered him.

"When?"

I pointed to my head. "In here."

"It doesn't make any sense," he said, and I could tell that he was trying to control his temper.

"What doesn't?"

"That you can turn your back on Kenya and go live on some ter-raformed planetoid, just because you want to wake up to the sight of a handful of animals grazing."

"I did not turn my back on Kenya, Edward," I said patiently. "Kenya turned its back on *us*."

"That simply isn't so," he said. "The President and most of his cabinet are Kikuyu. You *know* that."

"They call themselves Kikuyu," I said. "That does not make them Kikuyu."

"They *are* Kikuyu!" he insisted.

"The Kikuyu do not live in cities that were built by Europeans," I replied. "They do not dress as Europeans. They do not worship the Europeans' god. And they do not drive European machines," I added pointedly. "Your vaunted President is still a *kehee*—a boy who has not undergone the circumcision ritual."

"If he is a boy, then he is a fifty-seven-year-old boy."

"His age is unimportant."

"But his accomplishments are. He is responsible for the Turkana Pipeline, which has brought irrigation to the entire Northern Fron-tier District."

"He is a *kehee* who brings water to the Turkana and the Rendille and the Samburu," I agreed. "What is that to the Kikuyu?"

"Why do you persist in speaking like an ignorant old savage?" he demanded irritably. "You were schooled in Europe and America. You *know* what our President has accomplished."

"I speak the way I speak because I *have* been schooled in Europe and America. I have seen Nairobi grow into a second London, with all of that city's congestion and pollution, and Mombasa into another Miami, with all of that city's attendant dangers and diseases. I have seen our people forget what it means to be a Kikuyu, and speak proudly about being Kenyans, as if Kenya was anything more than an arbitrary set of lines drawn on a European map."

"Those lines have been there for almost three centuries," he pointed out.

I sighed. "As long as you have known me, you have never understood me, Edward."

"Understanding is a two-way street," he said with sudden bitterness. "When did you ever make an effort to understand *me?*"

"I raised you."

"But to this day you don't *know* me," he said, driving dangerously fast on the bumpy road. "Did we ever talk as father and son? Did you ever discuss anything but the Kikuyu with me?" He paused. "I was the only Kikuyu to play on the national basketball team, and yet you never once came to watch me."

"It is a European game."

"In point of fact, it is an *American* game."

I shrugged. "They are the same."

"And now it is an African game as well. I played on the only Kenyan team ever to defeat the Americans. I had hoped that would make you proud of me, but you never even mentioned it."

"I heard many stories of an Edward Kimante who played basketball against the Europeans and the Americans," I said. "But I knew that this could not be my son, for I gave my son the name Koriba."

"And my mother gave me the middle name of Edward," he said. "And since she spoke to me and shared my burdens, and you did not, I took the name she gave me."

"That is your right."

"I don't give a damn about my rights!" He paused. "It didn't have to be this way."

"I remained true to my convictions," I said. "It is you who tried to become a Kenyan rather than a Kikuyu."

"I *am* a Kenyan," he said. "I live here, I work here, I love my country. *All* of it, not just one tiny segment."

I sighed deeply. "You are truly your mother's son."

"You have not asked about her," he noted.

"If she were not well, you would have told me."

"And that's all you have to say about the woman you lived with for seventeen years?" he demanded.

"It was she who left to live in the city of the Europeans, not I," I replied.

He laughed humorlessly. "Nakuru is *not* a European city. It has two million Kenyans and less than twenty thousand whites."

"Any city is, by definition, European. The Kikuyu do not live in cities."

"Look around you," he said in exasperation. "More than ninety-five percent of them *do* live in cities."

"Then they are no longer Kikuyu," I said placidly.

He squeezed the steering wheel until his knuckles turned ash-gray.

"I do not wish to argue with you," he said, struggling to control his emotions. "It seems that is all we ever do anymore. You are my father, and despite all that has come between us, I love you—and I had hoped to make my peace with you today, since we shall never see each other again."

"I have no objection to that," I said. "I do not enjoy arguing."

"For a man who doesn't enjoy it, you managed to argue for twelve long years to get the government to sponsor this new world of yours."

"I did not enjoy the arguments, only the results," I replied.

"Have they decided what to name it yet?"

"Kirinyaga."

"Kirinyaga?" he repeated, surprised.

I nodded. "Does not Ngai sit upon His golden throne atop Kirinyaga?"

"Nothing sits atop Mount Kenya except a city."

"You see?" I said with a smile. "Even the name of the holy mountain has been corrupted by Europeans. It is time that we give Ngai a new Kirinyaga from which to rule the universe."

"Perhaps it *is* fitting, at that," he said. "There has been precious little room for Ngai in today's Kenya."

Suddenly he began slowing down, and a moment later we turned off the road and across a recently harvested field, driving very carefully so as not to damage his new car.

"Where are we going?" I asked.

"I told you: I have a surprise for you."

"What kind of surprise can there be in the middle of an empty field?" I asked.

"You will see."

Suddenly he came to a stop about twenty yards from a clump of thornbushes, and turned off the ignition.

"Look carefully," he whispered.

I stared at the bushes for a moment without seeing anything. Then there was a brief movement, and suddenly the whole picture came into view, and I could see two jackals standing behind the foliage, staring timidly at us.

"There have been no animals here in more than two decades," I whispered.

"They seem to have wandered in after the last rains," he replied softly. "I suppose they must be living off the rodents and birds."

"How did you find them?"

"*I* didn't," he answered. "A friend of mine in the Game Department told me they were here." He paused. "They'll be captured and relocated to a game park sometime next week, before they can do any lasting damage."

They seemed totally misplaced, hunting in tracks made by huge threshing and harvesting machines, searching for the safety of a savannah that had not existed for more than a century, hiding from cars rather than other predators. I felt a certain kinship to them.

We watched them in total silence for perhaps five minutes. Then Edward checked his timepiece and decided that we had to continue to the spaceport.

"Did you enjoy it?" he asked as we drove back onto the road.

"Very much," I said.

"I had hoped you would."

"They are being moved to a game park, you said?"

He nodded his head. "A few hundred miles to the north, I believe."

"The jackal walked this land long before the farmers arrived," I noted.

"But they are an anachronism," he replied. "They don't belong here anymore."

I nodded my head. "It is fitting."

"That the jackals go to a game park?" he asked.

"That the Kikuyu, who were here before the Kenyans, leave for a new world," I answered. "For we, too, are an anachronism that no longer belongs here."

He increased his speed, and soon we had passed through the farming area and entered the outskirts of Nairobi.

"What will you do on Kirinyaga?" he asked, breaking a long silence.

"We shall live as the Kikuyu were meant to live."

"I mean you, personally."

I smiled, anticipating his reaction. "I am to be the *mundumugu*."

"The witch doctor?" he repeated incredulously.

"That is correct."

"I can't believe it!" he continued. "You are an educated man. How can you sit cross-legged in the dirt and roll bones and read omens?"

"The *mundumugu* is also a teacher, and the custodian of the tribal customs," I said. "It is an honorable profession."

He shook his head in disbelief. "So I am to explain to people that my father has become a witch doctor."

"You need fear no embarrassment," I said. "You need only tell them that Kirinyaga's *mundumugu* is named Koriba."

"That is *my* name!"

"A new world requires a new name," I said. "You cast it aside to take a European name. Now I will take it back and put it to good use."

"You're serious about this, aren't you?" he said as we pulled into the spaceport.

"From this day forward, my name is Koriba."

The car came to a stop.

"I hope you will bring more honor to it than I did, my father," he said as a final gesture of conciliation.

"You have brought honor to the name you chose," I said. "That is quite enough for one lifetime."

"Do you really mean that?" he asked.

"Of course."

"Then why did you never say so before now?"

"Haven't I?" I asked, surprised.

We got out of the car and he accompanied me to the departure area. Finally he came to a stop.

"This is as far as I am permitted to go."

"I thank you for the ride," I said.

He nodded.

"And for the jackals," I added. "It was truly a perfect morning."

"I will miss you, my father," he said.

"I know."

He seemed to be waiting for me to say something, but I could think of nothing further to say.

For a moment I thought he was going to place his arms around me and hug me, but instead he reached out, shook my hand, muttered another farewell, and turned on his heel and left.

I thought he would go directly to his car, but when I looked through a porthole of the ship that would take us to Kirinyaga, I saw him standing at a huge, plate-glass window, waving his hand, while his other hand held a handkerchief.

That was the last sight I saw before the ship took off. But the image I held in my mind was of the two jackals, watching alien sights in a land that had itself become foreign to them. I hoped that they would adjust to their new life in the game park that had been artificially created for them.

Something told me that I soon would know.

1

KIRINYAGA

{AUGUST 2129}

In the beginning, Ngai lived alone atop the mountain called Kirinyaga. In the fullness of time He created three sons, who became the fathers of the Maasai, the Kamba, and the Kikuyu races, and to each son He offered a spear, a bow, and a digging stick. The Maasai chose the spear, and was told to tend herds on the vast savannah. The Kamba chose the bow, and was sent to the dense forests to hunt for game. But Gikuyu, the first Kikuyu, knew that Ngai loved the earth and the seasons, and chose the digging stick. To reward him for this Ngai not only taught him the secrets of the seed and the harvest, but gave him Kirinyaga, with its holy fig tree and rich lands.

The sons and daughters of Gikuyu remained on Kirinyaga until the white man came and took their lands away, and even when the white man had been banished they did not return, but chose to remain in the cities, wearing Western clothes and using Western machines and living Western lives. Even I, who am a *mundumugu*—a witch doctor—was born in the city. I have never seen the lion or the elephant or the rhinoceros, for all of them were extinct before my birth; nor have I seen Kirinyaga as Ngai meant it to be seen, for a bustling, overcrowded city of three million inhabitants covers its slopes, every year approaching closer and closer to Ngai's throne at the summit. Even the Kikuyu have forgotten its true name, and now know it only as Mount Kenya.

To be thrown out of Paradise, as were the Christian Adam and Eve, is a terrible fate, but to live beside a debased Paradise is infinitely worse. I think about them frequently, the descendants of Gikuyu who have forgotten their origin and their traditions and are now merely Kenyans, and I wonder why more of them did not join with us when we created the Eutopian world of Kirinyaga.

True, it is a harsh life, for Ngai never meant life to be easy; but it is also a satisfying life. We live in harmony with our environment, we offer sacrifices when Ngai's tears of compassion fall upon our fields and give sustenance to our crops, we slaughter a goat to thank him for the harvest.

Our pleasures are simple: a gourd of *pombe* to drink, the warmth of a *boma* when the sun has gone down, the wail of a newborn son or daughter, the footraces and spear-throwing and other contests, the nightly singing and dancing.

Maintenance watches Kirinyaga discreetly, making minor orbital adjustments when necessary, assuring that our tropical climate remains constant. From time to time they have subtly suggested that we might wish to draw upon their medical expertise, or perhaps allow our children to make use of their educational facilities, but they have taken our refusal with good grace, and have never shown any desire to interfere in our affairs.

Until I strangled the baby.

It was less than an hour later that Koinnage, our paramount chief, sought me out.

"That was an unwise thing to do, Koriba," he said grimly.

"It was not a matter of choice," I replied. "You know that."

"Of course you had a choice," he responded. "You could have let the infant live." He paused, trying to control his anger and his fear. "Maintenance has never set foot on Kirinyaga before, but now they will come."

"Let them," I said with a shrug. "No law has been broken."

"We have killed a baby," he replied. "They will come, and they will revoke our charter!"

I shook my head. "No one will revoke our charter."

"Do not be too certain of that, Koriba," he warned me. "You can bury a goat alive, and they will monitor us and shake their heads and speak contemptuously among themselves about our religion. You can leave the aged and the infirm out for the hyenas to eat, and they will look upon us with disgust and call us godless heathens. But I tell you that killing a newborn infant is another matter. They will not sit idly by; they will come."

"If they do, I shall explain why I killed it," I replied calmly.

"They will not accept your answers," said Koinnage. "They will not understand."

"They will have no choice but to accept my answers," I said. "This is Kirinyaga, and they are not permitted to interfere."

"They will find a way," he said with an air of certainty. "We must apologize and tell them that it will not happen again."

"We will not apologize," I said sternly. "Nor can we promise that it will not happen again."

"Then, as paramount chief, *I* will apologize."

I stared at him for a long moment, then shrugged. "Do what you must do," I said.

Suddenly I could see the terror in his eyes.

"What will you do to me?" he asked fearfully.

"I? Nothing at all," I said. "Are you not my chief?" As he relaxed, I added: "But if I were you, I would beware of insects."

"Insects?" he repeated. "Why?"

"Because the next insect that bites you, be it spider or mosquito or fly, will surely kill you," I said. "Your blood will boil within your body, and your bones will melt. You will want to scream out your agony, yet you will be unable to utter a sound." I paused. "It is not a death I would wish on a friend," I added seriously.

"Are we not friends, Koriba?" he said, his ebon face turning an ash-gray.

"I thought we were," I said. "But my friends honor our traditions. They do not apologize for them to the white man."

"I will not apologize!" he promised fervently. He spat on both his hands as a gesture of his sincerity.

I opened one of the pouches I kept around my waist and withdrew a small polished stone from the shore of our nearby river. "Wear this around your neck," I said, handing it to him, "and it shall protect you from the bites of insects."

"Thank you, Koriba!" he said with sincere gratitude, and another crisis had been averted.

We spoke about the affairs of the village for a few more minutes, and finally he left me. I sent for Mali, the infant's mother, and led her through the ritual of purification, so that she might conceive again. I also gave her an ointment to relieve the pain in her breasts, since they were heavy with milk. Then I sat down by the fire before my *boma* and made myself available to my people, settling disputes over the ownership of chickens and goats, and supplying charms against demons, and instructing my people in the ancient ways.

By the time of the evening meal, no one had a thought for the dead baby. I ate alone in my *boma*, as befitted my status, for the *mundu-mugu* always lives and eats apart from his people. When I had finished I wrapped a blanket around my body to protect me from the cold and walked down the dirt path to where all the other *bomas* were clustered. The cattle and goats and chickens were penned up for the night, and my people, who had slaughtered and eaten a cow, were now singing and dancing and drinking great quantities of *pombe*. As they made way for me, I walked over to the caldron and took a drink of *pombe*, and then, at Kanjara's request, I slit open a goat and read its entrails and saw that his youngest wife would soon conceive, which was cause for more celebration. Finally the children urged me to tell them a story.

"But not a story of Earth," complained one of the taller boys. "We hear those all the time. This must be a story about Kirinyaga."

"All right," I said. "If you will all gather around, I will tell you a story of Kirinyaga." The youngsters all moved closer. "This," I said, "is the story of the Lion and the Hare." I paused until I was sure that I had everyone's attention, especially that of the adults. "A hare was chosen by his people to be sacrificed to a lion, so that the lion would not bring disaster to their village. The hare might have run away, but he knew that sooner or later the lion would catch him, so instead he sought out the lion and walked right up to him, and as the lion opened his mouth to swallow him, the hare said, 'I apologize, Great Lion.'

"'For what?' asked the lion curiously.

"'Because I am such a small meal,' answered the hare. 'For that reason, I brought honey for you as well.'

"'I see no honey,' said the lion.

"'That is why I apologized,' answered the hare. 'Another lion stole it from me. He is a ferocious creature, and says that he is not afraid of you.'

"The lion rose to his feet. 'Where is this other lion?' he roared.

"The hare pointed to a hole in the earth. 'Down there,' he said, 'but he will not give you back your honey.'

"'We shall see about that!' growled the lion.

"He jumped into the hole, roaring furiously, and was never seen again, for the hare had chosen a very deep hole indeed. Then the hare went home to his people and told them that the lion would never bother them again."

Most of the children laughed and clapped their hands in delight, but the same young boy voiced his objection.

"That is not a story of Kirinyaga," he said scornfully. "We have no lions here."

"It *is* a story of Kirinyaga," I replied. "What is important about the story is not that it concerned a lion and a hare, but that it shows that the weaker can defeat the stronger if he uses his intelligence."

"What has that to do with Kirinyaga?" asked the boy.

"What if we pretend that the men of Maintenance, who have ships and weapons, are the lion, and that the Kikuyu are the hares?" I suggested. "What shall the hares do if the lion demands a sacrifice?"

The boy suddenly grinned. "Now I understand! We shall throw the lion down a hole!"

"But we have no holes here," I pointed out.

"Then what shall we do?"

"The hare did not know that he would find the lion near a hole," I replied. "Had he found him by a deep lake, he would have said that a large fish took the honey."

"We have no deep lakes."

"But we do have intelligence," I said. "And if Maintenance ever interferes with us, we will use our intelligence to destroy the lion of Maintenance, just as the hare used his intelligence to destroy the lion of the fable."

"Let us think how to destroy Maintenance right now!" cried the boy. He picked up a stick and brandished it at an imaginary lion as if it were a spear and he a great hunter.

I shook my head. "The hare does not hunt the lion, and the Kikuyu do not make war. The hare merely protects himself, and the Kikuyu do the same."

"Why would Maintenance interfere with us?" asked another boy, pushing his way to the front of the group. "They are our friends."

"Perhaps they will not," I answered reassuringly. "But you must always remember that the Kikuyu have no true friends except themselves."

"Tell us another story, Koriba!" cried a young girl.

"I am an old man," I said. "The night has turned cold, and I must have my sleep."

"Tomorrow?" she asked. "Will you tell us another tomorrow?"

I smiled. "Ask me tomorrow, after all the fields are planted and the cattle and goats are in their enclosures and the food has been made and the fabrics have been woven."

"But girls do not herd the cattle and goats," she protested. "What if my brothers do not bring all their animals to the enclosure?"

"Then I will tell a story just to the girls," I said.

"It must be a long story," she insisted seriously, "for we work much harder than the boys."

"I will watch you in particular, little one," I replied, "and the story will be as long or as short as your work merits."

The adults all laughed and suddenly she looked very uncomfortable, but then I chuckled and hugged her and patted her head, for it was necessary that the children learned to love their *mundumugu* as well as hold him in awe, and finally she ran off to play and dance with the other girls, while I retired to my *boma*.

Once inside, I activated my computer and discovered that a message was waiting for me from Maintenance, informing me that one of their number would be visiting me the following morning. I made a very brief reply—"Article II, Paragraph 5," which is the ordinance forbidding intervention—and lay down on my sleeping blanket, letting the rhythmic chanting of the singers carry me off to sleep.

I awoke with the sun the next morning and instructed my computer to let me know when the Maintenance ship had landed. Then I inspected my cattle and my goats—I, alone of my people, planted no crops, for the Kikuyu feed their *mundumugu*, just as they tend his herds and weave his blankets and keep his *boma* clean—and stopped by Siboki's *boma* to deliver a balm to fight the disease that was afflicting his joints. Then, as the sun began warming the earth, I returned to my own *boma*, skirting the pastures where the young men were tending their animals. When I arrived, I knew the ship had landed, for I found the droppings of a hyena on the ground near my hut, and that is the surest sign of a curse.

I learned what I could from the computer, then walked outside and scanned the horizon while two naked children took turns chasing a small dog and running away from it. When they began frightening my chickens, I gently sent them back to their own *shamba*, and then seated myself beside my fire. At last I saw my visitor from Maintenance, coming up the path from Haven. She was obviously uncomfortable in the heat, and she slapped futilely at the flies that circled her head. Her blonde hair was starting to turn gray, and I could tell by the ungainly way she negotiated the steep, rocky path that she was unused to such terrain. She almost lost her balance a number of times, and it was obvious that her proximity to so many animals frightened her, but she never slowed her pace, and within another ten minutes she stood before me.

"Good morning," she said.

"*Jambo*, Memsaab," I replied.

"You are Koriba, are you not?"

I briefly studied the face of my enemy; middle-aged and weary, it did not appear formidable. "I am Koriba," I replied.

"Good," she said. "My name is—"

"I know who you are," I said, for it is best, if conflict cannot be avoided, to take the offensive.

"You do?"

I pulled the bones out of my pouch and cast them on the dirt. "You are Barbara Eaton, born of Earth," I intoned, studying her reactions as I picked up the bones and cast them again. "You are married to Robert Eaton, and you have worked for Maintenance for nine years." A final cast of the bones. "You are forty-one years old, and you are barren."

"How did you know all that?" she asked with an expression of surprise.

"Am I not the *mundumugu*?"

She stared at me for a long minute. "You read my biography on your computer," she concluded at last.

"As long as the facts are correct, what difference does it make whether I read them from the bones or the computer?" I responded, refusing to confirm her statement. "Please sit down, Memsaab Eaton."

She lowered herself awkwardly to the ground, wrinkling her face as she raised a cloud of dust.

"It's very hot on Kirinyaga," she noted uncomfortably.

"It is very hot in Kenya," I replied.

"You could have created any climate you desired," she pointed out.

"We *did* create the climate we desired," I answered.

"Are there predators out there?" she asked, looking out over the savannah.

"A few," I replied.

"What kind?"

"Hyenas."

"Nothing larger?" she asked.

"There *is* nothing larger anymore," I said.

"I wonder why they didn't attack me?"

"Perhaps because you are an intruder," I suggested.

"Will they leave me alone on my way back to Haven?" she asked nervously, ignoring my comment.

"I will give you a charm to keep them away."

"I'd prefer an escort."

"Very well," I said.

"They're such ugly animals," she said with a shudder. "I saw them once when we were monitoring your world."

"They are very useful animals," I answered, "for they bring many omens, both good and bad."

"Really?"

I nodded. "A hyena left me an evil omen this morning."

"And?" she asked curiously.

"And here you are," I said.

She laughed. "They told me you were a sharp old man."

"They were mistaken," I replied. "I am a feeble old man who sits in front of his *boma* and watches younger men tend his cattle and goats."

"You are a feeble old man who graduated with honors from Cambridge and then acquired two postgraduate degrees from Yale," she replied.

"Who told you that?"

She smiled. "You're not the only one who reads biographies."

I shrugged. "My degrees did not help me become a better *mundumugu*," I said. "The time was wasted."

"You keep using that word. What, exactly, *is* a *mundumugu*?"

"You would call him a witch doctor," I answered. "But in truth the *mundumugu*, while he occasionally casts spells and interprets omens, is more a repository of the collected wisdom and traditions of his race."

"It sounds like an interesting occupation," she said.

"It is not without its compensations."

"And *such* compensations!" she said with false enthusiasm as a goat bleated in the distance and a young man yelled at it in Swahili. "Imagine having the power of life and death over an entire Eutopian world!"

So now it comes, I thought. Aloud I said: "It is not a matter of exercising power, Memsaab Eaton, but of maintaining traditions."

"I rather doubt that," she said bluntly.

"Why should you doubt what I say?" I asked.

"Because if it were traditional to kill newborn infants, the Kikuyus would have died out after a single generation."

"If the slaying of the infant arouses your disapproval," I said calmly, "I am surprised Maintenance has not previously asked about our custom of leaving the old and the feeble out for the hyenas."

"We know that the elderly and the infirm have consented to your treatment of them, much as we may disapprove of it," she replied. "We also know that a newborn infant could not possibly consent to its own death." She paused, staring at me. "May I ask why this particular baby was killed?"

"That *is* why you have come here, is it not?"

"I have been sent here to evaluate the situation," she replied, brushing an insect from her cheek and shifting her position on the ground. "A newborn child was killed. We would like to know why."

I shrugged. "It was killed because it was born with a terrible *thahu* upon it."

She frowned. "A *thahu*? What is that?"

"A curse."

"Do you mean that it was deformed?" she asked.

"It was not deformed."

"Then what was this curse that you refer to?"

"It was born feetfirst," I said.

"That's it?" she asked, surprised. "That's the curse?"

"Yes."

"It was murdered simply because it came out feetfirst?"

"It is not murder to put a demon to death," I explained patiently. "Our tradition tells us that a child born in this manner is actually a demon."

"You are an educated man, Koriba," she said. "How can you kill a perfectly healthy infant and blame it on some primitive tradition?"

"You must never underestimate the power of tradition, Memsaab Eaton," I said. "The Kikuyu turned their backs on their traditions once; the result is a mechanized, impoverished, overcrowded country that is no longer populated by Kikuyu, or Maasai, or Luo, or Wakamba, but by a new, artificial tribe known only as Kenyans. We here on Kirinyaga are true Kikuyu, and we will not make that mistake again. If the rains are late, a ram must be sacrificed. If a man's veracity is questioned, he must undergo the ordeal of the *githani* trial. If an infant is born with a *thahu* upon it, it must be put to death."

"Then you intend to continue to kill any children that are born feetfirst?" she asked.

"That is correct," I responded.

A drop of sweat rolled down her face as she looked directly at me and said: "I don't know what Maintenance's reaction will be."

"According to our charter, Maintenance is not permitted to interfere with us," I reminded her.

"It's not that simple, Koriba," she said. "According to your charter, any member of your community who wishes to leave your world is allowed free passage to Haven, from which he or she can board a ship to Earth." She paused. "Was the baby you killed given such a choice?"

"I did not kill a baby, but a demon," I replied, turning my head slightly as a hot breeze stirred up the dust around us.

She waited until the breeze died down, then coughed before speaking. "You do understand that not everyone in Maintenance may share that opinion?"

"What Maintenance thinks is of no concern to us," I said.

"When innocent children are murdered, what Maintenance thinks is of supreme importance to you," she responded. "I am sure you do not want to defend your practices in the Eutopian Court."

"Are you here to evaluate the situation, as you said, or to threaten us?" I asked calmly.

"To evaluate the situation," she replied. "But there seems to be only one conclusion that I can draw from the facts that you have presented to me."

"Then you have not been listening to me," I said, briefly closing my eyes as another, stronger breeze swept past us.

"Koriba, I know that Kirinyaga was created so that you could emulate the ways of your forefathers—but surely you must see the difference between the torture of animals as a religious ritual and the murder of a human baby."

I shook my head. "They are one and the same," I replied. "We cannot change our way of life because it makes *you* uncomfortable. We did that once before, and within a mere handful of years your culture had corrupted our society. With every factory we built, with every job we created, with every bit of Western technology we accepted, with every Kikuyu who converted to Christianity, we became something we were not meant to be." I stared directly into her eyes. "I am the *mundumugu*, entrusted with preserving all that makes us Kikuyu, and I will not allow that to happen again."

"There are alternatives," she said.

"Not for the Kikuyu," I replied adamantly.

"There *are*," she insisted, so intent upon what she had to say that she paid no attention to a black-and-gold centipede that crawled over her boot. "For example, years spent in space can cause certain physiological and hormonal changes in humans. You noted when I arrived that I am forty-one years old and childless. That is true. In fact, many of the women in Maintenance are childless. If you will turn the babies over to us, I am sure we can find families for them. This would effectively remove them from your society without the necessity of killing them. I could speak to my superiors about it; I think that there is an excellent chance that they would approve."

"That is a thoughtful and innovative suggestion, Memsaab Eaton," I said truthfully. "I am sorry that I must reject it."

"But why?" she demanded.

"Because the first time we betray our traditions this world will cease to be Kirinyaga, and will become merely another Kenya, a nation of men awkwardly pretending to be something they are not."

"I could speak to Koinnage and the other chiefs about it," she suggested meaningfully.

"They will not disobey my instructions," I replied confidently.

"You hold that much power?"

"I hold that much respect," I answered. "A chief may enforce the law, but it is the *mundumugu* who interprets it."

"Then let us consider other alternatives."

"No."

"I am trying to avoid a conflict between Maintenance and your people," she said, her voice heavy with frustration. "It seems to me that you could at least make the effort to meet me halfway."

"I do not question your motives, Memsaab Eaton," I replied, "but you are an intruder representing an organization that has no legal right to interfere with our culture. We do not impose our religion or our morality upon Maintenance, and Maintenance may not impose its religion or morality upon us."

"It's not that simple."

"It is precisely that simple," I said.

"That is your last word on the subject?" she asked.

"Yes."

She stood up. "Then I think it is time for me to leave and make my report."

I stood up as well, and a shift in the wind brought the odors of the village: the scent of bananas, the smell of a fresh caldron of *pombe*, even the pungent odor of a bull that had been slaughtered that morning.

"As you wish, Memsaab Eaton," I said. "I will arrange for your escort." I signaled to a small boy who was tending three goats and instructed him to go to the village and send back two young men.

"Thank you," she said. "I know it's an inconvenience, but I just don't feel safe with hyenas roaming loose out there."

"You are welcome," I said. "Perhaps, while we are waiting for the men who will accompany you, you would like to hear a story about the hyena."

She shuddered involuntarily. "They are such ugly beasts!" she said distastefully. "Their hind legs seem almost deformed." She shook her head. "No, I don't think I'd be interested in hearing a story about a hyena."

"You will be interested in *this* story," I told her.

She stared at me curiously, then shrugged. "All right," she said. "Go ahead."

"It is true that hyenas are deformed, ugly animals," I began, "but once, a long time ago, they were as lovely and graceful as the impala. Then one day a Kikuyu chief gave a hyena a young goat to take as a gift to Ngai, who lived atop the holy mountain Kirinyaga. The hyena took the goat between his powerful jaws and headed toward the distant mountain—but on the way he passed a settlement filled with Europeans and Arabs. It abounded in guns and machines and other wonders he had never seen before, and he stopped to look, fascinated. Finally an Arab noticed him staring intently and asked if he, too, would like to become a civilized man—and as he opened his mouth to say that he would, the goat fell to the ground and ran away. As the goat raced out of sight, the Arab laughed and explained that he was only joking, that of course no hyena could become a man." I paused for a moment, and then continued. "So the hyena proceeded to Kirinyaga, and when he reached the summit, Ngai asked him what had become of the goat. When the hyena told him, Ngai hurled him off the mountaintop for having the audacity to believe he could become a man. He did not die from the fall, but his rear legs were crippled, and Ngai declared that from that day forward, all hyenas would appear thus—and to remind them of the foolishness of trying to become something that they were not, He also gave them a fool's laugh." I paused again, and stared at her. "Memsaab Eaton, you do not hear the Kikuyu laugh like fools, and I will not let them become crippled like the hyena. Do you understand what I am saying?"

She considered my statement for a moment, then looked into my eyes. "I think we understand each other perfectly, Koriba," she said.

The two young men I had sent for arrived just then, and I instructed them to accompany her to Haven. A moment later they set off across the dry savannah, and I returned to my duties.

I began by walking through the fields, blessing the scarecrows. Since a number of the smaller children followed me, I rested beneath the trees more often than was necessary, and always, whenever we paused, they begged me to tell them more stories. I told them the tale of the Elephant and the Buffalo, and how the Maasai *elmoran* cut the rainbow with his spear so that it never again came to rest upon the earth, and why the nine Kikuyu tribes are named after Gikuyu's nine daughters, and when the sun became too hot I led them back to the village.

Then, in the afternoon, I gathered the older boys about me and explained once more how they must paint their faces and bodies for their forthcoming circumcision ceremony. Ndemi, the boy who had insisted upon a story about Kirinyaga the night before, sought me out privately to complain that he had been unable to slay a small gazelle with his spear, and asked for a charm to make its flight more accurate.

I explained to him that there would come a day when he faced a buffalo or a hyena with no charm, and that he must practice more before he came to me again. He was one to watch, this little Ndemi, for he was impetuous and totally without fear; in the old days, he would have made a great warrior, but on Kirinyaga we had no warriors. If we remained fruitful and fecund, however, we would someday need more chiefs and even another *mundumugu*, and I made up my mind to observe him closely.

In the evening, after I ate my solitary meal, I returned to the village, for Njogu, one of our young men, was to marry Kamiri, a girl from the next village. The bride-price had been decided upon, and the two families were waiting for me to preside at the ceremony.

Njogu, his faced streaked with paint, wore an ostrich-feather headdress, and looked very uneasy as he and his betrothed stood before me. I slit the throat of a fat ram that Kamiri's father had brought for the occasion, and then I turned to Njogu.

"What have you to say?" I asked.

He took a step forward. "I want Kamiri to come and till the fields of my *shamba*," he said, his voice cracking with nervousness as he spoke the prescribed words, "for I am a man, and I need a woman to tend to my *shamba* and dig deep around the roots of my plantings, that they may grow well and bring prosperity to my house."

He spit on both his hands to show his sincerity, and then, exhaling deeply with relief, he stepped back.

I turned to Kamiri.

"Do you consent to till the *shamba* of Njogu, son of Muchiri?" I asked her.

"Yes," she said softly, bowing her head. "I consent."

I held out my right hand, and the bride's mother placed a gourd of *pombe* in it.

"If this man does not please you," I said to Kamiri, "I will spill the *pombe* upon the ground."

"Do not spill it," she replied.

"Then drink," I said, handing the gourd to her.

She lifted it to her lips and took a swallow, then handed it to Njogu, who did the same.

When the gourd was empty, the parents of Njogu and Kamiri stuffed it with grass, signifying the friendship between the two clans.

Then a cheer rose from the onlookers, the ram was carried off to be roasted, more *pombe* appeared as if by magic, and while the groom took the bride off to his *boma*, the remainder of the people celebrated far into the night. They stopped only when the bleating of the goats told them that some hyenas were nearby, and then the women and children went off to their *bomas* while the men took their spears and went into the fields to frighten the hyenas away.

Koinnage came up to me as I was about to leave.

"Did you speak to the woman from Maintenance?" he asked.

"I did," I replied.

"What did she say?"

"She said that they do not approve of killing babies who are born feetfirst."

"And what did *you* say?" he asked nervously.

"I told her that we did not need the approval of Maintenance to practice our religion," I replied.

"Will Maintenance listen?"

"They have no choice," I said. "And *we* have no choice, either," I added. "Let them dictate one thing that we must or must not do, and soon they will dictate all things. Give them their way, and Njogu and Kamiri would have recited wedding vows from the Bible or the Koran. It happened to us in Kenya; we cannot permit it to happen on Kirinyaga."

"But they will not punish us?" he persisted.

"They will not punish us," I replied.

Satisfied, he walked off to his *boma* while I took the narrow, winding path to my own. I stopped by the enclosure where my animals were kept and saw that there were two new goats there, gifts from the bride's and groom's families in gratitude for my services. A few minutes later I was asleep within the walls of my own *boma*.

The computer woke me a few minutes before sunrise. I stood up, splashed my face with water from the gourd I keep by my sleeping blanket, and walked over to the terminal.

There was a message for me from Barbara Eaton, brief and to the point:

> It is the preliminary finding of Maintenance that infanticide, for any reason, is a direct violation of Kirinyaga's charter. No action will be taken for past offenses.
>
> We are also evaluating your practice of euthanasia, and may require further testimony from you at some point in the future.
>
> BARBARA EATON

A runner from Koinnage arrived a moment later, asking me to attend a meeting of the Council of Elders, and I knew that he had received the same message.

I wrapped my blanket around my shoulders and began walking to Koinnage's *shamba*, which consisted of his *boma*, as well as those of his three sons and their wives. When I arrived I found not only the local Elders waiting for me, but also two chiefs from neighboring villages.

"Did you receive the message from Maintenance?" demanded Koinnage, as I seated myself opposite him.

"I did."

"I warned you that this would happen!" he said. "What will we do now?"

"We will do what we have always done," I answered calmly.

"We cannot," said one of the neighboring chiefs. "They have forbidden it."

"They have no right to forbid it," I replied.

"There is a woman in my village whose time is near," continued the chief, "and all of the signs and omens point to the birth of twins. We have been taught that the firstborn must be killed, for one mother cannot produce two souls—but now Maintenance has forbidden it. What are we to do?"

"We must kill the firstborn," I said, "for it will be a demon."

"And then Maintenance will make us leave Kirinyaga!" said Koinnage bitterly.

"Perhaps we could let the child live," said the chief. "That might satisfy them, and then they might leave us alone."

I shook my head. "They will not leave you alone. Already they speak about the way we leave the old and the feeble out for the hyenas, as if this were some enormous sin against their god. If you give in on the one, the day will come when you must give in on the other."

"Would that be so terrible?" persisted the chief. "They have medicines that we do not possess; perhaps they could make the old young again."

"You do not understand," I said, rising to my feet. "Our society is not a collection of separate people and customs and traditions. No, it is a complex system, with all the pieces as dependent upon each other as the animals and vegetation of the savannah. If you burn the grass, you will not only kill the impala who feeds upon it, but the predator who feeds upon the impala, and the ticks and flies who live upon the predator, and the vultures and maribou storks who feed upon his remains when he dies. You cannot destroy the part without destroying the whole."

I paused to let them consider what I had said, and then continued speaking: "Kirinyaga is like the savannah. If we do not leave the old and the feeble out for the hyenas, the hyenas will starve. If the hyenas starve, the grass eaters will become so numerous that there is no land left for our cattle and goats to graze. If the old and the feeble do not die when Ngai decrees it, then soon we will not have enough food to go around."

I picked up a stick and balanced it precariously on my forefinger.

"This stick," I said, "is the Kikuyu people, and my finger is Kirinyaga. They are in perfect balance." I stared at the neighboring chief. "But what will happen if I alter the balance, and put my finger *here*?" I asked, gesturing to the end of the stick.

"The stick will fall to the ground."

"And here?" I asked, pointing to a stop an inch away from the center.

"It will fall."

"Thus is it with us," I explained. "Whether we yield on one point or all points, the result will be the same: The Kikuyu will fall as surely as the stick will fall. Have we learned nothing from our past? We *must* adhere to our traditions; they are all that we have!"

"But Maintenance will not allow us to do so!" protested Koinnage.

"They are not warriors, but civilized men," I said, allowing a touch of contempt to creep into my voice. "Their chiefs and their *mundumugus* will not send them to Kirinyaga with guns and spears. They will issue warnings and findings and declarations, and finally, when that fails, they will go to the Eutopian Court and plead their case, and the trial will be postponed many times and reheard many more times." I could see them finally relaxing, and I smiled confidently at them. "Each of you will have died from the burden of your years before Maintenance does anything other than talk. I am your *mundumugu*; I have lived among civilized men, and I tell you that this is the truth."

The neighboring chief stood up and faced me. "I will send for you when the twins are born," he pledged.

"I will come," I promised him.

We spoke further, and then the meeting ended and the old men began wandering off to their *bomas*, while I looked to the future, which I could see more clearly than Koinnage or the Elders.

I walked through the village until I found the bold young Ndemi, brandishing his spear and hurling it at a buffalo he had constructed out of dried grasses.

"*Jambo*, Koriba!" he greeted me.

"*Jambo*, my brave young warrior," I replied.

"I have been practicing, as you ordered."

"I thought you wanted to hunt the gazelle," I noted.

"Gazelles are for children," he answered. "I will slay *mbogo*, the buffalo."

"*Mbogo* may feel differently about it," I said.

"So much the better," he said confidently. "I have no wish to kill an animal as it runs away from me."

"And when will you go out to slay the fierce *mbogo*?"

He shrugged. "When I am more accurate." He smiled up at me. "Perhaps tomorrow."

I stared at him thoughtfully for a moment, and then spoke: "Tomorrow is a long time away. We have business tonight."

"What business?" he asked.

"You must find ten friends, none of them yet of circumcision age, and tell them to come to the pond within the forest to the south. They must come after the sun has set, and you must tell them that Koriba the *mundumugu* commands that they tell no one, not even their parents, that they are coming." I paused. "Do you understand, Ndemi?"

"I understand."

"Then go," I said. "Bring my message to them."

He retrieved his spear from the straw buffalo and set off at a trot, young and tall and strong and fearless.

You are the future, I thought, as I watched him run toward the village. *Not Koinnage, not myself, not even the young bridegroom Njogu, for their time will have come and gone before the battle is joined. It is you, Ndemi, upon whom Kirinyaga must depend if it is to survive.*

Once before the Kikuyu have had to fight for their freedom. Under the leadership of Jomo Kenyatta, whose name has been forgotten by most of your parents, we took the terrible oath of Mau Mau, and we maimed and we killed and we committed such atrocities that finally we achieved Uhuru, for against such butchery civilized men have no defense but to depart.

And tonight, young Ndemi, while your parents are asleep, you and your companions will meet me deep in the woods, and you in your turn and they in theirs will learn one last tradition of the Kikuyu, for I will invoke not only the strength of Ngai but also the indomitable spirit of Jomo Kenyatta. I will administer a hideous oath and force you to do unspeakable things to prove your fealty, and I will teach each of you, in turn, how to administer the oath to those who come after you.

There is a season for all things: for birth, for growth, for death. There is unquestionably a season for Utopia, but it will have to wait.

For the season of Uhuru is upon us.

2

FOR I HAVE TOUCHED THE SKY

{JANUARY 2131}

There was a time when men had wings.

Ngai, who sits alone on His golden throne atop Kirinyaga, gave men the gift of flight, so that they might reach the succulent fruits on the highest branches of the trees. But one man, a son of Gikuyu, who was himself the first man, saw the eagle and the vulture riding high upon the winds, and spreading his wings, he joined them. He circled higher and higher, and soon he soared far above all other flying things.

Then, suddenly, the hand of Ngai reached out and grabbed the son of Gikuyu.

"What have I done that you should grab me thus?" asked the son of Gikuyu.

"I live atop Kirinyaga because it is the top of the world," answered Ngai, "and no one's head may be higher than my own."

And so saying, Ngai plucked the wings from the son of Gikuyu, and then took the wings away from *all* men, so that no man could ever again rise higher than His head.

And that is why all of Gikuyu's descendants look at the birds with a sense of loss and envy, and why they no longer eat the succulent fruits from the highest branches of the trees.

We have many birds on the world of Kirinyaga, which was named for the holy mountain where Ngai dwells. We brought them along with our other animals when we received our charter from the Eutopian Council and departed from a Kenya that no longer had any meaning for true members of the Kikuyu tribe. Our new world is home to the maribou and the vulture, the ostrich and the fish eagle, the weaver and the heron, and many other species. Even I, who am the *mundumugu*, delight in their many colors, and find solace in their music. I have spent many afternoons seated in front of my *boma*, my back propped up against an ancient acacia tree, watching the profusion of colors and listening to the melodic songs as the birds come to slake their thirst in the river that winds through our village.

It was on one such afternoon that Kamari, a young girl who was not yet of circumcision age, walked up the long, winding path that separates my *boma* from the village, holding something small and gray in her hands.

"*Jambo*, Koriba," she greeted me.

"*Jambo*, Kamari," I answered her. "What have you brought to me, child?"

"This," she said, holding out a young pygmy falcon that struggled weakly to escape her grasp. "I found him in my family's *shamba*. He cannot fly."

"He looks fully fledged," I noted, getting to my feet. Then I saw that one of his wings was held at an awkward angle. "Ah!" I said. "He has broken his wing."

"Can you make him well, *mundumugu*?" asked Kamari.

I examined the wing briefly, while she held the young falcon's head away from me. Then I stepped back.

"I can make him well, Kamari," I said. "But I cannot make him fly. The wing will heal, but it will never be strong enough to bear his weight again. I think we will destroy him."

"No!" she exclaimed, pulling the falcon back. "You will make him live, and I will care for him!"

I stared at the bird for a moment, then shook my head. "He will not wish to live," I said at last.

"Why not?"

"Because he has ridden high upon the warm winds."

"I do not understand," said Kamari, frowning.

"Once a bird has touched the sky," I explained, "he can never be content to spend his days on the ground."

"I will *make* him content," she said with determination. "You will heal him and I will care for him, and he will live."

"I will heal him and you will care for him," I said. "But," I added, "he will not live."

"What is your fee, Koriba?" she asked, suddenly businesslike.

"I do not charge children," I answered. "I will visit your father tomorrow, and he will pay me."

She shook her head adamantly. "This is *my* bird. *I* will pay the fee."

"Very well," I said, admiring her spirit, for most children—and *all* adults—are terrified of their *mundumugu*, and would never openly contradict or disagree with him. "For one month you will clean my *boma* every morning and every afternoon. You will lay out my sleeping blankets, and keep my water gourd filled, and you will see that I have kindling for my fire."

"That is fair," she said after a moment's consideration. Then she added: "What if the bird dies before the month is over?"

"Then you will learn that a *mundumugu* knows more than a little Kikuyu girl," I said.

She set her jaw. "He will not die." She paused. "Will you fix his wing now?"

"Yes."

"I will help."

I shook my head. "You will build a cage in which to confine him, for if he tries to move his wing too soon, he will break it again and then I will surely have to destroy him."

She handed the bird to me. "I will be back soon," she promised, racing off toward her *shamba*.

I took the falcon into my hut. He was too weak to struggle very much, and he allowed me to tie his beak shut. Then I began the slow task of splinting his broken wing and binding it against his body to keep it motionless. He shrieked in pain as I manipulated the bones together, but otherwise he simply stared unblinking at me, and within ten minutes the job was finished.

Kamari returned an hour later, holding a small wooden cage in her hands.

"Is this large enough, Koriba?" she asked.

I held it up and examined it.

"It is almost too large," I replied. "He must not be able to move his wing until it has healed."

"He won't," she promised. "I will watch him all day long, every day."

"You will watch him all day long, every day?" I repeated, amused.

"Yes."

"Then who will clean my hut and my *boma*, and who will fill my gourd with water?"

"I will carry his cage with me when I come," she replied.

"The cage will be much heavier when the bird is in it," I pointed out.

"When I am a woman, I will carry far heavier loads on my back, for I shall have to till the fields and gather the firewood for my husband's *boma*," she said. "This will be good practice." She paused. "Why do you smile at me, Koriba?"

"I am not used to being lectured to by uncircumcised children," I replied with a smile.

"I was not lecturing," she answered with dignity. "I was *explaining*."

I held a hand up to shade my eyes from the afternoon sun.

"Are you not afraid of me, little Kamari?" I asked.

"Why should I be?"

"Because I am the *mundumugu*."

"That just means you are smarter than the others," she said with a shrug. She threw a stone at a chicken that was approaching her cage, and it raced away, squawking its annoyance. "Someday I shall be as smart as you are."

"Oh?"

She nodded confidently. "Already I can count higher than my father, and I can remember many things."

"What kind of things?" I asked, turning slightly as a hot breeze blew a swirl of dust about us.

"Do you remember the story of the honey bird that you told to the children of the village before the long rains?"

I nodded.

"I can repeat it," she said.

"You mean you can remember it."

She shook her head vigorously. "I can repeat every word that you said."

I sat down and crossed my legs. "Let me hear," I said, staring off into the distance and idly watching a pair of young men tending their cattle.

She hunched her shoulders, so that she would appear as bent with age as I myself am, and then, in a voice that sounded like a youthful replica of my own, she began to speak, mimicking my gestures.

"There is a little brown honey bird," she began. "He is very much like a sparrow, and as friendly. He will come to your *boma* and call to you, and as you approach him he will fly up and lead you to a hive, and then wait while you gather grass and set fire to it and smoke out the bees. But you must *always*"—she emphasized the word, just as I had done—"leave some honey for him, for if you take it all, the next time he will lead you into the jaws of *fisi*, the hyena, or perhaps into the desert where there is no water and you will die of thirst." Her story finished, she stood upright and smiled at me. "You see?" she said proudly.

"I see," I said, brushing away a large fly that had lit on my cheek.

"Did I do it right?" she asked.

"You did it right."

She stared at me thoughtfully. "Perhaps when you die, I will become the *mundumugu*."

"Do I seem that close to death?" I asked.

"Well," she answered, "you are very old and bent and wrinkled, and you sleep too much. But I will be just as happy if you do not die right away."

"I shall try to make you just as happy," I said ironically. "Now take your falcon home."

I was about to instruct her concerning his needs, but she spoke first.

"He will not want to eat today. But starting tomorrow, I will give him large insects, and at least one lizard every day. And he must always have water."

"You are very observant, Kamari."

She smiled at me again, and then ran off toward her *boma*.

She was back at dawn the next morning, carrying the cage with her. She placed it in the shade, then filled a small container with water from one of my gourds and set it inside the cage.

"How is your bird this morning?" I asked, sitting close to my fire, for even though the planetary engineers of the Eutopian Council had given Kirinyaga a climate identical to Kenya's, the sun had not yet warmed the morning air.

Kamari frowned. "He has not eaten yet."

"He will, when he gets hungry enough," I said, pulling my blanket more tightly around my shoulders. "He is used to swooping down on his prey from the sky."

"He drinks his water, though," she noted.

"That is a good sign."

"Can you not cast a spell that will heal him all at once?"

"The price would be too high," I said, for I had foreseen her question. "This way is better."

"How high?"

"*Too* high," I repeated, closing the subject. "Now, do you not have work to do?"

"Yes, Koriba."

She spent the next few minutes gathering kindling for my fire and filling my gourd from the river. Then she went into my hut to clean it and straighten my sleeping blankets. She emerged a moment later with a book in her hand.

"What is this, Koriba?" she asked.

"Who told you that you could touch your *mundumugu's* possessions?" I asked sternly.

"How can I clean them without touching them?" she replied with no show of fear. "What is it?"

"It is a book."

"What is a book, Koriba?"

"It is not for you to know," I said. "Put it back."

"Shall I tell you what I think it is?" she asked.

"Tell me," I said, curious to hear her answer.

"Do you know how you draw signs on the ground when you cast the bones to bring the rains? I think that a book is a collection of signs."

"You are a very bright little girl, Kamari."

"I *told* you that I was," she said, annoyed that I had not accepted her statement as a self-evident truth. She looked at the book for a moment, then held it up. "What do the signs mean?"

"Different things," I said.

"*What* things?"

"It is not necessary for the Kikuyu to know."

"But *you* know."

"I am the *mundumugu*."

"Can anyone else on Kirinyaga read the signs?"

"Your own chief, Koinnage, and two other chiefs can read the signs," I answered, sorry now that she had charmed me into this conversation, for I could foresee its direction.

"But you are all old men," she said. "You should teach me, so when you all die someone can read the signs."

"These signs are not important," I said. "They were created by the Europeans. The Kikuyu had no need for books before the Europeans came to Kenya; we have no need for them on Kirinyaga, which is our own world. When Koinnage and the other chiefs die, everything will be as it was long ago."

"Are they evil signs, then?" she asked.

"No," I said. "They are not evil. They just have no meaning for the Kikuyu. They are the white man's signs."

She handed the book to me. "Would you read me one of the signs?"

"Why?"

"I am curious to know what kind of signs the white men made."

I stared at her for a long minute, trying to make up my mind. Finally I nodded my assent.

"Just this once," I said. "Never again."

"Just this once," she agreed.

I thumbed through the book, which was a Swahili translation of Elizabethan poetry, selected one at random, and read it to her:

Come live with me and be my love,
And we will all the pleasures prove
That valleys, groves, hills, and fields,
Woods, or steepy mountains yields.

And we will sit upon the rocks,
Seeing the shepherds feed their flocks,
By shallow rivers to whose falls
Melodious birds sing madrigals.

There will I make thee bed of roses,
And a thousand fragrant posies,
A cap of flowers, and a kirtle
Embroidered all with leaves of myrtle.

A bed of straw and ivy buds,
With coral clasps and amber studs:
And if these pleasures may thee move,
Come live with me and be my love.

Kamari frowned. "I do not understand."

"I told you that you would not," I said. "Now put the book away and finish cleaning my hut. You must still work in your father's *shamba*, along with your duties here."

She nodded and disappeared into my hut, only to burst forth excitedly a few minutes later.

"It is a *story!*" she exclaimed.

"What is?"

"The sign you read! I do not understand many of the words, but it is a story about a warrior who asks a maiden to marry him!" She paused. "*You* would tell it better, Koriba. The sign doesn't even mention *fisi*, the hyena, and *mamba*, the crocodile, who dwell by the river and would eat the warrior and his wife. Still, it is a story! I had thought it would be a spell for *mundumugus*."

"You are very wise to know that it is a story," I said.

"Read another to me!" she said enthusiastically.

I shook my head. "Do you not remember our agreement? Just that once, and never again."

She lowered her head in thought, then looked up brightly. "Then teach *me* to read the signs."

"That is against the law of the Kikuyu," I said. "No woman is permitted to read."

"Why?"

"It is a woman's duty to till the fields and pound the grain and make the fires and weave the fabrics and bear her husband's children," I answered.

"But I am not a woman," she pointed out. "I am just a little girl."

"But you will become a woman," I said, "and a woman may not read."

"Teach me now, and I will forget how when I become a woman."

"Does the eagle forget how to fly, or the hyena to kill?"

"It is not fair."

"No," I said. "But it is just."

"I do not understand."

"Then I will explain it to you," I said. "Sit down, Kamari."

She sat down on the dirt opposite me and leaned forward intently.

"Many years ago," I began, "the Kikuyu lived in the shadow of Kirinyaga, the mountain upon which Ngai dwells."

"I know," she said. "Then the Europeans came and built their cities."

"You are interrupting," I said.

"I am sorry, Koriba," she answered. "But I already know this story."

"You do not know all of it," I replied. "Before the Europeans came, we lived in harmony with the land. We tended our cattle and plowed our fields, we produced just enough children to replace those who died of old age and disease, and those who died in our wars against the Maasai and the Wakamba and the Nandi. Our lives were simple but fulfilling."

"And *then* the Europeans came!" she said.

"Then the Europeans came," I agreed, "and they brought new ways with them."

"Evil ways."

I shook my head. "They were not evil ways for the Europeans," I replied. "I know, for I have studied in European schools. But they were not good ways for the Kikuyu and the Maasai and the Wakamba and the Embu and the Kisi and all the other tribes. We saw the clothes they wore and the buildings they erected and the machines they used, and we tried to become like Europeans. But we are not Europeans, and their ways are not our ways, and they do not work for us. Our cities became overcrowded and polluted, and our land grew barren, and our animals died, and our water became poisoned, and finally, when the Eutopian Council allowed us to move to the world of Kirinyaga, we left Kenya behind and came here to live according to the old ways, the ways that are good for the Kikuyu." I paused. "Long ago the Kikuyu had no written language, and did not know how to read, and since we are trying to create a Kikuyu world here on Kirinyaga, it is only fitting that our people do not learn to read or write."

"But what is good about not knowing how to read?" she asked. "Just because we didn't do it before the Europeans came doesn't make it bad."

"Reading will make you aware of other ways of thinking and living, and then you will be discontented with your life on Kirinyaga."

"But *you* read, and you are not discontented."

"I am the *mundumugu*," I said. "I am wise enough to know that what I read are lies."

"But lies are not always bad," she persisted. "You tell them all the time."

"The *mundumugu* does not lie to his people," I replied sternly.

"You call them stories, like the story of the lion and the hare, or the tale of how the rainbow came to be, but they are lies."

"They are parables," I said.

"What is a parable?"

"A type of story."

"Is it a true story?"

"In a way."

"If it is true in a way, then it is also a lie in a way, is it not?" she replied, and then continued before I could answer her. "And if I can listen to a lie, why can I not read one?"

"I have already explained it to you."

"It is not fair," she repeated.

"No," I agreed. "But it is true, and in the long run it is for the good of the Kikuyu."

"I still don't understand why it is good," she complained.

"Because we are all that remain. Once before the Kikuyu tried to become something that they were not, and we became not city-dwelling Kikuyu, or bad Kikuyu, or unhappy Kikuyu, but an entirely new tribe called Kenyans. Those of us who came to Kirinyaga came here to preserve the old ways—and if women start reading, some of them will become discontented, and they will leave, and then one day there will be no Kikuyu left."

"But I don't want to leave Kirinyaga!" she protested. "I want to become circumcised, and bear many children for my husband, and till the fields of his *shamba*, and someday be cared for by my grandchildren."

"That is the way you are supposed to feel."

"But I also want to read about other worlds and other times."

I shook my head. "No."

"But—"

"I will hear no more of this today," I said. "The sun grows high in the sky, and you have not yet finished your tasks here, and you must still work in your father's *shamba* and come back again this afternoon."

She arose without another word and went about her duties. When she finished, she picked up the cage and began walking back to her *boma*.

I watched her walk away, then returned to my hut and activated my computer to discuss a minor orbital adjustment with Maintenance, for it had been hot and dry for almost a month. They gave their consent, and a few moments later I walked down the long winding path into the center of the village. Lowering myself gently to the ground, I spread my pouchful of bones and charms out before me and invoked Ngai to cool Kirinyaga with a mild rain, which Maintenance had agreed to supply later in the afternoon.

Then the children gathered about me, as they always did when I came down from my *boma* on the hill and entered the village.

"*Jambo*, Koriba!" they cried.

"*Jambo*, my brave young warriors," I replied, still seated on the ground.

"Why have you come to the village this morning, Koriba?" asked Ndemi, the boldest of the young boys.

"I have come here to ask Ngai to water our fields with His tears of compassion," I said, "for we have had no rain this month, and the crops are thirsty."

"Now that you have finished speaking to Ngai, will you tell us a story?" asked Ndemi.

I looked up at the sun, estimating the time of day.

"I have time for just one," I replied. "Then I must walk through the fields and place new charms on the scarecrows, that they may continue to protect your crops."

"What story will you tell us, Koriba?" asked another of the boys.

I looked around, and saw that Kamari was standing among the girls.

"I think I shall tell you the story of the Leopard and the Shrike," I said.

"I have not heard that one before," said Ndemi.

"Am I such an old man that I have no new stories to tell?" I demanded, and he dropped his gaze to the ground. I waited until I had everyone's attention, and then I began:

"Once there was a very bright young shrike, and because he was very bright, he was always asking questions of his father.

" 'Why do we eat insects?' he asked one day.

" 'Because we are shrikes, and that is what shrikes do,' answered his father.

" 'But we are also birds,' said the shrike. 'And do not birds such as the eagle eat fish?'

" 'Ngai did not mean for shrikes to eat fish,' said his father, 'and even if you were strong enough to catch and kill a fish, eating it would make you sick.'

" 'Have you ever eaten a fish?' asked the young shrike.

" 'No,' said his father.

" 'Then how do you know?' said the young shrike, and that afternoon he flew over the river, and found a tiny fish. He caught it and ate it, and he was sick for a whole week.

" 'Have you learned your lesson now?' asked the shrike's father, when the young shrike was well again.

" 'I have learned not to eat fish,' said the shrike. 'But I have another question.'

" 'What is your question?' asked his father.

" 'Why are shrikes the most cowardly of birds?' asked the shrike. 'Whenever the lion or the leopard appears, we flee to the highest branches of the trees and wait for them to go away.'

" 'Lions and leopards would eat us if they could,' said the shrike's father. 'Therefore, we must flee from them.'

" 'But they do not eat the ostrich, and the ostrich is a bird,' said the bright young shrike. 'If they attack the ostrich, he kills them with his kick.'

" 'You are not an ostrich,' said his father, tired of listening to him.

" 'But I am a bird, and the ostrich is a bird, and I will learn to kick as the ostrich kicks,' said the young shrike, and he spent the next week practicing kicking any insects and twigs that were in his way.

"Then one day he came across *chui*, the leopard, and as the leopard approached him, the bright young shrike did not fly to the highest branches of the tree, but bravely stood his ground.

" 'You have great courage to face me thus,' said the leopard.

" 'I am a very bright bird, and I am not afraid of you,' said the shrike. 'I have practiced kicking as the ostrich does, and if you come any closer, I will kick you and you will die.'

" 'I am an old leopard, and cannot hunt any longer,' said the leopard. 'I am ready to die. Come kick me, and put me out of my misery.'

"The young shrike walked up to the leopard and kicked him full in the face. The leopard simply laughed, opened his mouth, and swallowed the bright young shrike.

" 'What a silly bird,' laughed the leopard, 'to pretend to be something that he was not! If he had flown away like a shrike, I would have gone hungry today—but by trying to be what he was never meant to be, all he did was fill my stomach. I guess he was not a very bright bird after all.' "

I stopped and stared straight at Kamari.

"Is that the end?" asked one of the other girls.

"That is the end," I said.

"Why did the shrike think he could be an ostrich?" asked one of the smaller boys.

"Perhaps Kamari can tell you," I said.

All the children turned to Kamari, who paused for a moment and then answered.

"There is a difference between wanting to be an ostrich, and wanting to know what an ostrich knows," she said, looking directly into my eyes. "It was not wrong for the shrike to want to know things. It was wrong for him to think he could become an ostrich."

There was a momentary silence while the children considered her answer.

"Is that true, Koriba?" asked Ndemi at last.

"No," I said, "for once the shrike knew what the ostrich knew, it forgot that it was a shrike. You must always remember who you are, and knowing too many things can make you forget."

"Will you tell us another story?" asked a young girl.

"Not this morning," I said, getting to my feet. "But when I come to the village tonight to drink *pombe* and watch the dancing, perhaps I will tell you the story about the bull elephant and the wise little Kikuyu boy. Now," I added, "do none of you have chores to do?"

The children dispersed, returning to their *shambas* and their cattle pastures, and I stopped by Siboki's hut to give him an ointment for his joints, which always bothered him just before it rained. I visited Koinnage and drank *pombe* with him, and then discussed the affairs of the village with the Council of Elders. Finally I returned to my own *boma*, for I always take a nap during the heat of the day, and the rain was not due for another few hours.

Kamari was there when I arrived. She had gathered more wood and water, and was filling the grain buckets for my goats as I entered my *boma*.

"How is your bird this afternoon?" I asked, looking at the pygmy falcon, whose cage had been carefully placed in the shade of my hut.

"He drinks, but he will not eat," she said in worried tones. "He spends all his time looking at the sky."

"There are things that are more important to him than eating," I said.

"I am finished now," she said. "May I go home, Koriba?"

I nodded, and she left as I was arranging my sleeping blanket inside my hut.

She came every morning and every afternoon for the next week. Then, on the eighth day, she announced with tears in her eyes that the pygmy falcon had died.

"I told you that this would happen," I said gently. "Once a bird has ridden upon the winds, he cannot live on the ground."

"Do all birds die when they can no longer fly?" she asked.

"Most do," I said. "A few like the security of the cage, but most die of broken hearts, for having touched the sky they cannot bear to lose the gift of flight."

"Why do we make cages, then, if they do not make the birds feel better?"

"Because they make *us* feel better," I answered.

She paused, and then said: "I will keep my word and clean your hut and your *boma*, and fetch your water and kindling, even though the bird is dead."

I nodded. "That was our agreement," I said.

True to her word, she came back twice a day for the next three weeks. Then, at noon on the twenty-ninth day, after she had completed her morning chores and returned to her family's *shamba*, her father, Njoro, walked up the path to my *boma*.

"*Jambo*, Koriba," he greeted me, a worried expression on his face.

"*Jambo*, Njoro," I said without getting to my feet. "Why have you come to my *boma*?"

"I am a poor man, Koriba," he said, squatting down next to me. "I have only one wife, and she has produced no sons and only two daughters. I do not own as large a *shamba* as most men in the village, and the hyenas killed three of my cows this past year."

I could not understand his point, so I merely stared at him, waiting for him to continue.

"As poor as I am," he went on, "I took comfort in the thought that at least I would have the bride-prices from my two daughters in my old age." He paused. "I have been a good man, Koriba. Surely I deserve that much."

"I have not said otherwise," I replied.

"Then why are you training Kamari to be a *mundumugu*?" he demanded. "It is well known that the *mundumugu* never marries."

"Has Kamari told you that she is to become a *mundumugu*?" I asked.

He shook his head. "No. She does not speak to her mother or myself at all since she has been coming here to clean your *boma*."

"Then you are mistaken," I said. "No woman may be a *mundumugu*. What made you think that I am training her?"

He dug into the folds of his *kikoi* and withdrew a piece of cured wildebeest hide. Scrawled on it in charcoal was the following inscription:

I AM KAMARI
I AM TWELVE YEARS OLD
I AM A GIRL

"This is writing," he said accusingly. "Women cannot write. Only the *mundumugu* and great chiefs like Koinnage can write."

"Leave this with me, Njoro," I said, taking the hide, "and send Kamari to my *boma*."

"I need her to work on my *shamba* until this afternoon."

"Now," I said.

He sighed and nodded. "I will send her, Koriba." He paused. "You are certain that she is not to be a *mundumugu*?"

"You have my word," I said, spitting on my hands to show my sincerity.

He seemed relieved, and went off to his *boma*. Kamari came up the path a few minutes later.

"*Jambo*, Koriba," she said.

"*Jambo*, Kamari," I replied. "I am very displeased with you."

"Did I not gather enough kindling this morning?" she asked.

"You gathered enough kindling."

"Were the gourds not filled with water?"

"The gourds were filled."

"Then what did I do wrong?" she asked, absently pushing one of my goats aside as it approached her.

"You broke your promise to me."

"That is not true," she said. "I have come every morning and every afternoon, even though the bird is dead."

"You promised not to look at another book," I said.

"I have not looked at another book since the day you told me that I was forbidden to."

"Then explain *this*," I said, holding up the hide with her writing on it.

"There is nothing to explain," she said with a shrug. "I wrote it."

"And if you have not looked at books, how did you learn to write?" I demanded.

"From your magic box," she said. "You never told me not to look at *it*."

"My magic box?" I said, frowning.

"The box that hums with life and has many colors."

"You mean my computer?" I asked, surprised.

"Your magic box," she repeated.

"And it taught you how to read and write?"

"*I* taught me—but only a little," she said unhappily. "I am like the shrike in your story—I am not as bright as I thought. Reading and writing are very difficult."

"I told you that you must not learn to read," I said, resisting the urge to comment on her remarkable accomplishment, for she had clearly broken the law.

Kamari shook her head.

"You told me I must not look at your books," she replied stubbornly.

"I told you that women must not read," I said. "You have disobeyed me. For this you must be punished." I paused. "You will continue your chores here for three more months, and you must bring me two hares and two rodents, which you must catch yourself. Do you understand?"

"I understand."

"Now come into my hut with me, that you may understand one thing more."

She followed me into the hut.

"Computer," I said. "Activate."

"Activated," said the computer's mechanical voice.

"Computer, scan the hut and tell me who is here with me."

The lens of the computer's sensor glowed briefly.

"The girl, Kamari wa Njoro, is here with you," replied the computer.

"Will you recognize her if you see her again?"

"Yes."

"This is a Priority Order," I said. "Never again may you converse with Kamari wa Njoro verbally or in any known language."

"Understood and logged," said the computer.

"Deactivate." I turned to Kamari. "Do you understand what I have done, Kamari?"

"Yes," she said, "and it is not fair. I did not disobey you."

"It is the law that women may not read," I said, "and you have broken it. You will not break it again. Now go back to your *shamba*."

She left, head held high, youthful back stiff with defiance, and I went about my duties, instructing the young boys on the decoration of their bodies for their forthcoming circumcision ceremony, casting a counterspell for old Siboki (for he had found hyena dung within his *shamba*, which is one of the surest signs of a *thahu*, or curse), instructing Maintenance to make another minor orbital adjustment that would bring cooler weather to the western plains.

By the time I returned to my hut for my afternoon nap, Kamari had come and gone again, and everything was in order.

For the next two months, life in the village went its placid way. The crops were harvested, old Koinnage took another wife and we had a two-day festival with much dancing and *pombe* drinking to celebrate the event, the short rains arrived on schedule, and three children were born to the village. Even the Eutopian Council, which had complained about our custom of leaving the old and the infirm out for the hyenas, left us completely alone. We found the lair of a family of hyenas and killed three whelps, then slew the mother when she returned. At each full moon I slaughtered a cow—not merely a goat, but a large, fat cow—to thank Ngai for His generosity, for truly He had graced Kirinyaga with abundance.

During this period I rarely saw Kamari. She came in the mornings when I was in the village, casting the bones to bring forth the weather, and she came in the afternoons when I was giving charms to the sick and conversing with the Elders—but I always knew she had been there, for my hut and my *boma* were immaculate, and I never lacked for water or kindling.

Then, on the afternoon after the second full moon, I returned to my *boma* after advising Koinnage about how he might best settle an argument over a disputed plot of land, and as I entered my hut I noticed that the computer screen was alive and glowing, covered with strange symbols. When I had taken my degrees in England and America I had learned English and French and Spanish, and of course I knew Kikuyu and Swahili, but these symbols represented no known language, nor, although they used numerals as well as letters and punctuation marks, were they mathematical formulas.

"Computer, I distinctly remember deactivating you this morning," I said, frowning. "Why does your screen glow with life?"

"Kamari activated me."

"And she forgot to deactivate you when she left?"

"That is correct."

"I thought as much," I said grimly. "Does she activate you every day?"

"Yes."

"Did I not give you a Priority Order never to communicate with her in any known language?" I said, puzzled.

"You did, Koriba."

"Can you then explain why you have disobeyed my directive?"

"I have not disobeyed your directive, Koriba," said the computer. "My programming makes me incapable of disobeying a Priority Order."

"Then what is this that I see upon your screen?"

"This is the Language of Kamari," replied the computer. "It is not among the one thousand seven hundred thirty-two languages and dialects in my memory banks, and hence does not fall under the aegis of your directive."

"Did you create this language?"

"No, Koriba. Kamari created it."

"Did you assist her in any way?"

"No, Koriba, I did not."

"Is it a true language?" I asked. "Can you understand it?"

"It is a true language. I can understand it."

"If she were to ask you a question in the Language of Kamari, could you reply to it?"

"Yes, if the question were simple enough. It is a very limited language."

"And if that reply required you to translate the answer from a known language to the Language of Kamari, would doing so be contrary to my directive?"

"No, Koriba, it would not."

"Have you, in fact, answered questions put to you by Kamari?"

"Yes, Koriba, I have," replied the computer.

"I see," I said. "Stand by for a new directive."

"Waiting . . ."

I lowered my head in thought, contemplating the problem. That Kamari was brilliant and gifted was obvious: she had not only taught herself to read and write, but had actually created a coherent and logical language that the computer could understand and in which it could respond. I had given orders, and without directly disobeying them she had managed to circumvent them. She had no malice within her, and wanted only to learn, which in itself was an admirable goal. All that was on the one hand.

On the other hand was the threat to the social order we had labored so diligently to establish on Kirinyaga. Men and women knew their responsibilities and accepted them happily. Ngai had given the Maasai the spear, and He had given the Wakamba the arrow, and He had given the Europeans the machine and the printing press, but to the Kikuyu He had given the digging stick and the fertile land surrounding the sacred fig tree on the slopes of Kirinyaga.

Once before we had lived in harmony with the land, many long years ago. Then had come the printed word. It turned us first into slaves, and then into Christians, and then into soldiers and factory workers and mechanics and politicians, into everything that the Kikuyu were never meant to be. It had happened before; it could happen again.

We had come to the world of Kirinyaga to create a perfect Kikuyu society, a Kikuyu Utopia. Could one gifted little girl carry within her the seeds of our destruction? I could not be sure, but it was a fact that gifted children grew up. They became Jesus, and Mohammed, and Jomo Kenyatta—but they also became Tippoo Tib, the greatest slaver of all, and Idi Amin, butcher of his own people. Or, more often, they became Friedrich Neitzsche and Karl Marx, brilliant men in their own right, but who influenced less brilliant, less capable men. Did I have the right to stand aside and hope that her influence upon our society would be benign when all history suggested that the opposite was more likely to be true?

My decision was painful, but it was not a difficult one.

"Computer," I said at last, "I have a new Priority Order that supercedes my previous directive. You are no longer allowed to communicate with Kamari under any circumstances whatsoever. Should she activate you, you are to tell her that Koriba has forbidden you to have any contact with her, and you are then to deactivate immediately. Do you understand?"

"Understood and logged."

"Good," I said. "Now deactivate."

When I returned from the village the next morning, I found my water gourds empty, my blanket unfolded, my *boma* filled with the dung of my goats.

The *mundumugu* is all-powerful among the Kikuyu, but he is not without compassion. I decided to forgive this childish display of temper, and so I did not visit Kamari's father, nor did I tell the other children to avoid her.

She did not come again in the afternoon. I know, because I waited beside my hut to explain my decision to her. Finally, when twilight came, I sent for the boy, Ndemi, to fill my gourds and clean my *boma*, and although such chores are woman's work, he did not dare disobey his *mundumugu*, although his every gesture displayed contempt for the tasks I had set for him.

When two more days had passed with no sign of Kamari, I summoned Njoro, her father.

"Kamari has broken her word to me," I said when he arrived. "If she does not come to clean my *boma* this afternoon, I will be forced to place a *thahu* upon her."

He looked puzzled. "She says that you have already placed a curse on her, Koriba. I was going to ask you if we should turn her out of our *boma*."

I shook my head. "No," I said. "Do not turn her out of your *boma*.

I have placed no *thahu* on her yet—but she must come to work this afternoon."

"I do not know if she is strong enough," said Njoro. "She has had neither food nor water for three days, and she sits motionless in my wife's hut." He paused. "*Someone* has placed a *thahu* on her. If it was not you, perhaps you can cast a spell to remove it."

"She has gone three days without eating or drinking?" I repeated. He nodded.

"I will see her," I said, getting to my feet and following him down the winding path to the village. When we reached Njoro's *boma* he led me to his wife's hut, then called Kamari's worried mother out and stood aside as I entered. Kamari sat at the farthest point from the door, her back propped against a wall, her knees drawn up to her chin, her arms encircling her thin legs.

"*Jambo,* Kamari," I said.

She stared at me but said nothing.

"Your mother worries for you, and your father tells me that you no longer eat or drink."

She made no answer.

"You also have not kept your promise to tend my *boma.*"

Silence.

"Have you forgotten how to speak?" I said.

"Kikuyu women do not speak," she said bitterly. "They do not think. All they do is bear babies and cook food and gather firewood and till the fields. They do not have to speak or think to do that."

"Are you that unhappy?"

She did not answer.

"Listen to my words, Kamari," I said slowly. "I made my decision for the good of Kirinyaga, and I will not recant it. As a Kikuyu woman, you must live the life that has been ordained for you." I paused. "However, neither the Kikuyu nor the Eutopian Council are without compassion for the individual. Any member of our society may leave if he wishes. According to the charter we signed when we claimed this world, you need only walk to that area known as Haven, and a

Maintenance ship will pick you up and transport you to the location of your choice."

"All I know is Kirinyaga," she said. "How am I to choose a new home if I am forbidden to learn about other places?"

"I do not know," I admitted.

"I don't *want* to leave Kirinyaga!" she continued. "This is my home. These are my people. I am a Kikuyu girl, not a Maasai girl or a European girl. I will bear my husband's children and till his *shamba*; I will gather his wood and cook his meals and weave his garments; I will leave my parents' *shamba* and live with my husband's family. I will do all this without complaint, Koriba, if you will just let me learn to read and write!"

"I cannot," I said sadly.

"But *why*?"

"Who is the wisest man you know, Kamari?" I asked.

"The *mundumugu* is always the wisest man in the village."

"Then you must trust to my wisdom."

"But I feel like the pygmy falcon," she said, her misery reflected in her voice. "He spent his life dreaming of soaring high upon the winds. I dream of seeing words upon the computer screen."

"You are not like the falcon at all," I said. "He was prevented from being what he was meant to be. You are prevented from being what you are not meant to be."

"You are not an evil man, Koriba," she said solemnly. "But you are wrong."

"If that is so, then I shall have to live with it," I said.

"But you are asking *me* to live with it," she said, "and that is your crime."

"If you call me a criminal again," I said sternly, for no one may speak thus to the *mundumugu*, "I shall surely place a *thahu* on you."

"What more can you do?" she said bitterly.

"I can turn you into a hyena, an unclean eater of human flesh who prowls only in the darkness. I can fill your belly with thorns, so that your every movement will be agony. I can—"

"You are just a man," she said wearily, "and you have already done your worst."

"I will hear no more of this," I said. "I order you to eat and drink what your mother brings to you, and I expect to see you at my *boma* this afternoon."

I walked out of the hut and told Kamari's mother to bring her banana mash and water, then stopped by old Benima's *shamba*. Buffalo had stampeded through his fields, destroying his crops, and I sacrificed a goat to remove the *thahu* that had fallen upon his land.

When I was finished I stopped at Koinnage's *boma*, where he offered me some freshly brewed *pombe* and began complaining about Kibo, his newest wife, who kept taking sides with Shumi, his second wife, against Wambu, his senior wife.

"You can always divorce her and return her to her family's *shamba*," I suggested.

"She cost twenty cows and five goats!" he complained. "Will her family return them?"

"No, they will not."

"Then I will not send her back."

"As you wish," I said with a shrug.

"Besides, she is very strong and very lovely," he continued. "I just wish she would stop fighting with Wambu."

"What do they fight about?" I asked.

"They fight about who will fetch the water, and who will mend my garments, and who will repair the thatch on my hut." He paused. "They even argue about whose hut I should visit at night, as if I had no choice in the matter."

"Do they ever fight about ideas?" I asked.

"Ideas?" he repeated blankly.

"Such as you might find in books."

He laughed. "They are *women*, Koriba. What need have they for ideas?" He paused. "In fact, what need have any of us for them?"

"I do not know," I said. "I was merely curious."

"You look disturbed," he noted.

"It must be the *pombe*," I said. "I am an old man, and perhaps it is too strong."

"That is because Kibo will not listen when Wambu tells her how to brew it. I really should send her away"—he looked at Kibo as she carried a load of wood on her strong, young back—"but she is so young and so lovely." Suddenly his gaze went beyond his newest wife to the village. "Ah!" he said. "I see that old Siboki has finally died."

"How do you know?" I asked.

He pointed to a thin column of smoke. "They are burning his hut."

I stared off in the direction he indicated. "That is not Siboki's hut," I said. "His *boma* is more to the west."

"Who else is old and infirm and due to die?" asked Koinnage.

And suddenly I knew, as surely as I knew that Ngai sits on His throne atop the holy mountain, that Kamari was dead.

I walked to Njoro's *shamba* as quickly as I could. When I arrived, Kamari's mother and sister and grandmother were already wailing the death chant, tears streaming down their faces.

"What happened?" I demanded, walking up to Njoro.

"Why do you ask, when it is you who destroyed her?" he replied bitterly.

"I did not destroy her," I said.

"Did you not threaten to place a *thabu* on her just this morning?" he persisted. "You did so, and now she is dead, and I have but one daughter to bring the bride-price, and I have had to burn Kamari's hut."

"Stop worrying about bride-prices and huts and tell me what happened, or you shall learn what it means to be cursed by a *mundu-mugu*!" I snapped.

"She hung herself in her hut with a length of buffalo hide."

Five women from the neighboring *shamba* arrived and took up the death chant.

"She hung herself in her hut?" I repeated.

He nodded. "She could at least have hung herself from a tree, so that her hut would not be unclean and I would not have to burn it."

"Be quiet!" I said, trying to collect my thoughts.

"She was not a bad daughter," he continued. "Why did you curse her, Koriba?"

"I did not place a *thahu* upon her," I said, wondering if I spoke the truth. "I wished only to save her."

"Who has stronger medicine than you?" he asked fearfully.

"She broke the law of Ngai," I answered.

"And now Ngai has taken His vengeance!" moaned Njoro fearfully. "Which member of my family will He strike down next?"

"None of you," I said. "Only Kamari broke the law."

"I am a poor man," said Njoro cautiously, "even poorer now than before. How much must I pay you to ask Ngai to receive Kamari's spirit with compassion and forgiveness?"

"I will do that whether you pay me or not," I answered.

"You will not charge me?" he asked.

"I will not charge you."

"Thank you, Koriba!" he said fervently.

I stood and stared at the blazing hut, trying not to think of the smoldering body of the little girl inside it.

"Koriba?" said Njoro after a lengthy silence.

"What now?" I asked irritably.

"We did not know what to do with the buffalo hide, for it bore the marks of your *thahu*, and we were afraid to burn it. Now I know that the marks were made by Ngai and not you, and I am afraid even to touch it. Will you take it away?"

"What marks?" I said. "What are you talking about?"

He took me by the arm and led me around to the front of the burning hut. There, on the ground, some ten paces from the entrance, lay the strip of tanned hide with which Kamari had hanged herself, and scrawled upon it were more of the strange symbols I had seen on my computer screen three days earlier.

I reached down and picked up the hide, then turned to Njoro. "If indeed there is a curse on your *shamba*," I said, "I will remove it and take it upon myself, by taking Ngai's marks with me."

"Thank you, Koriba!" he said, obviously much relieved.

"I must leave to prepare my magic," I said abruptly, and began the long walk back to my *boma*. When I arrived I took the strip of buffalo hide into my hut.

"Computer," I said. "Activate."

"Activated."

I held the strip up to its scanning lens.

"Do you recognize this language?" I asked.

The lens glowed briefly.

"Yes, Koriba. It is the Language of Kamari."

"What does it say?"

"It is a couplet:

I know why the caged birds die—
For, like them, I have touched the sky."

The entire village came to Njoro's *shamba* in the afternoon, and the women wailed the death chant all night and all of the next day, but before long Kamari was forgotten, for life goes on and she was, after all, just a little Kikuyu girl.

Since that day, whenever I have found a bird with a broken wing I have attempted to nurse it back to health. It always dies, and I always bury it next to the mound of earth that marks where Kamari's hut had been.

It is on those days, when I place the birds in the ground, that I find myself thinking of her again, and wishing that I was just a simple man, tending my cattle and worrying about my crops and thinking the thoughts of simple men, rather than a *mundumugu* who must live with the consequences of his wisdom.

3

BWANA

{ DECEMBER 2131–FEBRUARY 2132 }

Ngai rules the universe, and on His sacred mountain the beasts of the field roam free and share the fertile green slopes with His chosen people.

To the first Maasai He gave a spear, and to the first Kamba He gave a bow, but to Gikuyu, who was the first Kikuyu, He gave a digging stick and told him to dwell on the slopes of Kirinyaga. The Kikuyu, said Ngai, could sacrifice goats to read their entrails, and they could sacrifice oxen to thank Him for sending the rains, but they must not molest any of His animals that dwelt on the mountain.

Then one day Gikuyu came to Him and said, "May we not have the bow and arrow, so that we may kill *fisi*, the hyena, in whose body dwell the vengeful souls of evil men?"

And Ngai said that no, the Kikuyu must not molest the hyena, for the hyena's purpose was clear: He had created it to feed upon the lions' leavings, and to take the sick and the elderly from the Kikuyus' *shambas*.

Time passed, and Gikuyu approached the summit of the mountain again. "May we not have the spear, so that we can kill the lion and the leopard, who prey upon our own animals?" he said.

And Ngai said that no, the Kikuyu could not kill the lion or the leopard, for He had created them to hold the population of the grasseaters in check, so that they would not overrun the Kikuyus' fields.

Finally Gikuyu climbed the mountain one last time and said, "We must at least be allowed to kill the elephant, who can destroy a year's harvest in a matter of minutes—but how are we to do so when you have allowed us no weapons?"

Ngai thought long and hard, and finally spoke. "I have decreed that the Kikuyu should till the land, and I will not stain your hands with the blood of my other creatures," announced Ngai. "But because you are my chosen people, and are more important than the beasts that dwell upon my mountain, I will see to it that others come to kill these animals."

"What tribe will these hunters come from?" asked Gikuyu. "By what name will we know them?"

"You will know them by a single word," said Ngai.

When Ngai told him the word by which the hunters would be known, Gikuyu thought He had made a joke, and laughed aloud, and soon forgot the conversation.

But Ngai never jokes when He speaks to the Kikuyu.

We have no elephants or lions or leopards on the Eutopian world of Kirinyaga, for all three species were extinct long before we emigrated from the Kenya that had become so alien to us. But we took the sleek impala, and the majestic kudu, and the mighty buffalo, and the swift gazelle—and because we were mindful of Ngai's dictates, we took the hyena and the jackal and the vulture as well.

And because Kirinyaga was designed to be a Utopia in climate as well as in social organization, and because the land was more fertile than Kenya's, and because Maintenance made the orbital adjustments that assured us that the rains would always come on schedule, the wild animals of Kirinyaga, like the domestic animals and the people themselves, grew fruitful and multiplied.

It was only a matter of time before they came into conflict with us. Initially there would be sporadic attacks on our livestock by the hyenas, and once old Benima's entire harvest was destroyed by a herd of rampaging buffalo, but we took such setbacks with good grace, for Ngai had provided well for us and no one was ever forced to go hungry.

But then, as we reclaimed more and more of our terraformed veldt to be used as farmland, and the wild animals of Kirinyaga felt the pressure of our land-hungry people, the incidents grew more frequent and more severe.

I was sitting before the fire in my *boma*, waiting for the sun to burn the chill from the morning air and staring out across the acacia-dotted plains, when young Ndemi raced up the winding road from the village.

"Koriba!" he cried. "Come quickly!"

"What has happened?" I asked, rising painfully to my feet.

"Juma has been attacked by *fisi*!" he gasped, striving to regain his breath.

"By one hyena, or many?" I asked.

"One, I think. I do not know."

"Is he still alive?"

"Juma or *fisi*?" asked Ndemi.

"Juma."

"I think he is dead." Ndemi paused. "But you are the *mundumugu*. You can make him live again."

I was pleased that he placed so much faith in his *mundumugu*— but of course if his companion was truly dead there was nothing I could do about it. I went into my hut, selected some herbs that were especially helpful in combating infection, added a few *qat* leaves for Juma to chew (for we had no anesthetics on Kirinyaga, and the hallucinogenic trance caused by the *qat* leaves would at least make him forget his pain). All this I placed into a leather pouch that I hung about my neck. Then I emerged from my hut and nodded to Ndemi, who led the way to the *shamba* of Juma's father.

When we arrived, the women were already wailing the death chant, and I briefly examined what was left of poor little Juma's body. One bite from the hyena had taken away most of his face, and a second had totally removed his left arm. The hyena had then devoured most of Juma's torso before the villagers finally drove it away.

Koinnage, the paramount chief of the village, arrived a few moments later.

"*Jambo*, Koriba," he greeted me.

"*Jambo*, Koinnage," I replied.

"Something must be done," he said, looking at Juma's body, which was now covered by flies.

"I will place a curse on the hyena," I said, "and tonight I shall sacrifice a goat to Ngai, so that He will welcome Juma's soul."

Koinnage looked uneasy, for his fear of me was great, but finally he spoke: "It is not enough. This is the second healthy boy that the hyenas have taken this month."

"Our hyenas have developed a taste for men," I said. "It is because we leave the old and the infirm out for them."

"Then perhaps we should not leave the old and the sick out any longer."

"We have no choice," I replied. "The Europeans thought it was the mark of savages, and even Maintenance has tried to dissuade us—but we do not have medicine to ease their suffering. What seems barbarous to outsiders is actually an act of mercy. Ever since Ngai gave the first digging stick to the first Kikuyu, it has always been our tradition to leave the old and the infirm out for the hyenas when it is time for them to die."

"Maintenance has medicines," suggested Koinnage, and I noticed that two of the younger men had edged closer to us and were listening with interest. "Perhaps we should ask them to help us."

"So that they will live a week or a month longer, and then be buried in the ground like Christians?" I said. "You cannot be part Kikuyu and part European. That is the reason we came to Kirinyaga in the first place."

"But how wrong could it be to ask only for medicine for our elderly?" asked one of the younger men, and I could see that Koinnage looked relieved now that he himself did not have to pursue the argument.

"If you accept their medicine today, then tomorrow you will be accepting their clothing and their machinery and their god," I replied. "If history has taught us nothing else, it has taught us that." They still seemed unconvinced, so I continued: "Most races look ahead to their Utopia, but the Kikuyu must look *back*, back to a simpler time when we lived in harmony with the land, when we were not tainted with the customs of a society to which we were never meant to belong. I have lived among the Europeans, and gone to school at their universities, and I tell you that you must not listen to the siren song of their technology. What works for the Europeans did not work for the Kikuyu when we lived in Kenya, and it will not work for us here on Kirinyaga."

As if to emphasize my statement, a hyena voiced its eerie laugh far off in the veldt. The women stopped wailing and drew closer together.

"But we must do something!" protested Koinnage, whose fear of the hyena momentarily overrode his fear of his *mundumugu*. "We cannot continue to let the beasts of the field destroy our crops and take our children."

I could have explained that there was a temporary imbalance as the grasseaters lowered their birthrate to accommodate their decreased pasturage, and that the hyenas' birthrate would almost certainly adjust within a year, but they would not have understood or believed me. They wanted solutions, not explanations.

"Ngai is testing our courage, to see if we are truly worthy to live on Kirinyaga," I said at last. "Until the time of testing is over, we will arm our children with spears and have them tend the cattle in pairs."

Koinnage shook his head. "The hyenas have developed a taste for men—and two Kikuyu boys, even armed with spears, are no match for a pack of hyenas. Surely Ngai does not want His chosen people to become meals for *fisi*."

"No, He does not," I agreed. "It is the hyenas' nature to kill grasseaters, just as it is our nature to till the fields. I am your *mundumugu*. You must believe me when I tell you that this time of testing will soon pass."

"How soon?" asked another man.

I shrugged. "Perhaps two rains. Perhaps three." The rains come twice a year.

"You are an old man," said the man, mustering his courage to contradict his *mundumugu*. "You have no children, and it is this that gives you patience. But those of us with sons cannot wait for two or three rains wondering each day if they will return from the fields. We must do something *now*."

"I am an old man," I agreed, "and this gives me not only patience, but wisdom."

"You are the *mundumugu*," said Koinnage at last, "and you must face the problem in your way. But I am the paramount chief, and I must face it in mine. I will organize a hunt, and we will kill all the hyenas in the area."

"Very well," I said, for I had foreseen this solution. "Organize your hunt."

"Will you cast the bones and see if we shall be successful?"

"I do not need to cast the bones to foresee the results of your hunt," I replied. "You are farmers, not hunters. You will not be successful."

"You will not give us your support?" demanded another man.

"You do not need my support," I replied. "I would give you my patience if I could, for that is what you need."

"We were supposed to turn this world into a Utopia," said Koinnage, who had only the haziest understanding of the word, but equated it with good harvests and a lack of enemies. "What kind of Utopia permits children to be devoured by wild animals?"

"You cannot understand what it means to be full until you have been hungry," I answered. "You cannot know what it means to be warm and dry until you have been cold and wet. And Ngai knows, even if you do not, that you cannot appreciate life without death. This is His lesson for you; it will pass."

"It must end *now*," said Koinnage firmly, now that he knew I would not try to prevent his hunt.

I made no further comment, for I knew that nothing I could say would dissuade him. I spent the next few minutes creating a curse for the individual hyena that had killed Juma, and that night I sacrificed a goat in the middle of the village and read in the entrails that Ngai had accepted the sacrifice and welcomed Juma's spirit.

Two days later Koinnage led ten of the village men out to the veldt to hunt the hyenas, while I stayed in my *boma* and prepared for what I knew was inevitable.

It was in late morning that Ndemi—the boldest of the boys in the village, whose courage had made him a favorite of mine—came up the long, winding path to visit me.

"*Jambo*, Koriba," he greeted me unhappily.

"*Jambo*, Ndemi," I replied. "What is the matter?"

"They say that I am too young to hunt for *fisi*," he complained, squatting down next to me.

"They are right."

"But I have practiced my bushcraft every day, and you yourself have blessed my spear."

"I have not forgotten," I said.

"Then why can I not join the hunt?"

"It makes no difference," I said. "They will not kill *fisi*. In fact, they will be very lucky if all of them return unharmed." I paused. "*Then* the troubles will begin."

"I thought they had already begun," said Ndemi, with no trace of sarcasm.

I shook my head. "What has been happening is part of the natural order of things, and hence it is part of Kirinyaga. But when Koinnage does not kill the hyenas, he will want to bring a hunter to Kirinyaga, and that is *not* part of the natural order."

"You know he will do this?" asked Ndemi, impressed.

"I know Koinnage," I answered.

"Then you will tell him not to."

"I will tell him not to."

"And he will listen to you."

"No," I said. "I do not think he will listen to me."

"But you are the *mundumugu*."

"But there are many men in the village who resent me," I explained. "They see the sleek ships that land on Kirinyaga from time to time, and they hear stories about the wonders of Nairobi and Mombasa, and they forget why we have come here. They become unhappy with the digging stick, and they long for the Maasai's spear or the Kamba's bow or the European's machines."

Ndemi squatted in silence for a moment.

"I have a question, Koriba," he said at last.

"You may ask it."

"You are the *mundumugu*," he said. "You can change men into insects, and see in the darkness, and walk upon the air."

"That is true," I agreed.

"Then why do you not turn all the hyenas into honeybees and set fire to their hive?"

"Because *fisi* is not evil," I said. "It is his nature to eat flesh. Without him, the beasts of the field would become so plentiful that they would soon overrun our fields."

"Then why not kill just those *fisi* who kill us?"

"Do you not remember your own grandmother?" I asked. "Do you not recall the agony she suffered in her final days?"

"Yes."

"We do not kill our own kind. Were it not for *fisi*, she would have suffered for many more days. *Fisi* is only doing what Ngai created him to do."

"Ngai also created hunters," said Ndemi, casting me a sly look out of the corner of his eye.

"That is true."

"Then why do you not want hunters to come and kill *fisi*?"

"I will tell you the story of the Goat and the Lion, and then you will understand," I said.

"What do goats and lions have to do with hyenas?" he asked.

"Listen, and you will know," I answered. "Once there was a herd of black goats, and they lived a very happy life, for Ngai had provided them with green grass and lush plants and a nearby stream where they could drink, and when it rained they stood beneath the branches of large, stately trees where the raindrops could not reach them. Then one day a leopard came to their village, and because he was old and thin and weak, and could no longer hunt the impala and the water-buck, he killed a goat and ate it.

" 'This is terrible!' said the goats. 'Something must be done.'

" 'He is an old leopard,' said the wisest of the goats. 'If he regains his strength from the flesh he has eaten, he will go back to hunting for the impala, for the impala's flesh is much more nourishing than ours, and if he does not regain his strength, he will soon be dead. All we need do is be especially alert while he walks among us.'

"But the other goats were too frightened to listen to his counsel, and they decided that they needed help.

" 'I would beware of anyone who is not a goat and offers to help you,' said the wisest goat, but they would not hear him, and finally they sought out a huge black-maned lion.

" 'There is a leopard that is eating our people,' they said, 'and we are not strong enough to drive him away. Will you help us?'

" 'I am always glad to help my friends,' answered the lion.

" 'We are a poor race,' said the goats. 'What tribute will you exact from us for your help?'

" 'None,' the lion assured them. 'I will do this solely because I am your friend.'

"And true to his word, the lion entered the village and waited until next the leopard came to feed, and then the lion pounced upon him and killed him.

" 'Oh, thank you, great savior!' cried the goats, doing a dance of joy and triumph around the lion.

" 'It was my pleasure,' said the lion. 'For the leopard is my enemy as much as he is yours.'

" 'We shall sing songs and tell stories about you long after you leave,' continued the goats happily.

" 'Leave?' replied the lion, his eyes seeking out the fattest of the goats. 'Who is leaving?' "

Ndemi considered what I had said for a long moment, then looked up at me.

"You are not saying that the hunter will eat us as *fisi* does?"

"No, I am not."

He considered the implications further.

"Ah!" he said, smiling at last. "You are saying that if we cannot kill *fisi*, who will soon die or leave us, then we should not invite someone even stronger than *fisi*, someone who will not die or leave."

"That is correct."

"But why should a hunter of animals be a threat to Kirinyaga?" he continued thoughtfully.

"We are like the goats," I explained. "We live off the land, and we have not the power to kill our enemies. But a hunter is like the lion: It is his nature to kill, and he will be the only man on Kirinyaga who is skilled at killing."

"You think he will kill us, then?" asked Ndemi.

I shrugged. "Not at first. The lion had to kill the leopard before he could prey upon the goats. The hunter will kill *fisi* before he casts about for some other way to exercise his power."

"But you are our *mundumugu*!" protested Ndemi. "You will not let this happen!"

"I will try to prevent it," I said.

"If you try, you will succeed, and we will not send for a hunter."

"Perhaps."

"Are you not all-powerful?" asked Ndemi.

"I am all-powerful."

"Then why do you speak with such doubt?"

"Because I am not a hunter," I said. "The Kikuyu fear me because of my powers, but I have never knowingly harmed one of my people. I will not harm them now. I want what is best for Kirinyaga, but if their fear of *fisi* is greater than their fear of me, then I will lose."

Ndemi stared at the little patterns he had traced in the dirt with his finger.

"Perhaps, if a hunter does come, he will be a good man," he said at last.

"Perhaps," I agreed. "But he will still be a hunter." I paused. "The lion may sleep with the zebra in times of plenty. But in times of need, when both are starving, it is the lion who starves last."

Ten hunters had left the village, but only eight returned. Two had been attacked and killed by a pack of hyenas while they sat resting beneath the shade of an acacia tree. All day long the women wailed the death chant, while the sky turned black with the smoke, for it is our custom to burn the huts of our dead.

That very same night Koinnage called a meeting of the Council of Elders. I waited until the last rays of the sun had vanished, then painted my face and wrapped myself in my ceremonial leopardskin cloak, and made my way to his *boma*.

There was total silence as I approached the old men of the village. Even the night birds seemed to have taken flight, and I walked among them, looking neither right nor left, finally taking my accustomed place on a stool just to the left of Koinnage's personal hut. I could see his three wives clustered together inside his senior wife's hut, kneeling as close to the entrance as they dared while straining to see and hear what transpired.

The flickering firelight highlighted the faces of the Elders, most of them grim and filled with fear. By precedent no one—not even the *mundumugu*—could speak until the paramount chief had spoken, and since Koinnage had still not emerged from his hut, I amused myself by withdrawing the bones from the leather pouch about my neck and casting them on the dirt. Three times I cast them, and three times I frowned at what I saw. Finally I put them back in my pouch, leaving those Elders who were planning to disobey their *mundumugu* to wonder what I had seen.

At last Koinnage stepped forth from his hut, a long thin stick in his hand. It was his custom to wave the stick when he spoke to the Council, much as a conductor waves his baton.

"The hunt has failed," he announced dramatically, as if everyone in the village did not already know it. "Two more men have died because of *fisi*." He paused for dramatic effect, then shouted: "It must not happen again!"

"Do not go hunting again and it will not happen again," I said, for once he began to speak I was permitted to comment.

"You are the *mundumugu*," said one of the Elders. "You should have protected them!"

"I told them not to go," I replied. "I cannot protect those who reject my counsel."

"*Fisi* must die!" screamed Koinnage, and as he turned to face me I detected a strong odor of *pombe* on his breath, and now I knew why he had remained in his hut for so long. He had been drinking *pombe* until his courage was up to the task at hand, that of opposing his *mundumugu*. "Never again will *fisi* dine upon the flesh of the Kikuyu, nor will we hide in our *bomas* like old women until Koriba tells us that it is safe to come out! *Fisi* must die!"

The Elders took up the chant of "*Fisi* must die!" and Koinnage went through a pantomime of killing a hyena, using his stick as a spear.

"Men have reached the stars!" cried Koinnage. "They have built great cities beneath the sea. They have killed the last elephant and the last lion. Are we not men too—or are we old women to be terrified by unclean eaters of carrion?"

I got to my feet.

"What other men have achieved makes no difference to the Kikuyu," I said. "Other men did not cause our problem with *fisi*; other men cannot cure it."

"One of them can," said Koinnage, looking at the anxious faces that were distorted by the firelight. "A hunter."

The Elders muttered their approval.

"We must send for a hunter," repeated Koinnage, waving his stick wildly.

"It must not be a European," said an Elder.

"Nor can it be a Wakamba," said another.

"Nor a Luo," said a third.

"The Lumbwa and the Nandi are the enemies of our blood," added a fourth.

"It will be whoever can kill *fisi*," said Koinnage.

"How will you find such a man?" said an Elder.

"Hyenas still live on Earth," answered Koinnage. "We will find a hunter or a control officer from one of the game parks, someone who has hunted and killed *fisi* many times."

"You are making a mistake," I said firmly, and suddenly there was absolute silence again.

"We must have a hunter," said Koinnage adamantly, when he saw that no one else would speak.

"You would only be bringing a greater killer to Kirinyaga to slay a lesser killer," I responded.

"I am the paramount chief," said Koinnage, and I could tell from the way he refused to meet my gaze that the effects of the *pombe* had left him now that he was forced to confront me before the Elders. "What kind of chief would I be if I permitted *fisi* to continue to kill my people?"

"You can build traps for *fisi* until Ngai gives him back his taste for grasseaters," I said.

"How many more of us will *fisi* kill before the traps have been set?" demanded Koinnage, trying to work himself up into a rage again. "How many of us must die before the *mundumugu* admits that he is wrong, and that this is not Ngai's plan?"

"Stop!" I shouted, raising my hands above my head, and even Koinnage froze in his tracks, afraid to speak or to move. "I am your *mundumugu*. I am the book of our collected wisdom; each sentence I speak is a page. I have brought the rains on time, and I have blessed the harvest. Never have I misled you. Now I tell you that you must not bring a hunter to Kirinyaga."

And then Koinnage, who was literally shaking from his fear of me, forced himself to stare into my eyes.

"I am the paramount chief," he said, trying to steady his voice, "and I say we must act before *fisi* hungers again. *Fisi* must die! I have spoken."

The Elders began chanting "*Fisi* must die!" again, and Koinnage's courage returned to him as he realized that he was not the only one to openly disobey his *mundumugu*'s dictates. He led the frenzied chanting, walking from one Elder to the next and finally to me, yelling "*Fisi* must die!" and punctuating it with wild gesticulations of his stick.

I realized that I had lost for the very first time in council, yet I made no threats, since it was important that any punishment for disobeying the dictates of their *mundumugu* must come from Ngai and not from me. I left in silence, walking through the circle of Elders without looking at any of them, and returned to my *boma*.

The next morning two of Koinnage's cattle were found dead without a mark upon them, and each morning thereafter a different Elder awoke to two dead cattle. I told the villagers that this was undoubtedly the hand of Ngai, and that the corpses must be burned, and that anyone who ate of them would die under a horrible *thahu*, or curse, and they followed my orders without question.

Then it was simply a matter of waiting for Koinnage's hunter to arrive.

✻ ✻ ✻

He walked across the plain toward my *boma*, and it might have been Ngai Himself approaching me. He was tall, well over six and one-half feet, and slender, graceful as the gazelle and blacker than the darkest night. He was dressed in neither a *kikoi* nor in khakis, but in a light-weight pair of pants and a shortsleeved shirt. His feet were in sandals, and I could tell from the depth of their calluses and the straightness of his toes that he had spent most of his life without shoes. A small bag was slung over one shoulder, and in his left hand he carried a long rifle in a monogrammed gun case.

When he reached the spot where I was sitting he stopped, totally at ease, and stared unblinking at me. From the arrogance of his expression, I knew that he was a Maasai.

"Where is the village of Koinnage?" he asked in Swahili.

I pointed to my left. "In the valley," I said.

"Why do you live alone, old man?"

Those were his exact words. Not *mzee*, which is a term of respect for the elderly, a term that acknowledges the decades of accumulated wisdom, but *old man*.

Yes, I concluded silently, *there is no doubt that you are a Maasai.*

"The *mundumugu* always lives apart from other men," I answered loudly.

"So you are the witch doctor," he said. "I would have thought your people had outgrown such things."

"As yours have outgrown the need for manners?" I responded.

He chuckled in amusement. "You are not glad to see me, are you, old man?"

"No, I am not."

"Well, if your magic had been strong enough to kill the hyenas, I would not be here. *I* am not to blame for that."

"You are not to blame for anything," I said. "Yet."

"What is your name, old man?"

"Koriba."

He placed a thumb to his chest. "I am William."

"That is not a Maasai name," I noted.

"My full name is William Sambeke."

"Then I will call you Sambeke."

He shrugged. "Call me whatever you want." He shaded his eyes from the sun and looked off toward the village. "This isn't exactly what I expected."

"What did you expect, Sambeke?" I asked.

"I thought you people were trying to create a Utopia here."

"We are."

He snorted contemptuously. "You live in huts, you have no machinery, and you even have to hire someone from Earth to kill hyenas for you. That's not *my* idea of Utopia."

"Then you will doubtless wish to return to your home," I suggested.

"I have a job to do here first," he replied. "A job *you* failed to do."

I made no answer, and he stared at me for a long moment.

"Well?" he said at last.

"Well what?"

"Aren't you going to spout some mumbo-jumbo and make me disappear in a cloud of smoke, *mundumugu*?"

"Before you choose to become my enemy," I said in perfect English, "you should know that I am not as ineffectual as you may think, nor am I impressed by Maasai arrogance."

He stared at me in surprise, then threw back his head and laughed.

"There's more to you than meets the eye, old man!" he said in English. "I think we are going to become great friends!"

"I doubt it," I replied in Swahili.

"What schools did you attend back on Earth?" he asked, matching my change in languages again.

"Cambridge and Yale," I said. "But that was many years ago."

"Why does an educated man choose to sit in the dirt beside a grass hut?"

"Why does a Maasai accept a commission from a Kikuyu?" I responded.

"I like to hunt," he said. "And I wanted to see this Utopia you have built."

"And now you have seen it."

"I have seen Kirinyaga," he replied. "I have not yet seen Utopia."

"That is because you do not know how to look for it."

"You are a clever old man, Koriba, full of clever answers," said Sambeke, taking no offense. "Why have you not made yourself king of this entire planetoid?"

"The *mundumugu* is the repository of our traditions. That is all the power he seeks or needs."

"You could at least have had them build you a house, instead of living like this. No Maasai lives in a *manyatta* any longer."

"And after the house would come a car?" I asked.

"Once you built some roads," he agreed.

"And then a factory to build more cars, and another one to build more houses, and then an impressive building for our Parliament, and perhaps a railroad line?" I shook my head. "That is a description of Kenya, not of Utopia."

"You are making a mistake," said Sambeke. "On my way here from the landing field—what is it called?"

"Haven."

"On my way here from Haven, I saw buffalo and kudu and impala. A hunting lodge by the river overlooking the plains would bring in a lot of tourist money."

"We do not hunt our grasseaters."

"You wouldn't have to," he said meaningfully. "And think of how much their money could help your people."

"May Ngai preserve us from people who want to help us," I said devoutly.

"You are a stubborn old man," he said. "I think I had better go talk to Koinnage. Which *shamba* is his?"

"The largest," I answered. "He is the paramount chief."

He nodded. "Of course. I will see you later, old man."

I nodded. "Yes, you will."

"And after I have killed your hyenas, perhaps we will share a gourd of *pombe* and discuss ways to turn this world into a Utopia. I have been very disappointed thus far."

So saying, he turned toward the village and began walking down the long, winding trail to Koinnage's *boma*.

He turned Koinnage's head, as I knew he would. By the time I had eaten and made my way to the village, the two of them were sitting beside a fire in front of the paramount chief's *boma*, and Sambeke was describing the hunting lodge he wanted to build by the river.

"*Jambo*, Koriba," said Koinnage, looking up at me as I approached them.

"*Jambo*, Koinnage," I responded, squatting down next to him.

"You have met William Sambeke?"

"I have met Sambeke," I said, and the Maasai grinned at my refusal to use his European name.

"He has many plans for Kirinyaga," continued Koinnage, as some of the villagers began wandering over.

"How interesting," I replied. "You asked for a hunter, and they have sent you a planner instead."

"Some of us," interjected Sambeke, an amused expression on his face, "have more than one talent."

"Some of us," I said, "have been here for half a day and have not yet begun to hunt."

"I will kill the hyenas tomorrow," said Sambeke, "when their bellies are full and they are too content to race away at my approach."

"How will you kill them?" I asked.

He carefully unlocked his gun case and pulled out his rifle, which was equipped with a telescopic sight. Most of the villagers had never seen such a weapon, and they crowded around it, whispering to each other.

"Would you care to examine it?" he asked me.

I shook my head. "The weapons of the Europeans hold no interest for me."

"This rifle was manufactured in Zimbabwe, by members of the Shona tribe," he corrected me.

I shrugged. "Then they are black Europeans."

"Whatever they are, they make a splendid weapon," said Sambeke.

"For those who are afraid to hunt in the traditional way," I said.

"Do not taunt me, old man," said Sambeke, and suddenly a hush fell over the onlookers, for no man speaks thus to the *mundumugu*.

"I do not taunt you, Maasai," I said. "I merely point out why you have brought the weapon. It is no crime to be afraid of *fisi*."

"I fear nothing," he said heatedly.

"That is not true," I said. "Like all of us, you fear failure."

"I shall not fail with *this*," he said, patting the rifle.

"By the way," I asked, "was it not the Maasai who once proved their manhood by facing the lion armed with only a spear?"

"It was," he answered. "And it was the Maasai *and* the Kikuyu who lost most of their babies at birth, and who succumbed to every disease that passed through their villages, and who lived in shelters that could protect them from neither the rain nor the cold nor even the flesh-eaters of the veldt. It was the Maasai and the Kikuyu who learned from the Europeans, and who took back their land from the white man, and who built great cities where once there was only dust and swamps. Or, rather," he added, "it was the Maasai and *most* of the Kikuyu."

"I remember seeing a circus when I was in England," I said, raising my voice so that all could hear me, though I directed my remarks at Sambeke. "In it there was a chimpanzee. He was a very bright animal. They dressed him in human clothing, and he rode a human bicycle, and he played human music on a human flute—but that did not make him a human. In fact, he amused the humans because he was such a grotesque mockery of them ... just as the Maasai and Kikuyu who wear suits and drive cars and work in large buildings are not Europeans, but are instead a mockery of them."

"That is just your opinion, old man," said the Maasai, "and it is wrong."

"Is it?" I asked. "The chimpanzee had been tainted by his association with humans, so that he could never survive in the wild. And *you*, I notice, must have the Europeans' weapon to hunt an animal that your grandfathers would have gone out and slain with a knife or a spear."

"Are you challenging me, old man?" asked Sambeke, once again amused.

"I am merely pointing out why you have brought your rifle with you," I answered.

"No," he said. "You are trying to regain the power you lost when your people sent for me. But you have made a mistake."

"In what way?"

"You have made me your enemy."

"Will you shoot me with your rifle, then?" I asked calmly, for I knew he would not.

He leaned over and whispered to me, so that only I could hear him.

"We could have made a fortune together, old man. I would have been happy to share it with you, in exchange for you keeping your people in line, for a safari company will need many workers. But now you have publicly opposed me, and I cannot permit that."

"We must learn to live with disappointments," I said.

"I am glad you feel that way," he said. "For I plan to turn this world into a Utopia, rather than some Kikuyu dreamland."

Then, suddenly, he stood up.

"Boy," he said to Ndemi, who was standing at the outskirts of the crowd. "Bring me a spear."

Ndemi looked to me, and I nodded, for I could not believe that the Maasai would kill me with *any* weapon.

Ndemi brought the spear to Sambeke, who took it from him and leaned it against Koinnage's hut. Then he stood before the fire and slowly began removing all his clothes. When he was naked, with the firelight playing off his lean, hard body, looking like an African god, he picked up the spear and held it over his head.

"I go to hunt *fisi* in the dark, in the old way," he announced to the assembled villagers. "Your *mundumugu* has laid down the challenge, and if you are to listen to my counsel in the future, as I hope you will, you must know that I can meet any challenge he sets for me."

And before anyone could say a word or move to stop him, he strode boldly off into the night.

"Now he will die, and Maintenance will want to revoke our charter!" complained Koinnage.

"If he dies, it was his own decision, and Maintenance will not punish us in any way," I replied. I stared long and hard at him. "I wonder that you care."

"That I care if he should die?"

"That you care if Maintenance should revoke our charter," I answered. "If you listen to the Maasai, you will turn Kirinyaga into another Kenya, so why should you mind returning to the original Kenya?"

"He does not want to turn Kirinyaga into Kenya, but into Utopia," said Koinnage sullenly.

"We are already attempting to do that," I noted. "Does *his* Utopia include a big European house for the paramount chief?"

"We did not discuss it thoroughly," said Koinnage uneasily.

"And perhaps some extra cattle, in exchange for supplying him with porters and gun bearers?"

"He has good ideas," said Koinnage, ignoring my question. "Why should we carry our water from the river when he can create pumps and pipes to carry it for us?"

"Because if water is easy to obtain, it will become easy to waste, and we have no more water to waste here than we had in Kenya, where all the lakes have dried up because of farseeing men like Sambeke."

"You have answers for everything," said Koinnage bitterly.

"No," I said. "But I have answers for this Maasai, for his questions have been asked many times before, and always in the past the Kikuyu have given the wrong answer."

Suddenly we heard a hideous scream from perhaps half a mile away.

"It is finished," said Koinnage grimly. "The Maasai is dead, and now we must answer to Maintenance."

"It did not sound like a man," said Ndemi.

"You are just a *mtoto*—a child," said Koinnage. "What do you know?"

"I know what Juma sounded like when *fisi* killed him," said Ndemi defiantly. "That is what I know."

We waited in silence to see if there would be another sound, but none was forthcoming.

"Perhaps it is just as well that *fisi* has killed the Maasai," said old Njobe at last. "I saw the building that he drew in the dirt, the one he would make for visitors, and it was an evil building. It was not round and safe from demons like our own huts, but instead it had corners, and everyone knows that demons live in corners."

"Truly, there would be a curse upon it," agreed another of the Elders.

"What can one expect from one who hunts *fisi* at night?" added another.

"One can expect a dead *fisi*!" said Sambeke triumphantly, as he stepped out of the shadows and threw the bloody corpse of a large male hyena onto the ground. Everyone backed away from him in awe, and he turned to me, the firelight flickering off his sleek black body. "What do you say now, old man?"

"I say that you are a greater killer than *fisi*," I answered.

He smiled with satisfaction.

"Now," he said, "let us see what we can learn from this particular *fisi*." He turned to a young man. "Boy, bring a knife."

"His name is Kamabi," I said.

"I have not had time to learn names," replied Sambeke. He turned back to Kamabi. "Do as I ask, boy."

"He is a man," I said.

"It is difficult to tell in the dark," said Sambeke with a shrug.

Kamabi returned a moment later with an ancient hunting knife; it was so old and so rusty that Sambeke did not care to touch it, and so he merely pointed to the hyena.

"Kata hi ya tumbo," he said. "Slit the stomach here."

Kamabi knelt down and slit open the hyena's belly. The smell was terrible, but the Maasai picked up a stick and began prodding through the contents. Finally he stood up.

"I had hoped that we would find a bracelet or an earring," he said. "But it has been a long time since the boy was killed, and such things would have passed through *fisi* days ago."

"Koriba can roll the bones and tell if this is the one who killed Juma," said Koinnage.

Sambeke snorted contemptuously. "Koriba can roll the bones from now until the long rains come, but they will tell him nothing." He looked at the assembled villagers. "I have killed *fisi* in the old way to prove that I am no coward or European, to hunt only in the daylight and hide behind my gun. But now that I have shown you that I can do it, tomorrow I shall show you how many *fisi* I can kill in *my* way, and then you may decide which way is better, Koriba's or mine." He paused. "Now I need a hut to sleep in, so that I may be strong and alert when the sun rises."

Every villager except Koinnage immediately volunteered his hut. The Maasai looked at each man in turn, and then turned to the paramount chief. "I will take yours," he said.

"But—" began Koinnage.

"And one of your wives to keep me warm in the night." He stared directly into Koinnage's eyes. "Or would you deny me your hospitality after I have killed *fisi* for you?"

"No," said Koinnage at last. "I will not deny you."

The Maasai shot me a triumphant smile. "It is still not Utopia," he said. "But it is getting closer."

The next morning Sambeke went out with his rifle.

I walked down to the village in the morning to give Zindu ointment to help dry up her milk, for her baby had been stillborn. When I was finished, I went through the *shambas*, blessing the scarecrows, and before long I had my usual large group of children beside me, begging me to tell them a story.

Finally, when the sun was high in the sky and it was too hot to keep walking, I sat down beneath the shade of an acacia tree.

"All right," I said. "Now you may have your story."

"What story will you tell us today, Koriba?" asked one of the girls.

"I think I shall tell you the tale of the Unwise Elephant," I said.

"Why was he unwise?" asked a boy.

"Listen, and you shall know," I said, and they all fell silent.

"Once there was a young elephant," I began, "and because he was young, he had not yet acquired the wisdom of his race. And one day this elephant chanced upon a city in the middle of the savannah, and he entered it, and beheld its wonders, and thought it was quite the most marvelous thing he had ever seen. All his life he had labored day and night to fill his belly, and here, in the city, were wonderful machines that could make his life so much easier that he was determined to own some of them.

"But when he approached the owner of a digging stick, with which he could find buried acacia pods, the owner said, 'I am a poor man, and I cannot give my digging stick to you. But because you want it so badly, I will make a trade.'

" 'But I have nothing to trade,' said the elephant unhappily.

" 'Of course you do,' said the man. 'If you will let me have your ivory, so that I can carve designs on it, you may have the digging stick.'

"The elephant considered this offer, and finally agreed, for if he had a digging stick he would no longer need his tusks to root up the ground.

"And he walked a little farther, and he came to an old woman with a weaving loom, and he thought this was a wonderful thing, for with it he would be able to make a blanket for himself so that he could stay warm during the long nights.

"He asked the woman for her weaving loom, and she replied that she would not give it away, but that she would be happy to trade it.

" 'All I have to trade is my digging stick,' said the elephant.

" 'But I do not need a digging stick,' said the old woman. 'You must let me cut off one of your feet, that I may make a stool of it."

"The elephant thought for a long time, and he remembered how cold he had been the previous night, and finally he agreed, and the trade was made.

"Then he came to a man who had a net, and the elephant thought that the net would be a wonderful thing to have, for now he could catch the fruits when he shook a tree, rather than having to hunt for them on the ground.

" 'I will not give you the net, for it took me many days to make it,' said the man, 'but I will trade it to you for your ears, which will make excellent sleeping mats.'

"Again the elephant agreed, and finally he went back to the herd to show them the wonders he had brought from the city of men.

" 'What need have we for digging sticks?' asked his brother. 'No digging stick will last as long as our tusks.'

" 'It might be nice to have a blanket,' said his mother, 'but to make a blanket with a weaving loom we would need fingers, which we do not have.'

" 'I cannot see the purpose of a net for catching fruit from the trees,' said his father. 'For if you hold the net in your trunk, how will you shake the fruits loose from the tree, and if you shake the tree, how will you hold the net?'

" 'I see now that the tools of men are of no use to elephants,' said the young elephant. 'I can never be a man, so I will go back to being an elephant.'

"His father shook his head sadly. 'It is true that you are not a man—but because you have dealt with men, you are no longer an elephant either. You have lost your foot, and cannot keep up with the herd. You have given away your ivory, and you cannot dig for water, or churn up the ground to look for acacia pods. You have parted with your ears, and now you cannot flap them to cool your blood when the sun is high in the sky.'

"And so the elephant spent the rest of his unhappy life halfway between the city and the herd, for he could not become part of one and he was no longer part of the other."

I stopped, and stared off into the distance, where a small herd of impala was grazing just beyond one of our cultivated fields.

"Is that all?" asked the girl who had first requested the story.

"That is all," I said.

"It was not a very good story," she continued.

"Oh?" I asked, slapping a small insect that was crawling up my arm. "Why not?"

"Because the ending was not happy."

"Not all stories have happy endings," I said.

"I do not like unhappy endings," she said.

"Neither do I," I agreed. I paused and looked at her. "How do *you* think the story should end?"

"The elephant should not trade the things that make him an elephant, since he can never become a man."

"Very good," I said. "Would you trade the things that make you a Kikuyu, to try to be something you can never become?"

"Never!"

"Would any of you?" I asked my entire audience.

"No!" they cried.

"What if the elephant offered you his tusks, or the hyena offered you his fangs?"

"Never!"

I paused for just a moment before asking my next question.

"What if the Maasai offered you his gun?"

Most of the children yelled "No!", but I noticed that two of the older boys did not answer. I questioned them about it.

"A gun is not like tusks or teeth," said the taller of the two boys. "It is a weapon that men use."

"That is right," said the smaller boy, shuffling his bare feet in the dirt and raising a small cloud of dust. "The Maasai is not an animal. He is like us."

"He is not an animal," I agreed, "but he is not like us. Do the Kikuyu use guns, or live in brick houses, or wear European clothes?"

"No," said the boys in unison.

"Then if you were to use a gun, or live in a brick house, or wear European clothes, would you be a true Kikuyu?"

"No," they admitted.

"But would using a gun, or living in a brick house, or wearing European clothes, make you a Maasai or a European?"

"No."

"Do you see, then, why we must reject the tools and the gifts of outsiders? We can never become like them, but we can stop being Kikuyu, and if we stop being Kikuyu without becoming something else, then we are nothing."

"I understand, Koriba," said the taller boy.

"Are you sure?" I asked.

He nodded. "I am sure."

"Why are all your stories like this?" asked a girl.

"Like what?"

"They all have titles like the Unwise Elephant, or the Jackal and the Honeybird, or the Leopard and the Shrike, but when you explain them they are always about the Kikuyu."

"That is because I am a Kikuyu and you are a Kikuyu," I replied with a smile. "If we were leopards, then all my stories would really be about leopards."

I spent a few more minutes with them beneath the shade of the tree, and then I saw Ndemi approaching through the tall grass, his face alive with excitement.

"Well?" I said when he had joined us.

"The Maasai has returned," he announced.

"Did he kill any *fisi*?" I asked.

"Mingi sana," replied Ndemi. "Very many."

"Where is he now?"

"By the river, with some of the young men who served as his gun bearers and skinners."

"I think I shall go visit them," I said, getting carefully to my feet, for my legs tend to get stiff when I sit in one position for too long. "Ndemi, you will come with me. The rest of you children are to go back to your *shambas*, and to think about the story of the Unwise Elephant."

Ndemi's chest puffed up like one of my roosters when I singled him out to accompany me, and a moment later we were walking across the sprawling savannah.

"What is the Maasai doing at the river?" I asked.

"He has cut down some young saplings with a *panga*," answered Ndemi, "and he is instructing some of the men to build something, but I do not know what it is."

I peered through the haze of heat and dust, and saw a small party of men approaching us.

"*I* know what it is," I said softly, for although I had never seen a sedan chair, I knew what one looked like, and it was currently approaching us as four Kikuyu bore the weight of the sedan chair—and the Maasai—upon their sweating shoulders.

Since they were heading in our direction, I told Ndemi to stop walking, and we stood and waited for them.

"*Jambo*, old man!" said the Maasai when we were within earshot. "I have killed seven more hyenas this morning."

"*Jambo*, Sambeke," I replied. "You look very comfortable."

"It could use cushions," he said. "And the bearers do not carry it levelly. But I will make do with it."

"Poor man," I said, "who lacks cushions and thoughtful bearers. How did these oversights come to pass?"

"That is because it is not Utopia yet," he replied with a smile. "But it is getting very close."

"You will be sure to tell me when it arrives," I said.

"You will know, old man."

Then he directed his bearers to carry him to the village. Ndemi and I remained where we were, and watched him disappear in the distance.

That night there was a feast in the village to celebrate the slaying of the eight hyenas. Koinnage himself had slaughtered an ox, and there was much *pombe*, and the people were singing and dancing when I arrived, reenacting the stalking and killing of the animals by their new savior.

The Maasai himself was seated on a tall chair, taller even than Koinnage's throne. In one hand he held a gourd of *pombe*, and the leather case that held his rifle was laid carefully across his lap. He was clad now in the red robe of his people, his hair was neatly braided in his tribal fashion, and his lean body glistened with oils that had been rubbed onto it. Two young girls, scarcely past circumcision age, stood behind him, hanging upon his every word.

"*Jambo*, old man!" he greeted me as I approached him.

"*Jambo*, Sambeke," I said.

"That is no longer my name," he said.

"Oh? And have you taken a Kikuyu name instead?"

"I have taken a name that the Kikuyu will understand," he replied. "It is what the village will call me from this day forth."

"You are not leaving, now that the hunt is over?"

He shook his head. "I am not leaving."

"You are making a mistake," I said.

"Not as big a mistake as you made when you chose not to be my ally," he responded. Then, after a brief pause, he smiled and added: "Do you not wish to know my new name?"

"I suppose I should know it, if you are to remain here for any length of time," I agreed.

He leaned over and whispered the name word to me that Ngai had whispered to Gikuyu on the holy mountain millions of years earlier.

"Bwana?" I repeated.

He looked smugly at me, and smiled again.

"Now," he said, "it is Utopia."

Bwana spent the next few weeks making Kirinyaga a Utopia—for Bwana.

He took three young wives for himself, and he had the villagers build him a large house by the river, a house with windows and corners and verandas such as the colonial Europeans might have built in Kenya two centuries earlier.

He went hunting every day, collecting trophies for himself and providing the village with more meat than they had ever had before. At nights he went to the village to eat and drink and dance, and then, armed with his rifle, he walked through the darkness to his own house.

Soon Koinnage was making plans to build a house similar to Bwana's, right in the village, and many of the young men wanted the Maasai to procure rifles for them. This he refused to do, explaining that there could be only one Bwana on Kirinyaga, and it was their job to serve as trackers and cooks and skinners.

He no longer wore European clothes, but always appeared in traditional Maasai dress, his hair meticulously pleated and braided, his body bright and glistening from the oils that his wives rubbed on him each night.

I kept my own counsel and continued my duties, caring for the sick, bringing the rains, reading the entrails of goats, blessing the scarecrows, alleviating curses. But I did not say another word to Bwana, nor did he speak to me.

Ndemi spent more and more time with me, tending my goats and chickens, and even keeping my *boma* clean, which is woman's work but which he volunteered to do.

Finally one day he approached me while I sat in the shade, watching the cattle grazing in a nearby field.

"May I speak, *mundumugu?*" he asked, squatting down next to me.

"You may speak, Ndemi," I answered.

"The Maasai has taken another wife," he said. "And he killed Karanja's dog because its barking annoyed him." He paused. "And he calls everyone 'Boy,' even the Elders, which seems to me to be a term of disrespect."

"I know these things," I said.

"Why do you not do something, then?" asked Ndemi. "Are you not all-powerful?"

"Only Ngai is all-powerful," I said. "I am just the *mundumugu.*"

"But is not the *mundumugu* more powerful than a Maasai?"

"Most of the people in the village do not seem to think so," I said.

"Ah!" he said. "You are angry with them for losing faith in you, and *that* is why you have not turned him into an insect and stepped on him."

"I am not angry," I said. "Merely disappointed."

"When will you kill him?" asked Ndemi.

"It would do no good to kill him," I replied.

"Why not?"

"Because they believe in his power, and if he died, they would just send for another hunter, who would become another Bwana."

"Then will you do nothing?"

"I will do something," I answered. "But killing Bwana is not the answer. He must be humiliated before the people, so that they can see for themselves that he is not, after all, a *mundumugu* who must be listened to and obeyed."

"How will you do this?" asked Ndemi anxiously.

"I do not know yet," I said. "I must study him further."

"I thought you knew everything already."

I smiled. "The *mundumugu* does not know everything, nor does he have to."

"Oh?"

"He must merely know more than his people."

"But you already know more than Koinnage and the others."

"I must be sure I know more than the Maasai before I act," I said.

"You may know how large the leopard is, and how strong, and how fast, and how cunning—but until you have studied him further, and learned how he charges, and which side he favors, and how he tests the wind, and how he signals an attack by moving his tail, you are at a disadvantage if you hunt him. I am an old man, and I cannot defeat the Maasai in hand-to-hand combat, so I must study him and discover his weakness."

"And what if he has none?"

"Everything has a weakness."

"Even though he is stronger than you?"

"The elephant is the strongest beast of all, and yet a handful of tiny ants inside his trunk can drive him mad with pain to the point where he will kill himself." I paused. "You do not have to be stronger than your opponent, for surely the ant is not stronger than the elephant. But the ant knows the elephant's weakness, and I must learn the Maasai's."

He placed his hand to his chest.

"*I* believe in you, Koriba," he said.

"I am glad," I said, shielding my eyes as a hot breeze blew a cloud of dust across my hill. "For you alone will not be disappointed when I finally confront the Maasai."

"Will you forgive the men of the village?" he asked.

I paused before answering. "When they remember once more why we came to Kirinyaga, I will forgive them," I said at last.

"And if they do not remember?"

"I must make them remember," I said. I looked out across the savannah, following its contours as it led up the river and the woods. "Ngai has given the Kikuyu a second chance at Utopia, and we must not squander it."

"You and Koinnage, and even the Maasai, keep using that word, but I do not understand it."

"Utopia?" I asked.

He nodded. "What does it mean?"

"It means many things to many people," I replied. "To the true

Kikuyu, it means to live as one with the land, to respect the ancient laws and rituals, and to please Ngai."

"That seems simple enough."

"It does, doesn't it?" I agreed. "And yet you cannot begin to imagine how many millions of men have died because their definition of Utopia differed from their neighbor's."

He stared at me. "Truly?"

"Truly. Take the Maasai, for example. His Utopia is to ride upon his sedan chair, and to shoot animals, and to take many wives, and to live in a big house by the river."

"It does not sound like a bad thing," observed Ndemi thoughtfully.

"It is not a bad thing—for the Maasai." I paused briefly. "But do you suppose it is Utopia for the men who must carry the chair, or the animals that he kills, or the young men of the village who cannot marry, or the Kikuyu who must build his house by the river?"

"I see," said Ndemi, his eyes widening. "Kirinyaga must be a Utopia for all of us, or it cannot be a Utopia at all." He brushed an insect from his cheek and looked at me. "Is that correct, Koriba?"

"You learn quickly, Ndemi," I said, reaching a hand out and rubbing the hair atop his head. "Perhaps some day you yourself will become a *mundumugu.*"

"Will I learn magic then?"

"You must learn many things to be a *mundumugu,*" I said. "Magic is the least of them."

"But it is the most impressive," he said. "It is what makes the people fear you, and fearing you, they are willing to listen to your wisdom."

As I considered his words, I finally began to get an inkling of how I would defeat Bwana and return my people to the Utopian existence that we had envisioned when we accepted our charter for Kirinyaga.

"Sheep!" growled Bwana. "All sheep! No wonder the Maasai preyed on the Kikuyu in the old days."

I had decided to enter the village at night, to further observe my enemy. He had drunk much *pombe*, and finally stripped off his red cloak and stood naked before Koinnage's *boma*, challenging the young men of the village to wrestle him. They stood back in the shadows, shaking like women, in awe of his physical prowess.

"I will fight three of you at once!" he said, looking around for any volunteers. There were none, and he threw back his head and laughed heartily.

"And you wonder why I am Bwana and you are a bunch of boys!" Suddenly his eyes fell on me.

"*There* is a man who is not afraid of me," he announced.

"That is true," I said.

"Will *you* wrestle me, old man?"

I shook my head. "No, I will not."

"I guess you are just another coward."

"I do not fear the buffalo or the hyena, but I do not wrestle with *them*, either," I said. "There is a difference between courage and foolishness. You are a young man; I am an old one."

"What brings you to the village at night?" he asked. "Have you been speaking to your gods, plotting ways to kill me?"

"There is only one god," I replied, "and He disapproves of killing."

He nodded, an amused smile on his face. "Yes, it stands to reason that the god of sheep would disapprove of killing." Suddenly the smile vanished, and he stared contemptuously at me. "En-kai spits upon your god, old man."

"You call Him En-kai and we call him Ngai," I said calmly, "but it is the same god, and the day will come when we all must answer to Him. I hope you will be as bold and fearless then as you are now."

"I hope your Ngai will not tremble before *me*," he retorted, posturing before his wives, who giggled at his arrogance. "Did I not go naked into the night, armed with only a spear, and slay *fisi*? Have I not killed more than one hundred beasts in less than thirty days? Your Ngai had better not test my temper."

"He will test more than your temper," I replied.

"What does *that* mean?"

"It means whatever you wish it to mean," I said. "I am old and tired, and I wish to sit by the fire and drink *pombe*."

With that I turned my back on him and walked over to Njobe, who was warming his ancient bones by a small fire just outside Koinnage's *boma*.

Unable to find an opponent with whom to wrestle, Bwana drank more *pombe* and finally turned to his wives.

"No one will fight me," he said with mock misery. "And yet my fighting blood is boiling within my veins. Set me a task—any task— that I may do for your pleasure."

The three girls whispered together and giggled again, and finally one of them stepped forward, urged by the other two.

"We have seen Koriba place his hand in the fire without being burned," she said. "Can you do that?"

He snorted contemptuously. "A magician's trick, nothing more. Set me a true task."

"Set him an *easier* task," I said. "Obviously the fire is too painful."

He turned and glared at me. "What kind of lotion did you place on your hand before putting it in the fire, old man?" he asked in English.

I smiled at him. "That would be an *illusionist's* trick, not a magician's," I answered.

"You think to humiliate me before my people?" he said. "Think again, old man."

He walked to the fire, stood between Njobe and myself, and thrust his hand into it. His face was totally impassive, but I could smell the burning flesh. Finally he withdrew it and held it up.

"There is no magic to it!" he shouted in Swahili.

"But you are burned, my husband," said the wife who had challenged him.

"Did I cry out?" he demanded. "Did I cringe from pain?"

"No, you did not."

"Can any other man place his hand in the fire without crying out?"

"No, my husband."

"Who, then, is the greater man—Koriba, who protects himself with magic, or I, who need no magic to place my hand in the fire?"

"Bwana," said his wives in unison.

He turned to me and grinned triumphantly.

"You have lost again, old man."

But I had not lost.

I had gone to the village to study my enemy, and I had learned much from my visit. Just as a Kikuyu cannot become a Maasai, this Maasai could not become a Kikuyu. There was an arrogance that had been bred into him, an arrogance so great that it had not only elevated him to his current high status, but would prove to be his downfall as well.

The next morning Koinnage himself came to my *boma*.

"*Jambo,*" I greeted him.

"*Jambo,* Koriba," he replied. "We must talk."

"About what?"

"About Bwana," said Koinnage.

"What about him?"

"He has overstepped himself," said Koinnage. "Last night, after you left, he decided that he had drunk too much *pombe* to return home, and he threw me out of my own hut—*me*, the paramount chief!" He paused to kick at a small lizard that had been approaching his foot, and then continued. "Not only that, but this morning he announced that he was taking my youngest wife, Kibo, for his own!"

"Interesting," I remarked, watching the tiny lizard as it scurried under a bush, then turned and stared at us.

"Is that all you can say?" he demanded. "I paid twenty cows and five goats for her. When I told him that, do you know what he did?"

"What?"

Koinnage held up a small silver coin for me to see. "He gave me a *shilling* from Kenya!" He spat upon the coin and threw it onto the dry, rocky slope beyond my *boma*. "And now he says that whenever he stays in the village he will sleep in my hut, and that I must sleep elsewhere."

"I am very sorry," I said. "But I warned you against sending for a hunter. It is his nature to prey upon all things: the hyena, the kudu, even the Kikuyu." I paused, enjoying his discomfort. "Perhaps you should tell him to go away."

"He would not listen."

I nodded. "The lion may sleep with the goat, and he may feed upon him, but he very rarely listens to him."

"Koriba, we were wrong," said Koinnage, his face a mask of desperation. "Can you not rid us of this intruder?"

"Why?" I asked.

"I have already told you."

I shook my head slowly. "You have told me why *you* have cause to resent him," I answered. "That is not enough."

"What more must I say?" asked Koinnage.

I paused and looked at him. "It will come to you in the fullness of time."

"Perhaps we can contact Maintenance," suggested Koinnage. "Surely *they* have the power to make him leave."

I sighed deeply. "Have you learned nothing?"

"I do not understand."

"You sent for the Maasai because he was stronger than *fisi*. Now you want to send for Maintenance because they are stronger than the Maasai. If one man can so change our society, what do you think will happen when we invite many men? Already our young men talk of hunting instead of farming, and wish to build European houses with corners where demons can hide, and beg the Maasai to supply them with guns. What will they want when they have seen all the wonders that Maintenance possesses?"

"Then how are we to rid ourselves of the Maasai?"

"When the time comes, he will leave," I said.

"You are certain?"

"I am the *mundumugu*."

"When will this time be?" asked Koinnage.

"When you know *why* he must leave," I answered. "Now perhaps you should return to the village, lest you discover that he wants your other wives as well."

Panic spread across Koinnage's face, and he raced back down the winding trail to the village without another word.

I spent the next few days gathering bark from some of the trees at the edge of the savannah, and when I had gathered as much as I needed I added certain herbs and roots and mashed them to a pulp in an old turtle shell. I added some water, placed it in a cooking gourd, and began simmering the concoction over a small fire.

When I was done I sent for Ndemi, who arrived about half an hour later.

"*Jambo*, Koriba," he said.

"*Jambo*, Ndemi," I replied.

He looked at my cooking gourd and wrinkled his nose. "What is that?" he asked. "It smells terrible."

"It is not for eating," I replied.

"I hope not," he said devoutly.

"Be careful not to touch it," I said, walking over to the tree that grew within my *boma* and sitting down in its shade. Ndemi, giving the gourd a wide birth, joined me.

"You sent for me," he said.

"Yes, I did."

"I am glad. The village is not a good place to be."

"Oh?"

He nodded. "A number of the young men now follow Bwana everywhere. They take goats from the *shambas* and cloth from the huts, and nobody dares to stop them. Kanjara tried yesterday, but the young men hit him and made his mouth bleed while Bwana watched and laughed."

I nodded, for none of this surprised me.

"I think it is almost time," I said, waving my hand to scare away some flies that also sought shade beneath the tree and were buzzing about my face.

"Almost time for what?"

"For Bwana to leave Kirinyaga." I paused. "That is why I sent for you."

"The *mundumugu* wishes me to help him?" said Ndemi, his young face shining with pride.

I nodded.

"I will do anything you say," vowed Ndemi.

"Good. Do you know who makes the oils with which Bwana annoints himself?"

"Old Wambu makes them."

"You must bring me two gourds filled with them."

"I thought only the Maasai annoints himself," said Ndemi.

"Just do as I say. Now, have you a bow?"

"No, but my father does. He has not used it in many years, so he will not mind if I take it."

"I do not want anyone to know you have it."

Ndemi shrugged and idly drew a pattern in the dirt with his forefinger. "He will blame the young men who follow Bwana."

"And has your father any arrows with sharp tips?"

"No," said Ndemi. "But I can make some."

"I want you to make some this afternoon," I said. "Ten should be enough."

Ndemi drew an arrow in the dirt. "Like so?" he asked.

"A little shorter," I said.

"I can get the feathers for the arrows from the chickens in our *boma*," he suggested.

I nodded. "That is good."

"Do you want me to shoot an arrow into Bwana?"

"I told you once: the Kikuyu do not kill their fellow men."

"Then what do you want me to do with the arrows?"

"Bring them back here to my *boma* when you have made them," I said. "And bring ten pieces of cloth in which to wrap them."

"And then what?"

"And then we will dip them into the poison I have been making."

He frowned. "But you do not wish me to shoot an arrow into Bwana?" He paused. "What shall I shoot, then?"

"I will tell you when the time comes," I said. "Now return to the village and do what I have asked you to do."

"Yes, Koriba," he said, running out of my *boma* and down the hill on his strong young legs as a number of guinea fowl, squawking and screeching, moved resentfully out of his path.

It was less than an hour later that Koinnage once again climbed my hill, this time accompanied by Njobe and two other Elders, all wearing their tribal robes.

"*Jambo*, Koriba," said Koinnage unhappily.

"*Jambo*," I replied.

"You told me to come back when I understood why Bwana must leave," said Koinnage. He spat on the ground, and a tiny spider raced away. "I have come."

"And what have you learned?" I asked, raising my hand to shade my eyes from the sun.

He lowered his eyes to the ground, uncomfortable as a child being questioned by his father.

"I have learned that a Utopia is a delicate thing which requires protection from those who would force their will upon it."

"And you, Njobe?" I said. "What have you learned?"

"Our life here was very good," he answered. "And I believed that goodness was its own defense." He sighed deeply. "But it is not."

"Is Kirinyaga worth defending?" I asked.

"How can you, of all people, ask that?" demanded one of the other two Elders.

"The Maasai can bring many machines and much money to Kirinyaga," I said. "He seeks only to improve us, not destroy us."

"It would not be Kirinyaga any longer," said Njobe. "It would be Kenya all over again."

"He has corrupted everything he has touched," said Koinnage, his face contorted with rage and humiliation. "My own son has become one of his followers. No longer does he show respect for his father, or for our women or our traditions. He speaks only of money and guns now, and he worships Bwana as if he were Ngai Himself." He paused. "You must help us, Koriba."

"Yes," added Njobe. "We were wrong not to listen to you."

I stared at each of their worried faces in turn, and finally I nodded. "I will help you."

"When?"

"Soon."

"*How* soon?" persisted Koinnage, coughing as the wind blew a cloud of dust past his face. "We cannot wait much longer."

"Within a week the Maasai will be gone," I said.

"Within a week?" repeated Koinnage.

"That is my promise." I paused. "But if we are to purify our society, his followers may have to leave with him."

"You cannot take my son from me!" said Koinnage.

"The Maasai has already taken him," I pointed out. "I will have to decide if he will be allowed to return."

"But he is to be the paramount chief when I die."

"That is my price, Koinnage," I said firmly. "You must let me decide what to do with the Maasai's followers." I placed a hand to my heart. "I will make a just decision."

"I do not know," muttered Koinnage.

I shrugged. "Then live with the Maasai."

Koinnage stared intently at the ground, as if the ants and termites could tell him what to do. Finally he sighed.

"It will be as you say," he agreed unhappily.

"How will you rid us of the Maasai?" asked Njobe.

"I am the *mundumugu*," I answered noncommittally, for I wanted no hint of my plan to reach Bwana's ears.

"It will take powerful magic," said Njobe.

"Do you doubt my powers?" I asked.

Njobe would not meet my gaze. "No, but ..."

"But what?"

"But he is like a god. He will be difficult to destroy."

"We have room for only one god," I said, "and His name is Ngai."

They returned to the village, and I went back to blending my poison.

While I waited for Ndemi to return, I took a thin piece of wood and carved a tiny hole in it. Then I took a long needle, stuck it lengthwise through the entire length of the wood, and withdrew it.

Finally I placed the wood to my lips and blew into the hole. I could hear no sound, but the cattle in the pasture suddenly raised their heads, and two of my goats began racing frantically in circles. I tried my makeshift whistle twice more, received the same reaction, and finally put it aside.

Ndemi arrived in midafternoon, carrying the oil gourds, his father's ancient bow, and ten carefully crafted arrows. He had been unable to find any metal, but he had carved very sharp points at the end of each. I checked the bowstring, decided that it still had resiliency, and nodded my approval.

Then, very carefully making sure not to let any of the poison come in contact with my flesh, I dipped the head of each arrow into my solution, and wrapped them in the ten pieces of cloth Ndemi had brought.

"It is good," I said. "Now we are ready."

"What must I do, Koriba?" he asked.

"In the old days when we still lived in Kenya, only Europeans were allowed to hunt, and they used to be paid to take other Europeans on safari," I explained. "It was important to these white hunters that their clients killed many animals, for if they were disappointed, they would either not return or would pay a different white hunter to take them on their next safari." I paused. "Because of this, the hunters would sometimes train a pride of lions to come out and be killed."

"How would they do this, Koriba?" asked Ndemi, his eyes wide with wonder.

"The white hunter would send his tracker out ahead of the safari," I said, pouring the oil into six smaller gourds as I spoke. "The tracker would go into the veldt where the lions lived, and kill a wildebeest or a zebra, and slit open its belly, so that the odors wafted in the wind. Then he would blow a whistle. The lions would come, either because of the odors or because they were curious about the strange new sound.

"The tracker would kill another zebra the next day, and blow the whistle again, and the lions would come again. This went on every day until the lions knew that when they heard the whistle, there would be a dead animal waiting for them—and when the tracker had finally trained them to come at the sound of the whistle, he would return to the safari, and lead the hunter and his clients to the veldt where the lions dwelt, and then blow the whistle. The lions would run toward the sound, and the hunter's clients would collect their trophies."

I smiled at his delighted reaction, and wondered if anyone left on Earth knew that the Kikuyu had anticipated Pavlov by more than a century.

Then I handed Ndemi the whistle I had carved.

"This is your whistle," I said. "You must not lose it."

"I will place a thong around my neck and tie it to the thong," he said. "I will not lose it."

"If you do," I continued, "I will surely die a terrible death."

"You can trust me, *mundumugu*."

"I know I can." I picked up the arrows and handed them carefully to him. "These are yours," I said. "You must be very careful with them. If you cut your skin on them, or press them against a wound, you will almost certainly die, and not all of my powers will be able to save you."

"I understand," he said, taking the arrows gingerly and setting them on the ground next to his bow.

"Good," I said. "Do you know the forest that is half a mile from the house Bwana has built by the river?"

"Yes, Koriba."

"Each day I want you to go there and slay a grasseater with one of your poisoned arrows. Do not try to kill the buffalo, because he is too dangerous—but you may kill any other grasseater. Once it is dead, pour all the oil from one of these six gourds onto it."

"And then shall I blow the whistle for the hyenas?" he asked.

"Then you will climb a nearby tree, and only when you are safe in its branches are you to blow the whistle," I said. "They will come—slowly the first day, more rapidly the second and third, and almost instantly by the fourth. You will sit in the tree for a long time after they have eaten and gone, and then you will climb down and return to your *boma*."

"I will do as you ask, Koriba," he said. "But I do not see how this will make Bwana leave Kirinyaga."

"That is because you are not yet a *mundumugu*," I replied with a smile. "But I am not yet through instructing you."

"What else must I do?"

"I have one final task to set before you," I continued. "Just before sunrise on the seventh day, you will leave your boma and kill a seventh animal."

"I only have six gourds of oil," he pointed out.

"You will not need any on the seventh day. They will come simply because you whistle." I paused to make sure he was following my every word. "As I say, you will kill a grasseater before sunrise, but this time you will not spread oil on him, and you will not blow your whistle immediately. You will climb a tree that affords you a clear view of the plains between the woods and the river. At some point you will see me wave my hand *thus*"—I demonstrated a very definite rotating motion with my right hand—"and then you must blow the whistle *immediately*. Do you understand?"

"I understand."

"Good."

"And what you have told me to do will rid Kirinyaga of Bwana forever?" he asked.

"Yes."

"I wish I knew how," persisted Ndemi.

"This much I will tell you," I said. "Being a civilized man, he will expect two things: that I will confront him on my own territory, and that—because I, too, have been educated by the Europeans—I will use the Europeans' technology to defeat him."

"But you will not do what he expects?"

"No," I said. "He still does not understand that our traditions supply us with everything we need on Kirinyaga. I will confront him on his own battleground, and I will defeat him with the weapons of the Kikuyu and not the Europeans." I paused again. "And now, Ndemi, you must go slay the first of the grasseaters, or it will be dark before you go home, and I do not want you walking across the savannah at night."

He nodded, picked up his whistle and his weapons, and strode off toward the woods by the river.

On the sixth night I walked down to the village, arriving just after dark.

The dancing hadn't started yet, though most of the adults had already gathered. Four young men, including Koinnage's son, tried to block my way, but Bwana was in a generous mood, and he waved them aside.

"Welcome, old man," he said, sitting atop his tall stool. "It has been many days since I have seen you."

"I have been busy."

"Plotting my downfall?" he asked with an amused smile.

"Your downfall was predetermined by Ngai," I replied.

"And what will cause my downfall?" he continued, signaling one of his wives—he had five now—to bring him a fresh gourd of *pombe*.

"The fact that you are not a Kikuyu."

"What is so special about the Kikuyu?" he demanded. "They are a tribe of sheep who stole their women from the Wakamba and their cattle and goats from the Luo. Their sacred mountain, from which this world took its name, they stole from the Maasai, for *Kirinyaga* is a Maasai word."

"Is that true, Koriba?" asked one of the younger men.

I nodded. "Yes, it is true. In the language of the Maasai, *kiri* means *mountain*, and *nyaga* means *light*. But while it is a Maasai word, it is the Kikuyu's Mountain of Light, given to us by Ngai."

"It is the Maasai's mountain," said Bwana. "Even its peaks are named after Maasai chieftains."

"There has never been a Maasai on the holy mountain," said old Njobe.

"We owned the mountain first, or it would bear a Kikuyu name," responded Bwana.

"Then the Kikuyu must have slain the Maasai, or driven them away," said Njobe with a sly smile.

This remark angered Bwana, for he threw his gourd of *pombe* at a passing goat, hitting it on the flanks with such power that it bowled the goat over. The animal quickly got to its feet and raced through the village, bleating in terror.

"You are fools!" growled Bwana. "And if indeed the Kikuyu drove the Maasai from the mountain, then I will now redress the balance. I now proclaim myself Laibon of Kirinyaga, and declare that it is no longer a Kikuyu world."

"What is a laibon?" asked one of the men.

"It is the Maasai word for king," I said.

"How can this not be a Kikuyu world, when everyone except you is a Kikuyu?" Njobe demanded of Bwana.

Bwana pointed at his five young henchmen. "I hereby declare these men to be Maasai."

"You cannot make them Maasai just by calling them Maasai."

Bwana grinned as the flickering firelight cast strange patterns on his sleek, shining body. "I can do anything I want. I am the laibon."

"Perhaps Koriba has something to say about that," said Koinnage, for he knew that the week was almost up.

Bwana stared at me belligerently. "Well, old man, do you dispute my right to be king?"

"No," I said. "I do not."

"Koriba!" exclaimed Koinnage.

"You cannot mean that!" said Njobe.

"We must be realistic," I said. "Is he not our mightiest hunter?"

Bwana snorted. "I am your *only* hunter."

I turned to Koinnage. "Who else but Bwana could walk naked into the veldt, armed only with a spear, and slay *fisi*?"

Bwana nodded his head. "That is true."

"Of course," I continued, "none of us saw him do it, but I am sure he would not lie to us."

"Do you dispute that I killed *fisi* with a spear?" demanded Bwana heatedly.

"I do not dispute it," I said earnestly. "I have no doubt that you could do it again whenever you wished."

"That is true, old man," he said, somewhat assuaged.

"In fact," I continued, "perhaps we should celebrate your becoming laibon with another such hunt—but this time in the daylight, so that your subjects may see for themselves the prowess and courage of their king."

He took another gourd from his youngest wife and stared at me intently. "Why are you saying this, old man? What do you really want?"

"Only what I have said," I replied, spitting on my hands to show my sincerity.

He shook his head. "No," he said. "You are up to some mischief."

I shrugged. "Well, if you would rather not . . ."

"Perhaps he is afraid to," said Njobe.

"I fear nothing!" snapped Bwana.

"Certainly he does not fear *fisi*," I said. "That much should be evident by now."

"Right," said Bwana, still staring at me.

"Then if he does not fear *fisi*, what *does* he fear about a hunt?" asked Njobe.

"He does not wish to hunt because *I* suggested it," I replied. "He still does not trust me, and that is understandable."

"Why is that understandable?" demanded Bwana. "Do you think I fear your mumbo-jumbo like the other sheep do?"

"I have not said that," I answered.

"You have no magic, old man," he said, getting to his feet. "You have only tricks and threats, and these mean nothing to a Maasai." He paused, and then raised his voice so that everyone could hear him. "I will spend the night in Koinnage's hut, and then I will hunt *fisi* tomorrow morning, in the old way, so that all my subjects can see their laibon in combat."

"Tomorrow morning?" I repeated.

He glared at me, his Maasai arrogance chiseled in every feature of his lean, handsome face.

"At sunrise."

I awoke early the next morning, as usual, but this time, instead of building a fire and sitting next to it until the chill had vanished from my aged bones, I donned my *kikoi* and walked immediately to the village. All of the men were gathered around Koinnage's *boma*, waiting for Bwana to emerge.

Finally he came out of his hut, his body annointed beneath his red cloak. He seemed clear-eyed despite the vast quantities of *pombe* he had imbibed the previous night, and in his right hand he clutched the same spear he had used during his very first hunt on Kirinyaga.

Contemptuous of us all, he looked neither right nor left, but began walking through the village and out onto the savannah toward the river. We fell into step behind him, and our little procession continued until we were perhaps a mile from his house. Then he stopped and held a hand up.

"You will come no farther," he announced, "or your numbers will frighten *fisi* away."

He let his red cloak fall to the ground and stood, naked and glistening, in the morning sunlight.

"Now watch, my sheep, and see how a true king hunts."

He hefted his spear once, to get the feel of it, and then he strode off into the waist-high grass.

Koinnage sidled up to me. "You promised that he would leave today," he whispered.

"So I did."

"He is still here."

"The day is not yet over."

"You're *sure* he will leave?" persisted Koinnage.

"Have I ever lied to my people?" I responded.

"No," he said, stepping back. "No, you have not."

We fell silent again, looking out across the plains. For a long time we could see nothing at all. Then Bwana emerged from a clump of bushes and walked boldly toward a spot about fifty yards ahead of him.

And then the wind shifted and suddenly the air was pierced by the earsplitting laughter of hyenas as they caught scent of his oiled body. We could see grass swaying as the pack made their way toward Bwana, yelping and cackling as they approached.

For a moment he stood his ground, for he was truly a brave man, but then, when he saw their number and realized that he could kill no more than one of them, he hurled his spear at the nearest hyena and raced to a nearby acacia tree, clambering up it just before the first six hyenas reached its base.

Within another minute there were fifteen full-grown hyenas circling the tree, snarling and laughing at him, and Bwana had no choice but to remain where he was.

"How disappointing," I said at last. "I believed him when he said he was a mighty hunter."

"He is mightier than you, old man," said Koinnage's son.

"Nonsense," I said. "Those are just hyenas around his tree, not demons." I turned to Koinnage's son and his companions. "I thought you were his friends. Why do you not go to help him?"

They shifted uneasily, and then Koinnage's son spoke: "We are unarmed, as you can see."

"What difference does that make?" I said. "You are almost Maasai, and they are just hyenas."

"If they are so harmless, why don't *you* make them go away?" demanded Koinnage's son.

"This is not my hunt," I replied.

"You cannot make them go away, so do not chide us for standing here."

"I can make them go away," I said. "Am I not the *mundumugu*?"

"Then do so!" he challenged me.

I turned to the men of the village. "The son of Koinnage has put a challenge to me. Do you wish me to save the Maasai?"

"No!" they said almost as one.

I turned to the young man. "There you have it."

"You are lucky, old man," he said, a sullen expression on his face. "You could not have done it."

"*You* are the lucky one," I said.

"Why?" he demanded.

"Because you called me old man, rather than *mundumugu* or *mzee*, and I have not punished you." I stared unblinking at him. "But know that should you ever call me old man again, I will turn you into the smallest of rodents and leave you in the field for the jackals to feed upon."

I uttered my statement with such conviction that he suddenly seemed less sure of himself.

"You are bluffing, *mundumugu*," he said at last. "You have no magic."

"You are a foolish young man," I said, "for you have seen my magic work in the past, and you know it will work again in the future."

"Then make the hyenas disperse," he said.

"If I do so, will you and your companions swear fealty to me, and respect the laws and traditions of the Kikuyu?"

He considered my proposition for a long moment, then nodded.

"And the rest of you?" I asked, turning to his companions.

There were mumbled assents.

"Very well," I said. "Your fathers and the village Elders will bear witness to your agreement."

I began walking across the plain toward the tree where Bwana sat, glaring down at the hyenas. When I got within perhaps three hundred yards of them they noticed me and began approaching, constantly testing the wind and growling hungrily.

"In the name of Ngai," I intoned, "the *mundumugu* orders you to begone!"

As I finished the sentence, I waved my right arm at them in just the way I had demonstrated to Ndemi.

I heard no whistle, for it was above the range of human hearing, but instantly the entire pack turned and raced off toward the woods.

I watched them for a moment, then turned back to my people.

"Now go back to the village," I said sternly. "I will tend to Bwana."

They retreated without a word, and I approached the tree from which Bwana had watched the entire pageant. He had climbed down and was waiting for me when I arrived.

"I have saved you with my magic," I said, "but now it is time for you to leave Kirinyaga."

"It was a trick!" he exclaimed. "It was not magic."

"Trick or magic," I said, "what difference does it make? It will happen again, and next time I will not save you."

"Why should I believe you?" he demanded sullenly.

"I have no reason to lie to you," I said. "The next time you go hunting they will attack you again, so many *fisi* that even your European gun cannot kill them all, and I will not be here to save you." I paused. "Leave while you can, Maasai. They will not be back for half an hour. You have time to walk to Haven by then, and I will use my computer to tell Maintenance that you are waiting to be taken back to Earth."

He looked deep into my eyes. "You are telling the truth," he said at last.

"I am."

"How did you do it, old man?" he asked. "I deserve to know that much before I leave."

I paused for a long moment before answering him.

"I am the *mundumugu*," I replied at last, and, turning my back on him, I returned to the village.

We tore his house down that afternoon, and in the evening I called down the rains, which purified Kirinyaga of the last taint of the corruption that had been in our midst.

The next morning I walked down the long, winding path to the village to bless the scarecrows, and the moment I arrived I was surrounded by the children, who asked for a story.

"All right," I said, gathering them in the shade of an acacia tree. "Today I shall tell you the story of the Arrogant Hunter."

"Has it a happy ending?" asked one of the girls.

I looked around the village and saw my people contentedly going about their daily chores, then stared out across the tranquil green plains.

"Yes," I said. "This time it has."

4

THE MANAMOUKI

{MARCH–JULY 2133}

Many eons ago, the children of Gikuyu lived on the slopes of the holy mountain Kirinyaga.

There were many serpents on the mountain, but the sons and grandsons of Gikuyu found them repulsive, and they soon killed all but one.

Then one day the last serpent entered their village and killed and ate a young child. The children of Gikuyu sought out their *mundumugu* and asked him to destroy the menace.

The *mundumugu* rolled the bones and sacrificed a goat, and finally he created a poison that would kill the serpent. He slit open the belly of another goat, and placed the poison inside it, and left it beneath a tree, and the very next day the serpent swallowed the goat and died.

"Now," said the *mundumugu*, "you must cut the serpent into one hundred pieces and scatter them on the holy mountain, so that no demon can breathe life back into its body."

The children of Gikuyu did as they were instructed, and scattered the hundred pieces of the serpent across the slopes of Kirinyaga. But during the night, each piece came to life and became a new serpent, and soon the Kikuyu were afraid to leave their *bomas*.

The *mundumugu* ascended the mountain, and when he neared the highest peak, he addressed Ngai.

"We are beseiged by serpents," he said. "If you do not slay them, then the Kikuyu shall surely die as a people."

"I made the serpent, just as I made the Kikuyu and all other things," answered Ngai, who sat on His golden throne atop Kirinyaga. "And anything that I made, be it a man or a serpent or a tree or even an idea, is not repellent in My eyes. I will save you this one time, because you are young and ignorant, but you must never forget that you cannot destroy that which you find repulsive—for if you try to destroy it, it will always return one hundred times greater than before."

This is one of the reasons why the Kikuyu chose to till the soil rather than hunt the beasts of the jungle like the Wakamba, or make war on their neighbors like the Maasai, for they had no wish to see that which they destroyed return to plague them. It is a lesson taught by every *mundumugu* to his people, even after we left Kenya and emigrated to the terraformed world of Kirinyaga.

In the entire history of our tribe, only one *mundumugu* ever forgot the lesson that Ngai taught atop the holy mountain on that distant day.

And that *mundumugu* was myself.

When I awoke, I found hyena dung within the thorn enclosure of my *boma*. That alone should have warned me that the day carried a curse, for there is no worse omen. Also the breeze, hot and dry and filled with dust, came from the west, and all good winds come from the east.

It was the day that our first immigrants were due to arrive. We had argued long and hard against allowing any newcomers to settle on Kirinyaga, for we were dedicated to the old ways of our people, and we wanted no outside influences corrupting the society that we had created. But our charter clearly stated that any Kikuyu who pledged to obey our laws and made the necessary payments to the Eutopian Council could emigrate from Kenya, and after postponing the inevitable for as long as we could, we finally agreed to accept Thomas Nkobe and his wife.

Of all the candidates for immigration, Nkobe had seemed the best. He had been born in Kenya, had grown up in the shadow of the holy mountain, and after going abroad for his schooling, had returned and run the large farm his family had purchased from one of the last European residents. Most important of all, he was a direct descendant of Jomo Kenyatta, the great Burning Spear of Kenya who had led us to independence.

I trudged out across the hot, arid savannah to the tiny landing field at Haven to greet our new arrivals, accompanied only by Ndemi, my youthful assistant. Twice buffalo blocked our path, and once Ndemi had to hurl some stones to frighten a hyena away, but eventually we reached our destination, only to discover that the Maintenance ship that was carrying Nkobe and his wife had not yet arrived. I squatted down in the shade of an acacia tree, and a moment later Ndemi crouched down beside me.

"They are late," he said, peering into the cloudless sky. "Perhaps they will not come at all."

"They will come," I said. "The signs all point to it."

"But they are bad signs, and Nkobe may be a good man."

"There are many good men," I replied. "Not all of them belong on Kirinyaga."

"You are worried, Koriba?" asked Ndemi as a pair of crested cranes walked through the dry, brittle grass, and a vulture rode the thermals overhead.

"I am concerned," I said.

"Why?"

"Because I do not know why he wants to live here."

"Why shouldn't he?" asked Ndemi, picking up a dry twig and methodically breaking it into tiny pieces. "Is it not Utopia?"

"There are many different notions of Utopia," I replied. "Kirinyaga is the Kikuyu's."

"And Nkobe is a Kikuyu, so this is where he belongs," said Ndemi decisively.

"I wonder."

"Why?"

"Because he is almost forty years old. Why did he wait so long to come here?"

"Perhaps he could not afford to come sooner."

I shook my head. "He comes from a very wealthy family."

"They have many cattle?" asked Ndemi.

"Many," I said.

"And goats?"

I nodded.

"Will he bring them with him?"

"No. He will come empty-handed, as we all did." I paused, frowning. "Why would a man who owned a large farm and had many tractors and men to do his work turn his back on all that he possessed? That is what troubles me."

"You make it sound like the way he lived on Earth was better," said Ndemi, frowning.

"Not better, just different."

He paused for a moment. "Koriba, what *is* a tractor?"

"A machine that does the work of many men in the fields."

"It sounds truly wonderful," offered Ndemi.

"It makes deep wounds in the ground and stinks of gasoline," I said, making no effort to hide my contempt.

We sat in silence for another moment. Then the Maintenance ship came into view, its descent creating a huge cloud of dust and causing a great screeching and squawking by the birds and monkeys in the nearby trees. "Well," I said, "we shall soon have our answer."

I remained in the shade until the ship had touched down and

Thomas Nkobe and his wife emerged from its interior. He was a tall, well-built man dressed in casual Western clothes; she was slender and graceful, her hair elegantly braided, her khaki slacks and hunting jacket exquisitely tailored.

"Hello!" said Nkobe in English as I approached him. "I was afraid we might have to find our way to the village ourselves."

"*Jambo,*" I replied in Swahili. "Welcome to Kirinyaga."

"*Jambo,*" he amended, switching to Swahili. "Are you Koinnage?"

"No," I answered. "Koinnage is our paramount chief. You will live in his village."

"And you are?"

"I am Koriba," I said.

"He is the *mundumugu,*" added Ndemi proudly. "I am Ndemi." He paused. "Someday I will be a *mundumugu* too."

Nkobe smiled down at him. "I'm sure you will." Suddenly he remembered his wife. "And this is Wanda."

She stepped forward, smiled, and extended her hand. "A true *mundumugu!*" she said in heavily accented Swahili. "I'm thrilled to meet you!"

"I hope you will enjoy your new life on Kirinyaga," I said, shaking her hand.

"Oh, I'm certain I will," she replied enthusiastically, as the ship disgorged their baggage and promptly took off again. She looked around at the dry savannah, and saw a trio of maribou storks and a jackal patiently waiting for a hyena to finish gorging itself on the wildebeest calf it had killed earlier in the morning. "I love it already!" She paused, then added confidentially, "I'm really the one who got Tom to agree to come here."

"Oh?"

She nodded her head. "I just couldn't stand what Kenya has become. All those factories, all that pollution! Ever since I learned about Kirinyaga, I've wanted to move here, to come back to Nature and live the way we were meant to live." She inhaled deeply. "Smell that air, Tom! It will add ten years to your life."

"You don't have to sell me anymore," he said with a smile. "I'm here, aren't I?"

I turned to Wanda Nkobe. "You yourself are not Kikuyu, are you?"

"I am now," she replied. "Ever since I married Tom. But to answer your question, no, I was born and raised in Oregon."

"Oregon?" repeated Ndemi, brushing some flies away from his face with his hand.

"That's in America," she explained. She paused. "By the way, why are we speaking Swahili rather than Kikuyu?"

"Kikuyu is a dead language," I said. "Most of our people no longer know it."

"I had rather hoped it would still be spoken here," she said, obviously disappointed. "I've been studying it for months."

"If you had moved to Italy, you would not speak Latin," I replied. "We still use a few Kikuyu words, just as the Italians use a few Latin words."

She was silent for a moment, then shrugged. "At least I'll have the opportunity to improve my Swahili."

"I am surprised that you are willing to forego the amenities of America for Kirinyaga," I said, studying her closely.

"I was willing years ago," she answered. "It was Tom who had to be convinced, not me." She paused. "Besides, I gave up most of those so-called amenities when I left America and moved to Kenya."

"Even Kenya has certain luxuries," I noted. "We have no electricity here, no running water, no—"

"We camp out whenever we can," she said, and I placed a hand on Ndemi's shoulder before he could chide her for interrupting the *mundumugu*. "I'm used to roughing it."

"But you have always had a home to return to."

She stared at me, an amused smile on her face. "Are you trying to talk me out of moving here?"

"No," I replied. "But I wish to point out that nothing is immutable. Any member of our society who is unhappy and wishes to leave need only inform Maintenance of the fact and a ship will arrive at Haven an hour later."

"Not us," she said. "We're in for the long haul."

"The long haul?" I repeated.

"She means that we're here to stay," explained Nkobe, putting an arm around his wife's shoulders.

A hot breeze sent the dust swirling around us.

"I think I should take you to the village," I said, shielding my eyes. "You are doubtless tired and will wish to rest."

"Not at all," said Wanda Nkobe. "This is a brand-new world. I want to look around." Her gaze fell upon Ndemi, who was staring at her intently. "Is something wrong?" she asked.

"You are very strong and sturdy," said Ndemi approvingly. "That is good. You will bear many children."

"I certainly hope not," she said. "If there's one thing Kenya has more than enough of, it's children."

"This is not Kenya," said Ndemi.

"I will find other ways to contribute to the society."

Ndemi studied her for a moment. "Well," he said at last, "I suppose you can carry firewood."

"I'm glad I meet with your approval," she said.

"But you will need a new name," continued Ndemi. "Wanda is a European name."

"It is just a name," I said. "Changing it will not make her more of a Kikuyu."

"I have no objection," she interjected. "I'm starting a new life; I *ought* to have a new name."

I shrugged. "Which name will you take as your own?"

She smiled at Ndemi. "You choose one," she said.

He furrowed his brow for a long moment, then looked up at her. "My mother's sister, who died in childbirth last year, was named Mwange, and now there is no one in the village of that name."

"Then Mwange it shall be," she said. "Mwange wa Ndemi."

"But I am not your father," said Ndemi.

She smiled at him. "You are the father of my new name."

Ndemi puffed his chest up proudly.

"Well, now that *that's* settled," said Nkobe, "what about our luggage?"

"You will not need it," I said.

"Yes we will," said Mwange.

"You were told to bring nothing of Kenya with you."

"I've brought some *kikois* that I made myself," she said. "Surely that must be permissible, since I will be expected to weave my own fabrics and make my own clothes on Kirinyaga."

I considered her explanation for a moment, then nodded my consent. "I will send one of the village children for the bags."

"It's not that heavy," said Nkobe. "I can carry it myself."

"Kikuyu men do not fetch and carry," said Ndemi.

"What about Kikuyu women?" asked Mwange, obviously reluctant to leave the luggage behind.

"They carry firewood and grain, not bags of clothing," responded Ndemi. *"Those,"* he said, pointing contemptuously toward the two leather bags, "are for children."

"Then we might as well start walking," said Mwange. "There are no children here."

Ndemi beamed with pride and strutted forward.

"Let Ndemi go first," I said. "His eyes are young and clear. He will be able to see any snakes or hyenas hiding in the tall grass."

"Do you have poisonous snakes here?" asked Nkobe.

"A few."

"Why don't you kill them?"

"Because this is not Kenya," I replied.

I walked directly behind Ndemi, and Nkobe and Mwange followed us, remarking upon the scenery and the animals to each other. After about half a mile we came to an impala ram standing directly in our path.

"Isn't he beautiful?" whispered Mwange. "Look at the horns on him!"

"I wish I had my camera with me!" said Nkobe.

"We do not permit cameras on Kirinyaga," I said.

"I know," said Nkobe. "But to be perfectly honest, I can't see how something as simple as a camera could be a corrupting influence on your society."

"To have a camera, one needs film, and one must therefore have a factory that manufactures both cameras and films. To develop the film, one needs chemicals, and then one must find a place to dump those chemicals that haven't been used. To print the pictures, one needs photographic paper, and we have barely enough wood to burn in our fires." I paused. "Kirinyaga supplies us with all of our desires. That is why we came here."

"Kirinyaga supplies you with all of your *needs*," said Mwange. "That is not quite the same thing."

Suddenly Ndemi stopped walking and turned to her.

"This is your first day here, so you are to be forgiven your ignorance," he explained. "But no *manamouki* may argue with the *mundumugu*."

"*Manamouki?*" she repeated. "What is a *manamouki?*"

"*You* are," said Ndemi.

"I've heard that word before," said Nkobe. "I think it means *wife*."

"You are wrong," I said. "A *manamouki* is a female."

"You mean a woman?" asked Mwange.

I shook my head. "*Any* female property," I said. "A woman, a cow, a sow, a bitch, a ewe."

"And Ndemi thinks I'm some kind of property?"

"You are Nkobe's *manamouki*," said Ndemi.

She considered it for a moment, then shrugged with amusement. "What the hell," she said in English. "If Wanda was only a name, *manamouki* is only a word. I can live with it."

"I hope so," I replied in Swahili, "for you will have to."

She turned to me. "I know we are the first immigrants to come to Kirinyaga, and that you must have your doubts about us—but this is the life I've always wanted. I'm going to be the best damned *man-amouki* you ever saw."

"I hope so," I said, but I noticed that the wind still blew from the west.

I introduced Nkobe and Mwange to their neighbors, showed them their *shamba* where they would grow their food, pointed out their six cattle and ten goats and recommended that they lock them in their *boma* at night to protect them from the hyenas, told them how to reach the river to procure water, and left them at the entrance to their hut. Mwange seemed enthused about everything, and was soon engaged in animated conversation with the women who came by to look at her strange outfit.

"She is very nice," commented Ndemi as I walked through the fields, blessing the scarecrows. "Perhaps the omens you read were wrong."

"Perhaps," I said.

He stared at me. "But you do not think so."

"No."

"Well, *I* like her," he said.

"That is your right."

"Do you dislike her, then?"

I paused as I considered my answer.

"No," I said at last. "I fear her."

"But she is just a *manamouki*!" he protested. "She can do no harm."

"Under the proper circumstances, anything can do harm."

"I do not believe it," said Ndemi.

"Do you doubt your *mundumugu's* word?" I asked.

"No," he said uncomfortably. "If you say something, then it must be true. But I cannot understand how."

I smiled wryly. "That is because you are not yet a *mundumugu*."

He stopped and pointed to a spot some three hundred yards away, where a group of impala does were grazing.

"Can even *they* do harm?" he asked.

"Yes."

"But how?" he asked, frowning. "When danger appears, they do not confront it, but run away from it. Ngai has not blessed them with horns, so they cannot defend themselves. They are not large enough to destroy our crops. They cannot even kick an enemy, as can the zebra. I do not understand."

"I shall tell you the tale of the Ugly Buffalo, and then you will understand," I said.

Ndemi smiled happily, for he loved stories above all things, and I led him to the shade of a thorn tree, where we both squatted down, facing each other.

"One day a cow buffalo was wandering through the savannah," I began. "The hyenas had recently taken her first calf, and she was very sad. Then she came upon a newborn impala, whose mother had been killed by hyenas that very morning.

" 'I would like to take you home with me,' said the buffalo, 'for I am very lonely, and have much love in my heart. But you are not a buffalo.'

" 'I, too, am very lonely,' said the impala. 'And if you leave me here, alone and unprotected, I surely will not survive the night.'

" 'There is a problem,' said the buffalo. 'You are an impala, and we are buffalo. You do not belong with us.'

" 'I will become the best buffalo of all,' promised the impala. 'I will eat what you eat, drink what you drink, go where you go.'

" 'How can you become a buffalo? You cannot even grow horns.'

" 'Then I will wear the branches of a tree upon my head.'

" 'You do not wallow in the mud to protect your skin from parasites,' noted the buffalo.

" 'Take me home with you and I will cover myself with more mud than any other buffalo,' said the impala.

"For every objection the buffalo raised, the impala had an answer, and finally the buffalo agreed to take the impala back with her. Most of the members of the herd thought that the impala was the ugliest buffalo they had ever seen,"—Ndemi chuckled at that—"but because the impala tried so hard to act like a buffalo, they allowed her to remain.

"Then one day a number of young buffalo were grazing some distance from the herd, and they came to a deep mud wallow that blocked their way.

" 'We must return to the herd,' said one of the young buffalo.

" 'Why?' asked the impala. "There is fresh grass on the other side of the wallow."

" 'Because we have been warned that a deep wallow such as this can suck us down beneath the surface and kill us.'

" 'I do not believe it,' said the impala, and, bolder than her companions, she walked out to the center of the mud wallow.

" 'You see?' she said. 'I have not been sucked beneath the surface. It is perfectly safe.'

"Soon three of the young buffalo ventured out across the mud wallow, and each in turn was sucked beneath the surface and drowned.

" 'It is the ugly buffalo's fault,' said the king of the herd. 'It was she who told them to cross the mud wallow.'

" 'But she meant no harm,' said her foster mother. 'And what she told them was true: the wallow was safe for her. All she wants is to live with the herd and be a buffalo; please do not punish her.'

"The king was blessed with more generosity than wisdom, and so he forgave the ugly buffalo.

"Then, a week later, the ugly buffalo, who could leap as high as a tall bush, jumped up in the air and saw a pack of hyenas lurking in the grass. She waited until they were almost close enough to catch her, and then cried out a warning. All the buffalo began running, but the hyenas were able to catch the ugly buffalo's foster mother, and they pulled her down and killed her.

"Most of the other buffalo were grateful to the ugly buffalo for warning them, but during the intervening week there had been a new king, and this one was wiser than the previous one.

" 'It is the ugly buffalo's fault,' he said.

"'How can it be her fault?' asked one of the older buffalo. 'It was she who warned us of the hyenas.'

"'But she only warned you when it was too late,' said the king. 'Had she warned you when she first saw the hyenas, her mother would still be among us. But she forgot that we cannot run as fast as she can, and so her mother is dead.'

"And the new king, though his heart was sad, decreed that the ugly buffalo must leave the herd, for there is a great difference between being a buffalo and *wanting* to be a buffalo."

I leaned back against the tree, my story completed.

"Did the ugly buffalo survive?" asked Ndemi.

I shrugged and brushed a crawling insect from my forearm. "That is another story."

"She meant no harm."

"But she caused harm nonetheless."

Ndemi traced patterns in the dirt with his finger as he considered my answer, then looked up at me. "But if she had not been with the herd, the hyenas would have killed her mother anyway."

"Perhaps."

"Then it was not her fault."

"If I fall asleep against the tree, and you see a black mamba slithering through the grass toward me, and you make no attempt to wake me, and the mamba kills me, would you be to blame for my death?" I asked.

"Yes."

"Even though it would certainly have killed me had you not been here?"

Ndemi frowned. "It is a difficult problem."

"Yes, it is."

"The mud wallow was much easier," he said. "That was surely the ugly buffalo's fault, for without her urging, the other buffalo would never have entered it."

"That is true," I said.

Ndemi remained motionless for a few moments, still wrestling with the nuances of the story.

"You are saying that there are many different ways to cause harm," he announced.

"Yes."

"And that it takes wisdom to understand who is to blame, for the foolish king did not recognize the harm of the ugly buffalo's action, while the wise king knew that she was to blame for her inaction."

I nodded my head.

"I see," said Ndemi.

"And what has this to do with the *manamouki*?" I asked.

He paused again. "If harm comes to the village, you must use your wisdom to decide whether Mwange, who wants nothing more than to be a Kikuyu, is responsible for it."

"That is correct," I said, getting to my feet.

"But I still do not know what harm she can do."

"Neither do I," I answered.

"Will you know it when you see it?" he asked. "Or will it seem like a good deed, such as warning the herd that hyenas are near?"

I made no reply.

"Why are you silent, Koriba?" asked Ndemi at last.

I sighed heavily. "Because there are some questions that even a *mundumugu* cannot answer."

Ndemi was waiting for me, as usual, when I emerged from my hut five mornings later.

"*Jambo*, Koriba," he said.

I grunted a greeting and walked over to the fire that he had built, sitting cross-legged next to it until it removed the chill from my aging bones.

"What is today's lesson?" he asked at last.

"Today I will teach you how to ask Ngai for a fruitful harvest," I answered.

"But we did that last week."

"And we will do it next week, and many more weeks as well," I answered.

"When will I learn how to make ointments to cure the sick, or how to turn an enemy into an insect so that I may step on him?"

"When you are older," I said.

"I am already old."

"And more mature."

"How will you know when I am more mature?" he persisted.

"I will know because you will have gone an entire month without asking about ointments or magic, for patience is one of the most important virtues a *mundumugu* can possess." I got to my feet. "Now take my gourds to the river and fill them with water," I said, indicating two empty water gourds.

"Yes, Koriba," he said dejectedly.

While I was waiting for him, I went into my hut, activated my computer, and instructed Maintenance to make a minor orbital adjustment that would bring rain and cooler air to the western plains.

This done, I slung my pouch around my neck and went back out into my *boma* to see if Ndemi had returned, but instead of my youthful apprentice, I found Wambu, Koinnage's senior wife, waiting for me, bristling with barely controlled fury.

"*Jambo*, Wambu," I said.

"*Jambo*, Koriba," she replied.

"You wish to speak to me?"

She nodded. "It is about the Kenyan woman."

"Oh?"

"Yes," said Wambu. "You must make her leave!"

"What has Mwange done?" I asked.

"I am the senior wife of the paramount chief, am I not?" demanded Wambu.

"That is true."

"She does not treat me with the respect that is my due."

"In what way?" I asked.

"In *all* ways!"

"For example?"

"Her *khanga* is much more beautiful than mine. The colors are brighter, the designs more intricate, the fabric softer."

"She wove her *khanga* on her own loom, in the old way," I said.

"What difference does *that* make?" snapped Wambu.

I frowned. "Do you wish me to make her give you the *khanga*?" I asked, trying to understand her rage.

"No!"

"Then I do not understand," I said.

"You are no different than Koinnage!" she said, obviously frustrated that I could not comprehend her complaint. "You may be a *mundumugu*, but you are still a man!"

"Perhaps if you told me more," I suggested.

"Kibo was as silly as a child," she said, referring to Koinnage's youngest wife, "but I was training her to be a good wife. Now she wants to be like the Kenyan woman."

"But the Kenyan woman," I said, using her terminology, "wants to be like *you*."

"She cannot be like me!" Wambu practically shouted at me. "I am Koinnage's senior wife!"

"I mean that she wants to be a member of the village."

"Impossible!" scoffed Wambu. "She speaks of many strange things."

"Such as?"

"It does not matter! You must make her leave!"

"For wearing a pretty *khanga* and making a good impression on Kibo?" I said.

"Bah!" she snapped. "You are just like Koinnage! You pretend not to understand, but you know she must go!"

"I truly do not understand," I said.

"You are *my mundumugu*, not hers. I will pay you two fat goats to place a *thahu* on her."

"I will not place a curse on Mwange for the reasons you gave me," I said firmly.

She glared at me for a long moment, then spat on the ground, turned on her heel, and walked back down the winding path to the village, muttering furiously to herself, practically knocking Ndemi down as he returned with my water gourds.

I spent the next two hours instructing Ndemi in the harvest prayer, then told him to go into the village and bring Mwange back. An hour later Mwange, resplendent in her *khanga*, climbed up my hill, accompanied by Ndemi, and entered my *boma*.

"*Jambo,*" I greeted her.

"*Jambo,* Koriba," she replied. "Ndemi says that you wish to speak to me."

I nodded. "That is true."

"The other women seemed to think I should be frightened."

"I cannot imagine why," I said.

"Perhaps it is because you can call down the lightning, and change hyenas into insects, and kill your enemies from miles away," suggested Ndemi helpfully.

"Perhaps," I said.

"Why have you sent for me?" asked Mwange.

I paused for a moment, trying to think of how best to approach the subject. "There is a problem with your clothing," I said at last.

"But I am wearing a *khanga* that I wove on my own loom," she said, obviously puzzled.

"I know," I responded. "But the quality of the fabric and the subtlety of the colors have caused a certain ..." I searched for the proper word.

"Resentment?" she suggested.

"Precisely," I answered, grateful that she so quickly comprehended the situation. "I think it would be best if you were to weave some less colorful garments."

I half expected her to protest, but she surprised me by agreeing immediately.

"Certainly," she said. "I have no wish to offend my neighbors. May I ask who objected to my *khanga?*"

"Why?"

"I'd like to make her a present of it."

"It was Wambu," I said.

"I should have realized the effect my clothing would have. I am truly sorry, Koriba."

"Anyone may make a mistake," I said. "As long as it is corrected, no lasting harm will be done."

"I hope you're right," she said sincerely.

"He is the *mundumugu*," said Ndemi. "He is always right."

"I don't want the women to be resentful of me," continued Mwange. "Perhaps I could find some way to show my good intentions." She paused. "What if I were to offer to teach them to speak Kikuyu?"

"No *manamouki* may be a teacher," I explained. "Only the chiefs and the *mundumugu* may instruct our people."

"That's not very efficient," she said. "It may very well be that someone besides yourself and the chiefs has something to offer."

"It is possible," I agreed. "Now let me ask you a question."

"What is it?"

"Did you come to Kirinyaga to be efficient?"

She sighed. "No," she admitted. She paused for a moment. "Is there anything else?"

"No."

"Then I think I'd better go back and begin weaving my new fabric."

I nodded my approval, and she walked back down the long, winding path to the village.

"When I become *mundumugu*," said Ndemi, watching her retreating figure, "I will not allow any *manamoukis* to argue with *me*."

"A *mundumugu* must also show understanding," I said. "Mwange is new here, and has much to learn."

"About Kirinyaga?"

I shook my head. "About *manamoukis*."

* * *

Life proceeded smoothly and uneventfully for almost six weeks, until just after the short rains. Then one morning, just as I was preparing to go down into the village to bless the scarecrows, three of the women came up the path to my *boma*.

There was Sabo, the widow of old Kadamu, and Bori, the second wife of Sabana, and Wambu.

"We must speak with you, *mundumugu*," said Wambu.

I sat down, cross-legged, in front of my hut, and waited for them to seat themselves opposite me.

"You may speak," I said.

"It is about the Kenyan woman," said Wambu.

"Oh?" I said. "I thought the problem was solved."

"It is not."

"Did she not present you with her *khanga* as a gift?" I asked.

"Yes."

"You are not wearing it," I noted.

"It does not fit," said Wambu.

"It is only a piece of cloth," I said. "How can it not fit?"

"It does not fit," she repeated adamantly.

I shrugged. "What is this new problem?"

"She flaunts the traditions of the Kikuyu," said Wambu.

I turned to the other women. "Is this true?" I asked.

Sabo nodded. "She is a married woman, and she has not shaved her head."

"And she keeps flowers in her hut," added Bori.

"It is not the custom for Kenyan women to shave their heads," I replied. "I will instruct her to do so. As for the flowers, they are not in violation of our laws."

"But *why* does she keep them?" persisted Bori.

"Perhaps she thinks they are pleasing to the eye," I suggested.

"But now my daughter wants to grow flowers, and she answers with disrespect when I tell her it is more important to grow food to eat."

"And now the Kenyan woman has made a throne for her husband, Nkobe," put in Sabo.

"A throne?" I repeated.

"She put a back and arms on his sitting stool," said Sabo. "What man besides a chief sits upon a throne? Does she think Nkobe will replace Koinnage?"

"*Never!*" snarled Wambu.

"And she has made another throne for herself," continued Sabo. "Even Wambu does not sit atop a throne."

"These are not thrones, but chairs," I said.

"Why can she not use stools, like all the other members of the village?" demanded Sabo.

"I think she is a witch," said Wambu.

"Why do you say that?" I asked.

"Just look at her," said Wambu. "She has seen the long rains come and go thirty-five times, and yet her back is not bent, and her skin is not wrinkled, and she has all her teeth."

"Her vegetables grow better than ours," added Sabo, "and yet she spends less time planting and tending to them than we do." She paused. "I think she *must* be a witch."

"And although she carries with her the worst of all *thahus*, that of barrenness, she acts as if she is not cursed at all," said Bori.

"And her new garments are still more beautiful than ours," muttered Sabo sullenly.

"That is true," agreed Bori. "Now Sabana is displeased with me because his *kikoi* is not so bright and soft as Nkobe's."

"And my daughters all want thrones instead of sitting stools," added Sabo. "I tell them that we have scarcely enough wood for the fire, and they say that this is more important. She has turned their heads. They no longer respect their elders."

"The young women all listen to her, as if *she* were the wife of a chief instead of a barren *manamouki*," complained Wambu. "You must send her away, Koriba."

"Are you giving me an order, Wambu?" I asked softly, and the other two women immediately fell silent.

"She is an evil witch, and she must go," insisted Wambu, her outrage overcoming her fear of disobeying her *mundumugu*.

"She is not a witch," I said, "for if she were, then I, your *mundumugu*, would certainly know it. She is just a *manamouki* who is trying to learn our ways, and who, as you note, carries the terrible *thahu* of barrenness with her."

"If she is less than a witch, she is still more than a *manamouki*," said Sabo.

"More in what way?" I asked.

"Just more," she answered with a sullen expression.

Which totally summed up the problem.

"I will speak to her again," I said.

"And you will make her shave her head?" demanded Wambu.

"Yes."

"And remove the flowers from her hut?"

"I will discuss it."

"Perhaps you can tell Nkobe to beat her from time to time," added Sabo. "Then she would not act so much like a chief's wife."

"I feel very sorry for him," said Bori.

"For Nkobe?" I asked.

Bori nodded. "To be cursed with such a wife, and further, to have no children."

"He is a good man," agreed Sabo. "He deserves better than the Kenyan woman."

"It is my understanding that he is perfectly happy with Mwange," I said.

"That is all the more reason to pity him, for being so foolish," said Wambu.

"Have you come here to talk about Mwange or Nkobe?" I asked.

"We have said what we have come to say," replied Wambu, getting to her feet. "You must do something, *mundumugu*."

"I will look into the matter," I said.

She walked down the path to the village, followed by Sabo. Bori, her back bent from carrying firewood all her life, her stomach distended from producing three sons and five daughters, all but nine of her teeth missing, her legs permanently bowed from some childhood disease; Bori, who had seen but thirty-four long rains, stood before me for a moment.

"She really *is* a witch, Koriba," she said. "You have only to look at her to know it."

Then she, too, left my hill and returned to the village.

Once again I summoned Mwange to my *boma*.

She came up the path with the graceful stride of a young girl, lithe and lean and filled with energy.

"How old are you, Mwange?" I asked as she approached me.

"Thirty-eight," she replied. "I usually tell people that I'm thirty-five, though," she added with a smile. She stood still for a moment. "Is that why you asked me to come here? To talk about my age?"

"No," I said. "Sit down, Mwange."

She seated herself on the dirt by the ashes of my morning fire, and I squatted across from her.

"How are you adjusting to your new life on Kirinyaga?" I asked at last.

"Very well," she said enthusiastically. "I've made many friends, and I find that I don't miss the amenities of Kenya at all."

"Then you are happy here?"

"Very."

"Tell me about your friends."

"Well, my closest friend is Kibo, Koinnage's youngest wife, and I have helped Sumi and Kalena with their gardens, and—"

"Have you no friends among the older women?" I interrupted.

"Not really," she admitted.

"Why should that be?" I asked. "They are women of your own age."

"We don't seem to have anything to talk about."

"Do you find them unfriendly?" I asked.

She considered the question. "Ndemi's mother has always been very kind to me. The others could be a little friendlier, I suppose, but I imagine that's just because most of them are senior wives and are very busy running their households."

"Did it ever occur to you that there could be some other reason why they are not friendly?" I suggested.

"What are you getting at?" she asked, suddenly alert.

"There is a problem," I said.

"Oh?"

"Some of the older women resent your presence."

"Because I'm an immigrant?" she asked.

I shook my head. "No."

"Then why?" she persisted, genuinely puzzled.

"It is because we have a very rigid social order here, and you have not yet fit in."

"I thought I was fitting in very well," she said defensively.

"You were mistaken."

"Give me an example."

I looked at her. "You know that Kikuyu wives must shave their heads, and yet you have not done so."

She sighed and touched her hair. "I know," she replied. "I've been meaning to, but I'm very fond of it. I'll shave my head tonight." She seemed visibly relieved. "Is that what this is all about?"

"No," I said. "That is merely an outward sign of the problem."

"Then I don't understand."

"It is difficult to explain," I said. "Your *khangas* are more pleasing to the eye than theirs. Your garden grows better. You are as old as Wambu, but appear younger than her daughters. In their minds, these things set you apart from them and make you more than a *manamouki*. The corollary, which they have not yet voiced but must surely feel, is that if you are somehow *more*, then this makes them somehow *less*."

"What do you expect me to do?" she asked. "Wear rags and let my gardens go to seed?"

"No," I said. "I do not expect that."

"Then what can I do?" she continued. "You're telling me that they feel threatened because I am competent." She paused. "*You* are a competent man, Koriba. You have been schooled in Europe and America, you can read and write and work a computer. And yet I notice that you feel no need to hide your talents."

"I am a *mundumugu*," I said. "I live alone on my hill, removed from the village, and I am viewed with awe and fear by my people. This is the function of a *mundumugu*. It is not the function of a *manamouki*, who must live in the village and find her place in the social order of the tribe."

"That's what I am trying to do," she said in frustration.

"Do not try so hard."

"If you're not telling me to be incompetent, then I *still* don't understand."

"One does not fit in by being different," I said. "For example, I know that you bring flowers into your house. Doubtless they are fragrant and pleasing to the eye, but no other woman in the village decorates her hut with flowers."

"That's not true," she said defensively. "Sumi does."

"If so, then she does it because *you* do it," I pointed out. "Can you see that this is even more threatening to the older women than if you alone kept flowers, for it challenges their authority?"

She stared at me, trying to comprehend.

"They have spent their entire lives achieving their positions within the tribe," I continued, "and now you have come here and taken a position entirely outside of their order. We have a new world to populate: you are barren, but far from feeling shame or grief, you act as though this is not a terrible *thahu*. Such an attitude is contrary to their experience, just as decorating your house with flowers or creating *khangas* with intricate patterns is contrary to their experience, and thus they feel threatened."

"I still don't see what I can do about it," she protested. "I gave my original *khangas* to Wambu, but she refuses to wear them. And I have offered to show Bori how to get a greater yield from her gardens, but she won't listen."

"Of course not," I replied. "Senior wives will not accept advice from a *manamouki*, any more than a chief would accept advice from a newly circumcised young man. You must simply"—here I switched to English, for there is no comparable term in Swahili—"maintain a low profile. If you do so, in time the problems will go away."

She paused for a moment, considering what I had told her.

"I'll try," she said at last.

"And if you *must* do something that will call attention to yourself," I continued, reverting to Swahili, "try to do it in a way that will not offend."

"I didn't even know I *was* offending," she said. "How am I to avoid it if I'm calling attention to myself?"

"There are ways," I answered. "Take, for example, the chair that you built."

"Tom has had back spasms for years," she said. "I built the chair because he couldn't get enough support from a stool. Am I supposed to let my husband suffer because some of the women don't believe in chairs?"

"No," I said. "But you can tell the younger women that Nkobe ordered you to build the chair, and thus the stigma will not be upon you."

"Then it will be upon him."

I shook my head. "Men have far greater leeway here than women. There will be no stigma upon him for ordering his *manamouki* to see to his comfort." I paused long enough for the thought to sink in. "Do you understand?"

She sighed. "Yes."

"And you will do as I suggest?"

"If I'm to live in peace with my neighbors, I suppose I must."

"There is always an alternative," I said.

She shook her head vigorously. "I've dreamed of a place like this all my life, and nobody is going to make me leave it now that I'm here. I'll do whatever I have to do."

"Good," I said, getting to my feet to signify that the interview was over. "Then the problem will soon be solved."

But, of course, it wasn't.

I spent the next two weeks visiting a neighboring village whose chief had died quite suddenly. He had no sons and no brothers, and the line of succession was in doubt. I listened to all the applicants to the throne, discussed the situation with the Council of Elders until there was unanimity, presided at the ceremony that installed the new chief in his ceremonial robes and headdress, and finally returned to my own village.

As I climbed the path to my *boma*, I saw a female figure sitting just outside my hut. I drew closer and saw that it was Shima, Ndemi's mother.

"*Jambo*, Koriba," she said.

"*Jambo*, Shima," I responded.

"You are well, I trust."

"As well as an old man can feel after walking for most of the day," I responded, sitting down opposite her. I looked around my *boma*. "I do not see Ndemi."

"I sent him to the village for the afternoon, because I wished to speak to you alone."

"Does this concern Ndemi?" I asked.

She shook her head. "It is about Mwange."

I sighed wearily. "Proceed."

"I am not like the other women, Koriba," she began. "I have always been good to Mwange."

"So she has told me."

"Her ways do not bother me," she continued. "After all, someday I shall be the mother of the *mundumugu*, and while there can be many senior wives, there can be only one *mundumugu* and one *mundumugu*'s mother."

"This is true," I said, waiting for her to get to the point of her visit.

"Therefore, I have befriended Mwange, and have shown her many kindnesses, and she has responded in kind."

"I am pleased to hear it."

"And because I have befriended her," continued Shima, "I have felt great compassion for her, because as you know she carries the *thahu* of barrenness. And it seemed to me that, since Nkobe is such a wealthy man, that he should take another wife, to help Mwange with the work on the *shamba* and to produce sons and daughters." She paused. "My daughter Shuni, as you know, will be circumcised before the short rains come, and so I approached Mwange as a friend, and as the mother of the future *mundumugu*, to suggest that Nkobe pay the bride-price for Shuni." Here she paused again, and frowned. "She got very mad and yelled at me. You must speak to her, Koriba. A rich man like Nkobe should not be forced to live with only a barren wife."

"Why do you keep calling Nkobe a rich man?" I asked. "His *shamba* is small, and he has only six cattle."

"His family is rich," she stated. "Ndemi told me that they have many men and machines to do their planting and harvesting."

Thank you for nothing, little Ndemi, I thought irritably. Aloud I said: "All that is back on Earth. Here Nkobe is a poor man."

"Even if he is poor," said Shima, "he will not remain poor, for grain and vegetables grow for Mwange as for no one else, as if this is Ngai's blessing to make up for His *thahu* of barrenness." She stared at me. "You must talk to her, Koriba. This would be a good thing. Shuni is very obedient and hardworking, and she already likes Mwange very much. We will not demand a large bride-price, for we know that the *mundumugu*'s family will never go hungry."

"Why did you not wait for Nkobe to approach you, as is the custom?" I asked.

"I thought if I explained my idea to Mwange, she would see the wisdom of it and speak to Nkobe herself, for he listens to her more than most husbands listen to their wives, and surely the thought of a fertile woman who would share her chores would appeal to her."

"Well, you have presented your idea to her," I said. "Now it is up to Nkobe to make the offer or choose not to."

"But she says that she will permit him to marry no one else," answered Shima, more puzzled than outraged, "as if a *manamouki* could stop her husband from buying another wife. She is ignorant of our ways, Koriba, and for this reason you must speak with her. You must point out that she should be grateful to have another woman with whom to speak and share the work, and she should not want Nkobe to die without having fathered any children just because *she* has been cursed." She hesitated for a moment, and then concluded: "And you should remind her that Shuni will someday be sister to the *mundumugu.*"

"I am glad that you are so concerned about Mwange's future," I said at last.

She caught the trace of sarcasm in my voice.

"Is it so wrong to be concerned about my little Shuni as well?" she demanded.

"No," I admitted. "No, it is not wrong."

"Oh!" said Shima, as if she had suddenly remembered something important. "When you speak to Mwange, remind her that she is named for my sister."

"I do not intend to speak to Mwange at all."

"Oh?"

"No," I said. "As you yourself pointed out, this is not her concern. I will speak to Nkobe."

"And you will mention Shuni?" she persisted.

"I will speak to Nkobe," I answered noncommittally.

She got to her feet and prepared to leave.

"You can do me a favor, Shima," I said.

"Oh?"

I nodded. "Have Ndemi come to my *boma* immediately. I have many tasks for him to do here."

"How can you be sure, since you have only just returned?"

"I am sure," I said adamantly.

She looked across my *boma*, still the protective mother. "I can see no chores that have been left undone."

"Then I will find some," I said.

I went down to the village in the afternoon, for old Siboki needed ointments to keep the pain from his joints, and Koinnage had asked me to help him settle a dispute between Njoro and Sangora concerning the ownership of a calf that their jointly-owned cow had just produced.

When I had finished my business there, I placed charms on some of the scarecrows, and then, in midafternoon, I walked over to Nkobe's *shamba*, where I found him herding his cattle.

"*Jambo*, Koriba!" he greeted me, waving his hand.

"*Jambo*, Nkobe," I replied, approaching him.

"Would you like to come into my hut for some *pombe*?" he offered. "Mwange just brewed it yesterday."

"Thank you for the offer, but I do not care to drink warm *pombe* on a hot afternoon like this."

"It's actually quite cool," he said. "She buries the gourd in the ground to keep it that way."

"Then I will have some," I acquiesced, falling into step beside him as he drove his cattle toward his *boma*.

Mwange was waiting for us, and she invited us into the cool interior of the hut and poured our *pombe* for us, then began to leave, for *manamoukis* do not listen to the conversation of men.

"Stay here, Mwange," I said.

"You're sure?" she said.

"Yes."

She shrugged and sat on the floor, with her back propped up against a wall of the hut.

"What brings you here, Koriba?" asked Nkobe, sitting gingerly upon his chair, and I could see that his back was troubling him. "You have not paid us a visit before."

"The *mundumugu* rarely visits those who are healthy enough to visit *him*," I replied.

"Then this is a special occasion," said Nkobe.

"Yes," I replied, sipping my *pombe*. "This is a special occasion."

"What is it this time?" asked Mwange warily.

"What do you mean, 'this time'?" said Nkobe sharply.

"There have been some minor problems," I answered, "none of which concern you."

"Anything that affects Mwange concerns me," responded Nkobe. "I am not blind or deaf, Koriba. I know that the older women have refused to accept her—and I'm getting more than a little bit angry about it. She has gone out of her way to fit in here, and has met them more than halfway."

"I did not come here to discuss Mwange with you," I said.

"Oh?" he said suspiciously.

"Are you saying we have a problem that concerns *him*?" demanded Mwange.

"It concerns both of you," I replied. "That is why I have come here."

"All right, Koriba—what is it?" said Nkobe.

"You have made a good effort to fit into the community and to live as a Kikuyu, Nkobe," I said. "And yet there is one more thing that you will be expected to do, and it is this that I have come to discuss with you."

"And what is that?"

"Sooner or later, you will be expected to take another wife."

"I knew it!" said Mwange.

"I'm very happy with the wife I have," said Nkobe with unconcealed hostility.

"That may be," I said, draining the last of my *pombe*, "but you have no children, and as Mwange gets older she will need someone to help her with her duties."

"Now you listen to me!" snapped Nkobe. "I came here because I thought it would make Mwange happy. So far she's been ostracized and shunned and gossiped about, and now you're telling me that I have to take another wife into my house so that Mwange can keep from being spat on by the other women? We don't need this, Koriba! I was just as happy on my farm in Kenya. I can go back there any time I want."

"If that is the way you feel, then perhaps you should return to Kenya," I said.

"Tom," said Mwange, staring at him, and he fell silent.

"It is true that you do not have to stay," I continued. "But you are Kikuyus, living on a Kikuyu world, and if you do stay, you will be expected to act as Kikuyus."

"There's no law that says a Kikuyu man must take a second wife," said Nkobe sullenly.

"No, there is no such law," I admitted. "Nor is there a law that says a Kikuyu man must father children. But these are our traditions, and you will be expected to abide by them."

"To hell with them!" he muttered in English.

Mwange laid a restraining hand on his arm. "There is a coterie of young warriors who live beyond the forest," she said. "Why don't *they* marry some of the young women? Why should the men of the village monopolize them all?"

"They cannot afford wives," I said. "That is why they live alone."

"That's *their* problem," said Nkobe.

"I've made many sacrifices in the name of communal harmony," said Mwange, "but this is asking too much, Koriba. We are happy just the way we are, and we intend to stay this way."

"You will not remain happy."

"What does that mean?" she demanded.

"Next month is the circumcision ritual," I said. "When it is over, there will be many girls eligible for marriage, and since you are barren, it is only reasonable to suppose that a number of their families will suggest that Nkobe pay the bride-price for their daughters. He may refuse once, he may refuse twice, but if he continues to refuse, he will offend most of the village. They will assume that because he comes from Kenya he feels their women are not good enough for him, and they will be further offended by the fact that he refuses to have children with which to populate our empty planet."

"Then I'll explain my reasons to them," said Nkobe.

"They will not understand," I answered.

"No, they will not understand," agreed Mwange unhappily.

"Then they will have to learn to live with it," said Nkobe firmly.

"And you will have to learn to live with silence and animosity," I said. "Is this the life you envisioned when you came to Kirinyaga?"

"Of course not!" snapped Nkobe. "But nothing can make me—"

"We will think about it, Koriba," interrupted Mwange.

Nkobe turned to his wife, stunned. "What are you saying?"

"I am saying that we will think about it," repeated Mwange.

"That is all that I ask," I said, getting to my feet and walking to the door of the hut.

"You demand a lot, Koriba," said Mwange bitterly.

"I demand nothing," I replied. "I merely suggest."

"Coming from the *mundumugu*, is there a difference?"

I did not answer her, because in truth there was no difference whatsoever.

"You seem unhappy, Koriba," said Ndemi.

He had just finished feeding my chickens and my goats, and now he sat down beside me in the shade of my acacia tree.

"I am," I said.

"Mwange," he said, nodding his head.

"Mwange," I agreed.

Two weeks had passed since I had visited her and Nkobe.

"I saw her this morning, when I went to the river to fill your gourds," said Ndemi. "She, too, seems unhappy."

"She is," I said. "And there is nothing that I can do about it."

"But you are the *mundumugu*."

"I know."

"You are the most powerful of men," continued Ndemi. "Surely you can put an end to her sorrow."

I sighed. "The *mundumugu* is both the most powerful and the weakest of men. In Mwange's case, I am the weakest."

"I do not understand."

"The *mundumugu* is the most powerful of men when it comes to interpreting the law," I said. "But he is also the weakest of men, for it is he, of all men, who must be bound by that law, no matter what else happens." I paused. "I should allow her to be what she can be, instead of being merely a *manamouki*. And failing that, I should make her leave Kirinyaga and return to Kenya." I sighed again. "But she must behave like a *manamouki* if she is to have a life here, and she has broken no law that would allow me to force her to leave."

Ndemi frowned. "Being a *mundumugu* can be more difficult than I thought."

I smiled at him and placed a hand upon his head. "Tomorrow I will begin to teach you to make the ointments that cure the sick."

"Really?" he said, his face brightening.

I nodded. "Your last statement tells me that you are no longer a child."

"I have not been a child for many rains," he protested.

"Do not say any more," I told him with a wry smile, "or we will do more harvest prayers instead."

He immediately fell silent, and I looked out across the distant savannah, where a swirling tower of dust raced across the arid plain, and wondered, for perhaps the thousandth time, what to do about Mwange.

How long I sat thus, motionless, I do not know, but eventually I felt Ndemi tugging at the blanket I had wrapped around my shoulders.

"Women," he whispered.

"What?" I said, not comprehending.

"From the village," he said, gesturing toward the path that led to my *boma*.

I looked where he indicated and saw four of the village women approaching. There was Wambu, and Sabo, and Bori, and with them this time was Morina, the second wife of Kimoda.

"Should I leave?" asked Ndemi.

I shook my head. "If you are to become a *mundumugu*, it is time you started listening to a *mundumugu*'s problems."

The four women stopped perhaps ten feet away from me.

"*Jambo,*" I said, staring at them.

"The Kenyan witch must leave!" said Wambu.

"We have been through this before," I said.

"But now she has broken the law," said Wambu.

"Oh?" I said. "In what way?"

Wambu grabbed Morina by the arm and shoved her even closer to me. "Tell him," she said triumphantly.

"She has bewitched my daughter," said Morina, obviously uneasy in my presence.

"How has Mwange bewitched your daughter?" I asked.

"My Muri was a good, obedient child," said Morina. "She always helped me grind the grain, and she dutifully cared for her two younger brothers when I was working in the fields, and she never left the thorn gate open at night so that hyenas could enter our *boma* and kill our goats and cattle." She paused, and I could see that she was trying very hard not to cry. "All she could talk about since the last long rains was her forthcoming circumcision ceremony, and who she hoped would pay the bride-price for her. She was a perfect daughter, a daughter any mother would be proud of." Now a tear trickled down her cheek. "And then the Kenyan woman came, and Muri spent her time with her, and now"—suddenly the single tear became a veritable flood—"now she tells me that she refuses to be circumcised. She will never marry and she will die an old, barren woman!"

Morina could speak no more, and began beating her breasts with her clenched fists.

"That is not all," added Wambu. "The reason Muri does not wish to be circumcised is because the Kenyan woman herself has not been circumcised. And yet the Kenyan woman has married a Kikuyu man, and has tried to live among us as his *manamouki*." She glared at me. "She has broken the law, Koriba! We must cast her out!"

"I am the *mundumugu*," I replied sternly. "I will decide what must be done."

"You *know* what must be done!" said Wambu furiously.

"That is all," I said. "I will hear no more."

Wambu glared at me, but did not dare to disobey me, and finally, turning on her heel, she stalked back down the path to the village, followed by Sabo and the still-wailing Morina.

Bori stood where she was for an extra moment, then turned to me.

"It is as I told you before, Koriba," she said, almost apologetically. "She really *is* a witch."

Then she, too, began walking back to the village.

"What will you do, Koriba?" asked Ndemi.

"The law is clear," I said wearily. "No uncircumcised woman may live with a Kikuyu man as his wife."

"Then you will make her leave Kirinyaga?"

"I will offer her a choice," I said, "and I will hope that she chooses to leave."

"It is too bad," said Ndemi. "She has tried very hard to be a good *manamouki*."

"I know," I said.

"Then why is Ngai visiting her with such unhappiness?"

"Because sometimes trying is not enough."

We stood at Haven—Mwange, Nkobe, and I—awaiting the Maintenance ship's arrival.

"I am truly sorry that things did not work out," I said sincerely.

Nkobe glared at me, but said nothing.

"It didn't have to end this way," said Mwange bitterly.

"We had no choice," I said. "If we are to create our Utopia here on Kirinyaga, we must be bound by its rules."

"The fact that a rule exists does not make it right, Koriba," she said. "I gave up almost everything to live here, but I will not let them mutilate me in the name of some foolish custom."

"Without our traditions, we are not Kikuyu, but only Kenyans who live on another world," I pointed out.

"There is a difference between tradition and stagnation, Koriba," she said. "If you stifle every variation in taste and behavior in the name of the former, you achieve only the latter." She paused. "I would have been a good member of the community."

"But a poor *manamouki*," I said. "The leopard may be a stealthy hunter and fearsome killer, but he does not belong among a pride of lions."

"Lions and leopards have been extinct for a long time, Koriba," she said. "We are talking about human beings, not animals, and no matter how many rules you make and no matter how many traditions you invoke, you cannot make all human beings think and feel and act alike."

"It's coming," announced Nkobe as the Maintenance ship broke through the thin cloud cover.

"*Kwaheri*, Nkobe," I said, extending my hand.

He looked contemptuously at my hand for a moment, then turned his back and continued watching the Maintenance ship.

I turned to Mwange.

"I tried, Koriba," she said. "I really did."

"No one ever tried harder," I said. "*Kwaheri*, Mwange."

She stared at me, her face suddenly an emotionless mask.

"Good-bye, Koriba," she said in English. "And my name is Wanda."

The next morning Shima came to me to complain that Shuni had rejected the suitor that had been arranged for her.

Two days later Wambu complained to me that Kibo, Koinnage's youngest wife, had decorated her hut with colorful ribbons, and was beginning to let her hair grow.

And the morning after that, Kimi, who had only one son, announced that she wanted no more children.

"I thought it had ended," I said with a sigh as I watched Sangora, Kimi's distressed husband, walk back down the path to the village.

"That is because you have made a mistake, Koriba."

"Why do you say that?"

"Because you believed the wrong story," answered Ndemi with the confidence of youth.

"Oh?"

He nodded. "You believed the story about the Ugly Buffalo."

"And which story should I have believed?"

"The story of the *mundumugu* and the serpent."

"Why do you think one story is more worthy of belief than the other?" I asked him.

"Does not the story of the *mundumugu* and the serpent tell us that we cannot be rid of that which Ngai created simply because we find it repugnant or unsettling?"

"That is true," I said.

Ndemi smiled and held up three fingers. "Shuni, Kibo, Kimi," he said, counting them off. "Three serpents have returned already. There are ninety-seven yet to come."

And suddenly I had the awful premonition that he was right.

5

SONG OF A DRY RIVER

{JUNE–NOVEMBER 2134}

I will tell you why Ngai is the most cunning and powerful god of all.

Eons ago, when the Europeans were evil and their god decided to punish them, he caused it to rain for forty days and forty nights and covered the Earth with water—and because of this, the Europeans think that their god is more powerful than Ngai.

Certainly it is no small accomplishment to cover the Earth with water—but when the Kikuyu heard the story of Noah from the European missionaries, it did nothing to convince us that the god of the Europeans is more powerful than Ngai.

Ngai knows that water is the source of all life, and so when He wishes to punish us, He does not cover our lands with it. Instead He inhales deeply, and sucks the moisture from the air and the soil. Our rivers dry up, our crops fail, and our cattle and goats die of thirst.

The god of the Europeans may have created the flood—but it was Ngai who created the drought.

Can there be any doubt why He is the god that we fear and worship?

We emigrated from Kenya to the terraformed world of Kirinyaga to create a Kikuyu Utopia, a society that mirrored the simple, pastoral life we led before our culture was corrupted by the coming of the Europeans—and for the most part we have been successful.

Still, there are times when things seem to be coming apart, and it takes everything I can do in my capacity as *mundumugu* to keep Kirinyaga functioning as it was meant to function.

On the morning of the day that I brought the curse down upon my people, my youthful assistant, Ndemi, had overslept again and once more forgot to feed my chickens. Then I had to make the long trek to a neighboring village, where, in direct contradiction of my orders, they had begun planting maize in an overused field that I had decreed must lay fallow until after the long rains. I explained once more that the land needed time to rest and regain its strength, but as I left I had the distinct feeling that I would be back again the next week or the next month, giving them the same lecture.

On the way home, I had to settle a dispute between Ngona, who had diverted a small stream to irrigate his fields, and Kamaki, who claimed that his crops were suffering because the stream no longer carried enough water to them. This was the eleventh time someone had tried to divert the stream, and the eleventh time I had angrily explained that the water belonged to the entire village.

Then Sabella, who was to pay me two fat, healthy goats for presiding at his son's wedding, delivered two animals that were so underfed and scrawny that they didn't even look like goats. Ordinarily I might not have lost my temper, but I was tired of people keeping their best animals and trying to pay me with cattle and goats that looked half-dead, so I threatened to annul the marriage unless he replaced them.

Finally, Ndemi's mother told me that he was spending too much time studying to be a *mundumugu*, and that she needed him to tend his family's cattle; this in spite of the fact that he has three strong, healthy brothers.

A number of the women stared at me in amusement as I walked through the village, as if they knew some secret of which I was ignorant, and by the time I reached the long, winding path that led to the hill where I lived, I was annoyed with *all* of my people. I craved only the solitude of my *boma*, and a gourd of *pombe* to wash away the dust of the day.

When I heard the sound of a human voice singing on my hill, I assumed that it was Ndemi, carrying out his afternoon chores. But as I approached more closely, I realized that the voice was that of a woman.

I shaded my eyes from the sun and peered ahead, and there, halfway up my hill, a wrinkled old woman was busily erecting a hut beneath an acacia tree, weaving the twigs and branches together to form the walls, and singing to herself. I blinked in surprise, for it is well known that no one else may live on the *mundumugu's* hill.

The woman saw me and smiled. "*Jambo*, Koriba," she greeted me as if nothing was amiss. "Is it not a beautiful day?"

I saw now that she was Mumbi, the mother of Koinnage, who was the paramount chief of the village.

"What are you doing here?" I demanded as I approached her.

"As you see, I am building a hut," she said. "We are going to be neighbors, Koriba."

I shook my head. "I require no neighbors," I said, pulling my blanket more tightly around my shoulders. "And you already have a hut on Koinnage's *shamba*."

"I no longer wish to live there," said Mumbi.

"You may not live on my hill," I said. "The *mundumugu* lives alone."

"I have faced the doorway to the east," she said, turning to the broad, sprawling savannah beyond the river and ignoring my statement. "That way the rays of the sun will bring warmth into it in the morning."

"This is not even a true Kikuyu hut," I continued angrily. "A strong wind will blow it over, and it will protect you from neither the cold nor the hyenas."

"It will protect me from the sun and the rain," she responded. "Next week, when I have more strength, I will fill in the walls with mud."

"Next week you will be living with Koinnage, where you belong," I said.

"I will not," she said adamantly. "Before I would return to Koinnage's *shamba*, I would rather you left my withered old body out for the hyenas."

That can be arranged, I thought irritably, for I had seen enough foolishness for one day. But aloud I said: "Why do you feel this way, Mumbi? Does Koinnage no longer treat you with respect?"

"He treats me with respect," she admitted, trying to straighten her ancient body and placing a gnarled hand to the small of her back.

"Koinnage has three wives," I continued, slapping futilely at a pair of flies that circled my face. "If any of them have ignored you or treated you with disrespect, I will speak to them."

She snorted contemptuously. "Ha!"

I paused and stared at a small herd of impala grazing on the savannah, trying to decide upon the best way to approach the subject. "Have you fought with them?"

"I did not realize that the mornings were so cold on this hill," she said, rubbing her wrinkled chin with a gnarled hand. "I will need more blankets."

"You did not answer my question," I said.

"And firewood," she continued. "I will have to gather much firewood."

"I have heard enough," I said firmly. "You must return to your home, Mumbi."

"I will not!" she said, laying a protective hand on the walls of her hut. "*This* will be my home."

"This is the *mundumugu's* hill. I will not permit you to live here."

"I am tired of people telling me what I am not permitted to do," she said. Suddenly she pointed to a fish eagle that was lazily riding the thermals over the river. "Why should I not be as free as that bird? I will live here on this hill."

"Who else has told you what you cannot do?" I asked.

"It is not important."

"It must be important," I said, "or you would not be here."

She stared at me for a moment, then shrugged. "Wambu has said I may not help her cook the meals, and Kibo no longer lets me grind the maize or brew the *pombe*." She glared at me defiantly. "I am the mother of the paramount chief of the village! I will not be treated like a helpless baby."

"They are treating you as a respected elder," I explained. "You no longer have to work. You have raised your family, and now you have reached the point where they will care for you."

"I do not *want* to be cared for!" she snapped. "All my life I have run my *shamba*, and I have run it well. I am not ready to stop."

"Did not your own mother stop when her husband died and she moved into her son's *shamba*?" I asked, slapping at my cheek as one of the flies finally settled on it.

"My mother no longer had the strength to run her *shamba*," said Mumbi defensively. "That is not the case with me."

"If you do not step aside, how are Koinnage's wives ever to learn to run his *shamba*?"

"I will teach them," replied Mumbi. "They still have much to learn. Wambu does not cook the banana mash as good as I do, and as for Kibo, well …" She shrugged her shoulders, to indicate that Koinnage's youngest wife was beyond redemption.

"But Wambu is the mother of three sons and is soon to become a grandmother herself," I noted. "If she is not ready to run her husband's *shamba* by now, then she never will be."

A satisfied smile crossed Mumbi's leathery face. "So you agree with me."

"You misunderstand me," I said. "There comes a time when the old must make way for the young."

"*You* have not made way for anyone," she said accusingly.

"I am the *mundumugu*," I answered. "It is not my physical strength that I offer to the village, but my wisdom, and wisdom is the province of age."

"And I offer *my* wisdom to my son's wives," she said stubbornly.

"It is not the same thing," I said.

"It is precisely the same thing," she replied. "When we still lived in Kenya, I fought for Kirinyaga's charter as fiercely as you yourself did, Koriba. I came here in the same spaceship that brought you, and I helped clear the land and plant the fields. It is not fair that I should be cast aside now, just because I am old."

"You are not being cast aside," I explained patiently. "You came here to live the traditional life of the Kikuyu, and it is our tradition to care for our elders. You shall never want for food, or for a roof over your head, or for care when you are sick."

"But I don't *feel* like an elder!" she protested. She pointed to her loom and her pots, which she had brought up the hill from the village. "I can still weave cloth and repair thatch and cook meals. I am not too old to grind the maize and carry the water calabashes. If I am no longer permitted to do these things for my family, than I shall live here on this hill and do them for myself."

"That is unacceptable," I said. "You must return to your home."

"It is not *mine* anymore," she replied bitterly. "It is Wambu's."

I looked down at her stooped, wrinkled body. "It is the order of things that the old shall make way for the young," I said once again.

"Who will *you* make way for?" she asked bitterly.

"I am training young Ndemi to become the next *mundumugu*," I said. "When he is ready, I shall step aside."

"Who will decide when he is ready?"

"I will."

"Then *I* should decide when Wambu is ready to run my son's *shamba*."

"What you should do is listen to your *mundumugu*," I said. "Your shoulders are stooped and your back is bent from the burden of your years. The time has come to let your son's wives care for you."

Her jaw jutted out pugnaciously. "I will not let Wambu cook for me. I have always cooked for myself, ever since we lived beside the dry river in Kenya." She paused again. "I was very happy then," she added bitterly.

"Perhaps you must learn how to be happy again," I answered. "You have earned the right to rest, and to let others work for you. This should make you happy."

"But it doesn't."

"That is because you have lost sight of our purpose," I said. "We left Kenya and came to Kirinyaga because we wished to retain our customs and traditions. If I permit you to ignore them, then I must let everyone ignore them, and then we will no longer be a Kikuyu Utopia, but merely a second Kenya."

"You told us that in a Utopia, everyone is happy," she said. "Well, *I* am not happy, so something must be wrong with Kirinyaga."

"And running Koinnage's *shamba* will make it right?" I asked.

"Yes."

"But then Wambu and Kibo will be unhappy."

"Then perhaps there are no Utopias, and we must each be concerned with our own happiness," said Mumbi.

Why are old people so selfish and unfeeling? I wondered. *Here I am, hot and thirsty and tired, and all she can do is complain about how unhappy she is.*

"Come with me," I said. "We will go to the village together, and we will find a solution to your problem. You may not remain here."

She stared at me for a very long moment, then shrugged. "I will come with you, but we will not find a solution, and then I will return here to my new home."

The sun was low in the sky as we climbed down the hill and began walking along the winding path, and twilight had fallen by the time we reached the village and began walking by the various huts. A number of men and women had gathered at Koinnage's *shamba*, and most of them displayed the same amused expressions I had seen earlier in the day. As I approached Koinnage's *boma*, they followed me, eager to see what punishment I would mete out to Mumbi, as if her transgression and my anger were the highlight of their evening's entertainment.

"Koinnage!" I said in a loud, firm voice.

There was no response, and I called his name twice more before he finally emerged from his hut, a sheepish expression on his face.

"*Jambo*, Koriba," he said uneasily. "I did not know you were here."

I glared at him. "Did you also not know your mother was here?"

"This is her *shamba*: where else would she be?" he asked innocently.

"You know very well where she was," I said, as the light of the evening fires cast flickering shadows on his face. "I advise you to think very carefully of the consequences before you lie to your *mundumugu* again."

He seemed to shrink into himself for a moment. Then he noticed all the villagers behind me.

"What are *they* doing here?" he demanded. "Return to your *bomas*, all of you!"

They backed away a few steps, but did not leave.

Koinnage turned to Mumbi. "See how you shame me in front of my people? Why do you do this to me? Am I not the paramount chief?"

"I would think that the paramount chief could control his mother," I said sarcastically.

"I have tried," said Koinnage. "I do not know what has gotten into her." He glared at Mumbi. "I order you once again to return to your hut."

"No," said Mumbi.

"But I am the chief!" he insisted, half-furiously, half-whining. "You must obey me."

Mumbi stared defiantly at him. "No," she said again.

He turned back to me. "You see how it is," he said helplessly. "*You* are the *mundumugu*; *you* must order her to stay here."

"No one tells the *mundumugu* what he *must* do," I said severely, for I already knew what Mumbi's response to my order would be. "Summon your wives."

He seemed relieved to be sent away, however briefly, and he went off to the cooking hut, returning a moment later with Wambu, Sumi, and Kibo.

"You all know that a problem exists," I said. "Mumbi is so unhappy that she wishes to leave your *shamba* and live on my hill."

"It is a good idea," said Kibo. "It is too crowded here."

"It is a bad idea," I replied firmly. "She must live with her family."

"No one is stopping her," said Kibo petulantly.

"She wants to take a more active part in the daily life of the *shamba*," I continued. "Surely there is something she can do, so that the harmony of your *shamba* is preserved."

For a long moment no one spoke. Then Wambu, who is Koinnage's senior wife, stepped forward.

"I am sorry you are so unhappy, my mother," she said. "You may of course brew the *pombe* and weave the cloth."

"Those are *my* jobs!" protested Kibo.

"We must show respect for our husband's mother," said Wambu with a smug smile.

"Why do we not show her even more respect and let her supervise the cooking?" said Kibo.

"I am Koinnage's senior wife," said Wambu firmly. "*I* do the cooking."

"And *I* brew the *pombe* and weave the cloth," said Kibo stubbornly.

"And *I* pound the grain and fetch the water," added Sumi. "You must find something else for her to do."

Mumbi turned to me. "I told you that it wouldn't work, Koriba," she said. "I will gather the rest of my possessions and move into my new home."

"You will not," I said. "You will remain with your family, as mothers have always remained with their families."

"I am not ready to be cast aside as my grandchildren cast aside their toys," she replied.

"And *I* am not ready to allow you to break with the traditions of the Kikuyu," I said sternly. "You will stay here."

"I will not!" she replied, and I heard some of the villagers chuckling at this withered old lady who defied both her chief and her *mundumugu*.

"Koinnage," I said, directing him and his family inside the thorn fence of his *boma*, so that we might be farther away from the onlookers, "she is your mother. Speak to her and convince her to remain here, before she forces me to take some action that you will all regret."

"Do not continue to shame me in the eyes of the village, my mother," pleaded Koinnage. "You must remain in my *shamba*."

"I will not."

"You will!" said Koinnage heatedly, as the men and women of the village crowded closer to the *boma*'s entrance.

"And if I don't, what will you do to me?" she demanded, glaring at him. "Will you bind my hands and feet and force me to remain here in my hut?"

"I am the paramount chief," said Koinnage in obvious frustration. "I order you to stay here!"

"Hah!" she said, and now the people's chuckles became outright laughter. "You may be a chief, but you are still my son, and mothers do not take orders from their sons."

"But everyone must obey the *mundumugu*," he said, "and Koriba has ordered you to remain here."

"*I* will not obey him," she said. "I came to Kirinyaga to be happy, and I am unhappy in your *shamba*. I am going to live on the hill, and neither you nor Koriba will stop me."

Suddenly the laughter stopped, and was replaced by an awed silence, for no one may flaunt the *mundumugu*'s authority in such a manner. Under other circumstances I might have forgiven her, for she was very upset, but she had challenged me in front of the entire village, and it was the end of a long, irritating day.

My anger must have been reflected on my face, for Koinnage suddenly stepped between his mother and myself.

"Please, Koriba," he said, his voice unsteady. "She is an old woman, and she does not know what she is saying."

"I know what I am saying," said Mumbi. She glared at me defiantly. "If I cannot live as I like, then I prefer not to live at all. What will you do to me, *mundumugu*?"

"I?" I said innocently, aware of the many eyes that were focused upon me. "I will do nothing to you. As you yourself have pointed out, I am merely an old man." I paused and stared at her, as Koinnage and his wives shrank back in fear. "You speak fondly of the dry river we lived beside when we were children—but you have forgotten what it was like to live beside it. I will help you to remember." I raised my voice, so that all could hear. "Because you have chosen to ignore our tradition, and because the others have laughed, tonight I shall sacrifice a goat and ask Ngai to visit Kirinyaga with a drought such as it has never seen before, until the world is as dry and withered as you are yourself, Mumbi. I shall ask Him not to allow a single drop of rain to fall until you return to your *shamba* and agree to remain there."

"No!" said Koinnage.

"The cattle's tongues will swell in their heads until they cannot breathe, the crops will turn to dust, and the river will run dry." I looked angrily at the faces of my people, as if daring them to laugh again, but none of them had the courage to meet my gaze.

None but Mumbi, that is. She stared thoughtfully at me, and for a moment I thought she was going to retract her statement and agree to remain with Koinnage. Then she shrugged. "I have lived by a dry river before. I can do so again." She began walking away. "I am going to my hill now."

There was a stunned silence.

"Must you do this thing, Koriba?" asked Koinnage at last.

"You heard what your mother said to me, and yet you ask me that?" I demanded.

"But she is just an old woman."

"Do you think that only warriors can bring destruction upon us?" I responded.

"How can living on a hill destroy us?" asked Kibo.

"We are a society of laws and rules and traditions, and our survival as a people depends upon all of them being equally obeyed."

"Then you will really ask Ngai to bring a drought to Kirinyaga?" she said.

"I am tired of being doubted and contradicted by my people, who have all forgotten who we are and why we have come here," I replied irritably. "I have said I would ask Ngai to visit Kirinyaga with a drought, and I will." I spat on my hands to show my sincerity.

"How long will the drought last?"

"Until Mumbi leaves my hill and returns to her own hut on her own *shamba*."

"She is a very stubborn old woman," said Koinnage miserably. "She could stay there forever."

"That is her choice," I answered.

"Perhaps Ngai will not listen to your supplication," said Kibo hopefully.

"He will listen," I replied harshly. "Am I not the *mundumugu*?"

When I awoke the next morning, Ndemi had already built my fire and fed my chickens. I emerged from my hut into the cold morning air, my blanket wrapped around my shoulders.

"*Jambo*, Koriba," said Ndemi.

"*Jambo*, Ndemi," I answered.

"Why has Mumbi built a hut on your hill, Koriba?" he asked.

"Because she is a stubborn old woman," I replied.

"You do not wish her to live here?"

"No."

Suddenly he grinned.

"What do you find so amusing, Ndemi?" I asked.

"She is a stubborn old woman and you are a stubborn old man," said Ndemi. "This will be very interesting."

I stared at him, but made no answer. Finally I walked into my hut and activated my computer.

"Computer," I said, "calculate an orbital change that will bring a drought to Kirinyaga."

"Working ... done," replied the computer.

"Now transmit those changes to Maintenance and request that they enact them immediately."

"Working ... done." There was a moment's silence. "There is a voice-and-image message incoming from Maintenance."

"Put it through," I said.

The image of a middle-aged Oriental woman appeared on the computer's holographic screen.

"Koriba, I just received your instructions," she said. "Are you aware that such an orbital diversion will almost certainly bring a severe climactic change to Kirinyaga?"

"I am."

She frowned. "Perhaps I should word that more strongly. It will bring a *cataclysmic* change. This will precipitate a drought of major proportions."

"Have I the right to request such an orbital change or not?" I demanded.

"Yes," she answered. "According to your charter, you have the right. But ..."

"Then please do as I ask."

"You're sure you don't want to reconsider?"

"I am sure."

She shrugged. "You're the boss."

I am glad that someone remembers that, I thought bitterly as the connection was broken and the computer screen went blank.

* * *

"She talks too much, and I don't like the song she sings, but she has always seemed like a nice woman," remarked Ndemi, staring down the hill at Mumbi's hut after I had finished instructing him in the blessing of the scarecrows. "Why did Koinnage make her leave his *shamba*?"

"Koinnage did not make her leave," I answered. "She chose to leave."

Ndemi frowned, for such behavior was beyond his experience. "What reason did she have for leaving?"

"Her reason is not important," I said. "What *is* important is that the Kikuyu live as families, and she refuses to do so."

"Is she crazy?" asked Ndemi.

"No. Just stubborn."

"If she is not crazy, then she must think she has a good reason for living on your hill," he persisted. "What is it?"

"She still wants to do the work she has always done," I replied. "It is not crazy. In fact, in a way it is admirable—but in this society it is wrong."

"She is very foolish," said Ndemi. "When I am *mundumugu*, I will do no more work than you do."

Has everyone on Kirinyaga conspired to try my patience? I wondered. Aloud I said: "I work very hard."

"You work at your magic, and you call down the rains, and you bless the fields and the cattle," conceded Ndemi. "But you never carry water, or feed your animals, or clean your hut, or tend your gardens."

"The *mundumugu* does not do such things."

"That is why she is foolish. She could live like a *mundumugu* and have all these things done for her, and yet she chooses not to."

I shook my head. "She is foolish because she gave up everything she had to come to Kirinyaga and live the traditional life of the Kikuyu, and now she has broken with those traditions."

"You will have to punish her," said Ndemi thoughtfully.

"Yes."

"I hope the punishment is not a painful one," he continued, "for she is very much like you, and I do not think being punished will make her change her ways."

I looked down the hill at the old woman's hut and wondered if he was right.

Within a month Kirinyaga was feeling the effects of the drought. The days were long and hot and dry, and the river that ran through our village was very low.

Each morning I awoke to the sound of Mumbi singing to herself as she climbed the hill after filling her water gourd. Each afternoon I threw stones at her goats and chickens as they grazed closer and closer to my *boma*, and wondered how much longer it would be before she returned to her *shamba*. Each evening I received a message from Maintenance, asking if I wanted to make an orbital adjustment that would bring rain to my world.

From time to time Koinnage would trudge up the long, dusty path from the village and speak to Mumbi. I never eavesdropped, so I did not know the details of what they said to each other, but always it would end the same way: with Koinnage losing his temper and yelling at his mother, and with the old woman glaring at him obstinately as he walked back to the village, yelling imprecations over his shoulder.

One afternoon Shima, Ndemi's mother, came to my *boma*.

"*Jambo*, Shima," I greeted her.

"*Jambo*, Koriba," she said.

I waited patiently for her to tell me the purpose of her visit.

"Has Ndemi been a good assistant to you, Koriba?" she asked.

"Yes."

"And he learns his lessons well?"

"Very well."

"You have never questioned his loyalty?"

"I have never had cause to," I replied.

"Then why do you make his family suffer?" she asked. "Our cattle are weak, and our crops are dying. Why do you not bring the drought only to Koinnage's fields?"

"The drought will stop when Mumbi returns to her *shamba*," I said firmly. "She is the one who will decide when it ends, not I. Perhaps you should speak to her."

"I did," said Shima.

"And?"

"*She* told me to speak to *you*."

"She brought the drought to Kirinyaga," I said. "She can end it whenever she wishes."

"She is not the *mundumugu*. You are."

"I have acted to preserve our Utopia."

She smiled bitterly. "You have spent too long on your hill, *mundumugu*," she said. "Come down to the village. Look at the animals and the crops and the children, and then tell me how you are preserving our Utopia."

She turned and walked back down the hill before I could think of an answer.

Six weeks after the drought commenced, the Council of Elders came to my *boma* as I was giving Ndemi his daily instruction.

"*Jambo*," I greeted them. "I trust you are well?"

"We are not well, Koriba," said old Siboki, who seemed to be their spokesman.

"I am sorry to hear that," I said sincerely.

"We must talk, Koriba," continued Siboki.

"As you wish."

"We know that Mumbi is wrong," he began. "Once a woman has raised her children and seen her husband die, she must live with her son's family on his *shamba*, and allow them to care for her. It is the law, and it is foolish for her to want to live anywhere else."

"I agree," I said.

"We *all* agree," he said. "And if you must punish her to make her obey our laws, then so be it." He paused. "But you are punishing everyone, when only Mumbi has broken the law. It is not fair that we should suffer for her transgression."

"I wish things could be otherwise," I said sincerely.

"Then can you not intercede with Ngai on our behalf?" he persisted.

"I doubt that He will listen," I said. "It would be better if you spoke to Mumbi and convinced her to return to her *shamba*."

"We have tried," said Siboki.

"Then you must try again."

"We will," he said without much hope. "But will you at least *ask* Ngai to end the drought? You are the *mundumugu*, surely He will listen to you."

"I will ask Him," I said. "But Ngai is a harsh god. He brought forth the drought because Mumbi broke the law; He almost certainly will not bring the rains until she is ready to once again obey the law."

"But you will ask?"

"I will ask," I answered him.

They had nothing further to say, and after an awkward silence they left. Ndemi approached me when they were too far away to hear him.

"Ngai did not call forth the drought," he said. "You did, by speaking to the box in your hut."

I stared at him without replying.

"And if you brought the drought," he continued, "then surely you can end it."

"Yes, I can."

"Then why do you not do so, since it has brought suffering to many people, and not just to Mumbi?"

"Listen to me carefully, Ndemi," I said, "and remember my words, for someday you shall be the *mundumugu*, and this is your most important lesson."

"I am listening," he said, squatting down and staring at me intently.

"Of all the things on Kirinyaga, of all our laws and traditions and customs, the most important is this: The *mundumugu* is the most powerful man in our society. Not because of his physical strength, for as you see I am a wrinkled old man, but because he is the interpreter of our culture. It is he who determines what is right and what is wrong, and his authority must never be questioned."

"Are you saying that I cannot ask why you will not bring the rains?" asked Ndemi, confused.

"No," I said. "I am saying that the *mundumugu* is the rock upon which the Kikuyu build their culture, and because of that, he can never show weakness." I paused. "I wish I had not threatened to bring forth the drought. It had been a long, irritating day, and I was tired, and many people had been very foolish that day—but I *did* promise that there would be a drought, and now, if I show weakness, if I bring the rains, then sooner or later everyone in the village will challenge the *mundumugu's* authority ... and without authority, there is no structure to our lives." I looked into his eyes. "Do you understand what I am saying to you, Ndemi?"

"I think so," he said uncertainly.

"Someday it will be you, rather than I, who speaks to the computer. You must fully understand me before that day arrives."

There came a morning, three months into the drought, that Ndemi entered my hut and woke me by touching my shoulder.

"What is it?" I asked, sitting up.

"I cannot fill your gourds with water today," said Ndemi. "The river has dried up."

"Then we will dig a well at the foot of the hill," I said, walking out into my *boma* and wrapping my blanket around my shoulders to protect me from the dry, cold morning air.

Mumbi was singing to herself, as usual, as she lit a fire in front of her hut. I stared at her for a moment, then turned back to Ndemi.

"Soon she will leave," I said confidently.

"Will *you* leave?" he responded.

I shook my head. "This is my home."

"This is her home, too," said Ndemi.

"Her home is with Koinnage," I said irritably.

"She doesn't think so."

"She must have water to live. She will have to return to her *shamba* soon."

"Maybe," said Ndemi without much conviction.

"Why should you think otherwise?"

"Because I passed her well as I climbed the hill," he answered. He glanced down at Mumbi, who was now cooking her morning meal. "She is a very stubborn old woman," he added with more than a touch of admiration.

I made no answer.

"Your shade tree is dying, Koriba."

I looked up and saw Mumbi standing beside my *boma*.

"If you do not water it soon, it will wither, and you will be very uncomfortable." She paused. "I have extra thatch from my roof. You may have it and spread it across the branches of your acacia, if you wish."

"Why do you offer me this, when you yourself are responsible for the drought?" I asked suspiciously.

"To show you that I am your neighbor and not your enemy," she replied.

"You disobeyed the law," I said. "That makes you the enemy of our culture."

"It is an evil law," she replied. "For more than four months I have lived here on this hill. Every day I have gathered firewood, and I have woven two new blankets, and I have cooked my meals, and I fetched the water before the river ran dry, and now I bring water from my well. Why should I be cast aside when I can do all these things?"

"You are not being cast aside, Mumbi," I said. "It is precisely because you have done these things for so many years that you are finally allowed to rest and let others do them."

"But they are all I have," she protested. "What is the use of being alive if I cannot do the things that I know how to do?"

"The old have always been cared for by their families, as have the weak and the sick," I said. "It is our custom."

"It is a good custom," she said. "But I do not feel old." She paused. "Do you know the only time in my life I felt old? It was when I was not allowed to do anything in my own *shamba*." She frowned. "It was not a good feeling."

"You must come to terms with your age, Mumbi," I said.

"I did that when I moved to this hill," she replied. "Now *you* must come to terms with your drought."

The news began to reach my ears during the fourth month.

Njoro had slain his cattle and was now keeping gerunuk, which do not drink water but lick the dew off the leaves; this in spite of the fact that according to our tradition, the Kikuyu do not raise wild game.

Kambela and Njogu had taken their families and emigrated back to Kenya.

Kubandu, who lived in a neighboring village, had been found hoarding water that he had gathered before the river ran dry, and his neighbors burned his hut and killed his cattle.

A brush fire had broken out in the western plains and had destroyed eleven *shambas* before it was stopped.

Koinnage's visits to his mother became more frequent, more noisy, and more fruitless.

Even Ndemi, who previously had agreed that the *mundumugu* could, by definition, do no wrong, again began to question the need for the drought.

"Someday you will be the *mundumugu*," I said. "Remember all that I have taught you." I paused. "Now, if you should be confronted with the same situation, what will *you* do?"

He was silent for a moment. "I would probably let her live on the hill."

"That is contrary to our tradition."

"Perhaps," he said. "But she is living on the hill *now*, and all the Kikuyu who are not living on the hill are suffering." He paused thoughtfully. "Perhaps it is time to discard some traditions, rather than punish the whole world because one old woman chooses to ignore them."

"No!" I said heatedly. "When we lived in Kenya and the Europeans came, they convinced us to discard a tradition. And when we found out how easy it was, we discarded another, and then another, and eventually we discarded so many that we were no longer Kikuyu, but merely black Europeans." I paused and lowered my voice. "That is why we came to Kirinyaga, Ndemi—so that we could become Kikuyu once again. Have you listened to nothing I have said to you during the past two months?"

"I have listened," replied Ndemi. "I just do not understand how living on this hill makes her less of a Kikuyu."

"You had no trouble understanding it two months ago."

"My family was not starving two months ago."

"One has nothing to do with the other," I said. "She broke the law; she must be punished."

Ndemi paused. "I have been thinking about that."

"And?"

"Are there not degrees of lawbreaking?" said Ndemi. "Surely what she did is not the same as murdering a neighbor. And if there are degrees of lawbreaking, then should there not also be degrees of punishment?"

"I will explain it once again, Ndemi," I said, "for the day will come that you take my place as the *mundumugu*, and when that day arrives, your authority must be absolute. And that means that the punishment for anyone who refuses to recognize your authority must also be absolute."

He stared at me for a long moment. "This is wrong," he said at last.

"What is?"

"You have not called down the drought because she has broken the law," he answered. "You have brought this suffering to Kirinyaga because she disobeyed *you*."

"They are one and the same thing," I said.

He sighed deeply and furrowed his youthful brow in thought. "I am not sure of that."

That was when I knew that he would not be ready to be the *mundumugu* for a long, long time.

On the day that the drought was five months old, Koinnage made another trip to the hill, and this time there was no yelling. He stayed and spoke to Mumbi for perhaps five minutes, and then, without even looking toward me, he walked back to the village.

And twenty minutes later, Mumbi climbed up to the top of the hill and stood before the gate to my *boma*.

"I am returning to Koinnage's *shamba*," she announced.

An enormous surge of relief swept over me. "I knew that sooner or later you would see that you were wrong," I said.

"I am not returning because *I* am wrong," she said, "but because *you* are, and I cannot allow more harm to come to Kirinyaga because of it." She paused. "Kibo's milk has gone dry, and her baby is dying. My grandchildren have almost nothing left to eat." She glared at me. "You had better bring the rains today, old man."

"I will ask Ngai to bring the rains as soon as you have returned to your home," I promised her.

"You had better do more than *ask* Him," she said. "You had better *order* Him."

"That is blasphemy."

"How will you punish me for my blasphemy?" she said. "Will you bring forth a flood and destroy even more of our world?"

"I have destroyed nothing," I said. "It was you who broke the law."

"Look out at the dry river, Koriba," she said, pointing down the hill. "Study it well, for it is Kirinyaga, barren and unchanging."

I looked down upon the river. "Its changelessness is one of its virtues," I said.

"But it is a river," she said. "All *living* things change—even the Kikuyu."

"Not on Kirinyaga," I said adamantly.

"They change or they die," she continued. "I do not intend to die. You have won the battle, Koriba, but the war goes on."

Before I could answer her she turned and walked down the long, winding path to the village.

That afternoon I brought down the rains. The river filled with water, the fields turned green, the cattle and goats and the animals of the savannah slaked their thirst and renewed their strength, and the world of Kirinyaga returned to healthy, vigorous life.

But from that day forth, Njoro never again addressed me as *mzee*, the traditional term of respect the Kikuyu have always used to signify age and wisdom. Siboki built two large containers for water, each the size of a large hut, and threatened to harm anyone who came near them. Even Ndemi, who had previously absorbed everything I taught him without question, now seemed to consider and weigh each of my statements carefully before accepting it.

Kibo's baby had died, and Mumbi moved into her *boma* until Kibo regained her health, then built her own hut out in the fields of Koinnage's *shamba*. Since she was still officially living on his property, I chose to ignore it. She remained there until the next long rains, at which time she became so infirm that she finally had to move to the hut she had formerly occupied. Now that she needed the help of her family she accepted it, but Koinnage later told me that she never sang again after the day she left my hill.

As for myself, I spent many long days on my hill, watching the river flow past, clear and cool and unchanging, and wondering uneasily if I had somehow changed the course of that other, more important river through which we all must swim.

6

THE LOTUS AND THE SPEAR

{OCTOBER 2135}

Once, many eons ago, there was an elephant who climbed the slopes of Kirinyaga until he reached the very summit, where Ngai sat atop His golden throne.

"Why have you sought me out?" demanded Ngai.

"I have come to ask you to change me into something else," answered the elephant.

"I have made you the most powerful of beasts," said Ngai. "You need fear neither the lion nor the leopard nor the hyena. Wherever you walk, all My other creatures rush to move out of your path. Why do you no longer wish to be an elephant?"

"Because as powerful as I am, there are others of my kind who are more powerful," answered the elephant. "They keep the females to themselves, so that my seed will die within me, and they drive me away from the water holes and the succulent grasses."

"And what do you wish of me?" asked Ngai.

"I am not sure," said the elephant. "I would like to be like the giraffe, for there are so many treetops that no matter where he goes he finds sustenance. Or perhaps the warthog, for nowhere can he travel that there are no roots to be found. And the fish eagle takes one mate for life, and if he is not strong enough to defend her against others of his kind who would take her away from him, his vision is so keen that he can see them approaching from great distances and move her to safety. Change me in any way you wish," he concluded. "I will trust to Your wisdom."

"So be it," pronounced Ngai. "From this day forward, you shall have a trunk, so that the delicacies that grow atop the acacia trees will no longer be beyond your reach. And you shall have tusks, that you may dig in the ground for both roots and water no matter where you travel upon My world. And where the fish eagle has but a single superior sense, his vision, I shall give you two senses, those of smell and hearing, that will be greater than any other animal in My kingdom."

"How can I thank you?" asked the elephant joyously, as Ngai began the transformation.

"You may not wish to," answered Ngai.

"Why not?" asked the elephant.

"Because when all is said and done," said Ngai, "you will still be an elephant."

Some days it is easy to be the *mundumugu* on our terraformed world of Kirinyaga. On such days, I bless the scarecrows in the fields, distribute charms and ointments to the ailing, tell stories to the children, offer my opinions to the Council of Elders, and teach my youthful assistant, Ndemi, the lore of the Kikuyu people—for the *mundumugu* is more than a maker of charms and curses, more even than a voice of reason in the Council of Elders: he is the repository of all the traditions that make the Kikuyu what they are.

Some days it is difficult to be the *mundumugu*. When I must decide disputes, one side will always be unhappy with me. Or when there is an illness that I cannot cure, and I know that soon I will be telling the sufferer's family to leave him out for the hyenas. Or when Ndemi, who will someday be the *mundumugu*, gives every indication that he will not be ready to assume my duties when my body, already old and wrinkled, reaches the point, not too long off, when it is no longer able to function.

And, once in a long while, it is terrible to be the *mundumugu*, for I am presented with a problem against which all the accumulated wisdom of the Kikuyu seems like a reed in the wind.

Such a day begins like any other. I awake from my slumber and walk out of my hut into my *boma* with my blanket wrapped around my shoulders, for though it will soon be warm the sun has not yet removed the chill from the air. I light a fire and sit next to it, waiting for Ndemi, who will almost certainly be late. Sometimes I marvel at the facility of his imagination, for never has he given me the same excuse twice.

As I grow older, I have taken to chewing a *qat* leaf in the morning to start the blood flowing through my body. Ndemi disapproves, for he has been taught the uses of *qat* as a medicine and he knows that it is addictive. I will explain to him again that without it I would probably be in constant pain until the sun was overhead, that when you are as old as I am your muscles and joints do not always respond to your commands and can fill you with agony, and he will shrug and nod his head and forget again by the following morning.

Eventually he will arrive, my young assistant, and after he explains why he was late today, he will take my gourds down to the river and fill them with water, and then gather firewood and bring it to my *boma*. Then we will embark upon our daily lesson, in which perhaps I will explain to him how to make an ointment out of the pods of the acacia tree, and he will sit and try not to squirm and will demonstrate such self-control that he may well listen to me for ten or twelve minutes before asking when I will teach him how to turn an enemy into an insect so that he may stamp on him.

Finally I will take him into my hut, and teach him the rudiments of my computer, for after I am dead it will be Ndemi who will have to contact Maintenance and request the orbital adjustments that will affect the seasons, that will bring rain to the parched plains, that will make the days longer or shorter to give the illusion of seasonal changes.

Then, if it is to be an ordinary day, I will fill my pouch with charms and will begin walking through the fields, warding off any *thahu*, or curse, that has been placed on them, and assuring that they will continue to yield the food we need to survive, and if the rains have come and the land is green, perhaps I will slaughter a goat to thank Ngai for His beneficence.

If it is not to be an ordinary day, I usually know at the outset. Perhaps there will be hyena dung in my *boma*, a sure sign of a *thahu*, or the wind may come from the west, whereas all good winds blow from the east.

But on the day in question, there was no wind at all, and no hyenas had been in my *boma* the night before. It began like any other day. Ndemi was late—this time, he claimed, because there was a black mamba on the path up my hill, and he had to wait until it finally slithered off into the tall grasses—and I had just finished teaching him the prayer for health and long life that he must recite at the birth of a new baby, when Koinnage, the paramount chief of the village, walked up to my *boma*.

"*Jambo*, Koinnage," I greeted him, dropping my blanket to the ground, for the sun was now overhead and the air was finally warm.

"*Jambo*, Koriba," he replied, a worried frown on his face.

I looked at him expectantly, for it is very rare for Koinnage to climb my hill and visit me in my *boma*.

"It has happened again," he announced grimly. "This is the third time since the long rains."

"What has happened?" I asked, confused.

"Ngala is dead," said Koinnage. "He walked out naked and unarmed among the hyenas, and they killed him."

"Naked and unarmed?" I repeated. "Are you certain?"

"I am certain."

I squatted down near my dying fire, lost in thought. Keino was the first young man we had lost. We had thought it was an accident, that he had stumbled and somehow fallen upon his own spear. Then came Njupo, who burned to death when his hut caught fire while he was inside it.

Keino and Njupo lived with the young, unmarried men in a small colony by the edge of the forest, a few kilometers from the main village. Two such deaths might have been coincidence, but now there was a third, and it cast a new light on the first two. It was now obvious that, within the space of a few brief months, three young men had chosen to commit suicide rather than continue their lives on Kirinyaga.

"What are we to do, Koriba?" asked Koinnage. "My own son lives at the edge of the forest. He could be the next one!"

I took a round, polished stone from the pouch about my neck, stood up, and handed it to him.

"Place this beneath your son's sleeping blanket," I said. "It will protect him from this *thahu* that is affecting our young men."

"Thank you, Koriba," he said gratefully. "But can you not provide charms for *all* the young men?"

"No," I replied, still greatly disturbed by what I had heard. "That stone is only for the son of a chief. And just as there are all kinds of charms, there are all kinds of curses. I must determine who has placed this *thahu* on our young men, and why. Then and only then can I create strong enough magic to combat it." I paused. "Can Ndemi bring you some *pombe* to drink?"

He shook his head. "I must return to the village. The women are wailing the death chant, and there is much to be done. We must burn Ngala's hut and purify the ground upon which it rested, and we must post guards to make sure that the hyenas, having feasted so easily, do not come back in search of more human flesh."

He turned and took a few steps toward the village, then stopped.

"Why is this happening, Koriba?" he asked, his eyes filled with puzzlement. "And is the *thahu* limited just to the young men, or do the rest of us bear it, too?"

I had no answer for him, and after a moment he resumed walking down the path that led to the village.

I sat down next to my fire and stared silently out over the fields and savannah until Ndemi finally sat down next to me.

"What kind of *thahu* would make Ngala and Keino and Njupo all kill themselves, Koriba?" he asked, and I could tell from his tone that he was frightened.

"I am not sure yet," I replied. "Keino was very much in love with Mwala, and he was very unhappy when old Siboki was able to pay the bride-price for her before he himself could. If it were just Keino, I would say that he ended his life because he could not have her. But now two more have died, and I must find the reason for it."

"They all live in the village of young men by the edge of the forest," said Ndemi. "Perhaps *it* is cursed."

I shook my head. "They have not all killed themselves."

"You know," said Ndemi, "when Nboka drowned in the river two rains ago, we all thought it was an accident. But he, too, lived in the village of young men. Perhaps he killed himself as well."

I had not thought of Nboka in a long time. I thought of him now, and realized that he could very well have committed suicide. Certainly it made sense, for Nboka was known to be a very strong swimmer.

"I think perhaps you are right," I replied reluctantly.

Ndemi's chest puffed up with pride, for I do not often compliment him.

"What kind of magic will you make, Koriba?" he asked. "If it requires the feathers of the crested crane or the maribou stork, I could get them for you. I have been practicing with my spear."

"I do not know what magic I shall make yet, Ndemi," I told him. "But whatever it is, it will require thought and not spears."

"That is too bad," he said, shielding his eyes from the dust that a sudden warm breeze brought to us. "I thought I had finally found a use for it."

"For what?"

"For my spear," he said. "I no longer herd cattle on my father's *shamba*, now that I am helping you, so I no longer need it." He shrugged. "I think I shall leave it at home from now on."

"No, you must always take it with you," I said. "It is customary for all Kikuyu men to carry spears."

He looked inordinately proud of himself, for I had called him a man, when in truth he was just a *kehee*, an uncircumcised boy. But then he frowned again.

"Why do we carry spears, Koriba?" he asked.

"To protect us from our enemies."

"But the Maasai and Wakamba and other tribes, and even the Europeans, remain in Kenya," he said. "What enemies have we here?"

"The hyena and the jackal and the crocodile," I answered, and added silently: *And one other enemy, which must be identified before we lose any more of our young men, for without them there is no future, and ultimately no Kirinyaga.*

"It has been a long time since anyone needed a spear against a hyena," continued Ndemi. "They have learned to fear us and avoid us." He pointed to the domestic animals that were grazing in the nearby fields. "They do not even bother the goats and the cattle anymore."

"Did they not bother Ngala?" I asked.

"He *wanted* to be eaten by hyenas," said Ndemi. "That is different."

"Nonetheless, you must carry your spear at all times," I said. "It is part of what makes you a Kikuyu."

"I have an idea!" he said, suddenly picking up his spear and studying it. "If I *must* carry a spear, perhaps I should have one with a metal tip, so that it will never warp or break."

I shook my head. "Then you would be a Zulu, who live far to the south of Kenya, for it is the Zulus who carry metal-tipped spears, which they call *assagais*."

Ndemi looked crestfallen. "I thought it was my own idea," he said.

"Do not be disappointed," I said. "An idea can be new to you and old to someone else."

"Really?"

I nodded. "Take these young men who have killed themselves.

The idea of suicide is new to them, but they are not the first to think of it. We have *all* thought of killing ourselves at one time or another. What I must learn is not why they have finally thought of it, but why they have not rejected the thought, why it has become *attractive* to them."

"And then you will use your magic to make it unattractive?" asked Ndemi.

"Yes."

"Will you boil poisonous serpents in a pot with the blood of a freshly killed zebra?" he asked eagerly.

"You are a very bloodthirsty boy," I said.

"A *thahu* that can kill four young men requires powerful magic," he replied.

"Sometimes just a word or a sentence is all the magic one needs."

"But *if* you need more ..."

I sighed deeply. "If I need more, I will tell you what animals to slay for me."

He leaped to his feet, picked up his slender wooden spear, and made stabbing motions in the air. "I will become the most famous hunter ever!" he shouted happily. "My children and grandchildren will sing songs of praise to me, and the animals of the field will tremble at my approach!"

"But before that happy day arrives," I said, "there is still the water to be fetched and the firewood to be gathered."

"Yes, Koriba," he said. He picked up my water gourds and began walking down the hill, and I could tell that in his imagination he was still confronting charging buffalos and hurling his spear straight and true to the mark.

I gave Ndemi his morning lesson—the prayer for the dead seemed a proper topic—and then went down to the village to comfort Ngala's parents. His mother, Liswa, was inconsolable. He had been her first-born, and it was all but impossible to get her to stop wailing the death chant long enough for me to express my sorrow.

Kibanja, Ngala's father, stood off by himself, shaking his head in disbelief.

"Why would he do such a thing, Koriba?" he asked as I approached him.

"I do not know," I answered.

"He was the boldest of boys," he continued. "Even you did not frighten him." He stopped suddenly for fear that he had given offense.

"He was very bold," I agreed. "And bright."

"That is true," agreed Kibanja. "Even when the other boys would lie up beneath the shade trees during the heat of the day, my Ngala was always finding new games to play, new things to do." He looked at me through tortured eyes. "And now my only son is dead, and I do not know why."

"I will find out," I told him.

"It is wrong, Koriba," he continued. "It is against the nature of things. I was meant to die first, and then all that I own—my *shamba*, my cattle, my goats—everything would have been his." He tried to hold back his tears, for although the Kikuyu are not as arrogant as the Maasai, our men do not like to display such emotions in public. But the tears came anyway, making moist paths down his dusty cheeks before falling onto the dirt. "He did not even live long enough to take a wife and present her with a son. All that he was has died with him. What sin did he commit to merit such a dreadful *thahu*? Why could it not have struck *me* down and let him live?"

I remained with him a few more minutes, assured him that I would ask Ngai to welcome Ngala's spirit, and then I began walking to the colony of young men, which was about three kilometers beyond the village. It backed up to a dense forest, and was bordered to the south by the same river that wound through the village and broadened as it passed my hill.

It was a small colony, composed of no more than twenty young men. As each had undergone the circumcision ritual and passed into manhood, he had moved out from his father's *boma* and taken up residence here with the other bachelors of the village. It was a transitional dwelling place, for eventually each member would marry and take over part of his family's *shamba*, to be replaced by the next group of young men.

Most of the residents had gone to the village when they heard the death chants, but a few of them had remained behind to burn Ngala's hut and destroy the evil spirits within it. They greeted me gravely, as befitted the occasion, and asked me to utter the chant that would purify the ground so that they would not forever be required to avoid stepping on it.

When I was done, I placed a charm at the very center of the ashes, and then the young men began drifting away—all but Murumbi, who had been Ngala's closest friend.

"What can you tell me about this, Murumbi?" I asked when we were finally alone.

"He was a good friend," he replied. "We spent many long days together. I will miss him."

"Do you know why he killed himself?"

"He did not kill himself," answered Murumbi. "He was killed by hyenas."

"To walk naked and unarmed among the hyenas is to kill oneself," I said.

Murumbi continued staring at the ashes. "It was a stupid way to die," he said bitterly. "It solved nothing."

"What problem do you think he was trying to solve?" I asked.

"He was very unhappy," said Murumbi.

"Were Keino and Njupo also unhappy?"

He looked surprised. "You know?"

"Am I not the *mundumugu*?" I replied.

"But you said nothing when they died."

"What do you think I should have said?" I asked.

Murumbi shrugged his shoulders. "I don't know." He paused. "No, there was nothing you could have said."

"What about you, Murumbi?" I said.

"Me, Koriba?"

"Are you unhappy?"

"As you said, you are the *mundumugu*. Why ask questions to which you already know the answers?"

"I would like to hear the answer from your own lips," I replied.

"Yes, I am unhappy."

"And the other young men?" I continued. "Are they unhappy too?"

"Most of them are very happy," said Murumbi, and I noticed just the slightest edge of contempt in his tone. "Why should they not be? They are men now. They spend their days in idle talk, and painting their faces and their bodies, and at nights they go to the village and drink *pombe* and dance. Soon some of them will marry and sire children and start *shambas* of their own, and someday they will sit in the Council of Elders." He spat on the ground. "Indeed, there is no reason why they should not be happy, is there?"

"None," I agreed.

He stared defiantly at me.

"Perhaps you would like to tell me the reason for *your* unhappiness?" I suggested.

"Are you not the *mundumugu*?" he said caustically.

"Whatever else I am, I am not your enemy."

He sighed deeply, and the tension seemed to drain from his body, to be replaced by resignation. "I know you are not, Koriba," he said. "It is just that there are times when I feel like this entire world is my enemy."

"Why should that be?" I asked. "You have food to eat and *pombe* to drink, you have a hut to keep you warm and dry, there are only Kikuyu here, you have undergone the circumcision ritual and are now a man, you live in a world of plenty ... so why should you feel that such a world is your enemy?"

He pointed to a black she-goat that was grazing placidly a few yards away.

"Do you see that goat, Koriba?" he asked. "She accomplishes more with her life than I do with mine."

"Don't be silly," I said.

"I am being serious," he replied. "Every day she provides milk for the village, once a year she produces a kid, and when she dies it will almost certainly be as a sacrifice to Ngai. She has a purpose to her life."

"So have we all."

He shook his head. "That is not so, Koriba."

"You are bored?" I asked.

"If the journey through life can be likened to a journey down a broad river, then I feel that I am adrift with no land in sight."

"But you *have* a destination in sight," I said. "You will take a wife, and start a *shamba*. If you work hard, you will own many cattle and goats. You will raise many sons and daughters. What is wrong with that?"

"Nothing," he said, "if *I* had anything to do with it. But my wife will raise my children and till my fields, and my sons will herd my animals, and my daughters will weave the fabric for my garments and help their mothers cook my food." He paused. "And I ... I will sit around with the other men, and discuss the weather, and drink *pombe*, and someday, if I live long enough, I will join the Council of Elders, and the only thing that will change is that I will now talk to my friends in Koinnage's *boma* instead of my own. And then one day I will die. *That* is the life I must look forward to, Koriba."

He kicked the ground with his foot, sending up little flurries of dust. "I will *pretend* that my life has more meaning than that of a she-goat," he continued. "I will walk ahead of my wife while she carries the firewood, and I will tell myself that I am doing this to protect her from attack by the Maasai or the Wakamba. I will build my *boma* taller than a man's head and lay thorns across the top of it, and tell myself that this is to protect my cattle against the lion and the leopard, and I will try not to remember that there have never been any lions or leopards on Kirinyaga. I will never be without my spear, though I do nothing but lean on it when the sun is high in the sky, and I will tell myself that without it I could be torn to pieces by man or beast. All these things I will tell myself, Koriba ... but I will know that I am lying."

"And Ngala and Keino and Njupo felt the same way?" I said.

"Yes."

"Why did they kill themselves?" I asked. "It is written in our charter that anyone who wishes to leave Kirinyaga may do so. They need only have walked to that area known as Haven, and a Maintenance ship would have picked them up and taken them anywhere they wished to go."

"You still do not understand, do you?" he said.

"No, I do not," I admitted. "Enlighten me."

"Men have reached the stars, Koriba," he said. "They have medicines and machines and weapons that are beyond our imagining. They live in cities that dwarf our village." He paused again. "But here on Kirinyaga, we live the life that we lived before the Europeans came and brought the forerunners of such things with them. We live as the Kikuyu have always lived, as you say we were meant to live. How, then, can we go back to Kenya? What could we do? How would we feed and shelter ourselves? The Europeans changed us from Kikuyu into Kenyans once before, but it took many years and many generations. You and the others who created Kirinyaga meant no harm, you only did what you thought was right, but you have seen to it that I can never become a Kenyan. I am too old, and I am starting too far behind."

"What about the other young men of your colony?" I asked. "How do they feel?"

"Most of them are content, as I said. And why shouldn't they be? The hardest work they were ever forced to do was to nurse at their mothers' breasts." He looked into my eyes. "You have offered them a dream, and they have accepted it."

"And what is *your* dream, Murumbi?"

He shrugged. "I have ceased to dream."

"I do not believe that," I said. "Every man has a dream. What would it take to make you content?"

"Truly?"

"Truly."

"Let the Maasai come to Kirinyaga, or the Wakamba, or the Luo," he said. "I was trained to be a warrior. Therefore, give me a reason to carry my spear, to walk unfettered ahead of my wife when her back is bent under her burden. Let us raid their *shambas* and carry off their women and their cattle, and let them try to do the same for us. Do not *give* us new land to farm when we are old enough; let us *compete* for it with the other tribes."

"What you are asking for is war," I said.

"No," replied Murumbi. "What I am asking for is *meaning*. You mentioned my wife and children. I cannot afford the bride-price for a wife, nor will I be able to unless my father dies and leaves me his cattle, or asks me to move back to his *shamba*." He stared at me with reproachful eyes. "Don't you realize that the only result is to make me wish for his charity or his death? It is better far to steal women from the Maasai."

"That is out of the question," I said. "Kirinyaga was created for the Kikuyu, as was the original Kirinyaga in Kenya."

"I know that is what we believe, just as the Maasai believe that Ngai created Kilimanjaro for them," said Murumbi. "But I have been thinking about it for many days, and do you know what *I* believe? I believe that the Kikuyu and Maasai were created for each other, for when we lived side by side in Kenya, each of us gave meaning and purpose to the other."

"That is because you are not aware of Kenya's history," I said. "The Maasai came down from the north only a century before the Europeans. They are nomads, wanderers, who follow their herds from one grazing area to another. The Kikuyu are farmers, who have always lived beside the holy mountain. We lived side by side with the Maasai for only a handful of years."

"Then bring us the Wakamba, or the Luo, or the Europeans!" he said, trying to control his frustration. "You still don't understand what I am saying. It is not the Maasai I want, it is the challenge!"

"And this is what Keino and Njupu and Nboka wanted?"

"Yes."

"And will you kill yourself, as they did, should a challenge not materialize?"

"I do not know. But I do not want to live a life filled with boredom."

"How many others in the colony of young men feel as you do?"

"Right now?" asked Murumbi. "Only myself." He paused and stared unblinking at me. "But there have been others before; there will be again."

"I do not doubt it," I replied with a heavy sigh. "Now that I understand the nature of the problem, I will return to my *boma* and think about how best to solve it."

"This problem is beyond your ability to solve, *mundumugu*," said Murumbi, "for it is part of the society that you have fought so hard to preserve."

"No problem is incapable of solution," I said.

"This one is," answered Murumbi with absolute conviction.

I left him standing there by the ashes, not totally convinced that he was wrong.

For three days I sat alone on my hill. I neither went into the village nor conferred with the Elders. When old Siboki needed more ointment for his pain, I sent Ndemi down the path with it, and when it was time to place new charms on the scarecrows, I instructed Ndemi to tend to the matter, for I was wrestling with a far more serious problem.

In some cultures, I knew, suicide was an honorable way of dealing with certain problems, but the Kikuyu did not belong to such a culture.

Furthermore, we had built a Utopia here, and to admit that suicides would occur from time to time meant that it was not a Utopia for all our people, which in turn meant that it was not a Utopia at all.

But we had built our Utopia along the lines of a traditional Kikuyu society, that which existed in Kenya before the advent of the Europeans. It was the Europeans who forcefully introduced change into that society, not the Kikuyu, and therefore I could not allow Murumbi to change the way we lived, either.

The most obvious answer was to encourage him—and others like him—to emigrate to Kenya, but this seemed out of the question. I myself had received higher degrees in both England and America, but the majority of Kikuyu on Kirinyaga had been those (considered fanatics by a Kenyan government that was glad to be rid of them) who had insisted on living in the traditional way prior to coming to Kirinyaga. This meant that not only could they not cope with the technology that permeated every layer of Kenyan society, but also that they did not even possess the tools to learn, for they could neither read nor write.

So Murumbi, and those who would surely follow him, could not leave Kirinyaga for Kenya or any other destination. That meant they must remain.

If they remained, there were only three alternatives that I could see, all of them equally unpalatable.

First, they could eventually give up in despair and kill themselves, as four of their young comrades had. This I could not permit.

Second, they could eventually adjust to the life of ease and idleness that was the lot of the Kikuyu male, and come to enjoy and defend it as passionately as did the other men of the village. This I could not foresee.

Third, I could take Murumbi's suggestion and open up the northern plains to the Maasai or the Wakamba, but this would make a mockery of all our efforts to establish Kirinyaga as a world for and of the Kikuyu. This I could not even consider, for I would not allow a war that would destroy *our* Utopia in order to create *his*.

For three days and three nights I searched for another alternative.

On the morning of the fourth day, I emerged from my hut, my blanket wrapped tightly about me to protect me from the cold morning air, and lit my fire.

Ndemi was late, as usual. When he finally arrived, he was favoring his right foot, and explained that he had twisted it on his way up my hill—but I noticed, without surprise, that he limped on his left foot when he went off to fill my gourds with water.

When he returned, I watched him as he went about his duties, collecting firewood and removing fallen leaves from my *boma*. I had chosen him to be my assistant, and my eventual successor, because he was the boldest and brightest of the village children. It was Ndemi who always thought of new games for the others to play, and he himself was always the leader. When I would walk among them, he was the first to demand that I tell them a parable, and the quickest to understand the hidden meaning in it.

In short, he was a perfect candidate to commit suicide in a few more years, had I not averted that possibility by encouraging him to become my assistant.

"Sit down, Ndemi," I said as he finished collecting the last of the leaves and throwing them on the dying embers of my fire.

He sat down next to me. "What will we study today, Koriba?" he asked.

"Today we will just talk," I said. His face fell, and I added, "I have a problem, and I am hoping that you will provide me with an answer to it."

Suddenly he was alert and enthused. "The problem is the young men who killed themselves, isn't it?" he said.

"That is correct," I answered him. "Why do you suppose they did it?"

He shrugged his scrawny shoulders. "I do not know, Koriba. Perhaps they were crazy."

"Do you really think so?"

He shrugged again. "No, not really. Probably an enemy has cursed them."

"Perhaps."

"It must be so," he said firmly. "Is not Kirinyaga a Utopia? Why else would anyone not wish to live here?"

"I want you to think back, Ndemi, to the time before you started coming to my *boma* every day."

"I can remember," he said. "It was not that long ago."

"Good," I replied. "Now, can you also remember what you wanted to do?"

He smiled. "To play. And to hunt."

I shook my head. "I do not mean what you wanted to do *then*," I said. "Can you remember what you wanted to do when you were a man?"

He frowned. "Take a wife, I suppose, and start a *shamba*."

"Why do you frown, Ndemi?" I asked.

"Because that is not really what I wanted," he replied. "But it was all I could think of to answer."

"Think harder," I said. "Take as much time as you wish, for this is very important. I will wait."

We sat in silence for a long moment, and then he turned to me.

"I do not know. But I would not have wanted to live as my father and my brothers live."

"What *would* you have wanted?"

He shrugged helplessly. "Something different."

"Different in what way?"

"I do not know," he said again. "Something more ..."—he searched for the word—"more *exciting*." He considered his answer, then nodded, satisfied. "Even the impala grazing in the fields lives a more exciting life, for he must ever be wary of the hyena."

"But wouldn't the impala rather that there were no hyenas?" I suggested.

"Of course," said Ndemi, "for then he could not be killed and eaten." He furrowed his brow in thought. "But if there were no hyenas, he would not need to be fleet of foot, and if he were no longer fleet of foot, he would no longer be an impala."

And with that, I began to see the solution.

"So it is the hyena that makes the impala what he is," I said. "And therefore, even something that seems to be a bad or dangerous thing can be necessary to the impala."

He stared at me. "I do not understand, Koriba."

"I think that I must become a hyena," I said thoughtfully.

"Right now?" asked Ndemi excitedly. "May I watch?"

I shook my head. "No, not right now. But soon."

For if it was the threat of the hyena that defined the impala, then I had to find a way to define those young men who had ceased to be true Kikuyus and yet could not leave Kirinyaga.

"Will you have spots and legs and a tail?" asked Ndemi eagerly.

"No," I replied. "But I will be a hyena nonetheless."

"I do not understand," said Ndemi.

"I do not expect you to," I said. "But Murumbi will."

For I realized that what he needed was a challenge that could be provided by only one person on Kirinyaga.

And that person was myself.

I sent Ndemi to the village to tell Koinnage that I wanted to address the Council of Elders. Then, later that day, I put on my ceremonial headdress, painted my face to look its most frightening, and, filling my pouch with various charms, I made my way to the village, where Koinnage had assembled all the Elders in his *boma*. I waited patiently for him to announce that I had important matters to discuss with them—for even the *mundumugu* may not speak before the paramount chief—and then I got to my feet and faced them.

"I have cast the bones," I said. "I have read the entrails of a goat, and I have studied the pattern of the flies on a newly dead lizard. And now I know why Ngala walked unarmed among the hyenas, and why Keino and Njupo died."

I paused for dramatic effect, and made sure that I had everyone's attention.

"Tell us who caused the *thahu*," said Koinnage, "that we may destroy him."

"It is not that simple," I answered. "Hear me out. The carrier of the *thahu* is Murumbi."

"I will kill him!" cried Kibanja, who had been Ngala's father. "He is the reason my son is dead!"

"No," I said. "You must not kill him, for he is not the source of the *thahu*. He is merely the carrier."

"If a cow drinks poisoned water, she is not the source of her bad milk, but we must kill her anyway," insisted Kibanja.

"It is not Murumbi's fault," I said firmly. "He is as innocent as your own son, and he must not be killed."

"Then who *is* responsible for the *thahu*?" demanded Kibanja. "I will have blood for my son's blood!"

"It is an old *thahu*, cast upon us by a Maasai back when we still lived in Kenya," I said. "He is dead now, but he was a very clever *mundumugu*, for his *thahu* lives on long after him." I paused. "I have fought him in the spirit world, and most of the time I have won, but once in a while my magic is weak, and on those occasions the *thahu* is visited upon one of our young men."

"How can we know which of our young men bears the *thahu*?" asked Koinnage. "Must we wait for them to die before we know they have been cursed?"

"There are ways," I answered. "But they are known only to myself. When I have finished telling you what you must do, I will visit all the other villages and seek out the colonies of young men to see if any of them also bears the *thahu*."

"Tell us what we must do," said old Siboki, who had come to hear me despite the pain in his joints.

"You will not kill Murumbi," I repeated, "for it is not his fault that he carries this *thahu*. But we do not want him passing it to others, so from this day forward he is an outcast. He must be driven from his hut and never allowed back. Should any of you offer him food or shelter, the same *thahu* will befall you and your families. I want runners sent to all the nearby villages, so that by tomorrow morning they all know that he must be shunned, and I want them in turn to send out still more runners, so that within three days no village on Kirinyaga will welcome him."

"That is a terrible punishment," said Koinnage, for the Kikuyu are a compassionate people. "If the *thahu* is not his fault, can we not at least set food out for him at the edge of the village? Perhaps if he comes alone by night, and sees and speaks to no one else, the *thahu* will remain with him alone."

I shook my head. "It must be as I say, or I cannot promise that the *thahu* will not spread to all of you."

"If we see him in the fields, can we not acknowledge him?" persisted Koinnage.

"If you see him, you must threaten him with your spears and drive him away," I answered.

Koinnage sighed deeply. "Then it shall be as you say. We will drive him from his hut today, and we will shun him forever."

"So be it," I said, and left the *boma* to return to my hill.

All right, Murumbi, I thought. *Now you have your challenge. You have been raised not to use your spear; now you will eat only what your spear can kill. You have been raised to let your women build your huts; now you will be safe from the elements only in those huts that you yourself build. You have been raised to live a life of ease; now you will live only by your wits and your energies. No one will help you, no one will give you food or shelter, and I will not rescind my order. It is not a perfect solution, but it is the best I can contrive under the circumstances. You needed a challenge and an enemy; now I have provided you with both.*

I visited every village on Kirinyaga during the next month, and spent much time speaking to the young men. I found two more who had to be driven out and forced to live in the wilderness, and now, along with my other duties, such visits have become part of my regular schedule.

There have been no more suicides, and no more unexplained deaths among our young men. But from time to time I cannot help wondering what must become of a society, even a Utopia such as Kirinyaga, where our best and our brightest are turned into outcasts, and all that remains are those who are content to eat the fruit of the lotus.

7

A LITTLE KNOWLEDGE

{JULY 2136}

There was a time when animals could speak.

Lions and zebras, elephants and leopards, birds and men all shared the Earth. They labored side by side, they met and spoke of many things, they exchanged visits and gifts.

Then one day Ngai summoned all of His creations to meet with Him.

"I have done everything I can to make life good for all My creatures," said Ngai. The assembled animals and men began to sing His praises, but Ngai held up His hand, and they immediately stopped.

"I have made life *too* good for you," He continued. "None among you has died for the past year."

"What is wrong with that?" asked the zebra.

"Just as you are constrained by your natures," said Ngai, "just as the elephant cannot fly and the impala cannot climb trees, so I cannot be dishonest. Since no one has died, I cannot feel compassion for you, and without compassion, I cannot water the savannah and the forest with my tears. And without water, the grasses and the trees will shrivel and die."

There was much moaning and wailing from the creatures, but again Ngai silenced them.

"I will tell you a story," He said, "and you must learn from it.

"Once there were two colonies of ants. One colony was very wise, and one colony was very foolish, and they lived next to each other. One day they received word that an aardvark, a creature that eats ants, was coming to their land. The foolish colony went about their business, hoping that the aardvark would ignore them and attack their neighbors. But the wise colony built a mound that could withstand even the efforts of an aardvark, and they gathered sugar and honey, and stockpiled it in the mound.

"When the aardvark reached the kingdom of the ants, he immediately attacked the wise ants, but the mound withstood his greatest efforts, and the ants within survived by eating their sugar and honey. Finally, after many fruitless days, the aardvark wandered over to the kingdom of the foolish ants, and dined well that evening."

Ngai fell silent, and none of His creatures dared ask Him to speak further. Instead, they returned to their homes and discussed His story, and made their preparations for the coming drought.

A year passed, and finally the men decided to sacrifice an innocent goat, and that very day Ngai's tears fell upon the parched and barren land. The next morning Ngai again summoned His creatures to the holy mountain.

"How have you fared during the past year?" He asked each of them.

"Very badly," moaned the elephant, who was very thin and weak. "We did as you instructed us, and built a mound, and gathered sugar and honey—but we grew hot and uncomfortable within the mound, and there is not enough sugar and honey in all the world to feed a family of elephants."

"We have fared even worse," wailed the lion, who was even thinner, "for lions cannot eat sugar and honey at all, but must have meat."

And so it went, as each animal poured out its misery. Finally Ngai turned to the man and asked him the same question.

"We have fared very well," replied the man. "We built a container for water, and filled it before the drought came, and we stockpiled enough grain to last us to this day."

"I am very proud of you," said Ngai. "Of all my creatures, only you understood my story."

"It is not fair!" protested the other animals. "We built mounds and saved sugar and honey, as you told us to!"

"What I told you was a parable," said Ngai, "and you have mistaken the facts of it for the truth that lay beneath. I gave you the power to think, but since you have not used it, I hereby take it away. And as a further punishment, you will no longer have the ability to speak, for creatures that do not think have nothing to say."

And from that day forth, only man, among all Ngai's creations, has had the power to think and speak, for only man can pierce through the facts to find the truth.

You think you know a person when you have worked with him and trained him and guided his thinking since he was a small boy. You think you can foresee his reactions to various situations. You think you know how his mind works.

And if the person in question has been chosen by you, selected from the mass of his companions and groomed for something special, as young Ndemi was selected and groomed by me to be my successor as the *mundumugu* to our terraformed world of Kirinyaga, the one thing you think above all else is that you possess his loyalty and his gratitude.

But even a *mundumugu* can be wrong.

I do not know exactly when or how it began. I had chosen Ndemi to be my assistant when he was still a *kehee*—an uncircumcised child—and I had worked diligently with him to prepare him for the position he would one day inherit from me. I chose him not for his boldness, though he feared nothing, nor for his enthusiasm, which was boundless, but rather for his intellect, for with the exception of one small girl, long since dead, he was by far the brightest of the children on Kirinyaga. And since we had emigrated to this world to create a Kikuyu paradise, far from the corrupt imitation of Europe that Kenya had become, it was imperative that the *mundumugu* be the wisest of men, for the *mundumugu* not only reads omens and casts spells, but is also the repository for the collected wisdom and culture of his tribe.

Day by day I added to Ndemi's limited storehouse of knowledge. I taught him how to make medicine from the bark and pods of the acacia tree, I showed him how to create the ointments that would ease the discomfort of the aged when the weather turned cold and wet, I made him memorize the hundred spells that were used to bless the scarecrows in the field. I told him a thousand parables, for the Kikuyu have a parable for every need and every occasion, and the wise *mundumugu* is the one who finds the right parable for each situation.

And finally, after he had served me faithfully for six long years, coming up my hill every morning, feeding my chickens and goats, lighting the fire in my *boma*, and filling my empty water gourds before his daily lessons began, I took him into my hut and showed him how my computer worked.

There are only four computers on all of Kirinyaga. The others belong to Koinnage, the paramount chief of our village, and to two chiefs of distant clans, but their computers can do nothing but send and receive messages. Only mine is tied into the data banks of the Eutopian Council, the ruling body that had given Kirinyaga its charter, for only the *mundumugu* has the strength and the vision to be exposed to European culture without becoming corrupted by it.

One of the primary purposes of my computer was to plot the orbital adjustments that would bring seasonal changes to Kirinyaga, so that the rains would come on schedule and the crops would flourish and the harvest would be successful. It was perhaps the *mundumugu*'s most important obligation to his people, since it assured their survival. I spent many long days teaching Ndemi all the many intricacies of the computer, until he knew its workings as well as I myself did, and could speak to it with perfect ease.

The morning that I first noticed the change in him began like any other. I awoke, wrapped my blanket around my withered shoulders, and walked painfully out of my hut to sit by my fire until the warming rays of the sun took the chill from the air. And, as always, there was no fire.

Ndemi came up the path to my hill a few minutes later.

"*Jambo*, Koriba," he said, greeting me with his usual smile.

"*Jambo*, Ndemi," I said. "How many times have I explained to you that I am an old man, and that I must sit by my fire until the air becomes warmer?"

"I am sorry, Koriba," he said. "But as I was leaving my father's *shamba*, I saw a hyena stalking one of our goats, and I had to drive it off." He held his spear up, as if that were proof of his statement.

I could not help but admire his ingenuity. It was perhaps the thousandth time he had been late, and never had he given the same excuse twice. Still, the situation was becoming intolerable, and when he finished his chores and the fire had warmed my bones and eased my pain, I told him to sit down opposite me.

"What is our lesson for today?" he asked as he squatted down.

"The lesson will come later," I said, finally letting my blanket fall from my shoulders as the first warm breeze of the day blew a fine cloud of dust past my face. "But first I will tell you a story."

He nodded, and stared intently at me as I began speaking.

"Once there was a Kikuyu chief," I said. "He had many admirable qualities. He was a mighty warrior, and in council his words carried great weight. But along with his many good qualities, he also had a flaw.

"One day he saw a maiden tilling the fields in her father's *shamba*, and he was smitten with her. He meant to tell her of his love the very next day, but as he set out to see her, his way was blocked by an elephant, and he retreated and waited until the elephant had passed. When he finally arrived at the maiden's *boma*, he discovered that a young warrior was paying her court. Nevertheless, she smiled at him when their eyes met, and, undiscouraged, he made up his mind to visit her the following day. This time a deadly snake blocked his way, and once again, when he arrived he found the maiden being courted by his rival. Once more she gave him an encouraging smile, and so he decided to come back a third time.

"On the morning of the third day, he lay on his blanket in his hut, and thought about all the many things he wanted to tell her to impress her with his ardor. By the time he had decided upon the best approach to win her favor, the sun was setting. He ran all the way from his *boma* to that of the maiden, only to find that his rival had just paid her father five cattle and thirty goats for her hand in marriage.

"He managed to get the maiden alone for a moment, and poured forth his litany of love.

" 'I love you too,' she answered, 'but although I waited for you each day, and hoped that you would come, you were always late.'

" 'I have excuses to offer,' he said. 'On the first day I encountered an elephant, and on the second day a killer snake was in my path.' He did not dare tell her the real reason he was late a third time, so he said, 'And today a leopard confronted me, and I had to kill it with my spear before I could continue on my way.'

" 'I am sorry,' said the maiden, 'but I am still promised to another.'

" 'Do you not believe me?' he demanded.

" 'It makes no difference whether you are telling the truth or not,' she replied. 'For whether the lion and the snake and the leopard are real or whether they are lies, the result is the same: you have lost your heart's desire because you were late.' "

I stopped and stared at Ndemi. "Do you understand the moral of my story?" I asked.

He nodded. "It does not matter to you whether a hyena was stalking my father's goat or not. All that matters is that I was late."

"That is correct," I said.

This is where such things had always ended, and then we would begin his lessons. But not this day.

"It is a foolish story," he said, looking out across the vast savannah.

"Oh?" I asked. "Why?"

"Because it begins with a lie."

"What lie?"

"The Kikuyu had no chiefs until the British created them," he answered.

"Who told you that?" I asked.

"I learned it from the box that glows with life," he said, finally meeting my gaze.

"My computer?"

He nodded again. "I have had many long discussions about the Kikuyu with it, and I have learned many things." He paused. "We did not even live in villages until the time of the Mau Mau, and then the British *made* us live together so that we could be more easily watched. And it was the British who created our tribal chiefs, so that they could rule us through them."

"That is true," I acknowledged. "But it is unimportant to my story."

"But your story was untrue with its first line," he said, "so why should the rest of it be true? Why did you not just say, 'Ndemi, if you are late again, I will not care whether your reason is true or false. I will punish you.'"

"Because it is important for you to understand *why* you must not be late."

"But the story is a lie. Everyone knows that it takes more than three days to court and purchase a wife. So it began with a lie and it ended with a lie."

"You are looking at the surface of things," I said, watching a small insect crawl over my foot and finally flicking it off. "The truth lies beneath."

"The truth is that you do not want me to be late. What has that to do with the elephant and the leopard, which were extinct before we came to Kirinyaga?"

"Listen to me, Ndemi," I said. "When you become the *mundumugu*, you will have to impart certain values, certain lessons, to your people—and you must do so in a way that they understand. This is especially true of the children, who are the clay that you will mold into the next generation of Kikuyu."

Ndemi was silent for a long moment. "I think you are wrong, Koriba," he said at last. "Not only will the people understand you if you speak plainly to them, but stories like the one you just told me are filled with lies which they will think are true simply because they come from the *mundumugu*'s lips."

"No!" I said sharply. "We came to Kirinyaga to live as the Kikuyu lived before the Europeans tried to change us into that characterless tribe known as Kenyans. There is a poetry to my stories, a tradition to them. They reach out to our racial memory, of the way things were, and the way we hope to make them again." I paused to consider which path to follow, for never before had Ndemi so bluntly opposed my teachings. "You yourself used to beg me for stories, and of all the children you were the quickest to find the true meaning of them."

"I was younger then," he said.

"You were a Kikuyu then," I said.

"I am still a Kikuyu."

"You are a Kikuyu who has been exposed to European knowledge and European history," I said. "This is unavoidable, if you are to succeed me as the *mundumugu*, for we hold our charter at the whim of the Europeans, and you must be able to speak to them and work their machine. But your greatest challenge, as a Kikuyu and a *mundumugu*, is to avoid becoming corrupted by them."

"I do not *feel* corrupted," he said. "I have learned many things from the computer."

"So you have," I agreed, as a fish eagle circled lazily overhead and the breeze brought the smell of a nearby herd of wildebeest. "And you have forgotten many things."

"What have I forgotten?" he demanded, watching the fish eagle swoop down and grab a fish from the river. "You may test me and see how good my memory is."

"You have forgotten that the true value of a story is that the listener must bring something to it," I said. "I could simply order you not to be late, as you suggest—but the purpose of the story is to make you use your brain to understand *why* you should not be late." I paused. "You are also forgetting that the reason we do not try to become like the Europeans is because we tried once before, and became only Kenyans."

He was silent for a long time. Finally he looked up at me.

"May we skip today's lesson?" he asked. "You have given me much to think about."

I nodded my acquiescence. "Come back tomorrow, and we will discuss your thoughts."

He stood up and walked down the long, winding path that led from my hill to the village.

But though I waited for him until the sun was high in the sky the next day, he did not come back.

Just as it is good for fledgling birds to test their wings, it is good for young people to test *their* powers by questioning authority. I bore Ndemi no malice, but simply waited until the day that he returned, somewhat humbled, to resume his studies.

But the fact that I now had no assistant did not absolve me of my duties, and so each day I walked down to the village, and blessed the scarecrows, and took my place alongside Koinnage in the Council of Elders. I brought new ointment for old Siboki's joints, which were causing him discomfort, and I sacrificed a goat so that Ngai would look with favor upon the pending marriage of Maruta with a man of another clan.

As always, when I made my rounds, I was followed everywhere by the village children, who begged me to stop what I was doing and tell them a story. For two days I was too busy, for a *mundumugu* has many tasks to perform, but on the morning of the third day I had some time to spare, and I gathered them around me in the shade of an acacia tree.

"What kind of story would you like to hear?" I asked.

"Tell us of the old days, when we still lived in Kenya," said a girl.

I smiled. They always asked for stories of Kenya—not that they knew where Kenya was, or what it meant to the Kikuyu. But when we lived in Kenya the lion and the rhinoceros and the elephant were not yet extinct, and they loved stories in which animals spoke and displayed greater wisdom than men, a wisdom that they themselves assimilated as I repeated the stories.

"Very well," I said. "I will tell you the story of the Foolish Lion."

They all sat or squatted down in a semicircle, facing me with rapt attention, and I continued: "Once there was a foolish lion who lived on the slopes of Kirinyaga, the holy mountain, and because he was a foolish lion, he did not believe that Ngai had given the mountain to Gikuyu, the very first man. Then one morning—"

"That is wrong, Koriba," said one of the boys.

I focused my weak eyes on him, and saw that it was Mdutu, the son of Karenja.

"You have interrupted your *mundumugu*," I noted harshly. "And, even worse, you have contradicted him. Why?"

"Ngai did not give Kirinyaga to Gikuyu," said Mdutu, getting to his feet.

"He most certainly did," I replied. "Kirinyaga belongs to the Kikuyu."

"That cannot be so," he persisted, "for Kirinyaga is not a Kikuyu name, but a Maasai name. *Kiri* means *mountain* in the language of Maa, and *nyaga* means *light*. Is it not more likely that Ngai gave the mountain to the Maasai, and that our warriors took it away from them?"

"How do you know what these words mean in the language of

the Maasai?" I demanded. "That language is not known to anyone on Kirinyaga."

"Ndemi told us," said Mdutu.

"Well, Ndemi is wrong!" I shouted. "The truth has been passed on from Gikuyu through his nine daughters and his nine sons-in-law all the way down to me, and never has it varied. The Kikuyu are Ngai's chosen people. Just as He gave the spear and Kilimanjaro to the Maasai, He gave the digging stick and Kirinyaga to us. Kirinyaga has always belonged to the Kikuyu, and it always will!"

"No, Koriba, you are wrong," said a soft, high-pitched voice, and I turned to face my new assailant. It was tiny Thimi, the daughter of Njomu, barely seven years old, who rose to contradict me.

"Ndemi told us that many years ago the Kikuyu sold Kirinyaga to a European named John Boyes for six goats, and it was the British government that made him return it to us."

"Who do you believe?" I demanded severely. "A young boy who has lived for only fifteen long rains, or your *mundumugu*?"

"I do not know," she answered with no sign of fear. "He tells us dates and places, and you speak of wise elephants and foolish lions. It is very hard to decide."

"Then perhaps instead of the story of the Foolish Lion," I said, "I will tell you the story of the Arrogant Boy."

"No, no, the lion!" shouted some of the children.

"Be quiet!" I snapped. "You will hear what *I* want to tell you!"

Their protests subsided, and Thimi sat down again.

"Once there was a bright young boy," I began.

"Was his name Ndemi?" asked Mdutu with a smile.

"His name was Legion," I answered. "Do not interrupt again, or I shall leave and there will be no more stories until the next rains."

The smile vanished from Mdutu's face, and he lowered his head.

"As I said, this was a very bright boy, and he worked on his father's *shamba*, herding the goats and cattle. And because he was a bright young boy, he was always thinking, and one day he thought of a way to make his chores easier. So he went to his father and said that he had had a dream, and in this dream they had built a wire enclosure with sharp barbs on the wire, to keep the cattle in and the hyenas out, and he was sure that if he were to build such an enclosure, he would no longer have to herd the cattle but would be free to do other things.

" 'I am glad to see that you are using your brain,' said the boy's father, 'but that idea has been tried before, by the Europeans. If you wish to free yourself from your duties, you must think of some other way.'

" 'But why?' said the boy. 'Just because the Europeans thought of it does not make it bad. After all, it must work for *them* or they would not use it.'

" 'That is true,' said his father. 'But what works for the Europeans does not necessarily work for the Kikuyu. Now do your chores, and keep thinking, and if you think hard enough I am sure you will come up with a better idea.'

"But along with being bright, the boy was also arrogant, and he refused to listen to his father, even though his father was older and wiser and more experienced. So he spent all his spare time attaching sharp little barbs to the wire, and when he was done he built an enclosure and put his father's cattle into it, sure that they could not get out and the hyenas could not find a way in. And when the enclosure was completed, he went to sleep for the night."

I paused and surveyed my audience. Most of them were staring raptly at me, trying to figure out what came next.

"He awoke to screams of anger from his father and wails of anguish from his mother and sisters, and ran out to see what had happened. He found all of his father's cattle dead. During the night the hyenas, whose jaws can crush a bone, had bitten through the posts to which the wire was attached, and the cattle, in their panic, ran into the wire and were held motionless by the barbs while the hyenas killed and ate them.

"The arrogant boy looked upon the carnage with puzzlement. 'How can this have happened?' he said. 'The Europeans have used this wire, and it never happened to them.'

" 'There are no hyenas in Europe,' said his father. 'I told you that we are different from the Europeans, and that what works for them will not work for us, but you refused to listen, and now we must live our lives in poverty, for in a single night your arrogance cost me the cattle that it has taken me a lifetime to accumulate.' "

I fell silent and waited for a response.

"Is that all?" asked Mdutu at last.

"That is all."

"What did it mean?" asked another of the boys.

"You tell *me*," I said.

Nobody answered for a few moments. Then Balimi, Thimi's older sister, stood up.

"It means that only Europeans can use wire with barbs on it."

"No," I said. "You must not only listen, child, but *think*."

"It means that what works for the Europeans will not work for the Kikuyu," said Mdutu, "and that it is arrogant to believe that it will."

"That is correct," I said.

"That is *not* correct," said a familiar voice from behind me, and I turned to see Ndemi standing there. "All it means is that the boy was too foolish to cover the posts with the wire."

The children looked at him, and began nodding their heads in agreement.

"No!" I said firmly. "It means that we must reject all things European, including their ideas, for they were not meant for the Kikuyu."

"But why, Koriba?" asked Mdutu. "What is wrong with what Ndemi says?"

"Ndemi tells you only the facts of things," I said. "But because he, too, is an arrogant boy, he fails to see the truth."

"What truth does he fail to see?" persisted Mdutu.

"That if the wire enclosure were to work, then the next day the arrogant boy would borrow another idea from the Europeans, and yet another, until he had no Kikuyu ideas left, and he had turned his *shamba* into a European farm."

"Europe is an exporter of food," said Ndemi. "Kenya is an importer."

"What does that mean?" asked Thimi.

"It means that Ndemi has a little knowledge, and does not yet know that that is a dangerous thing," I answered.

"It means," responded Ndemi, "that European farms produce more than enough to feed their tribes, and Kenyan farms do not produce enough. And if that is the case, it means that some European ideas may be good for the Kikuyu."

"Perhaps you should wear shoes like the Europeans," I said angrily, "since you have decided to become one."

He shook his head. "I am a Kikuyu, not a European. But I do not wish to be an ignorant Kikuyu. How can we remain true to what we were, when your fables hide what we were from us?"

"No," I said. "They *reveal* it."

"I am sorry, Koriba," said Ndemi, "for you are a great *mundumugu* and I respect you above all men, but in this matter you are wrong." He paused and stared at me. "Why did you never tell us that the only time in our history the Kikuyu were united under the leadership of a single king, the king was a white man named John Boyes?"

The children gasped in amazement.

"If we do not know how it happened," continued Ndemi, "how can we prevent it from happening again? You tell us stories of our wars against the Maasai, and they are wonderful tales of courage and victory—but according to the computer, we lost every war we ever fought against them. Shouldn't we know that, so if the Maasai ever come to Kirinyaga, we are not deluded into fighting them because of the fables we have heard?"

"Koriba, is that true?" asked Mdutu. "Was our only king a European?"

"Did we never defeat the Maasai?" asked another of the children.

"Leave us for a moment," I said, "and then I will answer you."

The children reluctantly got up and walked away until they were out of earshot, then stood and stared at Ndemi and myself.

"Why have you done this?" I said to Ndemi. "You will destroy their pride in being Kikuyu!"

"I am not less proud for knowing the truth," said Ndemi. "Why should they be?"

"The stories I tell them are designed to make them distrust European ways, and to make them happy they are Kikuyu," I explained, trying to control my temper. "You will undermine the confidence they must have if Kirinyaga is to remain our Utopia."

"Most of us have never seen a European," answered Ndemi. "When I was younger, I used to dream about them, and in my dreams they had claws like a lion and shook the earth like an elephant when they walked. How does that prepare us for the day that we actually meet with them?"

"You will never meet them on Kirinyaga," I said. "And the purpose of my stories is to *keep* us on Kirinyaga." I paused. "Once before we had never seen Europeans, and we were so taken by their machines and their medicines and their religions that we tried to become Europeans ourselves, and succeeded only in becoming something other than Kikuyu. That must never happen again."

"But isn't it less likely to happen if you tell the children the truth?" persisted Ndemi.

"I *do* tell them the truth!" I said. "It is *you* who are confusing them with facts—facts that you got from European historians and a European computer."

"Are the facts wrong?"

"That is not the issue, Ndemi," I said. "These are *children*. They must learn as children do—as you yourself did."

"And after their circumcision rituals, when they become adults, will you tell them the facts then?"

That sentence was as close to rebellion as he had ever come—indeed, as *anyone* on Kirinyaga had ever come. Never had I been more fond of a young man than I was of Ndemi—not even of my own son, who had chosen to remain in Kenya. Ndemi was bright, he was bold, and it was hardly unusual for one of his age to question authority. Therefore, I decided to make another attempt to reason with him, rather than risk a permanent rift in our relationship.

"You are still the brightest young man on Kirinyaga," I said truthfully, "so I will pose you a question, and I will expect an honest answer. You seek after history, and I seek after truth. Which do you suppose is the more important?"

He frowned. "They are the same," he answered. "History *is* truth."

"No," I replied. "History is a compilation of facts and events, which is subject to constant reinterpretation. It begins with truth and evolves into fable. My stories begin with fable and evolve into truth."

"If you are right," he said thoughtfully, "then your stories are more important than history."

"Very well, then," I said, hoping that the matter was closed.

"But," he added, "I am not sure that you are right. I will have to think more about it."

"Do that," I said. "You are an intelligent boy. You will come to the right conclusion."

Ndemi turned and began walking off in the direction of his family's *shamba*. The children rushed back as soon as he was out of sight, and once more squatted in a tight semicircle.

"Have you an answer to my question, Koriba?" asked Mdutu.

"I cannot recall your question," I said.

"Was our only king a white man?"

"Yes."

"How could that be?"

I considered my response for a long moment.

"I will answer that by telling you the story of the little Kikuyu girl who became, very briefly, the queen of all the elephants," I said.

"What has that to do with the white man who became our king?" persisted Mdutu.

"Listen carefully," I instructed him, "for when I am done, I shall ask you many questions about my story, and before we are through, you will have the answer to your own question."

He leaned forward attentively, and I began reciting my fable.

I returned to my *boma* to take the noon meal. After I had finished it, I decided to take a nap during the heat of the day, for I am an old man and it had been a long, wearing morning. I let my goats and chickens loose on my hillside, secure in the knowledge that no one would take them away since they each carried the *mundumugu's* mark. I had just spread my sleeping blanket out beneath the branches of my acacia tree when I saw two figures at the foot of my hill.

At first I thought they were two village boys, looking for cattle that had strayed from their pastures, but when the figures began walking up the slopes of my hill I was finally able to focus my eyes on them. The larger figure was Shima, Ndemi's mother, and the smaller was a goat that she led by a rope that she had tied around its neck.

Finally she reached my *boma*, somewhat out of breath, for the goat was unused to the rope and constantly pulled against it, and opened the gate.

"*Jambo*, Shima," I said, as she entered the *boma*. "Why have you brought your goat to my hill? You know that only my own goats may graze here."

"It is a gift for you, Koriba," she replied.

"For me?" I said. "But I have done you no service in exchange for it."

"You can, though. You can take Ndemi back. He is a good boy, Koriba."

"But—"

"He will never be late again," she promised. "He truly did save our goat from a hyena. He would never lie to his *mundumugu*. He is young, but he can become a great *mundumugu* someday. I know he can, if you will just teach him. You are a wise man, Koriba, and you have made a wise choice in Ndemi. I do not know why you have banished him, but if you will just take him back he will never misbehave again. He wants only to become a great *mundumugu* like yourself. Though of course," she added hastily, "he could never be as great as you."

"Will finally you let me speak?" I asked irritably.

"Certainly, Koriba."

"I did not cast Ndemi out. He left of his own volition."

Her eyes widened. "*He* left *you?*"

"He is young, and rebellion is part of youth."

"So is foolishness!" she exclaimed furiously. "He has *always* been foolish. *And* late! He was even two weeks late being born when I carried him! He is always thinking, instead of doing his chores. For the longest time I thought we had been cursed, but then you made him your assistant, and I was to become the mother of the *mundumugu*—and now he has ruined everything!"

She let go of the rope, and the goat wandered around my *boma* as she began beating her breasts with her fists.

"Why am *I* so cursed?" she demanded. "Why does Ngai give me a fool for a son, and then stir my hopes by sending him to you, and then curse me doubly by returning him, almost a man and unable to perform any of the chores on our *shamba?* What will become of him? Who will accept a bride-price from such a fool? He will be late to plant our seed and late to harvest it, he will be late to choose a bride and late to make the payment on her, and he will end up living with the unmarried men at the edge of the forest and begging for food. With my luck he will even be late to die!" She paused for breath, then began wailing again, and finally screamed: "Why does Ngai hate me so?"

"Calm yourself, Shima," I said.

"It is easy for *you* to say!" she sobbed. "You have not lost all hope for your future."

"My future is of very limited duration," I said. "It is Kirinyaga's future that concerns me."

"See?" she said, wailing and beating her breasts again. "See? I am the mother of the boy who will destroy Kirinyaga!"

"I did not say that."

"What has he done, Koriba?" she said. "Tell me, and I will have his father and brothers beat him until he behaves."

"Beating him is not the solution," I said. "He is young, and he rebels against my authority. It is the way of things. Before long he will realize that he is wrong."

"I will explain to him all that he can lose, and he will know that he should never disagree with you, and he will come back."

"You might suggest it," I encouraged her. "I am an old man, and I have much left to teach him."

"I will do as you say, Koriba," she promised.

"Good," I said. "Now go back to your *shamba* and speak to Ndemi, for I have other things to do."

It was not until I awoke from my nap and returned to the village to sit at the Council of Elders that I realized just how many things I had to do.

Our daily business is always conducted in late afternoon, when the heat of the day has passed, at the *boma* of Koinnage, the paramount chief. One by one the Elders place their mats in a semicircle and sit on them, with my place being at Koinnage's right hand. The *boma* is cleared of all women, children, and animals, and when the last of us has arrived, Koinnage calls us into session. He announces what problems are to be considered, and then I ask Ngai to guide our judgment and allow us to come to just decisions.

On this particular day, two of the villagers had asked the Council of Elders to determine the ownership of a calf that was born to a cow they jointly owned; Sebana wanted permission to divorce his youngest wife, who had now been barren for three years; and Kijo's three sons were unhappy with the way his estate had been divided among them.

Koinnage consulted with me in low whispers after each petition had been heard, and took my advice, as always. The calf went to the man who had fed the cow during her pregnancy, with the understanding that the other man should own the next calf. Sebana was told that he could divorce his wife, but would not receive the bride-price back, and he elected to keep her. Kijo's sons were told that they could accept the division as it was, or if two of them agreed, I would place three colored stones in a gourd, and they could each withdraw a stone and own the *shamba* that it represented. Since each faced the possibility of ending up with the smallest *shamba*, only one brother voted for our solution, as I had foreseen, and the petition was dismissed.

At this point, Koinnage's senior wife, Wambu, would usually appear with a large gourd of *pombe*, and we would drink it and then return to our *bomas*, but this day Wambu did not come, and Koinnage turned nervously to me.

"There is one thing more, Koriba," he said.

"Oh?"

He nodded, and I could see the muscles in his face tensing as he worked up the courage to confront his *mundumugu*.

"You have told us that Ngai handed the burning spear to Jomo Kenyatta, that he might create Mau Mau and drive the Europeans from Kenya."

"That is true," I said.

"Is it?" he replied. "I have been told that he himself married a European woman, that Mau Mau did *not* succeed in driving the Europeans from the holy mountain, and that Jomo Kenyatta was not even his real name—that he was actually born with the European name Johnstone." He stared at me, half-accusing, half-terrified of arousing my wrath. "What have you to say to this, Koriba?"

I met his gaze and held it for a long time, until he finally dropped his eyes. Then, one by one, I looked coldly at each member of the Council.

"So you prefer to believe a foolish young boy to your own *mundumugu*?" I demanded.

"We do not believe the boy, but the computer," said Karenja.

"And have you spoken to the computer yourselves?"

"No," said Koinnage. "That is another thing we must discuss.

Ndemi tells me that your computer speaks to him and tells him many things, while *my* computer can do nothing but send messages to the other chiefs."

"It is a *mundumugu's* tool, not to be used by other men," I replied.

"Why?" asked Karenja. "It knows many things that we do not know. We could learn much from it."

"You *have* learned much from it," I said. "It speaks to me, and I speak to you."

"But it also speaks to Ndemi," continued Karenja, "and if it can speak to a boy barely past circumcision age, why can it not speak directly to the Elders of the village?"

I turned to Karenja and held my two hands in front of me, palms up. "In my left hand is the meat of an impala that I killed today," I said. "In my right is the meat of an impala that I killed five days ago and left to sit in the sun. It is covered with ants, worms crawl through it, and it stinks." I paused. "Which of the two pieces of meat will you eat?"

"The meat in your left hand," he answered.

"But both pieces of meat came from the same herd of impala," I pointed out. "Both animals were equally fat and healthy when they died."

"But the meat in your right hand is rotten," he said.

"That is true," I agreed. "And just as there can be good and bad meat, so there can be good and bad facts. The facts Ndemi has related to you come from books written by the Europeans, and facts can mean different things to them than they mean to us."

I paused while they considered what I had said, and then continued. "A European may look upon the savannah and envision a city, while a Kikuyu may look at the same savannah and see a *shamba*. A European may look at an elephant and see ivory trinkets, while a Kikuyu may look at the same elephant and see food for his village, or destruction for his crops. And yet they are looking at the same land, and the same animal.

"Now," I said, once again looking at each of them in turn, "I have been to school in Europe, and in America, and only I, of all the men and women on Kirinyaga, have lived among the white man. And I tell you that only I, your *mundumugu*, am capable of separating the good facts from the bad facts. It was a mistake to allow Ndemi to speak with my computer; I will not allow it again, until I have given him more of my wisdom."

I had thought my statement would put an end to the matter, but as I looked around I saw signs of discomfort, as if they wished to argue with me but lacked the courage. Finally Koinnage leaned forward and, without looking directly at me, said, "Do you not see what you are saying, Koriba? If the *mundumugu* can make a mistake by allowing a young boy to speak with his computer, can he not also make a mistake by not allowing the Elders to speak to it?"

I shook my head. "It is a mistake to allow *any* Kikuyu except the *mundumugu* to speak to it."

"But there is much that we can learn from it," persisted Koinnage.

"What?" I asked bluntly.

He shrugged helplessly. "If I knew, then I would already have learned it."

"How many times must I repeat this to you: there is nothing to be learned from the Europeans. The more you try to become like them, the less you remain Kikuyu. This is *our* Utopia, a *Kikuyu* Utopia. We must fight to preserve it."

"And yet," said Karenja, "even the word Utopia is European, is it not?"

"You heard that from Ndemi, too?" I asked without hiding the annoyance in my voice.

He nodded his head. "Yes."

"Utopia is just a word," I said. "It is the *idea* that counts."

"If the Kikuyu have no word for it and the Europeans do, perhaps it is a European idea," said Karenja. "And if we have built our world upon a European idea, perhaps there are other European ideas that we can also use."

I looked at their faces, and realized, for perhaps the first time, that most of the original Elders of Kirinyaga had died. Old Siboki remained, and I could tell by his face that he found European ideas even more abhorrent than I myself did, and there were two or three others, but this was a new generation of Elders, men who had come to maturity on Kirinyaga and could not remember the reasons we had fought so hard to come here.

"If you want to become black Europeans, go back to Kenya!" I snapped in disgust. "It is filled with them!"

"We are not black Europeans," said Karenja, refusing to let the matter drop. "We are Kikuyu who think it is possible that not all European ideas are harmful."

"Any idea that changes us is harmful," I said.

"Why?" asked Koinnage, his courage to oppose me growing as he realized that many of the Elders supported him. "Where is it written that a Utopia cannot grow and change? If that were the case, we would have ceased to be a Utopia the day the first baby was born on Kirinyaga."

"There are as many Utopias as there are races," I said. "None among you would argue that a Kikuyu Utopia is the same as a Maasai Utopia or a Samburu Utopia. By the same token, a Kikuyu Utopia cannot be a European Utopia. The closer you come to the one, the further you move from the other."

They had no answer to that, and I got to my feet.

"I am your *mundumugu*," I said. "I have never misled you. You have always trusted my judgment in the past. You must trust in it in this instance."

As I began walking out of the *boma*, I heard Karenja's voice behind me.

"If you were to die tomorrow, Ndemi would become our *mundumugu*. Are you saying we should trust his judgment as we trust yours?"

I turned to face him. "Ndemi is very young and inexperienced. You, as the Elders of the village, would have to use your wisdom to decide whether or not what he says is correct."

"A bird that has been caged all its life cannot fly," said Karenja, "just as a flower that has been kept from the sun will not blossom."

"What is your point?" I asked.

"Shouldn't we begin using our wisdom now, lest we forget how when Ndemi has become the *mundumugu*?"

This time it was I who had no answer, so I turned on my heel and began the long walk back to my hill.

For five days I fetched my own water and made my own fires, and then Ndemi returned, as I had known he would.

I was sitting in my *boma*, idly watching a herd of gazelles grazing across the river, when he trudged up the path to my hill, looking distinctly uncomfortable.

"*Jambo*, Ndemi," I said. "It is good to see you again."

"*Jambo*, Koriba," he replied.

"And how was your vacation?" I asked, but there is no Swahili word for *vacation* so I used the English term and the humor and sarcasm were lost on him.

"My father urged me to come back," he said, bending over to pet one of my goats, and I saw the welts on his back that constituted his "urging."

"I am glad to have you back, Ndemi," I said. "We have become like father and son, and it pains me when we argue, as I am sure it pains you."

"It *does* pain me," he admitted. "I do not like to disagree with you, Koriba."

"We have both made mistakes," I continued. "You argued with your *mundumugu*, and I allowed you access to information before you were mature enough to know what to do with it. We are both intelligent enough to learn from our mistakes. You are still my chosen successor. It shall be as if it never happened."

"But it *did* happen, Koriba," he said.

"We shall pretend it did not."

"I do not think I can do that," said Ndemi unhappily, protecting his eyes as a sudden wind blew dust across the *boma*. "I learned many things when I spoke to the computer. How can I unlearn them?"

"If you cannot unlearn them, then you will have to ignore them until you are older," I said. "*I* am your teacher. The computer is just a tool. You will use it to bring the rains, and to send an occasional message to Maintenance, and that is all."

A black kite swooped down and made off with a scrap of my morning meal that had fallen beside the embers of my fire. I watched it while I waited for Ndemi to speak.

"You appear troubled," I said, when it became apparent that he would not speak first. "Tell me what bothers you."

"It was you who taught me to think, Koriba," he said as various emotions played across his handsome young face. "Would you have me stop thinking now, just because I think differently than you do?"

"Of course I do not want you to stop thinking, Ndemi," I said, not without sympathy, for I understood the forces at war within him. "What good would a *mundumugu* be if he could not think? But just as there are right and wrong ways to throw a spear, there are right and wrong ways to think. I wish only to see you take the path of true wisdom."

"It will be greater wisdom if I come upon it myself," he said. "I must learn as many facts as I can, so that I can properly decide which are helpful and which are harmful."

"You are still too young," I said. "You must trust me until you are older, and better able to make those decisions."

"The facts will not change."

"No, but *you* will."

"But how can I know that change is for the good?" he asked. "What if you are wrong, and by listening to you until I become like you, I will be wrong too?"

"If you think I am wrong, why have you come back?"

"To listen, and decide," he said. "And to speak to the computer again."

"I cannot permit that," I said. "You have already caused great mischief among the tribe. Because of you, they are questioning everything I say."

"There is a reason for that."

"Perhaps you will tell me what it is?" I said, trying to keep the sarcasm from my voice, for I truly loved this boy and wished to win him back to my side.

"I have listened to your stories for many years now, Koriba," he said, "and I believe that I can use *your* method to show you the reason."

I nodded my head and waited for him to continue.

"This should be called the story of Ndemi," he said, "but because I am pretending to be Koriba, I shall call it the story of the Unborn Lion."

I plucked an insect from my cheek and rolled it between my fingers until the carapace cracked. "I am listening."

"Once there was an unborn lion who was very anxious to see the world," began Ndemi. "He spent much time talking about it to his unborn brothers. 'The world will be a wonderful place,' he assured them. 'The sun will always be shining, and the plains will be filled with fat, lazy impala, and all other animals will bow before us, for there shall be no animal mightier than us.'

"His brothers urged him to stay where he was. 'Why are you so anxious to be born?' they asked him. 'Here it is warm and safe, and we never hunger. Who knows what awaits us in the world?'

"But the unborn lion would hear none of it, and one night, while his mother and brethren slept, he stole out into the world. He could not see, so he nudged his mother and said, 'Where is the sun?' and she told him that the sun vanishes every evening, leaving the world cold and dark. 'At least when it comes back tomorrow, it will shine on fat, lazy impala that we will catch and eat,' he said, trying to console himself.

"But his mother said, 'There are no impala here, for they have migrated with the rains to the far side of the world. All that is left for us to eat is the buffalo. Their flesh is tough and tasteless, and they kill as many of us as we kill of them.'

" 'If my stomach is empty, at least my spirit will be full,' said the newly born lion, 'for all other animals will look upon us with fear and envy.'

" 'You are very foolish, even for a newly born cub,' said his mother. 'The leopard and the hyena and the eagle look upon you not as an object of envy, but rather as a tasty meal.'

" 'At least all of them will fear me when I am fully grown,' said the newly born lion.

" 'The rhinoceros will gore you with his horn,' said his mother, 'and the elephant will toss you high into the trees with his trunk. Even the black mamba will not step aside for you, and will kill you if you try to approach it.'

"The mother continued her list of all the animals that would neither fear nor envy the lion when he grew up, and finally he told her to speak no more.

" 'I have made a terrible mistake by being born,' he said. 'The world is not as I pictured it, and I will rejoin my brothers where they are warm and safe and comfortable.'

"But his mother merely smiled at him. 'Oh, no,' she said, not without compassion. 'Once you are born, whether it is of your own choosing or mine, you cannot ever go back to being an unborn lion. Here you are, and here you shall stay.' "

Ndemi looked at me, his story finished.

"It is a very wise story," I said. "I could not have done better myself. I knew the day I first made you my pupil that you would make a fine *mundumugu*."

"You still do not understand," he said unhappily.

"I understand the story perfectly," I replied.

"But it is a lie," said Ndemi. "I told it only to show you how easy it is to make up such lies."

"It is not easy at all," I corrected him. "It is an art, mastered by only a few—and now that I see that you have mastered it, it would be doubly hurtful to lose you."

"Art or not, it is a lie," he repeated. "If a child heard and believed it, he would be sure that lions could speak, and that babies can be born whenever they choose to be." He paused. "It would have been much simpler to tell you that once I have obtained knowledge, whether is was freely given or not, I cannot empty my mind and give it back. Lions have nothing to do with that." He paused for a long moment. "Furthermore, I do not *want* to give my knowledge back. I want to learn more things, not forget those that I already know."

"You must not say that, Ndemi," I urged him. "Especially now that I see that my teachings have taken root, and that your abilities as a creator of fables will someday surpass my own. You can be a great *mundumugu* if you will just allow me to guide you."

"I love and respect you as I do my own father, Koriba," he replied. "I have always listened and tried to learn from you, and I will continue to do so for as long as you will permit me. But you are not the only source of knowledge. I also wish to learn what your computer can teach me."

"When I decide you are ready."

"I am ready now."

"You are not."

His face reflected an enormous inner battle, and I could only watch until it was resolved. Finally he took a deep breath and let it out slowly.

"I am sorry, Koriba, but I cannot continue to tell lies when there are truths to be learned." He laid a hand on my shoulder. *"Kwaheri, mwalimu."* *Good-bye, my teacher.*

"What will you do?"

"I cannot work on my father's *shamba*," he said, "not after all that I have learned. Nor do I wish to live in isolation with the bachelors at the edge of the forest."

"What is left for you?" I asked.

"I shall walk to that area of Kirinyaga called Haven, and await the next Maintenance ship. I will go to Kenya and learn to read and write, and when I am ready, I will study to become an historian. And when I am a good enough historian, I will return to Kirinyaga and teach what I have learned."

"I am powerless to stop you from leaving," I said, "for the right to emigrate is guaranteed to all our citizens by our charter. But if you return, know that despite what we have been to one another, I will oppose you."

"I do not wish to be your enemy, Koriba," he said.

"I do not wish to have you as an enemy," I replied. "The bond between us has been a strong one."

"But the things I have learned are too important to my people."

"They are *my* people too," I pointed out, "and I have led them to this point by always doing what I think is best for them."

"Perhaps it is time for *them* to choose what is best."

"They are incapable of making that choice," I said.

"If they are incapable of making that choice, it is only because you have hoarded knowledge to which they have as much right as you do."

"Think very carefully before you do this thing," I said. "Despite my love for you, if you do anything to harm Kirinyaga, I will crush you like an insect."

He smiled sadly. "For six years I have asked you to teach me how to turn my enemies into insects so that I may crush them. Is this how I am finally to learn?"

I could not help but return his smile. I had an urge to stand up and throw my arms around him and hug him, but such behavior is unacceptable in a *mundumugu*, so I merely looked at him for a long moment and then said, "*Kwaheri*, Ndemi. You were the best of them."

"I had the best teacher," he replied.

And with that, he turned and began the long walk toward Haven.

The problems caused by Ndemi did not end with his departure.

Njoro dug a borehole near his hut, and when I explained that the

Kikuyu did not dig boreholes but carried their water from the river, he replied that surely *this* borehole must be acceptable, for the idea came not from the Europeans but rather the Tswana people far to the south of Kenya.

I ordered the boreholes to be filled in. When Koinnage argued that there were crocodiles in the river and that he would not risk the lives of our women simply to maintain what he felt was a useless tradition, I had to threaten him with a powerful *thahu*—that of impotency—before he agreed.

Then there was Kidogo, who named his firstborn Jomo, after Jomo Kenyatta, the Burning Spear. One day he announced that the boy was henceforth to be known as Johnstone, and I had to threaten him with banishment to another village before he relented. But even as he gave in, Mbura changed his own name to Johnstone and moved to a distant village even before I could order it.

Shima continued to tell anyone who would listen that I had forced Ndemi to leave Kirinyaga because he was occasionally late for his lessons, and Koinnage kept requesting a computer that was the equal of my own.

Finally, young Mdutu created his own version of a barbed-wire enclosure for his father's cattle, using woven grasses and thorns, making sure he wrapped them around the fenceposts. I had it torn down, and thereafter he always walked away when the other children circled around me to hear a story.

I began to feel like the Dutch boy in Hans Christian Andersen's fairy tale. As quickly as I put my finger in the dike to staunch the flow of European ideas, they would break through in another place.

And then a strange thing happened. Certain ideas that were *not* European, that Ndemi could not possibly have transmitted to the members of the village, began cropping up on their own.

Kibo, the youngest of Koinnage's three wives, rendered the fat from a dead warthog and began burning it at night, creating Kirinyaga's first lamp. Ngobe, whose arm was not strong enough to throw a spear with any accuracy, devised a very primitive bow and arrow, the first Kirinyagan ever to create such a weapon. Karenja created a wooden plow, so that his ox could drag it through the fields while his wives simply guided it, and soon all the other villagers were improvising plows and strangely shaped digging tools. Indeed, alien ideas that had been dormant since the creation of Kirinyaga were now springing forth on all fronts. Ndemi's words had opened a Pandora's box, and I did not know how to close it.

I spent many long days sitting alone on my hill, staring down at the village and wondering if a Utopia can evolve and still remain a Utopia.

And the answer was always the same: Yes, but it will not be the *same* Utopia, and it was my sacred duty to keep Kirinyaga a Kikuyu Utopia.

When I was convinced that Ndemi was not going to return, I began going down to the village each day, trying to decide which of the children was the brightest and most forceful, for it would take both brilliance and force to deflect the alien ideas that were infecting our world and turning it into something it was never meant to be.

I spoke only to the boys, for no female may be a *mundumugu*. Some, like Mdutu, had already been corrupted by listening to Ndemi—but those who had *not* been corrupted by Ndemi were even more hopeless, for a mind cannot open and close at will, and those who were unmoved by what he had to say were not bright enough for the tasks a *mundumugu* must perform.

I expanded my search to other villages, convinced that somewhere on Kirinyaga I would find the boy I sought, a boy who grasped the difference between facts, which merely informed, and parables, which not only informed but *instructed*. I needed a Homer, a Jesus, a Shakespeare, someone who could touch men's souls and gently guide them down the path that must be taken.

But the more I searched, the more I came to the realization that a Utopia does not lend itself to such tellers of tales. Kirinyaga seemed divided into two totally separate groups: those who were content with their lives and had no need to think, and those whose every thought led them further and further from the society we had labored to build. The unimaginative would never be capable of creating parables, and the imaginative would create their own parables, parables that would not reaffirm a belief in Kirinyaga and a distrust of alien ideas.

After some months I was finally forced to concede that, for whatever reason, there were no potential *mundumugus* waiting to be found and groomed. I began wondering if Ndemi had been truly unique, or if he would have eventually rejected my teachings even without exposure to the European influence of the computer. Was it possible that a true Utopia could not outlast the generation that founded it, that it was the nature of man to reject the values of the society into which he is born, even when those values are sacred?

Or was it just conceivable that Kirinyaga had *never* been a Utopia, that somehow we had deluded ourselves into believing that we could go back to a way of life that had forever vanished?

I considered that possibility for a long time, but eventually I rejected it, for if it were true, then the only logical conclusion was that it had vanished because the Europeans' values were more pleasing to Ngai than our own, and this I knew to be false.

No, if there was a truth anywhere in the universe, it was that Kirinyaga was exactly as it was meant to be—and if Ngai felt obligated to test us by presenting us with these heresies, that would make our ultimate victory over the lies of the Europeans all the more sweet. If minds were worth anything, they were worth fighting for, and when Ndemi returned, armed with his facts and his data and his numbers, he would find me waiting for him.

It would be a lonely battle, I thought as I carried my empty water gourds down to the river, but having given His people a second chance to build their Utopia, Ngai would not allow us to fail. Let Ndemi tempt our people with his history and his passionless statistics. Ngai had His own weapon, the oldest and truest weapon He possessed, the weapon that had created Kirinyaga and kept it pure and intact despite all the many challenges it had encountered.

I looked into the water and studied the weapon critically. It appeared old and frail, but I could also see hidden reservoirs of strength, for although the future appeared bleak, it could not fail as long as it was used in Ngai's service. It stared back at me, bold and unblinking, secure in the rightness of its cause.

It was the face of Koriba, the last storyteller among the Kikuyu, who stood ready to battle once again for the soul of his people.

8

WHEN THE OLD GODS DIE

{ MAY 2137 }

Ngai created the Sun and the Moon, and declared that they should
have equal domain over the Earth.

The Sun would bring warmth to the world, and all of Ngai's
creatures would thrive and grow strong in the light. And when the
light vanished and Ngai slept, He ordered the Moon to watch over
His creations.

But the Moon was duplicitous, and formed a secret alliance with
the Lion and the Leopard and the Hyena, and many nights, while
Ngai slept, it would turn only a part of its face to the Earth. At such
times the predators would go forth to maim and kill and eat their fellow creatures.

Finally one man, a *mundumugu*, realized that the Moon had tricked
Ngai, and he made up his mind to correct the problem. He might
have appealed to Ngai, but he was a proud man, and so he took it

upon himself to make certain that the flesh-eaters would no longer have a partnership with the darkness.

He retired to his *boma* and allowed no visitors. For nine days and nine nights he rolled his bones and arranged his charms and mixed his potions, and when he emerged on the morning of the tenth day, he was ready to do what must be done.

The Sun was overhead, and he knew that there could be no darkness as long as the Sun shone down upon the Earth. He uttered a mystic chant, and soon he was flying into the sky to confront the Sun.

"Halt!" he said. "Your brother the Moon is evil. You must remain where you are, lest Ngai's creatures continue to die."

"What is that to me?" responded the Sun. "I cannot shirk my duty simply because my brother shirks his."

The *mundumugu* held up a hand. "I will not let you pass," he said.

But the Sun merely laughed, and proceeded on its path, and when it reached the *mundumugu* it gobbled him up and spat out the ashes, for even the greatest *mundumugu* cannot stay the Sun from its course.

That story has been known to every *mundumugu* since Ngai created Gikuyu, the first man. Of them all, only one ignored it.

I am that *mundumugu*.

It is said that from the moment of birth, even of conception, every living thing has embarked upon an inevitable trajectory that culminates in its death. If this is true of all living things, and it seems to be, then it is also true of man. And if it is true of man, then it must be true of the gods who made man in their image.

Yet this knowledge does not lessen the pain of death. I had just come back from comforting Katuma, whose father, old Siboki, had finally died, not from disease or injury, but rather from the awful burden of his years. Siboki had been one of the original colonists on our terraformed world of Kirinyaga, a member of the Council of Elders, and though he had grown feeble in mind as well as body, I knew I would miss him as I missed few others.

As I walked back through the village, on the long, winding path by the river that eventually led to my own *boma*, I was very much aware of my own mortality. I was not that much younger than Siboki, and indeed was already an old man when we left Kenya and emigrated to Kirinyaga. I knew my death could not be too far away, and yet I hoped that it was, not from selfishness, but because Kirinyaga was not yet ready to do without me. The *mundumugu* is more than a shaman who utters curses and creates spells; he is the repository of all the moral and civil laws, all the customs and traditions, of the Kikuyu people, and I was not convinced that Kirinyaga had yet produced a competent successor.

It is a harsh and lonely life, the life of a *mundumugu*. He is more feared than loved by the people he serves. This is not his fault, but rather the nature of his position. He must do what he knows to be right for his people, and that means he must sometimes make unpopular decisions.

How strange, then, that the decision that brought me down had nothing at all to do with my people, but rather with a stranger.

Still, I should have had a premonition about it, for no conversation is ever truly random. As I was walking past the scarecrows in the fields on the way to my *boma*, I came across Kimanti, the young son of Ngobe, driving two of his goats home from their morning's grazing.

"*Jambo*, Koriba," he greeted me, shading his eyes from the bright overhead sun.

"*Jambo*, Kimanti," I said. "I see that your father now allows you to tend to his goats. Soon the day will come that he puts you in charge of his cattle."

"Soon," he agreed, offering me a water gourd. "It is a warm day. Would you like something to drink?"

"That is very generous of you," I said, taking the gourd and holding it to my mouth.

"I have always been generous to you, have I not, Koriba?" he said.

"Yes, you have," I replied suspiciously, wondering what favor he was preparing to request.

"Then why do you allow my father's right arm to remain shriveled and useless?" he asked. "Why do you not cast a spell and make it like other men's arms?"

"It is not that simple, Kimanti," I said. "It is not I who shriveled your father's arm, but Ngai. He would not have done so without a purpose."

"What purpose is served by crippling my father?" asked Kimanti.

"If you wish, I shall sacrifice a goat and ask Ngai why He has allowed it," I said.

He considered my offer and then shook his head. "I do not care to hear Ngai's answer, for it will change nothing." He paused, lost in thought for a moment. "How long do you think Ngai will be our god?"

"Forever," I said, surprised at his question.

"That cannot be," he replied seriously. "Surely Ngai was not our god when He was just a *mtoto*. He must have killed the old gods when He was young and powerful. But He has been god for a long time now, and it is time someone killed Him. Maybe the new god will show more compassion toward my father."

"Ngai created the world," I said. "He created the Kikuyu and the Maasai and the Wakamba, and even the European, and He created the holy mountain Kirinyaga, for which our world is named. He has existed since time began, and He will exist until it ends."

Kimanti shook his head again. "If He has been here that long, He is ready to die. It is just a matter of who will kill Him." He paused thoughtfully. "Perhaps I myself will, when I am older and stronger."

"Perhaps," I agreed. "But before you do, let me tell you the story of the King of the Zebras."

"Is this story about Ngai or zebras?" he asked.

"Why don't you listen?" I said. "Then, when I have finished, you can tell *me* what it was about."

I gently lowered myself to the ground, and he squatted down next to me.

"There was a time," I began, "when zebras did not have stripes.

They were as brown as the dried grasses on the savannah, as dull to the eye as the bole of the acacia tree. And because their color protected them, they were rarely taken by the lion and the leopard, who found it much easier to find and stalk the wildebeest and the topi and the impala.

"Then one day a son was born to the King of the Zebras—but it was not a normal son, for it had no nostrils. The King of the Zebras was first saddened for his son, and then outraged that such a thing should be allowed. The more he dwelt upon it, the more angry he became. Finally he ascended the holy mountain, and came at last to the peak, where Ngai ruled the world from His golden throne.

" 'Have you come to sing my praises?' asked Ngai.

" 'No!' answered the King of the Zebras. 'I have come to tell you that you are a terrible god, and that I am here to kill you.'

" 'What have I done to you that you should wish to kill me?' asked Ngai.

" 'You gave me a son who has no nostrils, so he cannot sense when the lion and the leopard are approaching him, and because of that they will surely find and kill him when at last he leaves his mother's side. You have been a god too long, and you have forgotten how to be compassionate.'

" 'Wait!' said Ngai, and suddenly there was such power in his voice that the King of the Zebras froze where he was. 'I will give your son nostrils, since that is what you want.'

" 'Why were you so cruel in the first place?' demanded the King of the Zebras, his anger not fully assuaged.

" 'Gods work in mysterious ways,' answered Ngai, 'and what seems cruel to you may actually be compassionate. Because you had been a good and noble king, I gave your son eyes that could see in the dark, that could see through bushes, that could even see around trees, so that he could never be surprised by the lion and the leopard, even should the wind's direction favor them. And because of this gift, he did not need his nostrils. I took them away so that he would not have to breathe in the dust that chokes his fellow zebras during the dry season. But now I have given him back his sense of smell, and taken away his special vision, because you have demanded it.'

" 'Then you *did* have a reason,' moaned the King of the Zebras. 'When did I become so foolish?'

" 'The moment you thought you were greater than me,' answered Ngai, rising to His true height, which was taller than the clouds. 'And to punish you for your audacity, I decree that from this moment forward you and all your kind shall no longer be brown like the dried grasses, but will be covered with black and white stripes that will attract the lion and the leopard from miles away. No matter where you go on the face of the world, you will never again be able to hide from them.'

"And so saying, Ngai waved a hand and every zebra in the world was suddenly covered with the same stripes you see today."

I stopped and stared at Kimanti.

"That is the end?" he asked.

"That is the end."

Kimanti stared at a millipede crawling in the dirt.

"The zebra was a baby and could not explain to its father that it had special eyes," he said at last. "My father's arm has been shriveled for many long rains, and the only explanation he has received is that Ngai works in mysterious ways. He has been given no special senses to make up for it, for if he had been he would surely know about them by now." Kimanti looked at me thoughtfully. "It is an interesting story, Koriba, and I am sorry for the King of the Zebras, but I think a new god must come along and kill Ngai very soon."

There we sat, the wise old *mundumugu* who had a parable for every problem, and the foolish young *kehee* who had no more knowledge of his world than a tadpole, in total opposition to each other.

Only a god with Ngai's sense of humor would have arranged for the *kehee* to be right.

It began when the ship crashed.

(There are those embittered men and women who would say it

began the day Kirinyaga received its charter from the Eutopian Council, but they are wrong.)

Maintenance ships fly among the Eutopian worlds, delivering goods to some, mail to others, services to a few. Only Kirinyaga has no traffic with Maintenance. They are permitted to observe us—indeed, that is one of the conditions of our charter—but they may not interfere, and since we have tried to create a Kikuyu Utopia, we have no interest in commerce with Europeans.

Still, Maintenance ships *have* landed on Kirinyaga from time to time. One of the conditions of our charter is that if a citizen is unhappy with our world, he need only walk to that area known as Haven, and a Maintenance ship will pick him up and take him either to Earth or to another Eutopian world. Once a Maintenance ship landed to disgorge two immigrants, and very early in Kirinyaga's existence Maintenance sent a representative to interfere with our religious practices.

I don't know why the ship was so close to Kirinyaga to begin with. I had not ordered Maintenance to make any orbital adjustments lately, for the short rains were not due for another two months, and it was right that the days passed, hot and bright and unchanging. To the best of my knowledge, none of the villagers had made the pilgrimage to Haven, so no Maintenance ship should have been sent to Kirinyaga. But the fact remains that one moment the sky was clear and blue, and the next there was a streak of light plunging down to the surface of the planetoid. An explosion followed; though I could not see it, I could both hear it and see the results, for the cattle became very nervous and herds of impala and zebra bolted this way and that in panic.

It was about twenty minutes later that young Jinja, the son of Kichanta, ran up the hill to my *boma*.

"You must come, Koriba!" he said as he gasped for breath.

"What has happened?" I asked.

"A Maintenance ship has crashed!" he said. "The pilot is still alive!"

"Is he badly hurt?"

Jinja nodded. "Very badly. I think he may die soon."

"I am an old man, and it would take me a very long time to walk to the pilot," I said. "It would be better for you to take three young men from the village and bring him back to me on a litter."

Jinja raced off while I went into my hut to see what I had that might ease the pilot's pain. There were some *qat* leaves, if he was strong enough to chew them, and a few ointments if he wasn't. I contacted Maintenance on my computer and told them that I would apprise them of the man's condition after I examined him.

In years past, I would have sent my assistant to the river to bring back water that I would boil in preparation for washing out the pilot's wounds, but I no longer had an assistant, and the *mundumugu* does not carry water, so I simply waited atop my hill, my gaze turned toward the direction of the crash. A grass fire had started, and a column of smoke rose from it. I saw Jinja and the others trotting across the savannah with the litter; I saw topi and impala and even buffalo race out of their way; and then I could not see them for almost ten minutes. When they once again came into view, they were walking, and it was obvious that they were carrying a man on the litter.

Before they reached my *boma*, however, Karenja came up the long, winding path from the village.

"*Jambo*, Koriba," he said.

"What are you doing here?" I asked.

"The whole village knows that a Maintenance ship has crashed," he replied. "I have never seen a European before. I came to see if his face is really as white as milk."

"You are doomed to be disappointed," I said. "We call them white, but in reality they are shades of pink and tan."

"Even so," he said, squatting down, "I have never seen one."

I shrugged. "As you will."

Jinja and the young men arrived a few minutes later with the litter. On it lay the twisted body of the pilot. His arms and legs were broken, and there was very little skin on him that was not burned. He had lost a lot of blood, and some still seeped through his wounds. He was unconscious, but breathing regularly.

"*Asante sana,*" I said to the four young men. "Thank you. You have done well this day."

I had one of them fill my gourds with water. The other three bowed and began walking down the hill, while I went through my various ointments, choosing the one that would cause the least discomfort when placed on the burns.

Karenja watched in rapt fascination. Twice I had to rebuke him for touching the pilot's blond hair in wonderment. As the sun changed positions in the sky, I had him help me move the pilot into the shade.

Then, after I had tended to the pilot's wounds, I went into my hut, activated my computer, and contacted Maintenance again. I explained that the pilot was still alive, but that all of his limbs were broken, his body was covered with burns, and that he was in a coma and would probably die soon.

Their answer was that they had already dispatched a medic, who would arrive within half an hour, and they told me to have someone waiting at Haven to guide the medic to my *boma*. Since Karenja was still looking at the pilot, I ordered him to greet the ship and bring the medic to me.

The pilot did not stir for the next hour. At least, I do not think he did, but I dozed with my back against a tree for a few minutes, so I cannot be sure. What woke me was a woman's voice speaking a language I had not heard for many years. I got painfully to my feet just in time to greet the medic that Maintenance had sent.

"You must be Koriba," she said in English. "I have been trying to communicate with the gentleman who accompanied me, but I don't think he understood a word I said."

"I am Koriba," I said in English.

She extended her hand. "I am Doctor Joyce Witherspoon. May I see the patient?"

I led her over to where the pilot lay.

"Do you know his name?" I asked. "We could not find any identification."

"Samuel or Samuels, I'm not sure," she said, kneeling down next to him. "He's in a bad way." She gave him a perfunctory examination, lasting less than a minute. "We could do much more for him back at Base, but I hate to move him in this condition."

"I can have him moved to Haven within an hour," I said. "The sooner you have him in your hospital, the better."

She shook her head. "I think he'll have to remain here until he's a little stronger."

"I will have to consider it," I said.

"There's nothing to consider," she said. "In my medical opinion, he's too weak to move." She pointed to a piece of his shinbone that had broken through the skin of his leg. "I need to set most of the broken bones, and make sure there's no infection."

"You could do this at your hospital," I said.

"I can do it here at much less cost to the patient's remaining vitality," she said. "What's the problem, Koriba?"

"The problem, *Memsaab* Witherspoon," I said, "is that Kirinyaga is a Kikuyu Utopia. This means a rejection of all things European, including your medicine."

"I'm not practicing it on any Kikuyu," she said. "I'm trying to save a Maintenance pilot who just happened to crash on your world."

I stared at the pilot for a long moment. "All right," I said at last. "That is a logical argument. You may minister to his wounds."

"Thank you," she said.

"But he must leave in three days' time," I said. "I will not risk contamination beyond that."

She looked at me as if she were about to argue, but said nothing. Instead, she opened the medical kit she had brought, and injected something—a sedative, I assumed, or a painkiller, or a combination of the two—into his arm.

"She is a witch!" said Karenja. "See how she punctures his skin with a metal thorn!" He stared at the pilot, fascinated. "Now he will surely die."

Joyce Witherspoon worked well into the night, cleansing the pilot's wounds, setting his broken bones, breaking his fever. I don't remember when I fell asleep, but when I woke up, shivering, in the cold morning air just after sunrise, she was sleeping and Karenja was gone.

I built a fire, then sat near it with my blanket wrapped around me until the sun began warming the air. Joyce Witherspoon woke up shortly thereafter.

"Good morning," she said when she saw me sitting a short distance away from her.

"Good morning, *Memsaab* Witherspoon," I replied.

"What time is it?" she asked.

"It is morning."

"I mean, what hour and minute is it?"

"We do not have hours and minutes on Kirinyaga," I told her. "Only days."

"I should look at Mr. Samuels."

"He is still alive," I said.

"Of course he is," she replied. "But the poor man will need skin grafts, and he may lose that right leg. He'll be a long time recovering." She paused and looked around. "Uh ... where do I wash up around here?"

"The river runs by the foot of my hill," I said. "Be sure you beat the water first, to frighten away the crocodiles."

"What kind of Utopia has crocodiles?" she asked with a smile.

"What Eden has no serpents?" I said.

She laughed and walked down the hill. I took a sip from my water gourd, then killed the fire and spread the ashes. One of the boys from the village came by to take my goats out to graze, and another brought firewood and took my gourds down to the river to fill them.

When Joyce Witherspoon returned from the river some twenty minutes later, she was not alone. With her was Kibo, the third and youngest wife of Koinnage, the paramount chief of the village, and in Kibo's arms was Katabo, her infant son. His left arm was swollen to twice its normal size and was badly discolored.

"I found this woman laundering her clothes by the river," said Joyce Witherspoon, "and I noticed that her child had a badly infected arm. It looks like some kind of insect bite. I managed through sign language to convince her to follow me up here."

"Why did you not bring Katabo to me?" I asked Kibo in Swahili.

"Last time you charged me two goats, and he remained sick for many days, and Koinnage beat me for wasting the goats," she said, so terrified she had made me angry that she could not think of a lie.

Even as Kibo spoke, Joyce Witherspoon began approaching her and Katabo with a syringe in her hand.

"This is a broad-spectrum antibiotic," she explained to me. "It also contains a steroid that will prevent itching or any discomfort while the infection remains."

"Stop!" I said harshly in English.

"What's the matter?"

"You may not do this," I said. "You are here to minister to the pilot only."

"This is a baby, and it's suffering," she said. "It'll take me two seconds to give it a shot and cure it."

"I cannot permit it."

"What's the matter with you?" she demanded. "I read your biography. You may dress like a savage and sit in the dirt next to your fire, but you were educated at Cambridge and received your postgraduate degrees from Yale. Surely you know how easily I can end this child's suffering."

"That's not the point," I said.

"Then what *is* the point?"

"You may not medicate this child. It seems like a blessing now— but once before we accepted the Europeans' medicine, and then their religion, and their clothing, and their laws, and their customs, and eventually we ceased to be Kikuyu and became a new race, a race of black Europeans known only as Kenyans. We came to Kirinyaga to make sure that such a thing does not happen to us again."

"*He* won't know why he feels better. You can credit it to your god or yourself for all I care."

I shook my head. "I appreciate your sentiment, but I cannot let you corrupt our Utopia."

"Look at him," she said, pointing to Katabo's swollen arm. "Is Kirinyaga a Utopia for *him*? Where is it written that Utopias must have sick and suffering children?"

"Nowhere."

"Well, then?"

"It is not written," I continued, "because the Kikuyu do not have a written language."

"Will you at least let the mother decide?"

"No," I said.

"Why not?"

"The mother will think only of her child," I answered. "*I* must think of an entire world."

"Perhaps her child is more important to her than your world is to you."

"She is incapable of making a reasoned decision," I said. "Only *I* can foresee all the consequences."

Suddenly Kibo, who understood not a word of English, turned to me.

"Will the European witch make my little Katabo better?" she asked. "Why are you two arguing?"

"The European witch is here only for the European," I answered. "She has no power to help the Kikuyu."

"Can she not try?" asked Kibo.

"*I* am your *mundumugu*," I said harshly.

"But look at the pilot," said Kibo, pointing to Samuels. "Yesterday he was all but dead. Today his skin is already healing, and his arms and legs are straight again."

"Her god is the god of the Europeans," I answered, "just as her magic is the magic of the Europeans. Her spells do not work on the Kikuyu."

Kibo fell silent, and clutched Katabo to her breast.

I turned to Joyce Witherspoon. "I apologize for speaking in Swahili, but Kibo knows no other language."

"It's all right," she said. "I had no difficulty following it."

"I thought you told me you only spoke English."

"Sometimes you needn't understand the words to translate. I believe you were saying, in essence, 'Thou shalt have no other gods before me.'"

The pilot moaned just then, and suddenly all of her attention was focused upon him. He was coming into a state of semiconsciousness, unfocused and unintelligible but no longer comatose, and she began administering medications into the tubes that were already attached to his arms and legs. Kibo watched in wonderment, but kept her distance.

I remained on my hill most of the morning. I offered to remove the curse from Katabo's arm and give him some soothing lotions, but Kibo refused, saying that Koinnage steadfastly refused to part with any more goats.

"I will not charge you this time," I said, for I wanted Koinnage on my side. I uttered a spell over the child, then treated his arm with a salve made from the pulped bark of the acacia tree. I ordered Kibo to return to her *shamba* with him, and told her that the child's arm would return to normal within five days.

Finally it was time for me to go into the village to bless the scarecrows and give Leibo, who had lost her baby, ointment to ease the pain in her breasts. I would meet with Bakada, who had accepted the bride-price for his daughter and wanted me to preside at the wedding, and finally I would join Koinnage and the Council of Elders as they discussed the weighty issues of the day.

As I walked down the long, winding path beside the river, I found myself thinking how much like the European's Garden of Eden this world looked.

How was I to know that the serpent had already arrived?

* * *

After I had tended to my chores in the village, I stopped at Ngobe's hut to share a gourd of *pombe* with him. He asked about the pilot, for by now everyone in the village had heard about him, and I explained that the European's *mundumugu* was curing him and would take him back to Maintenance headquarters in two more days.

"She must have powerful magic," he said, "for I am told that the man's body was badly broken." He paused. "It is too bad," he added wistfully, "that such magic will not work for the Kikuyu."

"My magic has always been sufficient," I said.

"True," he said uneasily. "But I remember the day when we brought Tabari's son back after the hyenas had attacked him and chewed off one of his legs. You eased his pain, but you could not save him. Perhaps the witch from Maintenance could have."

"The pilot had broken his legs, but they were not chewed off," I said defensively. "No one could have saved Tabari's son after the hyenas had finished with him."

"Perhaps you are right," he said.

My first inclination was to pounce on the word *"perhaps,"* but then I decided that he meant no insult by it, so I finished my *pombe*, cast the bones, read that he would have a successful harvest, and left his hut.

I stopped in the center of the village to recite a fable to the children, then went over to Koinnage's *shamba* and entered his *boma* for the daily meeting of the Council of Elders. Most of them were already there, grim-faced and silent. Finally Koinnage emerged from his hut and joined us.

"We have serious business to discuss today," he announced. "Perhaps the most serious we have *ever* discussed," he added, staring straight at me. Suddenly he faced his wives' huts. "Kibo!" he shouted. "Come here!"

Kibo emerged from her hut and walked over to us, carrying little Katabo in her arms.

"You all saw my son's arm yesterday," said Koinnage. "It was swollen to twice its normal size, and was the color of death." He took the child and held it above his head. "Now look at him!" he cried.

Katabo's arm was once again a healthy color, and almost all of the swelling had vanished.

"My medicine worked faster than I had anticipated," I said.

"This is not *your* medicine at all!" he said accusingly. "This is the European witch's medicine!"

I looked at Kibo. "I ordered you to leave my *boma* ahead of me!" I said sternly.

"You did not order me not to return," she said, her face filled with defiance as she stood next to Koinnage. "The witch pierced Katabo's arm with a metal thorn, and before I could climb back down your hill the swelling was already half gone."

"You disobeyed my command," I said ominously.

"I am the paramount chief, and I absolve her," interjected Koinnage.

"I am the *mundumugu*, and I do not!" I said, and suddenly Kibo's defiance was replaced by terror.

"We have more important things to discuss," snapped Koinnage. This startled me, for when I am angry, no one has the courage to confront or contradict me.

I pulled some luminescent powder, made from the ground-up bodies of night-stalking beetles, out of my pouch, held it on the palm of my hand, raised my hand to my mouth, and blew the powder in Kibo's direction. She screamed in terror and fell writhing to the ground.

"What have you done to her?" demanded Koinnage.

I have terrified her beyond your ability to comprehend, which is a just and fitting punishment for disobeying me, I thought. Aloud I said, "I have marked her spirit so that all the predators of the Other World can find it at night when she sleeps. If she swears never to disobey her *mundumugu* again, if she shows proper contrition for disobeying me today, then I shall remove the markings before she goes to sleep this evening. If not ..." I shrugged and let the threat hang in the air.

"Then perhaps the European witch will remove the markings," said Koinnage.

"Do you think the god of the Europeans is mightier than Ngai?" I demanded.

"I do not know," replied Koinnage. "But he healed my son's arm in moments, when Ngai would have taken days."

"For years you have told us to reject all things European," added Karenja, "yet I myself have seen the witch use her magic on the dying pilot, and I think it is stronger than *your* magic."

"It is a magic for Europeans only," I said.

"This is not so," answered Koinnage. "For did the witch not offer it to Katabo? If she can halt the suffering of our sick and our injured faster than Ngai can, then we must consider accepting her offer."

"If you accept her offer," I said, "before long you will be asked to accept her god, and her science, and her clothing, and her customs."

"Her science is what created Kirinyaga and flew us here," said Ngobe. "How can it be bad if it made Kirinyaga possible?"

"It is not bad for the Europeans," I said, "because it is part of their culture. But we must never forget why we came to Kirinyaga in the first place: to create a Kikuyu world and reestablish a Kikuyu culture."

"We must think seriously about this," said Koinnage. "For years we have believed that every facet of the Europeans' culture was evil, for we had no examples of it. But now that we see that even a female can cure our illness faster than Ngai can, it is time to reconsider."

"If her magic could have cured my withered arm when I was still a boy," added Ngobe, "why would that have been evil?"

"It would have been against the will of Ngai," I said.

"Does not Ngai rule the universe?" he asked.

"You know that He does," I replied.

"Then nothing that happens can be contrary to His wishes, and if she could have cured me, it would *not* have been against Ngai's will."

I shook my head. "You do not understand."

"We are trying to understand," said Koinnage. "Enlighten us."

"The Europeans have many wonders, and these wonders will entice you, as they are doing right now . . . but if you accept one European thing, soon they will insist you accept them all. Koinnage, their religion allows a man to have only one wife. Which two will you divorce?"

I turned to the others. "Ngobe, they will make Kimanti attend a school where he will learn to read and write. But since we do not have a written language, he will learn to write only in a European language, and the things and people he reads about and learns about will all be European."

I walked among the Elders, offering an example to each. "Karenja, if you do a service for Tabari, you will expect a chicken or a goat or perhaps even a cow in return, depending on the nature of the service. But the Europeans will make him reward you with paper money, which you cannot eat, and which cannot reproduce and make a man rich."

On and on I went, until I had run through all the Elders, pointing out what they would lose if they allowed the Europeans a toehold in our society.

"All that is on the one hand," said Koinnage when I had finished. He held his other hand out, palm up. "On the other hand is an end to illness and suffering, which is no small achievement in itself. Koriba has said that if we let the Europeans in, they will force us to change our ways. *I* say that some of our ways *need* changing. If their god is a greater healer than Ngai, who is to say that he may not also bring better weather, or more fertile cattle, or richer soil?"

"*No!*" I cried. "*You* may all have forgotten why we came here, but *I* have not. Our mandate was not to establish a European Utopia, but a Kikuyu one!"

"And *have* we established it?" asked Karenja sardonically.

"We are coming closer every day," I told him. "*I* am making it a reality."

"Do children suffer in Utopia?" persisted Karenja. "Do men grow up with withered arms? Do women die in childbirth? Do hyenas attack shepherds in Utopia?"

"It is a matter of balance," I said. "Unrestricted growth would eventually lead to unrestricted hunger. You have not seen what it has done on Earth, but *I* have."

Finally it was old Jandara who spoke.

"Do people *think* in a Utopia?" he asked me.

"Of course they do," I replied.

"If they think, are some of their thoughts new, just as some are old?"

"Yes."

"Then perhaps we should consider letting the witch tend to our illnesses and injuries," he said. "For if Ngai allows new thoughts in His Utopia, He must realize they will lead to change. And if change is not evil, then perhaps lack of change, such as we have striven for here, *is* evil, or at least wrong." He got to his feet. "You may debate the merits of the question. As for myself, I have had pain in my joints for many years, and Ngai has not cured it. I am climbing Koriba's hill to see if the god of the Europeans can end my pain."

And with that, he walked past me and out of the *boma*.

I was prepared to argue my case all day and all night if necessary, but Koinnage turned his back on me—on *me*, his *mundumugu*!—and began carrying his son back to Kibo's hut. That signaled the end to the meeting, and each of the Elders got up and left without daring to look me in the face.

There were more than a dozen villagers gathered at the foot of my hill when I arrived. I walked past them and soon reached my *boma*.

Jandara was still there. Joyce Witherspoon had given him an injection, and was handing him a small bottle of pills as I arrived.

"Who told you that you could treat the Kikuyu?" I demanded in English.

"I did not offer to treat them," she replied. "But I am a doctor, and I will not turn them away."

"Then *I* will," I said. I turned and looked down at the villagers. "You may not come up here!" I said sternly. "Go back to your *shambas*."

The adults all looked uneasy but stood their ground, while one small boy began climbing up the hill.

"Your *mundumugu* has forbidden you to climb this hill!" I said. "Ngai will punish you for your transgression!"

"The god of the Europeans is young and powerful," said the boy. "He will protect me from Ngai."

And now I saw that the boy was Kimanti.

"Stay back—I warn you!" I shouted.

Kimanti hefted his wooden spear. "Ngai will not harm me," he said confidently. "If He tries, I will kill Him with *this*."

He walked right by me and approached Joyce Witherspoon.

"I have cut my foot on a rock," he said. "If your god will heal me, I will sacrifice a goat to thank him."

She did not understand a word he said, but when he showed her his foot she began treating it.

He walked back down the hill, unmolested by Ngai, and when he was both alive and healed the next morning, word went out to other villages and soon there was a seemingly endless line of the sick and the lame, all waiting to climb my hill and accept European cures for Kikuyu ills.

Once again I told them to disperse. This time they seemed not even to hear me. They simply remained in line, neither arguing back as Kimanti had, nor even acknowledging my presence, each of them waiting patiently until it was their turn to be treated by the European witch.

I thought that when she left, things would go back to the way they had been, that the people would once again fear Ngai and show respect to their *mundumugu*—but this was not to be. Oh, they went about their daily chores, they planted their crops and tended to their cattle ... but they did not come to me with their problems as they always had done in the past.

At first I thought we had entered one of those rare periods in which no one in the village was ill or injured, but then one day I saw

Shanaka walking out across the savannah. Since he rarely left his *shamba*, and *never* left the village, I was curious about his destination and I decided to follow him. He walked due west for more than half an hour, until he reached the landing area at Haven.

"What is wrong?" I asked when I finally caught up with him.

He opened his mouth to reveal a serious abscess above one of his teeth. "I am in great pain," he said. "I have been unable to eat for three days."

"Why did you not come to me?" I asked.

"The god of the Europeans has defeated Ngai," answered Shanaka. "He will not help me."

"He will," I assured him.

Shanaka shook his head, then winced from the motion. "You are an old man, and Ngai is an old god, and both of you have lost your powers," he said unhappily. "I wish it were otherwise, but it is not."

"So you are deserting your wives and children because you have lost your faith in Ngai?" I demanded.

"No," he replied. "I will ask the Maintenance ship to take me to a European *mundumugu*, and when I am cured I will return home."

"*I* will cure you," I said.

He looked at me for a long moment. "There was a time when you could cure me," he said at last. "But that time has passed. I will go to the Europeans' *mundumugu*."

"If you do," I said sternly, "you may never call on me for help again."

He shrugged. "I never intend to," he said with neither bitterness nor rancor.

Shanaka returned the next day, his mouth healed.

I stopped by his *boma* to see how he was feeling, for I remained the *mundumugu* whether he wanted my services or not, and as I walked through the fields of his *shamba* I saw that he had two new scarecrows, gifts of the Europeans. The scarecrows had mechanical arms that flapped constantly, and they rotated so that they did not always face in one direction.

"*Jambo*, Koriba," he greeted me. Then, seeing that I was looking at his scarecrows, he added, "Are they not wonderful?"

"I will withhold judgment until I see how long they function," I said. "The more moving parts an object has, the more likely it is to break."

He looked at me, and I thought I detected a hint of pity in his expression. "They were created by the God of Maintenance," he said. "They will last forever."

"Or until their power packs are empty," I said, but he did not know what I meant, and so my sarcasm was lost on him. "How is your mouth?"

"It feels much better," he replied. "They pricked me with a magic thorn to end the pain, then cut away the evil spirits that had invaded my mouth." He paused. "They have very powerful gods, Koriba."

"You are back on Kirinyaga now," I said sternly. "Be careful how you blaspheme."

"I do not blaspheme," he said. "I speak the truth."

"And now you will want me to bless the Europeans' scarecrows, I suppose," I said with finely wrought irony.

He shrugged. "If it makes you happy," he said.

"If it makes *me* happy?" I repeated angrily.

"That's right," he said nonchalantly. "The scarecrows, being European, certainly do not *need* your blessings, but if you will feel better..."

I had often wondered what might happen if for some reason the *mundumugu* was no longer feared by the members of the village. I had never once considered what it might be like if he were merely tolerated.

Still more villagers went to Maintenance's infirmary, and each came back with some gift from the Europeans: time-saving gadgets for the most part. Western gadgets. Culture-killing gadgets.

Again and again I went into the village and explained why such things must be rejected. Day after day I spoke to the Council of Elders, reminding them why we had come to Kirinyaga—but most of the original settlers were dead, and the next generation, those who had become our Elders, had no memories of Kenya. Indeed, those of them who spoke to the Maintenance staff came home thinking that Kenya, rather than Kirinyaga, was some kind of Utopia, in which everyone was well fed and well cared for and no farm ever suffered from drought.

They were polite, they listened respectfully to me, and then they went right ahead with whatever they had been doing or discussing when I arrived. I reminded them of the many times I and I alone had saved them from themselves, but they seemed not to care; indeed, one or two of the Elders acted as if, far from keeping Kirinyaga pure, I had in some mysterious way been hindering its growth.

"Kirinyaga is not *supposed* to grow!" I argued. "When you achieve a Utopia, you do not cast it aside and say, 'What changes can we make tomorrow?' "

"If you do not grow, you stagnate," answered Karenja.

"We can grow by expanding," I said. "We have an entire world to populate."

"That is not growing, but breeding," he replied. "You have done your job admirably, Koriba, for in the beginning we needed order and purpose above all else ... but the time for your job is past. Now we have established ourselves here, and it is for *us* to choose how we will live."

"We have *already* chosen how to live!" I said angrily. "That is why we came here to begin with."

"I was just a *kehee*," said Karenja. "Nobody asked me. And I did not ask my son, who was born here."

"Kirinyaga was created for the purpose of becoming a Kikuyu Utopia," I said. "This purpose is the basis of our charter. It cannot be changed."

"No one is suggesting that we don't want to live in a Utopia,

Koriba," interjected Shanaka. "But the time has passed when you and you alone shall be the sole judge of what constitutes a Utopia."

"It is clearly defined."

"By *you*," said Shanaka. "Some of us have our own definitions of Utopia."

"You were one of the original founders of Kirinyaga," I said accusingly. "Why have you never spoken out before?"

"Many times I wanted to," admitted Shanaka. "But always I was afraid."

"Afraid of what?"

"Of Ngai. Or you."

"They are much the same thing," added Karenja.

"But now that Ngai has lost His battle to the God of Maintenance, I am no longer afraid to speak," continued Shanaka. "Why should I suffer with the pain in my teeth? How was it unholy or blasphemous for the European witches to cure me? Why should my wife, who is as old as I am and whose back is bent from years of carrying wood and water, continue to carry them when there are machines to carry things for her?"

"Why should you live on Kirinyaga at all, if that is the way you feel?" I asked bitterly.

"Because I have worked as hard to make Kirinyaga a home for the Kikuyu as you have!" he shot back. "And I see no reason to leave just because my definition of Utopia doesn't agree with yours. Why don't *you* leave, Koriba?"

"Because I was charged with establishing our Utopia, and I have not yet completed my assignment," I said. "In fact, it is false Kikuyu like you who have made my work that much harder."

Shanaka got to his feet and looked around at the Elders.

"Am I a false Kikuyu because I want my grandson to read?" he demanded. "Or because I want to ease my wife's burden? Or because I do not wish to suffer physical pain that can easily be avoided?"

"No!" cried the Elders as one.

"Be very careful," I warned them. "For if *he* is not a false Kikuyu, then you are calling *me* one."

"No, Koriba," said Koinnage, rising to his feet. "You are not a false Kikuyu." He paused. "But you are a mistaken one. Your day—and mine—has passed. Perhaps, for a fleeting second, we did achieve Utopia—but that second is gone, and the new moments and hours require new Utopias." Then Koinnage, who had looked at me with fear so many times in the past, suddenly looked at me with great compassion. "It was *our* dream, Koriba, but it is not *theirs*—and if we still have some feeble handhold on today, tomorrow surely belongs to them."

"I will hear none of this!" I said. "You cannot redefine a Utopia as a matter of convenience. We moved here in order to be true to our faith and traditions, to avoid becoming what so many Kikuyu had become in Kenya. I will not let us become black Europeans!"

"We are becoming *something*," said Shanaka. "Perhaps just once there was an instant when you felt we were perfect Kikuyu—but that instant has long since passed. To remain so, not one of us could have had a new thought, could have seen the world in a different way. We would have become the scarecrows you bless every morning."

I was silent for a very long time. Then, at last, I spoke. "This world breaks my heart," I said. "I tried so hard to mold it into what we had all wanted, and look at what it has become. What *you* have become."

"You can direct change, Koriba," said Shanaka, "but you cannot prevent it, and that is why Kirinyaga will always break your heart."

"I must go to my *boma* and think," I said.

"*Kwaheri*, Koriba," said Koinnage. *Good-bye, Koriba.* It had a sense of finality to it.

I spent many days alone on my hill, looking across the winding river to the green savannah and thinking. I had been betrayed by the people I had tried to lead, by the very world I had helped to create. I felt that I had surely displeased Ngai in some way, and that He would strike me dead. I was quite prepared to die, even willing ... but I did not die, for the gods draw their strength from their worshipers, and Ngai was now so weak that He could not even kill a feeble old man like myself.

Eventually I decided to go down among my people one last time, to see if any of them had rejected the enticements of the Europeans and come back to the ways of the Kikuyu.

The path was lined with mechanical scarecrows. The only meaningful way to bless *them* would be to renew their charges. I saw several women washing clothes by the river, but instead of pounding the fabrics with rocks, they were rubbing them on some artificial boards that had obviously been made for that purpose.

Suddenly I heard a ringing noise behind me, and, startled, I jumped, lost my footing, and fell heavily against a thornbush. When I was able to get my bearings, I saw that I had almost been run over by a bicycle.

"I am sorry, Koriba," said the rider, who turned out to be young Kimanti. "I thought you heard me coming."

He helped me gingerly to my feet.

"My ears have heard many things," I said. "The scream of the fish eagle, the bleat of the goat, the laugh of the hyena, the cry of the newborn baby. But they were never meant to hear artificial wheels going down a dirt hill."

"It is much faster and easier than walking," he replied. "Are you going anywhere in particular? I will be happy to give you a ride."

It was probably the bicycle that made up my mind. "Yes," I replied, "I am going somewhere, and no, I will not be taken on a bicycle."

"Then I will walk with you," he said. "Where are you going?"

"To Haven," I said.

"Ah," he said with a smile. "You, too, have business with Maintenance. Where do you hurt?"

I touched the left side of my chest. "I hurt *here*—and the only business I have with Maintenance is to get as far from the cause of that pain as I can."

"You are leaving Kirinyaga?"

"I am leaving what Kirinyaga has become," I answered.

"Where will you go?" he asked. "What will you do?"

"I will go elsewhere, and I will do other things," I said vaguely, for where *does* an unemployed *mundumugu* go?

"We will miss you, Koriba," said Kimanti.

"I doubt it."

"We will," he repeated with sincerity. "When we recite the history of Kirinyaga to our children, you will not be forgotten." He paused. "It is true that you were wrong, but you were necessary."

"Is that how I am to be remembered?" I asked. "As a necessary evil?"

"I did not call you evil, just wrong."

We walked the next few miles in silence, and at last we came to Haven.

"I will wait with you if you wish," said Kimanti.

"I would rather wait alone," I said.

He shrugged. "As you wish. *Kwaheri*, Koriba."

"Kwaheri," I replied.

After he left I looked around, studying the savannah and the river, the wildebeest and the zebras, the fish eagles and the marabou storks, trying to set them in my memory for all time to come.

"I am sorry, Ngai," I said at last. "I have done my best, but I have failed you."

The ship that would take me away from Kirinyaga forever suddenly came into view.

"You must view them with compassion, Ngai," I said as the ship approached the landing strip. "They are not the first of your people to be bewitched by the Europeans."

And it seemed, as the ship touched down, that a voice spoke into my ear and said, *You have been my most faithful servant, Koriba, and so*

I shall be guided by your counsel. Do you really wish me to view them with compassion?

I looked toward the village one last time, the village that had once feared and worshiped Ngai, and which had sold itself, like some prostitute, to the god of the Europeans.

"No," I said firmly.

"Are you speaking to me?" asked the pilot, and I realized that the hatch was open and waiting for me.

"No," I replied.

He looked around. "I don't see anyone else."

"He is very old and very tired," I said. "But He is here."

I climbed into the ship and did not look back.

Epilogue

THE LAND OF NOD

{AUGUST–SEPTEMBER 2137}

Once, many years ago, there was a Kikuyu warrior who left his village and wandered off in search of adventure. Armed only with a spear, he slew the mighty lion and the cunning leopard. Then one day he came upon an elephant. He realized that his spear was useless against such a beast, but before he could back away or find cover, the elephant charged.

His only hope was divine intervention, and he begged Ngai to find him and pluck him from the path of the elephant.

But Ngai did not respond, and the elephant picked the warrior up with its trunk and hurled him high into the air, and he landed in a distant thorn tree. His skin was badly torn by the thorns, but at least he was safe, since he was on a branch some twenty feet above the ground.

After he was sure the elephant had left the area, the warrior climbed down. Then he returned home and ascended the holy mountain to confront Ngai.

"What is it that you want of me?" asked Ngai, when the warrior had reached the summit.

"I want to know why you did not come," said the warrior angrily. "All my life I have worshiped you and paid tribute to you. Did you not hear me ask for your help?"

"I heard you," answered Ngai.

"Then why did you not come to my aid?" demanded the warrior. "Are you so lacking in godly powers that you could not find me?"

"After all these years you still do not understand," said Ngai sternly. "It is *you* who must search for *me*."

My son Edward picked me up at the police station on Biashara Street just after midnight. The sleek British vehicle hovered a few inches above the ground while I got in, and then his chauffeur began taking us back to his house in the Ngong Hills.

"This is becoming tedious," he said, activating the shimmering privacy barrier so that we could not be overheard. He tried to present a judicial calm, but I knew he was furious.

"You would think they would tire of it," I agreed.

"We must have a serious talk," he said. "You have been back only two months, and this is the fourth time I have had to bail you out of jail."

"I have broken no Kikuyu laws," I said calmly, as we raced through the dark, ominous slums of Nairobi on our way to the affluent suburbs.

"You have broken the laws of Kenya," he said. "And like it or not, that is where you now live. I'm an official in the government, and I will not have you constantly embarrassing me!" He paused, struggling with his temper. "Look at you! I have offered to buy you a new wardrobe. Why must you wear that ugly old *kikoi*? It smells even worse than it looks."

"Is there now a law against dressing like a Kikuyu?" I asked him.

"No," he said, as he commanded the miniature bar to appear from beneath the floor and poured himself a drink. "But there *is* a law against creating a disturbance in a restaurant."

"I paid for my meal," I noted, as we turned onto Langata Road and headed out for the suburbs. "In the Kenya shillings that you gave me."

"That does not give you the right to hurl your food against the wall, simply because it is not cooked to your taste." He glared at me, barely able to contain his anger. "You're getting worse with each offense. If I had been anyone else, you'd have spent the night in jail. As it is, I had to agree to pay for the damage you caused."

"It was eland," I explained. "The Kikuyu do not eat game animals."

"It was *not* eland," he said, setting his glass down and lighting a smokeless cigarette. "The last eland died in a German zoo a year after you left for Kirinyaga. It was a modified soybean product, genetically enhanced to *taste* like eland." He paused, then sighed deeply. "If you thought it was eland, why did you order it?"

"The server said it was steak. I assumed he meant the meat of a cow or an ox."

"This has got to stop," said Edward. "We are two grown men. Why can't we reach an accommodation?" He stared at me for a long time. "I can deal with rational men who disagree with me. I do it at Government House every day. But I cannot deal with a fanatic."

"I am a rational man," I said.

"Are you?" he demanded. "Yesterday you showed my wife's nephew how to apply the *githani* test for truthfulness, and he practically burned his brother's tongue off."

"His brother was lying," I said calmly. "He who lies faces the red-hot blade with a dry mouth, whereas he who has nothing to fear has enough moisture on his tongue so that he cannot be burned."

"Try telling a seven-year-old boy that he has nothing to fear when he's being approached by a sadistic older brother who is brandishing a red-hot knife!" snapped my son.

A uniformed watchman waved us through to the private road where my son lived, and when we reached our driveway the chauffeur pulled our British vehicle up to the edge of the force field. It identified us and vanished long enough for us to pass through, and soon we came to the front door.

Edward got out of the vehicle and approached his residence as I followed him. He clenched his fists in a physical effort to restrain his anger. "I agreed to let you live with us, because you are an old man who was thrown off his world—"

"I left Kirinyaga of my own volition," I interrupted calmly.

"It makes no difference why or how you left," said my son. "What matters is that you are *here* now. You are a very old man. It has been many years since you have lived on Earth. All of your friends are dead. My mother is dead. I am your son, and I will accept my responsibilities, but you *must* meet me halfway."

"I am trying to," I said.

"I doubt it."

"I am," I repeated. "Your own son understands that, even if you do not."

"My own son has had quite enough to cope with since my divorce and remarriage. The last thing he needs is a grandfather filling his head with wild tales of some Kikuyu Utopia."

"It is a failed Utopia," I corrected him. "They would not listen to me, and so they are doomed to become another Kenya."

"What is so wrong with that?" said Edward. "Kenya is my home, and I am proud of it." He paused and stared at me. "And now it is *your* home again. You must speak of it with more respect."

"I lived in Kenya for many years before I emigrated to Kirinyaga," I said. "I can live here again. Nothing has changed."

"That is not so," said my son. "We have built a transport system beneath Nairobi, and there is now a spaceport at Watamu on the coast. We have closed down the nuclear plants; our power is now entirely thermal, drawn from beneath the floor of the Rift Valley. In fact," he added with the pride that always accompanied the descriptions of his new wife's attainments, "Susan was instrumental in the changeover."

"You misunderstood me, Edward," I replied. "Kenya remains unchanged in that it continues to ape the Europeans rather than remain true to its own traditions."

The security system identified us and opened his house to us. We walked through the foyer, past the broad, winding staircase that led to the bedroom wing. The servants were waiting for us, and the butler took Edward's coat from him. Then we passed the doorways to the lounge and drawing room, both of which were filled with Roman statues and French paintings and rows of beautifully bound British books. Finally we came to Edward's study, where he turned and spoke in a low tone to the butler.

"We wish to be alone."

The servants vanished as if they had been nothing but holograms.

"Where is Susan?" I asked, for my daughter-in-law was nowhere to be seen.

"We were at a party at the Cameroon ambassador's new home when the call came through that you had been arrested again," he answered. "You broke up a very enjoyable bridge game. My guess is that she's in the tub or in bed, cursing your name."

I was about to mention that cursing my name to the god of the Europeans would not prove effective, but I decided that my son would not like to hear that at this moment, so I was silent. As I looked at my surroundings, I reflected that not only had all of Edward's belongings come from the Europeans, but that even his house had been taken from them, for it consisted of many rectangular rooms, and all Kikuyu knew—or should have known—that demons dwell in corners and the only proper shape for a home is round.

Edward walked briskly to his desk, activated his computer and read his messages, and then turned to me.

"There is another message from the government," he announced. "They want to see you next Tuesday at noon."

"I have already told them I will not accept their money," I said. "I have performed no service for them."

He put on his Lecture Face. "We are no longer a poor country," he said. "We pride ourselves that none of our infirm or elderly go hungry."

"I will not go hungry, if the restaurants will stop trying to feed me unclean animals."

"The government is just making sure that you do not become a financial burden to me," said Edward, refusing to let me change the subject.

"You are my son," I said. "I raised you and fed you and protected you when you were young. Now I am old and you will do the same for me. That is our tradition."

"Well, it is our government's tradition to provide a financial safety net to families who are supporting elderly members," he said, and I could tell that the last trace of Kikuyu within him had vanished, that he was entirely a Kenyan.

"You are a wealthy man," I pointed out. "You do not need their money."

"I pay my taxes," he said, lighting another smokeless cigarette to hide his defensiveness. "It would be foolish not to accept the benefits that accrue to us. You may live a very long time. We have every right to that money."

"It is dishonorable to accept what you do not need," I replied. "Tell them to leave us alone."

He leaned back, half sitting on his desk. "They wouldn't, even if I asked them to."

"They must be Wakamba or Maasai," I said, making no effort to hide my contempt.

"They are Kenyans," he answered. "Just as you and I are."

"Yes," I said, suddenly feeling the weight of my years. "Yes, I must work very hard at remembering that."

"You will save me more trips to the police station if you can," said my son.

I nodded and went off to my room. He had supplied me with a bed and mattress, but after so many years of living in my hut on Kirinyaga, I found the bed uncomfortable, so every night I removed the blanket and placed it on the floor, then lay down and slept on it.

But tonight sleep would not come, for I kept reliving the past two months in my mind. Everything I saw, everything I heard, made me remember why I had left Kenya in the first place, why I had fought so long and so hard to obtain Kirinyaga's charter.

I rolled onto my side, propped my head on my hand, and looked out the window. Hundreds of stars were twinkling brightly in the clear, cloudless sky. I tried to imagine which of them was Kirinyaga. I had been the *mundumugu*—the witch doctor—who was charged with establishing our Kikuyu Utopia.

"I served you more selflessly than any other," I whispered, staring at a flickering, verdant star, "and you betrayed me. Worse, you have betrayed Ngai. Neither He nor I shall ever seek you out again."

I laid my head back down, turned away from the window, and closed my eyes, determined to look into the skies no more.

In the morning, my son stopped by my room.

"You have slept on the floor again," he noted.

"Have they passed a law against that now?" I demanded.

He sighed deeply. "Sleep any way you want."

I stared at him. "You look very impressive ..." I began.

"Thank you."

"... in your European clothes," I concluded.

"I have an important meeting with the Finance Minister today." He looked at his timepiece. "In fact, I must leave now or I will be late." He paused uneasily. "Have you considered what we spoke about yesterday?"

"We spoke of many things," I said.

"I am referring to the Kikuyu retirement village."

"I have lived in a village," I said. "And that is not one. It is a twenty-story tower of steel and glass, built to imprison the elderly."

"We have been through all this before," said my son. "It would be a place for you to make new friends."

"I have a new friend," I said. "I shall be visiting him this evening."

"Good!" he said. "Maybe he'll keep you out of trouble."

I arrived at the huge titanium-and-glass laboratory complex just before midnight. The night had turned cool, and a breeze was blowing gently from the south. The moon had passed behind a cloud, and it was difficult to find the side gate in the darkness. Eventually I did find it, though, and Kamau was waiting for me. He deactivated a small section of the electronic barrier long enough for me to step through.

"*Jambo, mzee,*" he said. *Hello, wise old man.*

"*Jambo, mzee,*" I replied, for he was almost as old as I myself was. "I have come to see with my own eyes if you were telling the truth."

He nodded and turned, and I followed him between the tall, angular buildings that hovered over us, casting eerie shadows along the narrow walkways and channeling all the noises of the city in our direction. Our path was lined with Whistling Thorn and Yellow Fever trees, cloned from the few remaining specimens, rather than the usual introduced European shrubbery. Here and there were ornamental displays of grasses from the vanished savannahs.

"It is strange to see so much true African vegetation here in Kenya," I remarked. "Since I have returned from Kirinyaga, my eyes have hungered for it."

"You have seen a whole world of it," he replied with unconcealed envy.

"There is more to a world than greenery," I said. "When all is said and done, there is little difference between Kirinyaga and Kenya. Both have turned their backs on Ngai."

Kamau came to a halt, and gestured around him at the looming metal and glass and concrete buildings that totally covered the cool swamps from which Nairobi took its name. "I do not know how you can prefer *this* to Kirinyaga."

"I did not say I preferred it," I replied, suddenly aware that the ever-present noises of the city had been overshadowed by the droning hum of machines.

"Then you *do* miss Kirinyaga."

"I miss what Kirinyaga might have been. As for these," I said, indicating the immense structures, "they are just buildings."

"They are European buildings," he said bitterly. "They were built by men who are no longer Kikuyu or Luo or Embu, but merely Kenyans. They are filled with corners." He paused, and I thought, approvingly, *How much you sound like me! No wonder you sought me out when I returned to Kenya.* "Nairobi is home to eleven million people," he continued. "It stinks of sewage. The air is so polluted there are days when you can actually see it. The people wear European clothes and worship the Europeans' god. How could you turn your back on Utopia for this?"

I held up my hands. "I have only ten fingers."

He frowned. "I do not understand."

"Do you remember the story of the little Dutch boy who put his finger in the dike?"

Kamau shook his head and spat contemptuously on the ground. "I do not listen to European stories."

"Perhaps you are wise not to," I acknowledged. "At any rate, the dike of tradition with which I had surrounded Kirinyaga began to spring leaks. They were few and easily plugged at first, but as the society kept evolving and growing they became many, and soon I did not have enough fingers to plug them all." I shrugged. "So I left before I was washed away."

"Have they another *mundumugu* to replace you?" he asked.

"I am told that they have a doctor to cure the sick, and a Christian minister to tell them how to worship the god of the Europeans, and a computer to tell them how to react to any situation that might arise," I said. "They no longer need a *mundumugu.*"

"Then Ngai has forsaken them," he stated.

"No," I corrected him. "*They* have forsaken Ngai."

"I apologize, *mundumugu*," he said with deference. "You are right, of course."

He began walking again, and soon a strong, pungent odor came to my nostrils, a scent I had never encountered before, but which stirred some memory deep within my soul.

"We are almost there," said Kamau.

I heard a low rumbling sound, not like a predator growling, but rather like a vast machine purring with power.

"He is very nervous," continued Kamau, speaking in a soft monotone. "Make no sudden movements. He has already tried to kill two of his daytime attendants."

And then we were there, just as the moon emerged from its cloud cover and shone down on the awesome creature that stood facing us.

"He is magnificent!" I whispered.

"A perfect replication," agreed Kamau. "Height, ten feet eight inches at the shoulder, weight seven tons—and each tusk is exactly one hundred forty-eight pounds."

The huge animal stared at me through the flickering force field that surrounded it and tested the cool night breeze, striving to pick up my scent.

"Remarkable!" I said.

"You understand the cloning process, do you not?" asked Kamau.

"I understand what cloning *is*," I answered. "I know nothing of the exact process."

"In this case, they took some cells from his tusks, which have been on display in the museum for more than two centuries, created the proper nutrient solution, and this is the result: Ahmed of Marsabit, the only elephant ever protected by Presidential Decree, lives again."

"I read that he was always accompanied by two guards no matter where he roamed on Mount Marsabit," I said. "Have they also ignored tradition? I see no one but you. Where is the other guard?"

"There are no guards. The entire complex is protected by a sophisticated electronic security system."

"Are you not a guard?" I asked.

He kept the shame from his voice, but he could not banish it from his face; even in the moonlight I could see it. "I am a paid companion."

"Of the elephant?"

"Of Ahmed."

"I am sorry," I said.

"We cannot all be *mundumugus*," he answered. "When you are my age in a culture that worships youth, you take what is offered to you."

"True," I said. I looked back at the elephant. "I wonder if he has any memories of his former life? Of the days when he was the greatest of all living creatures, and Mount Marsabit was his kingdom."

"He knows nothing of Marsabit," answered Kamau. "But he knows something is wrong. He knows he was not born to spend his life in a tiny yard, surrounded by a glowing force field." He paused. "Sometimes, late at night, he faces the north and lifts his trunk and cries out his loneliness and misery. To the technicians it is just an annoyance. Usually they tell me to feed him, as if food will assuage his sorrow. It is not even *real* food, but something they have concocted in their laboratories."

"He does not belong here," I agreed.

"I know," said Kamau. "But then, neither do you, *mzee*. You should be back on Kirinyaga, living as the Kikuyu were meant to live."

I frowned. "No one on Kirinyaga is living as the Kikuyu were meant to live." I sighed deeply. "I think perhaps the time for *mundumugus* is past."

"This cannot be true," he protested. "Who else can be the repository of our traditions, the interpreter of our laws?"

"Our traditions are as dead as *his*," I said, gesturing toward Ahmed. Then I turned back to Kamau. "Do you mind if I ask you a question?"

"Certainly not, *mundumugu*."

"I am glad you sought me out, and I have enjoyed our conversations since I returned to Kenya," I told him. "But something puzzles me: since you feel so strongly about the Kikuyu, why did I not know you during our struggle to find a homeland? Why did you remain behind when we emigrated to Kirinyaga?"

I could see him wrestling with himself to produce an answer. Finally the battle was over, and the old man seemed to shrink an inch or two.

"I was terrified," he admitted.

"Of the spaceship?" I asked.

"No."

"Then what frightened you?"

Another internal struggle, and then an answer: "*You* did, *mzee*."

"Me?" I repeated, surprised.

"You were always so sure of yourself," he said. "Always such a perfect Kikuyu. You made me afraid that I wasn't good enough."

"That was ridiculous," I said firmly.

"Was it?" he countered. "My wife was a Catholic. My son and daughter bore Christian names. And I myself had grown used to European clothes and European conveniences." He paused. "I was afraid if I went with you—and I wanted to; I have been cursing myself for my cowardice ever since—that soon I would complain about missing the technology and comfort I had left behind, and that you would banish me." He would not meet my gaze, but stared at the ground. "I did not wish to become an outcast on the world that was the last hope of my people."

You are wiser than I suspected, I thought. Aloud I uttered a compassionate lie: "You would not have been an outcast."

"You are sure?"

"I am sure," I said, laying a comforting hand on his bony shoulder. "In fact, I wish you had been there to support me when the end came."

"What good would the support of an old man have been?"

"You are not just *any* old man," I answered. "The word of a descendant of Johnstone Kamau would have carried much weight among the Council of Elders."

"That was another reason I was afraid to come," he replied, the words flowing a little more easily this time. "How could I live up to my name—for everyone knows that Johnstone Kamau became Jomo Kenyatta, the great Burning Spear of the Kikuyu. How could I possibly compare to such a man as that?"

"You compare more favorably than you think," I said reassuringly. "I could have used the passion of your belief."

"Surely you had support from the people," he said.

I shook my head. "Even my own apprentice, whom I was preparing to succeed me, abandoned me; in fact, I believe he is at the university just down the road even as we speak. In the end, the people rejected the discipline of our traditions and the teachings of Ngai for the miracles and comforts of the Europeans. I suppose I should not be surprised, considering how many times it has happened here in Africa." I looked thoughtfully at the elephant. "I am as much an anachronism as Ahmed. Time has forgotten us both."

"But Ngai has not."

"Ngai, too, my friend," I said. "Our day has passed. There is no place left for us, not in Kenya, not on Kirinyaga, not anywhere."

Perhaps it was something in the tone of my voice, or perhaps in some mystic way Ahmed understood what I was saying. Whatever the reason, the elephant stepped forward to the edge of the force field and stared directly at me.

"It is lucky we have the field for protection," remarked Kamau.

"He would not hurt me," I said confidently.

"He has hurt men whom he had less reason to attack."

"But not me," I said. "Lower the field to a height of five feet."

"But . . ."

"Do as I say," I ordered him.

"Yes, *mundumugu*," he replied unhappily, going to a small control box and punching in a code.

Suddenly the mild visual distortion vanished at eye level. I reached out a reassuring hand, and a moment later Ahmed ran the tip of his trunk gently across my face and body, then sighed deeply and stood there, swaying gently as he transferred his weight from one foot to the other.

"I would not have believed it if I had not seen it!" said Kamau almost reverently.

"Are we not all Ngai's creations?" I said.

"Even Ahmed?" asked Kamau.

"Who do *you* think created him?"

He shrugged again and did not answer.

I remained for a few more minutes, watching the magnificent creature, while Kamau returned the force field to its former position. Then the night air became uncomfortably cold, as so often happened at this altitude, and I turned to Kamau.

"I must leave now," I said. "I thank you for inviting me here. I would not have believed this miracle had I not seen it with my own eyes."

"The scientists think it is *their* miracle," he said.

"You and I know better," I replied.

He frowned. "But why do you think Ngai has allowed Ahmed to live again, at this time and in this place?"

I paused for a long moment, trying to formulate an answer, and found that I couldn't.

"There was a time when I knew with absolute certainty why Ngai did what He did," I said at last. "Now I am not so sure."

"What kind of talk is that from a *mundumugu*?" demanded Kamau.

"It was not long ago that I would wake up to the song of birds," I said as we left Ahmed's enclosure and walked to the side gate through which I had entered. "And I would look across the river that wound by my village on Kirinyaga and see impala and zebra grazing on the savannah. Now I wake up to the sound and smell of modern Nairobi and then I look out and see a featureless gray wall that separates my son's house from that of his neighbor." I paused. "I think this must be my punishment for failing to bring Ngai's word to my people."

"Will I see you again?" he asked as we reached the gate and he deactivated a small section long enough for me to pass through.

"If it will not be an imposition," I said.

"The great Koriba an imposition?" he said with a smile.

"My son finds me so," I replied. "He gives me a room in his house, but he would prefer I lived elsewhere. And his wife is ashamed of my bare feet and my *kikoi*; she is constantly buying European shoes and clothing for me to wear."

"*My* son works inside the laboratory," said Kamau, pointing to his son's third-floor office with some pride. "He has seventeen men working for him. Seventeen!"

I must not have looked impressed, for he continued, less enthusiastically, "It is he who got me this job, so that I *wouldn't* have to live with him."

"The job of paid companion," I said.

A bittersweet expression crossed his face. "I love my son, Koriba, and I know that he loves me—but I think that he is also a little bit ashamed of me."

"There is a thin line between shame and embarrassment," I said. "My son glides between one and the other like the pendulum of a clock."

Kamau seemed grateful to hear that his situation was not unique. "You are welcome to live with me, *mundumugu*," he said, and I could tell that it was an earnest offer, not just a polite lie that he hoped I would reject. "We would have much to talk about."

"That is very considerate of you," I said. "But it will be enough if I may visit you from time to time, on those days when I find Kenyans unbearable and must speak to another Kikuyu."

"As often as you wish," he said. "*Kwaheri, mzee.*"

"*Kwaheri,*" I responded. *Farewell.*

I took the slidewalk down the noisy, crowded streets and boulevards that had once been the sprawling Athi Plains, an area that had swarmed with a different kind of life, and got off when I came to the airbus platform. An airbus glided up a few minutes later, almost empty at this late hour, and began going north, floating perhaps ten inches above the ground.

The trees that lined the migration route had been replaced by a dense angular forest of steel and glass and tightly bonded alloys. As I peered through a window into the night, it seemed for a few moments that I was also peering into the past. Here, where the titanium-and-glass courthouse stood, was the very spot where the Burning Spear had first been arrested for having the temerity to suggest that his country did not belong to the British. Over there, by the new eight-story post office building, was where the last lion had died. Over there, by the water recycling plant, my people had vanquished the Wakamba in glorious and bloody battle some three hundred years ago.

"We have arrived, *mzee*," said the driver, and the bus hovered a few inches above the ground while I made my way to the door. "Aren't you chilly, dressed in just a blanket like that?"

I did not deign to answer him, but stepped out to the sidewalk, which did not move here in the suburbs as did the slidewalks of the city. I preferred it, for man was meant to walk, not be transported effortlessly by miles-long beltways.

I approached my son's enclave and greeted the guards, who all knew me, for I often wandered through the area at night. They passed me through with no difficulty, and as I walked I tried to look across the centuries once more, to see the mud-and-grass huts, the *bomas* and *shambas* of my people, but the vision was blotted out by enormous mock-Tudor and mock-Victorian and mock-Colonial and mock-contemporary houses, interspersed with needlelike apartment buildings that reached up to stab the clouds.

I had no desire to speak to Edward or Susan, for they would question me endlessly about where I had been. My son would once again warn me about the thieves and muggers who prey on old men after dark in Nairobi, and my daughter-in-law would try to subtly suggest that I would be warmer in a coat and pants. So I went past their house and walked aimlessly through the enclave until all the lights in the house had gone out. When I was sure they were asleep, I went to a side door and waited for the security system to identify my retina and skeletal structure, as it had on so many similar nights. Then I quietly made my way to my room.

Usually I dreamed of Kirinyaga, but this night the image of Ahmed haunted my dreams. Ahmed, eternally confined by a force field; Ahmed, trying to imagine what lay beyond his tiny enclosure; Ahmed, who would live and die without ever seeing another of his own kind.

And gradually, my dream shifted to myself; to Koriba, attached by invisible chains to a Nairobi he could no longer recognize; Koriba, trying futilely to mold Kirinyaga into what it might have been; Koriba, who once led a brave exodus of the Kikuyu until one day he looked around and found that he was the only Kikuyu remaining.

In the morning I went to visit my daughter on Kirinyaga—not the terraformed world, but the *real* Kirinyaga, which is now called Mount Kenya. It was here that Ngai gave the digging stick to Gikuyu, the first man, and told him to work the earth. It was here that Gikuyu's nine daughters became the mothers of the nine tribes of the Kikuyu, here that the sacred fig tree blossomed. It was here, millennia later, that Jomo Kenyatta, the great Burning Spear of the Kikuyu, would invoke Ngai's power and send the Mau Mau out to drive the white man back to Europe.

And it was here that a steel-and-glass city of five million inhabitants sprawled up the side of the holy mountain. Nairobi's overstrained water and sewer system simply could not accommodate any more people, so the government offered enormous tax incentives to any business that would move to Kirinyaga, in the hope that the people would follow them—and the people accommodated them.

Vehicles spewed pollution into the atmosphere, and the noise of the city at work was deafening. I walked to the spot where the fig tree had once stood; it was now covered by a lead foundry. The slopes where the bongo and the rhinoceros once lived were hidden beneath the housing projects. The winding mountain streams had all been diverted and redirected. The tree beneath which Deedan Kimathi had been killed by the British was only a memory, its place taken by a fast-food restaurant. The summit had been turned into a park, with tram service leading to a score of souvenir shops.

And now I realized why Kenya had become intolerable. Ngai no longer ruled the world from His throne atop the mountain, for there was no longer any room for Him there. Like the leopard and the golden sunbird, like I myself many years ago, He too had fled before this onslaught of black Europeans.

Possibly my discovery influenced my mood, for the visit with my daughter did not go well. But then, they never did: she was too much like her mother.

I entered my son's study late that same afternoon.

"One of the servants said you wished to see me," I said.

"Yes, I do," said my son as he looked up from his computer. Behind him were paintings of two great leaders, Martin Luther King, Jr. and Julius Nyerere, black men both, but neither one a Kikuyu. "Please sit down."

I did as he asked.

"On a chair, my father," he said.

"The floor is satisfactory."

He sighed heavily. "I am too tired to argue with you. I have been brushing up on my French." He grimaced. "It is a difficult language."

"Why are you studying French?" I asked.

"As you know, the ambassador from Cameroon has bought a house in the enclave. I thought it would be advantageous to be able to speak to him in his own tongue."

"That would be Bamileke or Ewondo, not French," I noted.

"He does not speak either of those," answered Edward. "His family is ruling class. They only spoke French in his family compound, and he was educated in Paris."

"Since he is the ambassador to our country, why are you learning *his* language?" I asked. "Why does he not learn Swahili?"

"Swahili is a street language," said my son. "English and French are the languages of diplomacy and business. His English is poor, so I will speak to him in French instead." He smiled smugly. "*That* ought to impress him!"

"I see," I said.

"You look disapproving," he observed.

"I am not ashamed of being a Kikuyu," I said. "Why are you ashamed of being a Kenyan?"

"I am not ashamed of anything!" he snapped. "I am proud of being able to speak to him in his own tongue."

"More proud than he, a visitor to Kenya, is to speak to you in *your* tongue," I noted.

"You do not understand!" he said.

"Evidently," I agreed.

He stared at me silently for a moment, then sighed deeply. "You drive me crazy," he said. "I don't even know how we came to be discussing this. I wanted to see you for a different reason." He lit a smokeless cigarette, took one puff, and threw it into the atomizer. "I had a visit from Father Ngoma this morning."

"I do not know him."

"You know his parishioners, though," said my son. "A number of them have come to you for advice."

"That is possible," I admitted.

"Damn it!" said Edward. "I have to live in this neighborhood, and he is the parish priest. He resents your telling his flock how to live, especially since what you tell them is in contradiction to Catholic dogma."

"Am I to lie to them, then?" I asked.

"Can't you just refer them to Father Ngoma?"

"I am a *mundumugu*," I said. "It is my duty to advise those who come to me for guidance."

"You have not been a *mundumugu* since they made you leave Kirinyaga!" he said irritably.

"I left of my own volition," I replied calmly.

"We are getting off the subject again," said Edward. "Look, if you want to stay in the *mundumugu* business, I'll rent you an office, or"—he added contemptuously—"buy you a patch of dirt on which to sit and make pronouncements. But you cannot practice in my house."

"Father Ngoma's parishioners must not like what he has to say," I observed, "or they would not seek advice elsewhere."

"I do not want you speaking to them again. Is that clear?"

"Yes," I said. "It is clear that you do not want me to speak to them again."

"You know exactly what I mean!" he exploded. "No more verbal games! Maybe they worked on Kirinyaga, but they won't work here! I know you too well!"

He went back to staring at his computer.

"It is most interesting," I said.

"What is?" he asked suspiciously, glaring at me.

"Here you are, surrounded by English books, studying French, and arguing on behalf of the priest of an Italian religion. Not only are you not Kikuyu, I think perhaps you are no longer even Kenyan."

He glared at me across his desk. "You drive me crazy," he repeated.

After I left my son's study I left the house and took an airbus to the park in Muthaiga, miles from my son and the neighbors who were interchangeable with him. Once lions had stalked this terrain. Leopards had clung to overhanging limbs, waiting for the opportunity to pounce upon their prey. Wildebeest and zebra and gazelles had rubbed shoulders, grazing on the tall grasses. Giraffes had nibbled the tops of acacia trees, while warthogs rooted in the earth for tubers. Rhinos had nibbled on thornbushes, and charged furiously at any sound or sight they could not immediately identify.

Then the Kikuyu had come and cleared the land, bringing with them their cattle and their oxen and their goats. They had dwelt in huts of mud and grass, and lived the life that we aspired to on Kirinyaga.

But all that was in the past. Today the park contained nothing but a few squirrels racing across the imported Kentucky Blue Grass and a pair of hornbills that had nested in one of the transplanted European trees. Old Kikuyu men, dressed in shoes and pants and jackets, sat on the benches that ran along the perimeter. One man was tossing crumbs to an exceptionally bold starling, but most of them simply sat and stared aimlessly.

I found an empty bench, but decided not to sit on it. I didn't want to be like these men, who saw nothing but the squirrels and the birds, when I could see the lions and the impala, the war-painted Kikuyu and the red-clad Maasai, who had once stalked across this same land.

I continued walking, suddenly restless, and despite the heat of the day and the frailty of my ancient body, I walked until twilight. I decided I could not endure dinner with my son and his wife, their talk of their boring jobs, their continual veiled suggestions about the retirement home, their inability to comprehend either why I went to Kirinyaga or why I returned—so instead of going home I began walking aimlessly through the crowded city.

Finally I looked up at the sky. *Ngai*, I said silently, *I still do not understand. I was a good* mundumugu. *I obeyed Your law. I honored Your rituals. There must have come a day, a moment, a second, when together we could have saved Kirinyaga if You had just manifested Yourself. Why did You abandon it when it needed You so desperately?*

I spoke to Ngai for minutes that turned into hours, but He did not answer.

When it was ten o'clock at night, I decided it was time to start making my way to the laboratory complex, for it would take me more than an hour to get there, and Kamau began working at eleven.

As before, he deactivated the electronic barrier to let me in, then escorted me to the small grassy area where Ahmed was kept.

"I did not expect to see you back so soon, *mzee*," he said.

"I have no place else to go," I answered, and he nodded, as if this made perfect sense to him.

Ahmed seemed nervous until the breeze brought my scent to him. Then he turned to face the north, extending his trunk every few moments.

"It is as if he seeks some sign from Mount Marsabit," I remarked, for the great creature's former home was hundreds of miles north of Nairobi, a solitary green mountain rising out of the blazing desert.

"He would not be pleased with what he found," said Kamau.

"Why do you say that?" I asked, for no animal in our history was ever more identified with a location than the mighty Ahmed with Marsabit.

"Do you not read the papers, or watch the news on the holo?"

I shook my head. "What happens to black Europeans is of no concern to me."

"The government has evacuated the town of Marsabit, which sits next to the mountain. They have closed the Singing Wells, and have ordered everyone to leave the area."

"Leave Marsabit? Why?"

"They have been burying nuclear waste at the base of the mountain for many years," he said. "It was just revealed that some of the containers broke open almost six years ago. The government hid the fact from the people, and then failed to properly clean up the leak."

"How could such a thing happen?" I asked, though of course I knew the answer. After all, how does *anything* happen in Kenya?

"Politics. Payoffs. Corruption."

"A third of Kenya is desert," I said. "Why did they not bury it there, where no one lives or even thinks to travel, so when this kind of disaster occurs, as it always does, no one is harmed?"

He shrugged. "Politics. Payoffs. Corruption," he repeated. "It is our way of life."

"Ah, well, it is nothing to me anyway," I said. "What happens to a mountain five hundred kilometers away does not interest me, any more than I am interested in what happens to a world named after a different mountain."

"It interests *me*," said Kamau. "Innocent people have been exposed to radiation."

"If they live near Marsabit, they are Pokot and Rendille," I pointed out. "What does that matter to the Kikuyu?"

"They are *people*, and my heart goes out to them," said Kamau.

"You are a good man," I said. "I knew that from the moment we first met." I pulled some peanuts from the pouch that hung around my neck, the same pouch in which I used to keep charms and magical tokens. "I bought these for Ahmed this afternoon," I said. "May I . . . ?"

"Certainly," answered Kamau. "He has few enough pleasures. Even a peanut will be appreciated. Just toss them at his feet."

"No," I said, walking forward. "Lower the barrier."

He lowered the force field until Ahmed was able to reach his trunk out over the top. When I got close enough, the huge beast gently took the peanuts from my hand.

"I am amazed!" said Kamau when I had rejoined him. "Even *I* cannot approach Ahmed with impunity, yet you actually fed him by hand, as if he were a family pet."

"We are each the last of our kind, living on borrowed time," I said. "He senses a kinship."

I remained a few more minutes, then went home to another night of troubled sleep. I felt Ngai was trying to tell me something, trying to impart some message through my dreams, but though I had spent years interpreting the omens in other people's dreams, I was ignorant of my own.

Edward was standing on the beautifully rolled lawn, staring at the blackened embers of my fire.

"I have a beautiful fire pit on the terrace," he said, trying unsuccessfully to hide his anger. "Why on earth did you build a fire in the middle of the garden?"

"That is where a fire belongs," I answered.

"Not in *this* house, it doesn't!"

"I shall try to remember."

"Do you know what the landscaper will charge me to repair the damage you caused?" A look of concern suddenly crossed his face. "You haven't sacrificed any animals, have you?"

"No."

"You're sure none of the neighbors is missing a dog or a cat?" he persisted.

"I know the law," I said. And indeed, Kikuyu law required the sacrifice of goats and cattle, not dogs and cats. "I am trying to obey it."

"I find that difficult to believe."

"But *you* are not obeying it, Edward," I said.

"What are you talking about?" he demanded.

I looked at Susan, who was staring at us from a second-story window.

"You have two wives," I pointed out. "The younger one lives with you, but the older one lives many kilometers away, and sees you only when you take your children away from her on weekends. This is unnatural: a man's wives should all live together with him, sharing the household duties."

"Linda is no longer my wife," he said. "You know that. We were divorced many years ago."

"You can afford both," I said. "You should have kept both."

"In this society, a man may have only one wife," said Edward. "What kind of talk is this? You have lived in England and America. You know that."

"That is their law, not ours," I said. "This is Kenya."

"It is the same thing."

"The Moslems have more than one wife," I replied.

"I am not a Moslem," he said.

"A Kikuyu man may have as many wives as he can afford," I said. "It is obvious that you are also not a Kikuyu."

"I've had it with this smug superiority of yours!" he exploded. "You deserted my mother because she was not a true Kikuyu," he continued bitterly. "You turned your back on my sister because she was not a true Kikuyu. Since I was a child, every time you were displeased with me you have told me that I am not a true Kikuyu. Now you have even proclaimed that none of the thousands who followed you to Kirinyaga are true Kikuyus." He glared furiously at me. "Your standards are higher than Kirinyaga itself! Can there possibly be a true Kikuyu anywhere in the universe?"

"Certainly," I replied.

"Where can such a paragon be found?" he demanded.

"Right here," I said, tapping myself on the chest. "You are looking at him."

My days faded one into another, the dullness and drudgery of them broken only by occasional nocturnal visits to the laboratory complex. Then one night, as I met Kamau at the gate, I could see that his entire demeanor had changed.

"Something is wrong," I said promptly. "Are you ill?"

"No, *mzee*, it is nothing like that."

"Then what is the matter?" I persisted.

"It is Ahmed," said Kamau, unable to stop tears from rolling down his withered cheeks. "They have decided to put him to death the day after tomorrow."

"Why?" I asked, surprised. "Has he attacked another keeper?"

"No," said Kamau bitterly. "The experiment was a success. They know they can clone an elephant, so why continue to pay for his upkeep when they can line their pockets with the remaining funds of the grant?"

"Is there no one you can appeal to?" I demanded.

"Look at me," said Kamau. "I am an eighty-six-year-old man who was given his job as an act of charity. Who will listen to me?"

"We must do something," I said.

He shook his head sadly. "They are *kehees*," he said. "Uncircumcised boys. They do not even know what a *mundumugu* is. Do not humiliate yourself by pleading with them."

"If I did not plead with the Kikuyu on Kirinyaga," I replied, "you may be sure I will not plead with the Kenyans in Nairobi." I tried to ignore the ceaseless hummings of the laboratory machines as I considered my options. Finally I looked up at the night sky: the moon glowed a hazy orange through the pollution. "I will need your help," I said at last.

"You can depend on me."

"Good. I shall return tomorrow night."

I turned on my heel and left, without even stopping at Ahmed's enclosure.

All that night I thought and planned. In the morning, I waited until my son and his wife had left the house, then called Kamau on the vidphone to tell him what I intended to do and how he could help. Next, I had the computer contact the bank and withdraw my money, for though I disdained shillings and refused to cash my government checks, my son had found it easier to shower me with money than respect.

I spent the rest of the morning shopping at vehicle rental agencies, until I found exactly what I wanted. I had the saleswoman show me how to manipulate it, practiced until nightfall, hovered opposite the laboratory until I saw Kamau enter the grounds, and then maneuvered up to the side gate.

"Jambo, mundumugu!" whispered Kamau as he deactivated enough of the electronic barrier to accommodate the vehicle, which he scrutinized carefully. I backed up to Ahmed's enclosure, then opened the back and ordered the ramp to descend. The elephant watched with an uneasy curiosity as Kamau deactivated a ten-foot section of the force field and allowed the bottom of the ramp through.

"Njoo, Tembo," I said. *Come, elephant.*

He took a tentative step toward me, then another and another. When he reached the edge of his enclosure he stopped, for always he had received an electrical "correction" when he tried to move beyond this point. It took almost twenty minutes of tempting him with peanuts before he finally crossed the barrier and then clambered awkwardly up the ramp, which slid in after him. I sealed him into the hovering vehicle, and he instantly trumpeted in panic.

"Keep him quiet until we get out of here," said a nervous Kamau as I joined him at the controls, "or he'll wake up the whole city."

I opened a panel to the back of the vehicle and spoke soothingly, and strangely enough the trumpeting ceased and the scuffling did stop. As I continued to calm the frightened beast, Kamau piloted the vehicle out of the laboratory complex. We passed through the Ngong Hills twenty minutes later, and circled around Thika in another hour. When we passed Kirinyaga—the true, snowcapped Kirinyaga, from which Ngai once ruled the world—ninety minutes after that, I did not give it so much as a glance.

We must have been quite a sight to anyone we passed: two seemingly crazy old men, racing through the night in an unmarked cargo vehicle carrying a six-ton monster that had been extinct for more than two centuries.

"Have you considered what effect the radiation will have on him?" asked Kamau as we passed through Isiolo and continued north.

"I questioned my son about it," I answered. "He is aware of the incident, and says that the contamination is confined to the lower levels of the mountain." I paused. "He also tells me it will soon be cleaned up, but I do not think I believe him."

"But Ahmed must pass through the radiation zone to ascend the mountain," said Kamau.

I shrugged. "Then he will pass through it. Every day he lives is a day more than he would have lived in Nairobi. For as much time as Ngai sees fit to give him, he will be free to graze on the mountain's greenery and drink deep of its cool waters."

"I hope he lives many years," he said. "If I am to be jailed for breaking the law, I would at least like to know that some lasting good came of it."

"No one is going to jail you," I assured him. "All that will happen is that you will be fired from a job that no longer exists."

"That job supported me," he said unhappily.

The Burning Spear would have no use for you, I decided. *You bring no honor to his name. It is as I have always known: I am the last true Kikuyu.*

I pulled my remaining money out of my pouch and held it out to him. "Here," I said.

"But what about yourself, *mzee?*" he said, forcing himself not to grab for it.

"Take it," I said. "I have no use for it."

"Asante sana, mzee," he said, taking it from my hand and stuffing it into a pocket. *Thank you, mzee.*

We fell silent then, each occupied with his own thoughts. As Nairobi receded farther and farther behind us, I compared my feelings with those I had experienced when I had left Kenya behind for Kirinyaga. I had been filled with optimism then, certain that we would create the Utopia I could envision so clearly in my mind.

The thing I had not realized is that a society can be a Utopia for only an instant—once it reaches a state of perfection it cannot change and still be a Utopia, and it is the nature of societies to grow and evolve. I do not know when Kirinyaga became a Utopia; the instant came and went without my noticing it.

Now I was seeking Utopia again, but this time of a more limited, more realizable nature: a Utopia for one man, a man who knew his own mind and would die before compromising. I had been misled in the past, so I was not as elated as the day we had left for Kirinyaga; being older and wiser, I felt a calm, quiet certitude rather than more vivid emotions.

An hour after sunrise, we came to a huge, green, fog-enshrouded mountain set in the middle of a bleached desert. A single swirling dust devil was visible against the horizon.

We stopped, then unsealed the elephant's compartment. We stood back as Ahmed stepped cautiously down the ramp, his every movement tense with apprehension. He took a few steps, as if to convince himself that he was truly on solid ground again, then raised his trunk to examine the scents of his new—and ancient—home.

Slowly the great beast turned toward Marsabit, and suddenly his whole demeanor changed. No longer cautious, no longer fearful, he spent almost a full minute eagerly examining the smells that wafted down to him. Then, without a backward glance, he strode confidently to the foothills and vanished into the foliage. A moment later we heard him trumpet, and then he was climbing the mountain to claim his kingdom.

I turned to Kamau. "You had better take the vehicle back before they come looking for it."

"Are you not coming with me?" he asked, surprised.

"No," I replied. "Like Ahmed, I will live out my days on Marsabit."

"But that means you, too, must pass through the radiation."

"What of it?" I said with an unconcerned shrug. "I am an old man. How much time can I have left—weeks? Months? Surely not a year. Probably the burden of my years will kill me long before the radiation does."

"I hope you are right," said Kamau. "I should hate to think of you spending your final days in agony."

"I have seen men who live in agony," I told him. "They are the old *mzees* who gather in the park each morning, leading lives devoid of purpose, waiting only for death to claim another of their number. I will not share their fate."

A frown crossed his face like an early-morning shadow, and I could see what he was thinking: he would have to take the vehicle back and face the consequences alone.

"I will remain here with you," he said suddenly. "I cannot turn my back on Eden a second time."

"It is not Eden," I said. "It is only a mountain in the middle of a desert."

"Nonetheless, I am staying. We will start a new Utopia. It will be Kirinyaga again, only done right this time."

I have work to do, I thought. *Important work. And you would desert me in the end, as they have all deserted me. Better that you leave now.*

"You must not worry about the authorities," I said in the same reassuring tones with which I spoke to the elephant. "Return the vehicle to my son and he will take care of everything."

"Why should he?" asked Kamau suspiciously.

"Because I have always been an embarrassment to him, and if it were known that I stole Ahmed from a government laboratory, I would graduate from an embarrassment to a humiliation. Trust me: he will not allow this to happen."

"If your son asks about you, what shall I tell him?"

"The truth," I answered. "He will not come looking for me."

"What will stop him?"

"The fear that he might find me and have to bring me back with him," I said.

Kamau's face reflected the battle that was going on inside him, his terror of returning alone pitted against his fear of the hardships of life on the mountain.

"It is true that my son would worry about me," he said hesitantly, as if expecting me to contradict him, perhaps even hoping that I would. "And I would never see my grandchildren again."

You are the last Kikuyu, indeed the last human being, that I shall ever see, I thought. *I will utter one last lie, disguised as a question, and if you do not see through it, then you will leave with a clear conscience and I will have performed a final act of compassion.*

"Go home, my friend," I said. "For what is more important than a grandchild?"

"Come with me, Koriba," he urged. "They will not punish you if you explain why you kidnapped him."

"I am not going back," I said firmly. "Not now, not ever. Ahmed and I are both anachronisms. It is best that we live out our lives here, away from a world we no longer recognize, a world that has no place for us."

Kamau looked at the mountain. "You and he are joined at the soul," he concluded.

"Perhaps," I agreed. I laid my hand on his shoulder. "*Kwaheri,* Kamau."

"Kwaheri, mzee," he replied unhappily. "Please ask Ngai to forgive me for my weakness."

It seemed to take him forever to activate the vehicle and turn it toward Nairobi, but finally he was out of sight, and I turned and began ascending the foothills.

I has wasted many years seeking Ngai on the wrong mountain. Men of lesser faith might believe Him dead or disinterested, but I knew that if Ahmed could be reborn after all others of his kind were long dead, then Ngai must surely be nearby, overseeing the miracle. I would spend the rest of the day regaining my strength, and then, in the morning, I would begin searching for Him again on Marsabit.

And this time, I knew I would find Him.

Author's Afterword

How does one go about writing the most honored science-fiction book in history?

Well, not on purpose, believe me.

It all began back in 1987, when Orson Scott Card asked me to contribute a story to his shared-world anthology, *Eutopia*. He postulated a number of artificial planetoids that were chartered by groups that wanted to create Utopian societies, and he had a pair of conditions that made it very challenging.

First, anyone who wished to leave could walk to an area called Haven and promptly be picked up by a Maintenance ship. This meant there could be no revolts against Big Brother and a Utopia gone wrong; if you didn't like your world you simply left, and no one stopped you.

Second, the story had to be told by an insider who believed in the

Utopia. There could be no simplistic "wonder tour" by a visitor who codifies what he sees and then goes home.

Because of my love of Africa, and my knowledge of East Africa in particular, I chose to write about a Kikuyu Utopia. The story was "Kirinyaga," and I handed it to Scott at the 1987 World Science Fiction Convention in Brighton, England, where I stopped for a few days on my way down to Kenya for yet another safari.

I felt I had written a pretty good story, but writers are notoriously insecure, and I half thought Scott might reject it. He didn't, and he also gave me permission to sell it to *The Magazine of Fantasy and Science Fiction*, where it appeared as the November 1988 cover story, and won me my first Hugo Award the next year.

But long before that happened, even before Scott let me know he was buying it, I took my Kenya safari—and a strange thing happened. Maybe it was because I had just written "Kirinyaga" a couple of weeks earlier and it was still fresh in my mind, maybe it was because my subconscious is a lot smarter than my conscious mind, but whatever the reason, I realized that "Kirinyaga" was not a stand-alone story, but rather the first chapter in a book. Everywhere I looked I saw material for more Kirinyaga episodes, and by the time the safari was over, I had outlined the entire book that you hold in your hands. From that day to this, the only change I made was to one of the titles: "The Last Storyteller" became "A Little Knowledge."

I decided to write the book a chapter at a time, and to sell each chapter as a short story (or novelette, or novella, depending on length), but never to lose sight of the fact that these stories were really chapters in a novel, which, when completed, would build to a climax as a novel does, and have a coda after the climax, as so many of my own novels do.

I confess that I am not the most modest, self-effacing man in the world, but even I was stunned by the reaction.

The first story chronologically (which, since it is set in Kenya rather than Kirinyaga, serves as a prologue to the novel), and the only one to be written and appear out of sequence, was "One Perfect Morning, With Jackals." Its various nominations and awards were:

Hugo Award Nominee
Nebula Preliminary Ballot
Science Fiction Chronicle Poll Runner-up
Alexander Award Nominee
Year's Best SF—9th Annual Collection selection

The second story/chapter was "Kirinyaga," which seems to have made my reputation (or, rather, remade it, since before its appearance I was known almost exclusively for my novels). Its various nominations and awards were:

Hugo Award Winner
Hugo Award Nominee
Nebula Award Nominee
Nebula Preliminary Ballot
Science Fiction Chronicle Poll Winner
Hayakawa SF Award Finalist
Locus Poll Runner-up
Year's Best SF—6th Annual Collection selection

The third story/chapter—and my personal favorite—was "For I Have Touched the Sky," which has actually been anthologized more often than "Kirinyaga." Its various nominations and awards were:

Hugo Award Nominee
Nebula Award Nominee
Nebula Preliminary Ballot
Hayakawa SF Award Winner
Science Fiction Chronicle Poll Winner
Japanese Hugo *(Sieun-Sho)* Nominee
Year's Best SF—7th Annual Collection selection

The fourth story/chapter was "Bwana." It was not nominated for a Hugo, probably because it was in competition that year with my own *Bully!*, which was a stronger story. Also, I think it's the weakest of the Kirinyaga stories, primarily because there's a lack of the usual ambiguities: you know from the first line that Koriba is in the right, and you root for him to triumph. Its various nominations and awards were:

Japanese Hugo *(Sieun-Sho)* Nominee
HOMer Award Nominee
Nebula Preliminary Ballot
Year's Best SF—8th Annual Collection, Honorable Mention

The fifth story/chapter was "The Manamouki," which won me my second Hugo—and by the end of it, readers could see that Koriba's Utopia was starting to crumble around the edges. Its various nominations and awards were:

Hugo Award Winner
Hugo Award Nominee
Nebula Award Nominee
Nebula Preliminary Ballot
Golden Pagoda Award Winner
Science Fiction Chronicle Poll Winner
HOMer Award Nominee
HOMer Award Winner
Year's Best SF—8th Annual Collection, Honorable Mention

The sixth story/chapter was "Song of a Dry River." It was not nominated for a Hugo, but I think the reason was technical rather than because of a lack of quality. When I was the Guest of Honor at a science-fiction convention called Boskone, the convention published a hardcover collection of my African stories and articles, and asked if I would contribute a brand-new Kirinyaga story to it. I wrote "Song of a Dry River" and it appeared in the book. I then sold it to *Asimov's*, but due to scheduling problems it did not appear in *Asimov's* during the same calendar year, so that by the time most readers encountered it, it had already used up its eligibility for most of the major awards. Its various nominations and awards were:

HOMer Award Winner
HOMer Award Nominee
Hayakawa SF Award Finalist
Year's Best SF—10th Annual Collection, Honorable Mention

The seventh story/chapter was "The Lotus and the Spear," and by now Koriba's solutions were less elegant and his long-term prospects less reassuring. Its various nominations and awards were:
Hugo Award Nominee
Nebula Preliminary Ballot
HOMer Award Nominee
Year's Best SF—10th Annual Collection, Honorable Mention

The eighth story/chapter was "A Little Knowledge." It dealt with one of my favorite subjects—the difference an artist finds between facts and truth—and I really thought it had a shot at a Hugo. But that was the year I wrote "Seven Views of Olduvai Gorge," which ran off with the Hugo and the Nebula and just about every other award in the field, and the voters evidently thought that was honor enough for one year. "A Little Knowledge's" various nominations and awards were:
Hugo Award Nominee
Nebula Preliminary Ballot
HOMer Award Nominee
Year's Best SF—12th Annual Collection, Honorable Mention

In the ninth story/chapter, "When the Old Gods Die," the inevitable comes to pass, and Koriba and his Utopia reject each other. I was afraid the readers might be getting tired of Kirinyaga, but "When the Old Gods Die" obviously hit a responsive chord. Its various nominations and awards were:
Hugo Nominee
Nebula Nominee
Nebula Preliminary Ballot
Locus Award Winner

HOMer Award Winner
HOMer Award Nominee
Science Fiction Weekly Poll Winner
Year's Best SF—13th Annual Collection, Honorable Mention

I had been waiting for nine years to write the "The Land of Nod," which had been plotted out back in 1987. I took a much longer time with it than usual, because the ongoing Kirinyaga fable had already won more honors than any other science fiction in history and I knew that the final story—which became an epilogue for the same reason "One Perfect Morning, With Jackals" was a prologue: they are each set in Kenya, and form literary bookends around the eight episodes that take place on Kirinyaga—would be subject to considerable scrutiny. My wife, Carol, who has been my uncredited collaborator for close to a third of a century, thinks it is the best Kirinyaga tale of them all. I still prefer "For I Have Touched the Sky," but Koriba's final story did exactly what I wanted it to do, and I am well pleased with it. I am writing this in early June of 1997, and many of the awards haven't been determined yet. Thus far, its various nominations and awards are:

Hugo Nominee
Nebula Preliminary Ballot
HOMer Award Nominee
Year's Best SF—14th Annual Collection selection

And what, I hear you ask, ever became of *Eutopia?* Well, the fact of the matter is that, for various reasons, it is still awaiting publication a full decade after it was contracted—but I'll be forever grateful to it, and to Orson Scott Card, for without *Eutopia* there would be no *Kirinyaga.*

—Mike Resnick

© Carol Resnick

About the Author

MIKE RESNICK'S outstanding work has won numerous awards—including three Hugos and one Nebula—and has been nominated for dozens more.

Resnick has traveled extensively in Africa, the setting for *Kirinyaga*. He divides his time between Cincinnati, Ohio, and Orlando, Florida.